DO YOU
FEEL IT
TOO?

ALSO BY NICOLA RENDELL

Shimmy Bang Sparkle

So Good

Just Like That

Hail Mary

Confessed

Professed

DO YOU FEEL IT TOO?

NICOLA
RENDELL

Montlake
Romance

Text copyright © 2018 Lux Holdings LLC

Published by Montlake Romance, Seattle

www.apub.com

Amazon, the Amazon logo, and Montlake Romance are trademarks of Amazon.com, Inc., or its affiliates.

ISBN-13: 9781503903500
ISBN-10: 1503903508

Cover design by Letitia Hasser

Cover photography by Wander Aguiar

Printed in the United States of America

To P.

1

GABE

The first time I saw her, there were fireworks—*actual* fireworks. It was the Fourth of July on River Street in Savannah. It had been a long time since I'd spent the Fourth in the States. A year ago I'd been in the Yukon Province chasing down the yeti; the year before I was outside Nogales hunting for the chupacabra. I'd missed the hell out of Fourth of July fireworks, but all the explosions in the sky that night had *nothing* on her.

She was across the park from me, maybe fifty feet away. The hot and humid night air made halos around the dimmed park lights. She was like an angel out there, like a goddamned vision. Red shorts. White T-shirt. Sneakers. She had long dark hair arranged over one shoulder. Sexy tanned thighs and a delicate line of cleavage.

Fuck, she was gorgeous.

She knelt down, like she'd dropped a contact or an earring. I began to stand to go help her but stopped myself. She wasn't searching; she was working—peeling a line of duct tape off an audio cable on the ground. Before the fireworks, the mayor had given a speech in Emmet Park and a brass quartet had played as the sun set. It looked to me like she'd been the one doing the audio for it. In one hand she gathered the tape into a ball, and with the other she made neat loops of the cord that it had been covering. She followed the tape and wire to the edge of the sidewalk and over the curb to the back of a white van. Her curves and softness disappeared behind its open back doors so that all I could see were her calves and her navy-blue Converse. By the light of a series of fireworks exploding overhead, I saw the van's logo. It was a flower with microphones as petals and an extension cord as the stem. Under that were the words:

SOUNDS GOOD
Turning Savannah Up to Eleven Since 2011!

When a whistle filled the air, I kept my eyes trained on the back of the van. But when the sky lit up again with a *pop*, she wasn't there. I scanned the edge of the park again and spotted her next to the bandstand, loading a speaker onto a handcart. On the back of her shirt was the same flower-shaped logo. She crouched down to secure the speaker with a bungee cord. Her position accentuated her waist and showed off a narrow strip of skin at the small of her back. I ran my hand down my stubble and growled into my palm when I saw the lacy edge of her panties peeking out.

She wheeled the dolly a few feet and paused to grab a mic stand. Rather than carrying it by its top, she knelt down in front of it and reached back to balance it on her shoulder. It reminded me of Huck Finn, carrying his rucksack on a branch. Off she went, zipping across the path that ran diagonally across the edge of the park.

Watching a beautiful woman move heavy equipment by herself was the pinnacle of douchebaggery. I was a lot of things, but to the best of my knowledge, douchebag wasn't one of them. Whether she needed a hand or not, I was sure as hell going to offer one. Just because I wasn't Southern didn't mean I couldn't be a gentleman.

I tossed my go cup into the trash and made my way toward her, trying to time myself so our paths would cross right before she got to the van. In show business, they call it the meet-cute. Best way to get sparks to fly. I might not have been in the rom-com business, but I was going to meet-cute the hell out of her. Her *and* her sexy thighs.

A series of smaller fireworks exploded overhead, and the crowd *oohed* and *ahhed* like a soundtrack as I ran my eyes over her body. A spray of star-shaped explosions lit up the park, and she raised her face to the sky, smiling. Now that I was closer to her, I could make out white stars on her red shorts. Her hair was pushed back from her forehead with a rolled blue bandanna.

Cute as a button and sexier still.

But right as I was about to offer to help her, the fireworks flamed out, sending us into darkness. She was so close that I could hear her sneakers on the pavement. A breeze carried her perfume over to me. Vanilla, maybe. But even though she smelled good enough to eat, I stayed where I was. Creeping up behind beautiful women in the dark wasn't the type of shit that would get me onto *People* magazine's list of Most Eligible Bachelors, thanks.

When another firework exploded, turning everything deep red, I took another step toward her. She had her back to me. She'd put the dolly down and was checking something on her phone. The light from the screen illuminated the lines of her hourglass curves and highlighted the elegant curve where her neck met her shoulder. It was go time. "Can I give you a hand?" I asked.

She swung around to face me, pivoting on her toes. As she did, time kind of . . . slowed down, as if everything were moving at a quarter speed. I saw her welcoming smile. Her dimples. Her full and shiny lips. But on my left, in my periphery, I also noticed something else. Something big, dark, and something—

Wham!

The bones in my skull rattled, my molars jiggled, and I stumbled backward. I pressed my hands to my face and staggered blindly back into the dark. Everything was spinning, and the neon necklaces the city

3

had handed out to the children whizzed by like I was in the middle of a glow-in-the-dark roller rink.

Blinking hard against the sting of sudden tears and the general feeling that my brain was sloshing around like too-watery Jell-O salad in a bowl, I tried to figure out what in the ever-loving fuck had just . . .

The mic stand. She'd coldcocked me in the face with the god-damned mic stand.

"Oh my *God!*" she shrieked and lunged to help me. Unfortunately, this also made the mic stand clatter to the ground. The base spun around like a quarter on a table, making the pole end gather just enough speed to whack me across the shins like a karate chop into a cinder block.

I dropped to my knees and growled out, *"Jesus!"*

"Oh *no!*" she said, clapping her hands to the sides of her head.

"I'm good!" I told her, my voice muffled by my palm. "Totally good!" She was coming to help me, but out of pure protective instinct, I waved her away. Next thing I knew, I'd be getting beaten with her handbag. "I've got this. Totally!"

But she wasn't dissuaded. She grabbed my shoulders and steered me toward a bench to sit down. Her grip was firm and confident, which was way more than I could say for my backward flailing. Once I was sitting, she crouched in front of me. Just then, the finale of the fireworks kicked into high gear—patriotic trombones, cannon fire, soaring strings. The works. Dozens of fireworks exploded behind her, showing off all of her beauty. Her big, warm eyes. Her enticing lips. Her concerned grimace. As far as I could tell, she didn't recognize me. I was pretty relieved; for a guy who spent his professional life on camera, it was still damned uncomfortable for me whenever anybody said, *Hang on! Aren't you* . . .

Which meant it would've been a perfect moment if not for all the goddamned spinning.

By the light of the finale, she checked my pupils, leaning in so close that I felt the heat of her body against mine. Even through the brainpan-rattling pain, I knew she was even more beautiful than I'd thought at first. Once she seemed reasonably sure that I wasn't obviously concussed, she knelt down at my feet. She placed one hand on my leg and the other hand to her rosy cheek. "I am *so* sorry. I had no idea you were standing behind me. Are you OK?"

OK was debatable. There was a nonzero chance I was missing some teeth. Keeping my nose shielded with my hand, I felt around my mouth with my tongue. It seemed like they were all there. Probably. The front ones were there, anyway. Bonus. And as an even bigger bonus, there was still no sign that she recognized me *at all*. To her, I was just some poor sucker she'd almost knocked unconscious, and I didn't mind that one bit. "You could take that swing to the major leagues."

She cringed, and it made her nose crinkle adorably. She placed her hand on my cheek, tipping her body forward so her cleavage brushed against my knees. Her palm was soft and cool, and her expression was worried and pained. "Come on. Let me get a closer look at the damage."

I wasn't too hot on the idea, but she was gently persistent. She held my forearm, slowly tightening her grip to say *please*. Very carefully I lifted my hand. When she peeked underneath, she sucked in a breath between gritted teeth. I cupped my nose again and watched her blink a few times in rapid succession. Then the grimace transformed into an agonized smile. "Nothing a bag of frozen peas won't fix!" she said.

I wasn't buying it. She looked like she'd just seen a five-car pileup that featured a diaper truck in the middle. I touched my knuckle to my nostril and saw a smudge of blood. "Any chance you've got a Kleenex?"

She smacked her thighs with her palms. "Yes, yes, yes! Of course! One sec!" She scurried back to her van and leaned inside. When she did, one leg lifted up behind her like a ballerina, revealing the soft inside of her thigh. The sight of her silk-soft skin was like a shot of morphine. All my pain disappeared. But then I made the mistake of sniffing.

Mother*fuck* it.

She hustled back to me with her purse in hand. This she upended at my feet, covering the grass with all manner of shit, including lipsticks, a bruised banana, a paperback book, knitting needles, and a whole shitload of tangled yarn. She jiggled her bag, searched through the stuff at my feet, and growled, "No wonder this thing was on clearance." She rummaged around through the pockets and finally emerged with a small pack of flower-printed tissues. "Here!" She thrust them out to me. I began to reach for them, but she snatched them back. "What am I thinking! I'll get it. You hold tight." Instead of pulling one tissue from the pack, she ripped the whole damned thing apart and they fluttered to the ground. With a few tissues in hand, she came up from her crouch and sat next to me, her thigh pressing against my leg.

"Here, put your head back a little." She placed one of her hands on the back of my head, and I felt the featherlight touch of her fingertips above my collar. "Now, easy does it," she said softly. She dabbed at my upper lip with the corner of the tissue. But when she touched the edge of my nostril, I hissed before I could stop myself.

"Sorry!" she whispered and pulled the tissue away to let me recover. I blinked hard, forcing the wave of pain to subside, and then leaned back into her. While she tended to me, I got a chance to study her up close. Around her neck, she wore a delicate necklace with a charm in the shape of what might've been a slice of pie. Or an ice cream cone. Or wait. Nope. It was a microphone. Of course. "Be honest," I said. "Got a lot of experience bludgeoning strangers?"

She blinked thoughtfully. "They teach it at the Y," she said without missing a beat. "Every Tuesday after Hairspray as Offensive Weapon."

How you *doin'?* It was one thing to be pretty, but it was another to be both quick *and* funny in the middle of a small disaster. "Serves me right for sneaking up behind a beautiful woman in the dark."

She paused with the tissue an inch from my face. She pressed her lips together and gave me an adorable smile. "Well," she said, a little embarrassed, "I don't know about the beautiful woman part, but I do know you certainly didn't deserve to get hit in the face." She scooted closer, and I got a hit of her perfume—definitely vanilla. But the real deal. Like the vanilla bean orchid that grew wild in New Guinea. Exotic, rare, and utterly intoxicating.

"Maybe I should take you to the ER." She grabbed a fresh tissue. "It's the least I could do."

It wasn't exactly how I'd envisioned my first night in town, and I'd definitely survived crazier shit without medical attention. Like the time a lumberjack chased me off his property and I fell into a ravine. Or the time I had dinner with a rancher in the middle of Nowhere, Mexico, and ate a little orange pepper that sent me into an unstoppable cycle of hiccups, dry heaves, and uncontrollable weeping. I could handle this . . . *especially* if she was going to play nurse. "I'm Gabe." I began to reach out my right hand to shake hers, but since it was probably smudged with blood, I opted for my left hand.

Her eyes twinkled. Rather than try to shake it, she gave my fingers a squeeze. "Hi, Gabe," she said softly. "I'm Lily." She patted her name on the front of her shirt, and it made her gorgeous breasts jiggle. "But now"—she moved her head side to side as she peered at my face—"I think we should make double sure I don't need to drive you to the doctor. Give me a sec to do some light googling." She took my hand and pressed it to the tissue and then grabbed her phone from her pile of purse stuff on the grass at my feet.

While she did her light googling, I did some light Lily studying. No wedding ring and no engagement ring. On her home screen was a photograph of a chubby, laughing infant in a onesie that said I LOVE MY AUNTIE LILY! She tapped in her security code and flipped through her apps. The background image was a sepia-filtered photo of the same kid, but this time sitting in an old-fashioned stroller with thin and oversize wheels. He wore an old-fashioned getup, like a tiny sailor's costume, complete with an old-timey white hat.

The light from her phone screen illuminated her features. Soft cheekbones, full lips. As she typed away with her thumbs, she pushed her eyebrows together so hard that a ridge appeared between them, and all the while she nibbled on her lip. On her screen in big, bold letters appeared the header "Broken Nose Treatment."

"OK! Found a symptom checker. 'When to go see a health-care provider for a broken nose.'"

"I'm sure it's not broken." Actually, I wasn't completely sure about that at all, but I didn't want to make her feel too bad about it. "Sprained, maybe."

She glanced up from the screen and pursed her lips. "Shush, now. You're the patient, I'm the pretend internet doctor. In WebMD we trust. Bullet one: 'You cannot stop the nose from bleeding.'"

I pulled the flowery tissue back from my nose. She leaned in, still with her eyebrows rumpled. She was unselfconscious about her expressions—no pretense, no shyness. No sense that she'd been practicing her expressions in a mirror for years, like half the women in LA did. That authenticity made her ten times more alluring. "Mmm. We're fine. Just a little droplet. That's good at least." She held up her phone and read, "'The nostril or nasal septum is crooked or out of place.'"

With one finger I touched the ridge of my nose, then my septum. I'd never actually felt for the shape of my own nose, but it didn't seem *obviously* messed up. "I think we're good."

Lily pursed her lips. "I'm not so sure. I have no point of reference. Unless you've got a selfie handy!" she teased, squinting at my nose and then meeting my eyes for a beat. "But I don't suppose that's your jam."

Actually, my jam was hosting my own show investigating urban legends, mysteries, and generally strange shit around the world. *The Powers of Suggestion*, hosted by yours truly, Gabe Powers. New episodes aired every Thursday from 9:30 to 10:30 p.m. on Destination America, reruns every Friday between Bear Grylls and *A Haunting*, and all-day marathons every third Saturday. All she had to do was turn her light googling skills on my name and she'd see my face all over place. But I wasn't about to just say all that. Because again, not a douchebag. *Not a douchebag.* "I never think to take them."

She sighed. "Well, you do seem OK. Everything seems pretty much . . ." Her eyes moved over my face. At first she was focused on my nose. But after a few seconds, it was clear to me that I wasn't the only one feeling some chemistry. She was *totally* checking me out. So I gave her a lift of my chin to say, *I see you, sexy.* The chin flick made my nose throb, but it was worth it. Because in return, I got a big smile paired with a shy little giggle. She zipped the charm on her necklace back and forth and then returned to her phone. "Next bullet. 'There is a grapelike swelling inside the nose.'"

"*Grapelike,*" I said. "Jesus Christ. What does that even mean, grapelike?"

Lily scooted closer to me. "I don't know. WebMD is so scary," she said, using the screen of her phone as a flashlight to examine me. "Sore throat? Get your affairs in order. Splotches on your fingernails? Might as well grab a white sheet, call an Uber, and head to the cemetery."

My laugh came out as a painful mix between a cough and a bark. "I once hit a spin class too hard and looked up *leg cramps.* Scared the living shit out of myself."

She huffed. "I *know*, right? You either need to eat a banana or you've got a rare degenerative muscle disease. Potato, potahto." She tipped my head back, examining me with serious concern, before finally leaning away. "But I think that's a negative. No grapelike swelling."

I took a fresh tissue from her lap and ripped it into quarters. I made tight twists out of two of them and put one into each nostril. A wave of pain made my eyes water. *Man the fuck up, Powers.* "Hundred percent."

She grimaced. Clearly, I wasn't looking 100 percent. By the light of her phone and the park lamp, I saw a blush creep up on her cheeks. There was a gentle kindness about her that was incredibly hard to resist. "I feel just terrible. At least let me pay to have your shirt cleaned." She pressed her hand to my arm and gave it a firm squeeze. Firm enough to hijack all my goddamned thoughts.

The chemistry between us was white-hot. One squeeze and I knew what I wanted. As if there'd been any doubt.

I wasn't a guy to think about a good idea for long. Dicking around wasn't my thing. I had gut instincts, and I listened to them. Here was a beautiful woman, and I was feeling it. If I didn't grab this chance, I might never see her again. There was no way in hell I was going to let that happen. "How about I take you out for a drink?"

Her eyes flashed in the lamplight. "I almost knocked you unconscious, and we haven't even checked on your shins."

I nodded, and the torn edges of the Kleenex wads tickled my lip. "You said you wanted to make it up to me, right? So. A drink. We can call it even."

Again she nibbled on her lip. She sized me up, like she was deciding what to make of me. She traced the edge of her phone case with her fingertip. "But I don't even know you."

Some problems could be solved on the spot. "I'm Gabe. I'll be forty next year. I'm an Aquarius. I'm a lefty, but I can use regular scissors. I actually really do like long walks on the beach. Big fan of spaghetti and meatballs. I'm here for a while on business, and I'd really like to get to know you better." I dusted off my hands. "Boom. Done."

She pressed her tongue against her teeth, like she was stifling a giggle. "Fess up now. You stole that from a Tinder profile."

Zing! But actually, no, I hadn't. When it came down to it, I was just a dude like every other. Mostly. "You'll never know unless you let me take you out."

She crossed her legs, pressing her bare thighs together. She tucked the fingers of one hand between them. What I wouldn't give for that to be my hand. Somehow, I managed to pull my eyes off that gap. But my gaze landed on her cleavage, and I dragged it away from there too. Every part of her was like a damned eye magnet. I made myself focus on her eyes. But those were most alluring of all. For a second we faced off in a badly lit game of chicken. She had no idea who she was up against. If there was one thing I'd learned in my line of work, it was unending, unflinching patience. Along with the ability to stay stationary for *hours*. "I could literally do this all night. Let me know if you want a break."

Her eyes flashed, as if she liked that challenge. "All night?"

I lifted my eyebrow. "All. Night. Long."

Her rapid blinks were followed by a stare and a press of her hand to her chest. *So* Southern belle. Fuck. But she relented, at last. "All right. Yes. It's yes to a drink."

"And dinner."

Her mouth dropped open, and she stopped zipping her necklace. But I could tell she loved it. So I didn't back down.

I ran my hand down my jaw and watched her. "Have some mercy, bruiser. Throw a guy a bone."

She gave me a half wince, half smile. "Dinner and drinks, then. But it'll have to be tomorrow. I have to get home soon. I'm not used to being whisked off for spontaneous dates."

"Maybe you should get used to it."

And she swallowed hard enough for me to hear the *gulp*.

The look in her eyes gave me a rush of adrenaline that I hadn't felt in a long, long time. There was no fangirl fawning—just pure, plain old desire. Admittedly, I'd been closer to having a date with the yeti than a beautiful woman in the last few months. But there was something going on between us, and it felt damned good. "You pick the spot, my treat. Seven thirty tomorrow."

One last firework whistled and went off in the air. It exploded in a shower of bright-white pinpricks right above us. Both of us looked up to watch it, and as the embers tumbled down into the river, she asked, "You're *sure* you're OK?"

"Lily."

"All right! All right!" she giggled. "It's a date."

An hour later, I was lying in the bedroom of my allegedly haunted Airbnb on Abercorn Street with enough bags of frozen peas, corn, and green beans scattered around me that I could have gone into business as a vegetable soup tycoon. In spite of the throbbing pain in my nose, I could not stop thinking about her. She'd given me her number, and I'd sent her a text so she had mine too. I moved a dripping bag of slightly thawed peas aside so I could see my phone and opened the chat window. In reply, she'd said I'm so glad I didn't mace you!, which she'd tapped out as I sat next to her. Cute. Now the blank space was begging me to answer with a *Can't wait to see you*, or *I'm totally fine, don't worry at all*, or *The peas are definitely helping*. It didn't even matter that they weren't, I just wanted to say *something, anything*, because 7:30 p.m. tomorrow felt way too far away.

But before I could type in a single letter, my phone started vibrating and my producer's face appeared on the screen. There was a brief instant as I stared at his contact photo—a shot of him in Groucho Marx glasses with attached mustache—when I thought *very* seriously about hitting the decline button. I'd had a great night. I was thinking about Lily. I was in bed. The last thing I needed was him and his harebrained ideas killing this buzz.

His name was Mark Markowitz, and he was like an overcaffeinated Woody Allen with a near-religious devotion to spandex bike shorts. He drank green smoothies and used Bluetooth headsets and drove a yellow Prius with a license plate that said PRODUCE, which made his trips to the farmers' market like an Abbott and Costello sketch. Some lady with a hippie skirt and a basketful of beet greens would look him up and down in the parking lot, zero in on his god-awful bike shorts, and say, *What kind of produce do you grow? Let me guess—those tiny bananas!*

Markowitz was the king of the Idea Fart. Every idea, large or small, had two things in common: urgency and inconvenient timing. He made like we had to act on all the Idea Farts *right now* before we got scooped. Sometimes I felt like he approached my career like an infomercial sales-man hawking carpet cleaner at one in the morning. *Act now and get a free bottle of foaming enzymatic carpet spray with your next television show!*

But I'd done well, and I owed a lot of that to him and his terrier-like persistence. So I took a deep breath and answered the call on speaker. The big master bedroom was filled instantly with the sound of *very* heavy breathing. *Fool me once, shame on me. Fool me twice, and I'm on to your workout schedule.* "How's spin class?"

"Kicking my ass! The burn, Powers! The burn!"

Spin classes at 9:00 p.m. on the Fourth of July. Los Angeles was *the weirdest.* "It's like midnight here, man. What's on your mind?"

"So," he panted, "I was reading up on this ghost-hunting thing."

Here we go. I put my phone faceup on my chest and mashed some corn into my eye socket. "I've got it covered. Seriously. I'm in a haunted house right now." I looked up at the high ceilings and the ornate crown molding. I didn't believe in ghosts, of course. And I sure as hell didn't think they were in this beautiful house.

"Seems like they all pick up EV somethings on their RadioShack tape recorders. Been reading up, Powers! Been busting my chops! I think we can do better! I'm thinking we should hire someone to help you out! Someone local! Someone who will know where to find the ghosts *and* get you some good audio!"

That was the other thing about Markowitz. He only responded to sentences that let him steer the conversation where he wanted it to go. Sometimes it was like he hadn't even heard anything I'd said, like one of those robocalls that sounded real until you said, "Stop calling me," and they responded with, "Refinancing your home is really very simple!"

"Like I told you, I'm in a haunted house. Right now."

"EVPs! That's what they're called! Electro something somethings! We need someone professional for that!"

Though he presented this like a fresh Idea Fart, it was one of the oldest in his repertoire. He was absolutely determined to get me to believe that I needed to have a film crew for my show. He wanted my shoots to get bigger and better. *More action, more stunts, more wide-angle panorama shots!* I was equally determined to prove that if Les goddamned Stroud could spend a month in the fucking Norwegian tundra *by himself*, subsisting off nothing but pinecones, snowmelt, and frozen sparrow wings, I could certainly manage to film a few episodes about ghosts in one of the prettiest cities in America. And I most certainly didn't need a film crew following me around with seven hundred pounds of equipment and six Starbucks runs a day to do it. "We've been through this like nine hundred times. I can handle it myself. It's cheaper, it's easier, and it's my *thing*."

"Powers!" he panted. "My thing involves a webcam and coconut oil, but you don't see me making a career out of it, do you?"

Why. Just . . . *why*? "I'm gonna wire this place up tomorrow. See if I can get anything on video. I'm good, man. I've got this thing covered." *Exactly like everything I've ever done.* I rubbed my temples and squished a pea between my forehead and thumb. "I'll share the files when they're ready. Don't forget to hold your stretches, man," I said and hung up the phone.

In the silence, I briefly considered doing the only new-age California thing that I'd actually found I liked—meditation. I was a big fan, and I'd tried all kinds. I'd practiced tonglen with Buddhist monks in a mountaintop temple in Nepal and transcendentalism with David Lynch in an overcrowded conference room in a slightly dilapidated Hilton in downtown LA. Hands down the best guided meditation I'd found for dealing with Markowitz was a two-and-a-half-minute video of pure genius on YouTube: "Fuck That: An Honest Meditation." But I knew that tonight, I wouldn't need to meditate. Because as I closed my eyes, there she was—those curves, those hips, that face, that Lily.

Fuck that? Fuck yeah.

2

LILY

The next morning, I was doing some breakfast-time nephew watching at my sister's apartment so that she could enjoy her coffee, get rid of her grays, and generally have a baby-free morning to herself. While my nephew crawled around on the television room rug, I attempted to knit a hat for him—the fifteenth time *had* to be a charm—but no matter how many purls and knits I tried to string together, I found that I still couldn't shake my thoughts of Gabe, the Possibly Broken-Nosed Hunk.

Even with the marked facial swelling, he'd been positively dreamy. I really and truly did feel awful for almost knocking him unconscious with the mic stand. That sort of thing wasn't my style *at all*. When it came to men, I preferred to reject them by slowly failing to reply to their text messages. I preferred to go out with a fizzle rather than a bang. But he was so sexy, I found myself thinking less about fizzling and a whole lot more about . . . banging. Because that face. That jawline. Those shoulders. *My goodness.*

He was tall, dark, handsome, and also strangely familiar. But I couldn't place the face. Maybe he had one of those faces, I thought, as I tried to remember if I was supposed to be purling or knitting. Rugged stubble, cheekbones. One of those faces that *really* belonged on television. I refocused on my needles. Was that a purl? Did I even really know how to purl? Or . . . "Oh, for God's sake," I muttered at my yarn as I ripped out a row.

My nephew planted his hands on the pink shag carpeting and dragged his knees along, occasionally off-gassing with the effort of this newfound mode of transportation. He made my heart ache with love. I was more than his auntie, really; after his dad left my sister, I'd stepped in as sort of auntie/father/all-purpose-coparent. His birth father was named Boris—a suspiciously dashing Russian photographer who'd done a midnight flit back to Mother Russia on an airline that nobody had ever heard of, never to be heard from again. But to his credit, he'd left behind the most fabulous little boy on the planet. He was named Ivan. After the czar.

Obviously.

Though I hated my sister's ex, I loved the stuffing out of Ivan. Sometimes I even raised my sweet tea and said a secret *nostrovia* to Boris as a thank-you.

Ivan toppled onto his side by the sofa and found a dusty Cheerio by the sofa leg. My standards about floor foods were *not* up to snuff, as per my sister. She adhered almost militantly to the five-second rule *and* insisted everything get rinsed off. I wasn't so particular. As long as it was identifiable and hadn't been left unrefrigerated for a dangerous amount of time, it seemed safe enough. And anyway, what was I going to do, pry the Cheerio out of his chubby, sticky, wet little hands?

That wasn't how I earned my #1 Auntie hoodie. No, it was not.

He looked up at me and slowly moved his drooly hand toward his drooly mouth. For a second, he paused and watched me for my verdict. I too paused with the tip of my needle about to drop a stitch. Or move a stitch, or . . . *Maybe I should take up origami.* "Go for it, little bean," I whispered and then ripped out another row of too-tight stitches.

It was then that my phone rang, making a grating *grr-grr-grr* on the kitchen table. I set down my knitting and bolted for it. Maybe it was Gabe, or maybe it was someone calling to hire me for a job. Either way, I wasn't about to let it go to voice mail. On the screen was a number I didn't recognize with an unfamiliar out-of-town area code. I hit the answer button and put my phone to my ear. "Sounds Good. This is Lily."

"I'm looking for Lily!" hollered a nasally voice on the other end of the line. It sounded a bit like my dentist, except for the heavy breathing.

"Speaking. Yes. Hello. This is Lily Jameson."

"My name is Mark Markowitz. I'm the producer for a show called *The Powers of Suggestion*. Ever heard of it?"

I almost didn't think I'd heard him right. A producer. A show. As in . . . a *television* show? Holy moly. Move over, hourly bingo gigs! "I . . . I don't think so?" Actually, I knew so. In the last few months, my watching diet consisted almost entirely of cartoons for Ivan and YouTube tutorials from women who knew how to knit and who talked reassuringly like I could learn too. Bless their sweet angel lying hearts. "How can I help you, Mr. Markowitz?"

"Investigating weird shit in far-flung places," Mr. Markowitz said, like he hadn't even heard my question. "Half survivalist, half legend hunter. Ring any bells?"

I was still a no on that. But even though it didn't ring *my* bell, it would *definitely* ring my sister's. Daisy was the queen of *Unsolved Mysteries* and whatever that ghost show was that was comprised entirely of badly lit and low-budget reenactments, all filmed on the same set, regardless of the episode. As if we wouldn't notice that every scene had an identical sofa! "Not my cup of tea, exactly. Though it sounds very exciting!"

A *rrrrrrr* sound caught my attention, and I turned to Ivan. He'd gotten a hold of his hat and was now gleefully pulling it apart—yarn flew in every direction. He made small *kaa-kaa-kaaaaa* noises and banged my knitting needles against the coffee table.

"I've got a problem, Ms. Jameson. I need your help. Filming starts on the show this evening, down in your city of Savannah. Normally, we shoestring it. My guy is hell-bent on being a one-man deal. But *this* time, we're going to need legit audio. We're doing ghosts, and we can't be doing it half-assed, you feel me?"

"I'm with you so far," I told him as I pried one of my needles out of Ivan's hand.

"You believe in ghosts, Ms. Jameson?"

The question was hardly unexpected. Being from Savannah meant that everybody believed you automatically checked two boxes. One: a deep and undying passion for sweet tea.

A *check* so hard and enthusiastic it would've ripped right through the survey.

And two: believing in ghosts.

I still had my pencil hovering over that box.

I wasn't sure if I believed or if I didn't. It was one of those mysterious things. Like Jesus. Or Buddha. Or a totally mistake-free home manicure. Just because I hadn't *seen* them didn't mean they didn't exist. And even if I *had* had a reason to be skeptical, I had the very serious disadvantage of eight generations of Jamesons from Savannah, gathering around the dining table, looking at old photos and wondering if that flash on the mirror was Great-Aunt Velma or if those strange sounds from the radiator were actually Grandpa Frank trying to communicate with Morse code.

In Savannah, *everything* was said to be haunted. And I mean everything: Churches built in the 1800s. The Outback Steakhouse built in 1999. Some old lady's root cellar. The boys' locker room at my high school. The bank teller's station wagon. *Everything.* All I could say for certain was that the closest I'd ever gotten to a ghost was when I'd cut eye holes in a dish towel and put it over Ivan's head. "That's a bit complicated. I don't really *believe*, but that doesn't mean that—"

"Probably for the best! Can't have our audio technician getting the yips, can we?"

If I'd known what the yips were, that would have helped. But I got the gist. "I'd be delighted to do whatever I can."

"Tremendous. I'd like to hire you to record some sound in a house over on, lemme find the street . . ." Some papers rustled around on the other end of the line. "Abercrombie. Abraham. Corncob . . ."

"Abercorn?"

"That's the spot! Three o'clock today!"

I spun around to check the clock on my sister's oven. It was almost nine in the morning. But business wasn't exactly booming these days. The next gig I had was next Saturday evening at the Universalist church, and they paid me in pasta salad. And yet, I didn't want to seem *too* eager. If there was one thing I'd learned as a small business owner, it was that gasping *Oh thank God!* didn't exactly bring the clients flocking. "Let me see, hang on one second . . ." I meandered around the kitchen, twirling on the tiles on my tiptoes and then straightening my sister's shopping list on the fridge. I put some bottles on the drying rack and wiped something sticky off the counter and then tried to get it off my finger. "Umm, let's . . . oh, you know, you're in luck! I just had this afternoon open up!"

Ivan tossed my yarn aside and pulled himself up alongside the coffee table. He smacked the tabletop with his hand, making *na-na-na* noises as he drummed on the magazines. I hustled over to help him before he made a mess of my sister's *People* magazine. Hell hath no fury like Daisy when she found a photo of Jamie Dornan ripped in half. "I'll be there. Thank you!"

"Fab. Bring your equipment. I'll pay you double your rate to help my guy film his pilot. Just the one episode. One and done. How's that suit you?"

What I said, in my head, was, *Double. My. Rate?* But I played it cool and calm and small-businessy. "That'll be fine, Mr. Markowitz. I really appreciate your generosity. I can promise that the audio will be—"

Ivan smacked the remote, and the television turned on with a staticky click. And there, staring back at me from my sister's television screen, was a man who looked an *awful* lot like Gabe.

He was shirtless. His skin was dewy with sweat, tanned and delicious. He was in a jungle, gesturing at something behind him. The camera bobbled as he turned to look over his shoulder, revealing a dark and sexy tattoo on his back. He held the camera out farther from his body, and I saw a row of muscular, rock-solid abs and a broad and rippling chest. Then he smiled.

And I gasped.

It was him. Even in the half-light last night, I'd seen that smile. I'd never forget that smile.

Though the volume was down low, it was just loud enough for me to hear him say, "I start our search for the mysterious Zambian swamp creature, known as the 'boat breaker' or the kongamato, right now on . . ."

An opening montage filled the screen, accompanied by a theme song that was manly and heavy on the electric guitar riffs. On the screen flashed Gabe, talking to the camera, in his swim trunks. There was Gabe, running through the snow, the snowflakes accentuating the salt and pepper in his sideburns. Gabe, eating something that looked like a roasted quail next to a campfire. There was Gabe bailing out a canoe in the dark. The image faded to black; the music kicked up a notch. Then there it was. Confirmation. He didn't just *look* like he belonged on television. He was actually *on* television.

THE POWERS OF SUGGESTION
WITH GABE POWERS

"Mr. Markowitz." I stared at the screen. How was I going to *work* with that man? I could barely keep the drool inside my mouth. Gabe leaped off a dock into a pristine African lake, and I bit my knuckle. He resurfaced, sparkling with water and beaming. "I think we might have a problem . . ." I gaped at the rather spectacular bulge in his swim trunks. "A *big* problem."

"Three p.m., Ms. Jameson! Corner of Abercorn and Hull!"

3

GABE

The crawl space under the porch of my Airbnb was full of dusty old pool noodles, busted sprinklers, and an incomplete troop of faded Christmas gnomes, the remaining members of which each held a letter to spell **ERRY CHRI M !**

With the right light and the right filter, the house would look spooky as hell. In reality, it was actually stunningly beautiful. It was called the Willows, and it had a minor entry in two of the ghost-hunting books I'd used to gather information on Savannah. Built in 1802, it was three stories—six bedrooms and four baths. There was a big wraparound porch, a knocker in the shape of a horseshoe, and a garden thick with vines and flowers. In addition to being an Airbnb, it was also for sale. That morning as I drank my coffee, I'd looked it up on Zillow and checked out the real estate brochure in the front hallway. Original woodwork, new roof, updated wiring and heating and cooling systems. *Modern conveniences with historic charm.* It was, in fact, just the sort of house I would have loved to own . . . if I were a different dude with a different job and a whole different life completely.

But I wasn't a different dude. I was a television host sweating my balls off in Georgia in July. And I had a pilot to film.

I army-crawled between the noodles and the gnomes and turned on the camera that was attached to my helmet. My face in the camera's flip screen confirmed what I'd known already—the frozen veggies had helped with the pain, but I still looked pretty messed up. My nose was swollen, and there was a cut across the side. On the upside, I didn't have a black eye, I could still smell, and Markowitz had made it plenty clear that the rough-and-tumble angle played pretty well with the twenty-four-to-thirty-six-year-old female demographic. Normally, demographic data was background noise to me. But now, the sweetheart demographic had a face.

Lily.

Even now I couldn't stop thinking about her. Or the way her shorts fit her. Or the way her cleavage had looked under her hand when she'd pressed it to her chest.

But I snapped out of my Lily daydream and refocused on the camera. I hit record, made sure I didn't have anything between my teeth, and then counted back from three. And *action*.

"I'm coming at you from underneath a house on Abercorn, known as the most haunted street in Savannah. Records indicate that this house was built in 1802 by a local developer named William Jeremiah Beaumont. Apparently, he and his wife spent every afternoon on the porch drinking lemonade and holding hands. The legend is that they're still there." I panned up to the floorboards above me, with rays of sunlight streaming in between the planks. "Just going to have a poke around down here to make sure that all this can't be explained by something logical, like a family of raccoons or some issue with the gas meter."

I planted my elbows and wriggled forward on my stomach, adjusting my camera on my helmet. It was then that I heard a car door swing shut. It sounded nearby. Mailman, probably. But then I heard footsteps coming up the walkway. I lifted my head to see through the diamond gaps in the lattice, and there she was. In a cute half sundress, half jumper printed with tiny flowers. The sweetheart demographic herself.

Lily.

But just hang on a second. *Lily?*

Her light and peppy footsteps moved up the porch steps, and she headed for the front door. She rapped a few times on the glass window, a soft but confident knock.

I crawled forward a few feet to get a better look at her as she stood there waiting. Between the slats I saw a smooth calf, a soft thigh. And a little bit of her underwear. Her shorts were loose enough and her stance was *just* wide enough for me to see them: bright yellow with white polka dots.

Fuuuuuck.

She lifted up onto her tiptoes to reach the knocker on the front door. As she did, the summer wind kicked up and showed me the spot where her ass made a ball-busting crease with her thighs.

Double fuuuuuuck.

But what the hell was I going to do now? Do my best Barry White impression and hit her with, *Hey, baby, right here below you, looking up your shorts.*

Nice, Powers. Real nice. Man of the year right there.

I stopped filming and stayed low. It had worked with the lumberjack yeti trespassing thing, and it might work here. Maybe she'd head back to her van and I could crawl my way out of gnomeland without seeming like a Peeping Tom.

But she didn't go back to her van. Instead, she sat on the porch swing, directly above me. Her thighs pressed against the wooden slats, and her shorts rode up enough to make me *almost* groan out loud. She was fucking delicious. And I wanted to nibble every damned inch of her.

She pulled her phone from her bag. The sounds of her typing were barely audible, a faint *click-click-click* above the breeze, followed by the airplane sound effect of a message being sent.

One second later my phone chirped in my pocket. As I shot my hand out to silence it, my elbow clipped the first of the gnomes. Which knocked over the second. Which knocked over the third. Pretty soon the whole goddamned line of the little bastards was toppling over and rolling around, with jingle bells jangling and toy drums banging.

Overhead, Lily leaped off the swing with a thump. "Who's down there? I've got my pepper spray! You've been warned!" She dropped to her knees and peered through the knothole in the slats.

God*damn* it. "It's me, Gabe." I unclipped the chin strap of my filming helmet. "Just doing some light crawl-space investigation."

She blinked once and stared at me. Then she hit me with that smile. "Hi."

I pulled off my helmet. The thing was incredibly useful, but it had the slight disadvantage of making me look like both a geek and a storm trooper. "What the hell are you doing here?"

"You first," she said. "Lemme guess. Going spelunking?"

I was going to have to tell her something. I was under a porch with a camera on an articulating arm bolted to my helmet. *Just hanging out* wasn't gonna cut it. "Yeah, so. I'm actually . . ." See, I *hated* this part. As far as I could tell, there was no way to explain what I did without sounding like a total prick. "I'm actually on television. I have a television show."

It didn't seem to faze her at all. "I know. I was teasing about the spelunking." She pinned her tongue between her teeth as she smiled. "I happened to stumble upon your show for the first time this morning. You were in Zambia hunting for the kongamato lizard thingy. You look *really* nice in swim trunks."

Awww, fuck yeah. I might not love being recognized, but this was different. That new desire in her eyes? Gimme. Some. Of. That. Sugar. "Glad you think so."

"And I really liked your show. Which is good because, apparently, I'm your new audio tech."

Markowitz! Asshole! But it was no mystery to me what he'd done—it was his standard MO. He'd googled "audio engineers in Savannah" and clicked on the top result. That was how he always did his research. She probably had like four hundred five-star reviews with everybody saying, "We love Lily!"

Totally understandable.

Lily pressed her eye closer to the hole in the floorboards. "Your nose looks pretty good! I brought you some arnica cream. And some sweet tea. Have you had sweet tea yet?"

Like she'd doused me with a bucket of water, my Markowitz annoyance subsided. Her smile made me smile. If that was what *help* looked like, it might be exactly what I needed. "Not yet."

"Then you're in for a treat."

She was goddamned right about that.

4

LILY

Gabe crawled out from under the porch, dusting himself off as he walked up the wooden steps. I handed him the tea I'd gotten for him on the way over—I'd hemmed and hawed over flavored or plain before finally taking a gamble on him liking peach. Instead of drinking it from the straw, he popped the lid off and took a few greedy gulps.

The ice in the plastic cup clattered as he wiped his mouth on his forearm. In a few seconds, he'd gulped down what took me half a morning to drink. "Fuck, that's good," he said.

But as he said it, his eyes moved all over me, making it abundant clear that he wasn't actually talking about the tea.

Everything got a bit swirly when I looked straight at him. Like when I got off the teacup ride at the fair with Ivan. I hooked my arm around one of the porch posts and hung on tight.

"So," I said, gripping the wood and clutching my tea to my chest, feeling the sweaty coolness of the condensation against my skin, "you're staying here? And filming here?" I glanced up at the porch ceiling, painted baby blue in the old-fashioned way. When I looked back at him, I found he'd been staring right at me the whole time. My knees felt a bit wobbly, so I gripped the post a little tighter and wedged my tush up against the railing.

"That's the idea." He reached into his pants pocket, pulled out a key, and opened the front door. "After you, beautiful."

I stepped underneath his rippling outstretched arm into the foyer. I was met with a wave of cool air-conditioning and a faint whiff of furniture polish. The house was even prettier inside than it was outside. Dark, shiny woodwork was offset with immaculate paint in elegant colors that nobody used anymore—mauve and chartreuse and olive green. Sitting on the side table in the foyer was a sales brochure with photos of the house. I peeked inside and saw an eye-popping row of zeros. It wasn't just expensive. It was a fairy tale. And standing there in the reflection of the foyer mirror was this fairy tale's rugged, dashing prince. He checked something on his phone, and the muscles of his jaw fluttered.

What was happening to me? I was getting all hot and bothered over *jaw* muscles? I blamed the fact that I'd been binge-watching him all morning. *The Powers of Suggestion* wasn't just sexy and exciting, it was also playfully cheeky, and it let me get a delightful glimpse at Gabe's personality. He didn't take himself too seriously and always investigated the mystery du jour with a respectful curiosity. He never exploited anybody's fear or superstition but tackled everything with an almost boyish zest. *Cutie patooootie.* It wasn't *my* fault that my hormones were shooting through me like an exploding cartoon thermometer.

It took real strength to stop myself from staring at him, but for the sake of not being a total weirdo, I managed to turn my attention to a ring of old skeleton keys hanging on the newel post. It weighed about five pounds, and it had a small silver tag engraved with the words *The Willows*.

The house had a name. I'd always loved the idea of a house with a name.

"This place is incredible," I said, admiring the way the staircase curved and wound up the floors. The steps and landings made a concentric series of rectangles with a sparkling chandelier in the center, suspended from the ceiling of the top floor.

"Right? Sitting right there on Airbnb." He was close enough for me to feel the heat and warmth of his body and to smell some sort of sexy musky something. Maybe cologne, or maybe a dash of hair product. I looked at his thick dark hair for any sign of gel. I didn't see any. But really, I'd *have* to touch it to know. Lord.

Oblivious to my lusty thoughts about his hair-care regimen, he went on. "I found it mentioned in a few books when I was doing research. I couldn't hit *book trip* fast enough." He glanced at me. "I can't imagine owning a house like this. When I was growing up, my dad was in the army and we moved a ton. One cinder-block ranch house after another. This place is like a palace."

I nodded slowly, watching him like I'd watched him on television. When I was watching his reruns, I'd been mesmerized thinking of him doing ordinary things—bringing his effortless sexiness to grocery shopping, and making scrambled eggs, and taking out the recycling. *I'll bet he's a very conscientious recycler.* Now that same thing was happening again except in reverse—what I was actually seeing fuzzed into a sexy daydream. *Army* had apparently been the keyword. I envisioned him in fatigues being brave and dashing. Shirtless—definitely shirtless. *Hello, soldier!*

Clearing my throat, I hooked the keys back over the post. I looked at Gabe again but this time zeroed in on what I imagined was the only imperfection on his entire body. The cut across the nose that I'd given him. Nice. Leave it to me to deface a masterpiece! Maybe later that afternoon I could pop over to the Telfair museum and dump nail polish all over the *Bird Girl* statue.

I dug the tube of arnica cream out of my purse and unscrewed the cap. I put a little dollop on my fingertip, got up on my tiptoes, and gently dabbed it on the bruise and the small cut. He watched me the whole time. Never winced, never grimaced. Just focused right on me with those deep-brown eyes of his. There was an expression I'd read about in my smutty romances. *Bedroom eyes.* I'd never known what that meant . . .

Until now.

He was so intense about the very act of staring at me that I didn't even know what to say. So I just smiled awkwardly at him, feeling like my lips were sticking to my teeth. I rubbed the extra arnica into my hand and managed to whisper, "That should help."

"Feels better already." For a few seconds, we stayed locked in stop-motion. This time he turned away first and raked his hand through his hair. It was exactly what he'd done when he'd popped out of the lake in Africa. I'd freeze-framed that moment more times that I cared to admit. Same smile and everything. His shirt pulled tight over his biceps, and I realized that if he moved his hand a little bit farther, I might get a glimpse of *the muscles*. I didn't know what they were actually called, but I knew he had them. *The muscles.* The man muscles. The V muscles. With veins!

The thought of them made me groan. Out loud. A sound that I think I'd only ever come close to making when I licked cake batter directly from the beater.

"What was that?" He cocked his head slightly, smiling. "Was that you?"

My cheeks went from hot to *on fire*. I was about point-five seconds from tumbling into his arms or tackling him on the steps as I roared, *Not all Southern girls are polite!* But instead, I clasped my hands, clenched my thighs, and squeaked, "Ghosts. Had to be the ghosts."

He followed me around as I wired up the house, wearing my rolls of gaffer's tape on his forearm. We put mics and recording devices in each room so that no sound would go uncaptured. He carried my ladder like it weighed nothing at all and never griped when we had to move it a few feet this way, or that way, or back again. But the thing with the tape was what was really getting to me. It meant that every time I needed a piece, I had to get really close. Close enough to be within grabbing distance, which made me want grab his fashionably wrinkled black linen shirt in my fists and send his buttons pinging all over the . . .

Hoooo-boy. I was going to have to get ahold of myself here, and quick. I'd already whacked him up upside the face. I couldn't be ripping off his buttons too. "Could you hand me that wire?" I said, trying desperately to sound professional. "The thin one? With the white line in the middle?" I pulled a plastic hook and removable foamy backing from my pocket. I peeled the paper backing off the wall side of the squishy adhesive strip and affixed it to the plaster, pressing the plastic hook in place. Gabe reached into the hallway for the cord, still keeping one hand on the ladder to make sure I didn't fall. He tightened his grip on the middle rung, and the veins in his forearm grew even more noticeable.

I tried to think if I had ever been so close to anybody so sexy. I mean, unless I counted one of the personal trainers at the gym, whose attention I had only ever gotten by falling off a yoga ball, I think it was a resounding, deafening no. "Did you model before you got into television?"

Oh, Lily, Lily, Lily. I clutched the top step of the ladder, hooking my fingers over the plastic cap. "That was supposed to be an inside thought. I think maybe I need a snack."

Gabe laughed a lovely embarrassed laugh. "I'm no model. Just a guy who likes to make home movies and somehow managed to make a career out of it."

With burning cheeks, I hooked my patch cable up with the mic as he watched me. Normally when I did my work, I didn't think in particularly techy terms. But today I did, and I watched the male end slide into the female end. *Mmmm-hmmmm.*

I made my way down the ladder, each step surprisingly unsure because my thighs were literally trembling. When I was back on the ground, he took a step toward me and I held on to the side of the ladder, frozen with desire as he got closer and closer. He leaned in and reached out his hand so that his fingertips were brushing my cheeks. *He's going to kiss me. Oh my God, he's going to* . . . I inhaled, fluttering my eyelids closed and raising my lips to his.

"Here," he said.

When I opened my eyes, I saw he'd only been pulling a piece of backing paper from my hair.

"Right, yes." I rubbed my lips together and glued my eyes to a nearby light switch. I was horrified. He'd been trying to help me, and I'd turned into some kissy-faced wanton woman. One pint of ice cream in my pajamas wasn't even going to put a dent in this embarrassment; I was going to have to stop by the grocery and get one of those plastic buckets of cheap Neapolitan. *What is wrong with me?* I jammed the little piece of paper into my pocket and straightened my shoulders. And wiped my sweaty hands on my bare legs. "Well! I think that does it!"

Gabe shook his head. "One more room." He pointed behind me. "Master bedroom."

I glanced over my shoulder and into the bedroom across the hall-way. It was beautiful, spacious, and luxurious. There was a massive plaster fireplace on the wall and a gigantic old wooden bed in the middle. The bed had fancy sheets, like something out of an overpriced home-wares magazine. But the covers were a bit rumpled, and I spotted a cell phone charging cord plugged into the wall and an empty glass on the nightstand. It was the room where he was staying. It was the bed where he had slept. I envisioned him with his waist barely covered by the sheet, like in a soap opera. Cue the *Young and the Restless* theme song.

"Of course," I squeaked and grabbed the last of the mics. Feeling frazzled and embarrassed, I scurried toward the room before realizing I needed one more sticky hook from my bag. I spun around to grab it.

When I did, I smacked right into him, and the air left my lungs with a *whoosh*.

I stayed there. Frozen. The longer he held my stare, the more bedroomy his eyes became. But I had no idea what to do with a man as handsome as he was. I couldn't make a move on him—I could hardly look right at him. So I chickened out and tried to pretend that I was actually trying to grab a piece of tape from the roll on his arm. But I got distracted when I touched his skin, and I slid my hand off the tape and onto his forearm instead.

As soon as I touched him, I saw something wild in his expression. Something so intense, it sent a prickle of goose bumps right through me. It was as if I'd fired a starting pistol. He took one more step toward me and said, "I want to kiss you, Lily. Better stop me right now before I can't stop myself."

I wasn't used to this kind of treatment at all. I was used to men who confused chivalry with going dutch and thought unbridled desire was some sign of disrespect. False! What I'd always wanted was *a man*. But I'd never imagined a man quite like this.

And I wasn't about to stop him. No, siree.

He gripped my hips and shoved me up against the wall. The plaster was cold against my skin, and the chair rail dug into my tush. He pressed his hips into my stomach and pulled my face toward his. He wasn't shy about it. He was aggressive and furious and unrelentingly *male*. Knotting my hair around his fingers, he cupped my jaw, looked hard into my eyes, and kissed me. Oh *God* and heaven above, did he kiss me. Kissed me like I'd never been kissed before. Our teeth clashed, my lip got pinched, my tongue got swept aside. He growled into my mouth and dug his fingers into my thighs.

It was electric, dizzying, and disorienting. I opened my eyes to make sure I didn't miss a thing, not a second of this beautiful man kissing me. I'd been watching him all day, and I couldn't stop now. I watched him devour me, get lost in me, savor me. This time, reality didn't fuzz into the dream. The dream became the reality.

Gabe really let me feel his strength, pinning me with such force that I came up onto my tiptoes and whimpered. We pawed at each other, so frenzied that I didn't know whose breath was whose. I pushed him back from me an inch and let my fingertips slide across the bare skin above his belt under his shirt. I traced the lines of the hills and valleys of his abs and the very top of his treasure trail. And the muscles. Oh, glory, glory, glory. There they were.

The muscles.

When he felt me tracing them down past his belt line, he inhaled hard and pressed me against the wall even harder. He took his hand away from my hip just long enough to slam the bedroom door. With his other hand he drew my knee up, like we were about to tango. Standing on one foot, hanging on to him for support, I thought how easy, how simple, how *natural* it would be for him to hoist me right up off the floor, and . . .

Whoa, nelly, this was *bananas*!

I flattened my hand and pushed him away, sucking in a breath. "I . . . ," I said, locking eyes with him. "We *have* to slow down . . ."

My skin stung from the coarseness of his stubble. He looked greedy, and his stare was intense. Almost a warning. Like I might not be able to stop him now that he'd gotten started. "Why?" he growled, letting me feel his hardness against my thigh. A lot of hardness. *Big* hardness.

The gruffness of his voice and the pressure of him against me just about made me lose my resolve. But still, I stayed strong and sensible. I was no prude, but I was no wanton woman either. "It's the heat." I tried not to let him hear that I was, in fact, *panting*. I smoothed one of the fist-shaped puckers I'd made on his shirt. "Makes people do crazy things."

Gabe told my cleavage, "It's not the heat."

Feeling flustered, shy, and more than a little annoyed with myself for not having the guts to go headlong into what was surely going to be the most delightful of afternoon delights, I reached for the carved-crystal doorknob. Except when I tried to turn it, nothing happened. I jiggled it back and forth, but it didn't turn. Gabe let out a breathy laugh behind me, and I looked at him over my shoulder, still holding on to the knob.

"Suppose that explains the keys downstairs," he said and adjusted his pants to accommodate his now much more noticeable bulge. *Gaaaaah!*

Only the tiniest thread of common sense was preventing me from shoving him backward onto the bed, climbing on top of him, and saying, "I'll sew your buttons back on myself!" as I sent them pinging around the room like a handful of M&Ms.

He took a step toward me. I was actually trembling with desire—it was buzzing through me, through every muscle and bone. "For the record," Gabe said, "I want to take you. Right here, right now."

My breath came out as a shudder. If he came at me again, I was going to crack like an overstuffed taco shell. Just one more scoop of Gabe and I was a goner. "Noted," I whispered.

He hooked my chin with his brawny finger and made me raise my eyes to his. "But instead I'll get us out of here, take you to dinner, and pretend like fucking you hasn't been the only item on the agenda since you nearly knocked me out. We clear?"

I was stunned with desire. Shivering with need. Pulsing with *please, please, please.* Yet somehow, in the midst of all of it, I hung on tight to the antique doorknob and managed to whisper out the only word that was left in my head. *"Crystal."*

5

GABE

She was one hell of a kisser, and I couldn't wait to taste her again. Her lips were kiss-reddened from my stubble, and she was blushing hard. And Jesus, I wanted her. I wanted her in bed, naked. I wanted to take her through sunset and halfway through the night. But she'd stopped me, and I respected that. For now.

I took one last look at her fantastic cleavage and turned around, adjusting my hard-on with my back to her. The struggle was real. My inseam was *not* prepared for her, not even close.

Once I got myself situated, I focused on how to get us out of the bedroom. I didn't have my phone, and as I could tell by looking at the pockets of that tiny little flowered number she was wearing—fuck *me*—neither did she. We were on the second floor, with a view of the big overgrown yard. Right below the window was the roof of the back porch. That made it easy. "I'll climb down and get the keys." I unlocked the metal latch on the window, gripped the sash with both hands, and gave it a push.

The damned thing didn't budge at all.

Lily gave it a try, but it was the same result. Not even a rattle. "Humidity," she said. "Or else it's painted shut. But there's that . . ." She spun around, pointing at the door.

Above it was a louvered window, one of those old-fashioned things that has a hinge on the top. Walking across the room, I cracked my knuckles and then hooked my fingers over the top of the doorjamb, getting ready to pull myself up.

Lily tugged on one of my belt loops and wagged her finger at me. "There's no way you and all this"—she gave me a glance up and down—"are going to fit through there. I'll go." She kicked off her sandals. "Give me a boost."

I let go of the jamb and raised my eyebrow at her. "You think *I'm* gonna let you be the hero?"

She gave me an equally sassy eyebrow lift. "That way you won't get stuck in the window, and you might even get to cop a feel." She sealed the deal with a shimmy of her hips that made her boobs shake.

The way they shook reminded me of the way flan jiggled, like the kind I'd had in Spain. I liked flan. But I liked her boobs *way* better. "Sold." I crouched down and intertwined my fingers. Using my shoulder for support, she nestled her heel in the cradle of my hands. The skin of her calf was smooth and soft, and I noticed a tan line on her foot in the shape of her sandal. It was V-shaped, like the straps of her flip-flop. It was also the same shape as her panty line, now at eye level. I ground my teeth, thinking how badly I wanted to yank those suckers off her. I could hear the lace ripping already.

"Ready?" Lily asked.

You've got no idea, sweetheart. I cleared my throat and looked away from that enticing, mouthwatering ridge. "Count of one, two, three," I said and gave her a boost like we were doing some sort of cheerleading move.

She rose up into the air with a squeal. She wasn't heavy at all, but the position was awkward, and as I hoisted her up I had to step into her. My forehead was against her ass, and my face was between her legs. "I take it back. This was fucking brilliant."

Lily giggled above me. I inhaled deeply. There was the faintest hit of something other than her perfume and her lotion. That scent, that salty warmth, gave me a pulse of desire right through my balls.

Her toes curled slightly as she leveraged herself against my hand. Yet again, I was painfully hard in my pants. With her free leg, she anchored herself against the doorknob. The change in position put my nose right on the edge of her shorts. I pressed my forehead against her ass and suppressed a growl.

"Well, hello," she said, all low and sultry.

Now she decides to have her way with me. "Hurry up before I can't help myself and sink my teeth into you."

"OK!" she giggled. "OK," she said again, with more focus. She wobbled a bit, but I kept her steady. I heard the window creak open above me, and with her free leg she tried to get a toehold on the door, but her foot slid right down the shiny off-white paint.

"Give me a little more," she said. "Please."

Maybe it wasn't supposed to sound dirty, but Jesus, that's how I heard it. My mind was in the gutter, and it was there to stay. I hoisted her heel up farther, but it wasn't enough. She was halfway out the window, with her torso out and her hips still on my side. There was no way for me to get enough leverage by boosting her heels alone. It meant one thing.

I was going to have to put my hands on that ass.

"All right. I'd apologize if I were sorry, but I'm not," I said. "I'm going to have to . . ." Very gently, I put one hand in the center of her magnificent ass cheeks.

"Oh *Lord.*"

Under my palms, her skin was so soft and voluptuous that all I could think of doing was giving it a flat-handed spank. I could almost hear the *crack* of my palm against her. I gripped her hips and gave her a push. It got her about halfway through, up to her waist.

"Keep going," she told me, getting into it now. "Don't be shy. I won't break."

Now I didn't even try to suppress my growl.

Her laugh echoed through the hallway. "Harder, Mr. Powers. *Harder.*"

She was killing me. "Don't know, Lily. You might have to hang out there for a while so I can do a safety check." I dug my hands more firmly into her ass.

"Give me one more good thrust, you animal," she said through another wonderful giggle. "I can take it."

Fuck. I gave her one more shove, and she finally wedged her knee out of the window. She wriggled through the opening, hung on to the sill with her fingers and thudded down onto the floor. "One enormous set of ancient skeleton keys, coming right up," she said as she pitter-pattered down the hallway.

What a cutie.

The keyhole gave me a peekaboo view of her face and her cleavage, but the scene cut to black as she tried the first key. She gave it a twist, but it answered with a *clack* and she pulled it out, giving me a new angle on her beautiful face. "So tell me about this show you're filming," she said.

Her spaghetti strap slid down, revealing her bra strap underneath. Beneath that was the faint, pale edge of a tan line. I saw the top of her bra—the delicate scalloped edge was pink trimmed with white. Because she didn't know I was watching, she didn't fix it, and I pressed my fist to my mouth to stop myself from groaning. She tried another key, and the keyhole went dark again. She huffed and pulled it out, giving me my perfect view once more. "Gabe?"

Focus, Powers. Focus. Answer the goddamned question. "This is for the pilot," I explained. "I've found it's a hell of a lot easier to actually film an episode than pitch an idea on paper."

She nodded and wrinkled up her eyebrows, as animated as if I was sitting across from her. "Makes sense. Does that mean you'll do more episodes? If they . . ." She trailed off and looked up at the ceiling like she might find the word up there. "*Give you the go-ahead* or whatever the lingo is?"

"Yeah. That's the idea."

She tried another key, and the hole went dark again. Again she gave it a twist, but the lock didn't shift. "So the guy who I talked to this morning?" she asked. "That was . . ."

"My producer." I realized I didn't sound nearly as annoyed about him as I sometimes felt. The fact was, even if he was an occasional pain in my ass, he'd made it so I got to spend the day with Lily. And I had zero complaints about that. "Markowitz. But let me ask you something. Do you believe in these Savannah ghosts everybody's always talking about?"

She froze with the keys swinging from the ring. "I don't really know. I think so." She wrinkled up her eyebrows again. "But I've never seen one or anything. It's really just stories for me."

Now there was an idea. "Maybe I can get you on camera telling some of those stories."

Her eyes widened and then scrunched shut with a cringe. "Oh, I don't know about that." She shook her head and smiled. "No, I don't think . . . That's very nice of you. But no. I'll leave the television stuff to you." Now she actually fanned herself. "Lord knows, you know what you're doing."

The idea of her watching my show was *intensely* hot to me. A kink I never knew I had.

The next key on the ring was a long and thin one, slimmer and shinier than the rest. She placed it in the lock, slid it into the keyhole . . .

And poked me right in the goddamned eye.

I lunged backward, trying to catch myself before I fell. But no dice. The bare floors were slippery, and I clocked the back of my head on the hardwood. "Fuck," I groaned, clasping my eye with one hand and my head with the other.

"Oh my God, are you OK?" she asked as the jingling got more urgent. "Hold on! It's got to be one of these!"

"Totally fine." I blinked hard against my palm and felt my eye welling up with tears. "Just getting comfortable."

I blinked up at the circular plaster chandelier medallion as tears streamed down my cheek. What the hell was going on here? I'd spent my whole career avoiding dangerous situations. I get within ten feet of Lily and it's one disaster after another. She was like the Bermuda Triangle.

Lily finally found the right key and came bursting in. Through the blur of the tears, I watched her try to put together why the hell I was lying on the floor. She looked at me and the door and the ring of keys in her hand. "What *happened*?"

You happened. "Listen. Why don't we go get dinner now? Then we can come on back here to do some taping." I rubbed my eye with knuckle. "We can make a night of it."

In response, she gave me an openmouthed, wide-eyed stare. "Ummm . . ."

Granted, *dinner and work* didn't exactly have the same ring of romance as *dinner and drinks*, but it didn't seem *that* bad. And anyway, she'd been the one who'd told me we had to slow down. "Or . . . not?"

But Lily shook her head. "Working tonight is just fine! But I . . . thought we said seven thirty."

I craned my neck to check the grandfather clock in the hallway. "It's already five. The sooner we eat, the sooner we can get back here to do some recording." *And possibly find our way back to this room.*

Lily played with the keys a little nervously. "OK," she said slowly. "That's fine. Sure. But don't you have something you need to do? Don't you have to, I don't know, maybe . . ." Her babbles were getting faster and more urgent. ". . . shower or change or something?" She cringed again and face-palmed her forehead. "Not because you *need* to. Sorry. I'm just saying, no need to rough it on my account."

In my book, roughing it was washing my boxers in a piranha-infested tributary of the Amazon. Going straight to dinner with her in downtown Savannah wasn't. I was pretty sure she was trying to distract me from something or that there was something she didn't want me to know about. That was when I remembered the wallpapers on her cell phone—that chubby little boy. Maybe she had babysitting duty. "You worried about kids? I love kids. I take care of my nieces whenever I get a chance to visit them."

She shook her head quickly. "Not kids."

"Dogs? I love dogs. And cats. All animals, really."

She looked sternly at me. Seriously focused and genuinely worried. "*All* animals?"

I mean . . . "Unless it's some kind of man-eating Malaysian jungle lizard, we're all good."

She offered her hand to help me up. Still, she seemed *very* concerned. The eyebrow rumple ridge was in full form. "It's not Malaysian. And it's not a lizard. But the jury is still out on man-eating."

6

LILY

When it came to my dating life, the General was a living, breathing deal breaker. The men he hated were the ones I thought I might end up being able to tolerate for a while; the ones he liked were the ones I knew were headed for the old heave-ho. It wasn't like I was some Tinder-queen floozy; I went on promising dates about as often as I had to get my teeth cleaned. But each encounter with the General wasn't merely *memorable*—it was painfully unforgettable. And if the General didn't like them, that meant trouble. Because God help me, the idea of having a lasting, meaningful relationship while being constantly heckled by a parrot who viewed every man as his rival was not exactly how I envisioned my happily ever after.

In spite of his strong opinions about my dating life, I adored the General. He was good company and full of delightful, unexpected surprises. But it seemed as though he didn't want to share me. Ever. Sometimes my sister sent me articles about things like *the mate-seeking habits of territorial fowl* with suggestive winky emojis. She definitely had a point. What other thirtysomething woman would he be able to con into buying organic vegetables for the rest of his wonderfully long lifespan?

Now I was going to introduce him to Gabe. Sexy, aggressive, scrumptious Gabe. But I had a feeling that the General was going to be pretty suspicious about Gabe's confidence and cocky swagger. Of course, I didn't *have* to introduce them just yet. Gabe surely wasn't going to be in town for long, and I didn't want to ruffle any feathers. Literally or figuratively. But I also wanted to be polite—my idea of Southern hospitality wasn't asking Gabe to hang out on the porch while I negotiated with my beloved resident terrorist. And anyway, as my grandma often said, *"If you're worried about the General, honey, take it from FDR: the only thing to fear is fear itself. Seven out of ten times!"*

So we left Gabe's truck at the Willows, and I drove us back to my house in my van. I didn't live far, and Gabe kept up the third degree for the whole drive as he made sexy adjustments to the rolled-up sleeves of the dress shirt he'd changed into before we left. Unsurprisingly, given his line of work, he knew all about dangerous and semi-dangerous animals. He cycled through them like he was reading from a Wikipedia entry. "Is it a ferret? Ferrets can be *really* intense."

"Definitely not a ferret."

"Pot-bellied pig?"

"Smaller. Less friendly."

"Turtle?"

I pictured his beady eyes. His prehistoric toes. The way he trundled across the floor when he didn't feel like flying. "Close, but fatter and fluffier."

A few minutes later, we pulled into my driveway and I saw my sister peeking out of her window on the first floor. Ivan was in her arms and yanking on her hair like a bell pull. I loved my sister to bits, but introducing Gabe to one member of my family with strong opinions about my dating life at a time was enough. So I gave Daisy wide eyes and a tiny shake of my head, and she disappeared behind the lace curtain.

I led Gabe up the stairs to the second floor of the house I shared with my sister; each floor had been converted into its own apartment by my grandmother, who really only believed in two things: sugar cookies and saving money. She'd rented out the second floor to offset her property tax payments. When she passed away, she left the house to me and my sister jointly, one floor each. To me alone had she bequeathed the General. He was sweet on me, and I liked him a lot. In the world of African gray parrots and humans, that made us an unbreakable love match. Like Richard Burton and Elizabeth Taylor, though. Sometimes it was bliss. Sometimes it was chaos.

"This place is fantastic," Gabe said, trailing behind me, looking up at the crown molding and the plasterwork on the ceiling. "It's like out of a movie."

A movie, yes. Sure. But what *kind* of movie? I thought, as I fumbled for my house keys. Rom-com?

Or horror?

We were about to find out. I said a private little *Please don't let this be too awful* to whoever might be listening upstairs and opened the door.

The General had his back to us. He was in his cage, gazing out the window at the street. When he heard the door creak, he turned to look back at us over his shoulder. Any other bird—a canary, a parakeet, even one of the scary-huge crows that lived off fried chicken out of the dumpster at the grocery store—would have hopped around to face us straight on. That was what *regular, normal, ordinary-IQ* birds did. But not the General. He was the master of the over-the-shoulder glare. Like Dracula.

"Hi!" I said, as cheerfully as possible. In one of my many books about living with African gray parrots, which tended to tilt more toward self-help than informational in tone, I'd learned that they can "sense signs of microdiscomfort in the human voice." I'd also heard the very same thing about Mother Teresa *and* Ted Bundy. The General was a many-sided mystery.

He turned away to look out the window and mimicked the sound of me locking the door right before I actually locked the door. It made it sound like the house was full of echoes.

Gabe glanced at me, clearly a bit puzzled. "Lily. That's just a parrot."

I set down my keys and hung my purse on the hook next to the door. It was a logical enough thing to say. But logic didn't really apply to a creature that could distinguish between organic and nonorganic cauliflower. "And Jaws was just a shark."

That was when the General did hop around to face us. He lowered his head and lifted his little rounded shoulders to face off with us. I felt like a toreador walking into a bullring. "How's my Mr. Potato?" I asked.

He gave me a warm coo but then went silent as he zeroed in on Gabe. He ducked down slightly to get a better angle on the new human in the room, peering out from under a pair of primary-colored plastic keys that he'd stolen from Ivan. He poked his head between two of the keys and puffed up his feathers so he looked like a great big gray pinecone.

I'd known the General since I was a kid. I knew that puff. It meant he was about to say something brand-spanking-new.

I rewound through the handful of words that Gabe and I had said since we walked in. I looked him hard in the tiny black eyes.

"Daaaaa-dun . . ." sang the General. Oh my God, it was *Jaws*. He was singing the theme from *Jaws*.

"You've never even seen it!" I whisper-barked.

He shook his narrow shoulders. He lifted his beak. "Daaaa-dun!"

Why was I even surprised? For reasons we'd never know, he had the Gettysburg Address down pat. He knew my grandma's sugar cookie recipe by heart. On days when there was no garbage pickup and I was sleeping in, he mimicked the sound of a garbage truck so I'd go flying out of bed, confused and gathering up recycling. Of course he had *Jaws* in that little walnut brain. Of course he did.

"Hey, man," Gabe said and began approaching him.

He leaped up one rung and hung his head. "Da-dun! Da-dun! Da-dun-da-dun-da-dun-da . . ." He snatched the keys off their hook and gave them an almighty cage-rattling shake. "Intruder!" he barked around the plastic ring. "Thief! Interloper!"

One floor directly below, Ivan was just going down for the night. "Shhhh!" I put my finger to my lips. "Do you want your dinner or not?"

The General silenced his cries and dropped his keys. Next to me, Gabe snickered, and the General glared at him.

For a moment, I thought the worst might've passed. If we got out of this with a new theme song and some scattered insults, it'd be a total win. At least he hadn't made the Noise.

Gabe studied him curiously, with an adorable little smirk. His eyes twinkled with interest, not fear. A definite bonus. "Is he an African gray?" Gabe asked.

I nodded. "He's a Timneh. Chubbier and calmer than the Congo gray. I inherited him from my grandma with a shoebox full of cash for vet bills. She rescued him from an estate sale. Before that . . ." I thought back to the time he'd seen a clip of Martin Luther King Jr. on television and said *It was very nice to meet you!* ". . . it's really anybody's guess."

"He's awesome," Gabe said, studying him closely. "I've never seen one in person. How old is he?"

This was one of those questions that was probably best left to the General himself. "How old are you, Mr. Potato?"

"Wouldn't you like to know!" the General chirped back.

"No way!" Gabe laughed. But as he leaned in closer, he gently placed his hand on the small of my back.

Uh-oh . . .

I watched the General's eyes widen in disgust, and he screamed, "Unhand my lady, you swarthy villain! Unhand her this instant!"

I grabbed the old tablecloth from where I'd draped it over the back of one of my kitchen chairs. Unfurling it with a *snap* worthy of any cut-rate magic show, I let it fall down over the cage. As he was plunged into partial darkness, he made a disappointed, "Wah-wahhhhhhh." Exactly like a slide whistle.

"I'll get your dinner, OK?" I said to the tablecloth.

"Potatoes?" he replied and then made the sound of the can opener cranking. He preferred canned potatoes and always had. "Nom-nom-nom!"

"Not for dinner."

"Booooooooo!"

Next to me, Gabe pressed his fist to his mouth to stifle a laugh. I fiddled with the tablecloth and said softly, "Sorry."

He didn't seem weirded out or even spooked. He seemed totally delighted, and I was *so* relieved. "It's OK," he snickered. "What a riot."

The General went back to his just-for-me warbles and coos. I'd always thought he was a riot too, but I'd gotten awfully used to apologizing for him to everybody who came by. It was really refreshing not to have to do that this time. "I'll get his dinner squared away. Make yourself comfy."

"Getting comfy here isn't going to be a problem." He glanced around my place—at my houseplants, at my sofa, at my piles of yarn, and also at my drying rack lined with my favorite and least sexy bras—and smiled.

That'll teach me! I hustled over to the drying rack and hurriedly tossed handfuls of bras into my bedroom. "Do you want a drink or something?" I asked as I scurried back to the kitchen and flung open the fridge, feeling a bit embarrassed that he now knew I had a fondness for gray racerbacks. Hardly the stuff of erotica. "I probably have a beer in here somewhere." I bent down to check the half shelf below the cheese drawer where all my hardly used things ended up, like single beers and flavors of yogurt that I didn't mean to buy. But then I felt his hand on the small of my back again and I straightened up. He pointed at the big pitcher on the top shelf. "Is that lemonade?"

He was so close that I could see the chiseled line of his pecs through his shirt. I swallowed hard. "Ginger mint."

"You made it?" he asked.

I hoisted the pitcher from the fridge with both hands. "It's my favorite."

"Then that's what I'll have," he said as he very slowly began to run his eyes over my face. And my body. It was sexy, it was sensuous, and it just melted me. Like a Popsicle on a July day. Or a pat of butter on a hot pancake. Or . . . I stared at my trusty old cookie sheet by the sink. That was it. That was the feeling.

Like the chocolate on a freshly baked snickerdoodle.

7

GABE

Her house smelled like cookies, and her lemonade tasted *almost* as delicious as she did. As she prepared the General's dinner—a rainbow assortment of fresh veggies on a beak-battered plastic plate—I took stock of her kitchen. It was bright, clean, and messy. Everything about it said *home*. My apartment back in California was like an IKEA showroom, and on the few nights when I'd been there that year, I had ordered in because I didn't even have a damned pan in the cupboard. Her place, though, was exactly how a home should be. Cluttered with cookbooks and memories. From the furniture to the plates, it felt like everything in it had a story. A pan next to the sink still had the circular marks from a dozen cookies; the oven had been used and cleaned so often, the numbers on the dials had been rubbed off. On the fridge were lots of photographs of her with the little boy I'd seen on her phone. There was a big one in the middle of the freezer of him sitting on the edge of a pool in inflatable orange floaties. His chubby stomach poked out over his swim diaper. On each side of him was a tanned, sexy calf, but the top of the photo was covered by a set of pizza coupons. Like they'd been strategically placed there.

I glanced over my shoulder and saw Lily was busy slicing a carrot. Using my fingertip, I carefully shifted the coupons aside. There she was, in all her glory, wearing a pink polka-dot bikini. Sun-kissed and laughing. I ran my eyes over her soft lines. Her belly button. Her cleavage. Her thighs. Damn, damn, damn.

I replaced the sheet of coupons and moved on to the other photos. In some, she was with the little boy by herself. In others, there was another woman who looked a bit like Lily, but a little older. It had to be her sister. And I remembered the onesie that little boy had been wearing in the photo on her phone. "I'm guessing this is your nephew?"

Lily spun around with a carrot in hand. "Yes! That's Ivan. He lives right downstairs with Daisy, my sister." She gestured down with the carrot as a pointer. "The cutest little muffin *ever*. Ivan, I mean. Not my sister. Obviously. My sister doesn't look like a muffin at all."

Her awkwardness was adorable and somehow made me feel even more comfortable with her. She wiped off the vegetable knife on a dish towel and approached the General's cage. He made some happy noises, and I watched her smile as she moved the cloth away and placed her fingertips on the door.

"I need you to stay in there, OK?" she said.

He warbled again and bobbed his head.

"OK?" she repeated.

"OK!" the General echoed back and landed with a thud on the floor of his cage. Lily slowly opened the door and put his plate of veggies on a small ledge on the side. She made a perch of her finger and lowered it in front of him. He hopped on and made noises that, honest to God, could only be described as pure happiness. He opened his mouth wide, like a Muppet, and Lily laughed a little. Then he did a waddling dance on her finger, releasing one foot and then the other as he swayed back and forth. Like a bird polka. She raised him up to the bar level with the food, and he hopped off. "Thank you!" he said as she closed the door.

"Welcome!" she said back.

"Love you!" he said.

"Love you too," she answered.

And he buried his face in the veggie medley.

When she turned back toward me, I saw a warmth in her expression that I found intoxicating. A pure, nurturing joy that was irresistible. I wasn't used to being around someone like her. I was used to women who had their careers and their yoga studios—their expensive stilettos and their watery green smoothies. She was different. A world apart, and a world I really wanted to get to know.

She washed the cutting board and dried her hands on a dish towel. "I'm just going to run and get changed. Is that OK?"

Only if I can watch. "You bet. I'm not going anywhere."

Lily took a step into me and got up on her tiptoes. Her cheek brushed against mine, and the cool curtain of her hair swept along my bare arm. Into my ear, she whispered, "Leave the cloth over the cage and he won't even know you're here. Where do you want to go for dinner? That way I'll know what to wear."

Last night I'd told her it was her choice and my treat, and that was still the deal. "Where's your favorite place to eat in town?" I asked, nice and low and deep in her ear.

Her laugh came on the outbreath, gentle and cool. "It's not fancy. But it's a little bit expensive."

With my nose nestled in her hair, I asked, "Think that fucking matters to me?"

She leaned into me, and her breasts compressed against my chest. "I like that. The way you talk. The way you act."

"Oh yeah?"

She pulled her face back from mine. The setting sun made her irises sparkle like fool's gold. "Yeah."

"So tell me where I'm taking you."

"It's a fondue place. I think you'll like it." She sounded tentative, like she wasn't used to asking for what she wanted. But she damned well better get used to it. "Is that OK?"

She could've said anything—pizza and beer, wine and steaks, oysters and champagne—and my answer would've been the same. "Of course it is." I pressed her up against the countertop, keeping her close with one hand just above her ass. I pulled her hair back from her face and went in for another kiss.

But before my lips could even brush against hers, the General screamed, "I said unhand her, swarthy villain!"

And Lily dissolved into giggles in my arms.

Lily topped up my lemonade and hustled down the hallway. I watched her ass the whole way and didn't even pretend that I hadn't been staring when she turned over her shoulder to glance back at me. She spun around and put her hand on her hip. "Were you watching me?"

Watching. *Fantasizing.* "Big fan of that outfit."

She smiled, rocked back on her heels, and lifted her toes up off the floor. "Well, I'll see if I can outdo myself, then. Be back in a jiff."

Once she closed her bedroom door, I wandered into her living room and looked around. It seemed like she was really into knitting. I didn't see any afghans or anything, but there were lots of just-started things that hadn't quite taken shape yet. There was a whole hell of a lot of yarn, and on the bookshelves I saw all sorts of how-to knitting guides, as well as audio-engineering manuals and a whole shelf of books on the African gray parrot. On a table beside the old fireplace was a big glass jar with folded pieces of paper inside. I peered at them, trying to figure out what they might be. Some of the folded paper squares were slightly open, and I could see handwritten words on them like *sunshine* and *pink* and *gummy bears*. I glanced down the hallway to make sure the coast was clear and picked up the jar, giving it a shake. A piece of paper was taped to the inside of the bottom. Though the letters were backward, it was clear enough. *Gratitude Jar!*

I shook it again and saw *Daisy* and *Ivan* and *rain*. I really dug that idea, the thought of taking the time be grateful for something each day. To write it down. To have that ritual. I gave the jar another shake to see if I could see anything else, but the General interrupted my snooping with a "Tsk-tsk-tsk."

Setting the jar down, I turned toward his cage. It sat on a small table near the window. Of course, the right thing to do would be to leave him alone. But the little dude fascinated me, and I couldn't resist a peek. I approached the cage quietly and lifted the edge of the tablecloth. It was like he'd been waiting for me, like he'd known where I'd pick up the cover. He stared at me with a piece of raw corn in his beak. When he saw me, he dropped the corn and began a low, menacing growl. Like a pit bull. Or a jaguar. Or a Komodo dragon.

"Hey there," I said.

The growl quieted down. He tilted his head to the side, scratching his chest feathers with his prehistoric foot.

There was something about him that was spooky-intense. Right up my alley. He was mostly gray, with a reddish plume of feathers at the bottom of his tail. For all the urban legends and crazy shit I'd chased around in my day, I'd never come face-to-face with an animal that could actually talk back to me.

So here goes nothing. "I'm Gabe."

He hopped up one more bar. He cocked his head the other way and leaned down to pick up a piece of carrot without breaking my stare.

"Nice to meet you."

"Nice to meet you," he responded, in exactly my same voice. And then he asked, "Where are you from?"

Whoa. He wasn't just parroting what I was saying; he was having thoughts of his own. He was actually steering the conversation. Holy *shit.*

When I didn't answer right away, he asked again, "Where are you from?"

It should've been an easy one for me to answer, but it wasn't. Being the son of a career army man meant we'd moved more than we'd ever stayed still. The General was waiting for an answer, though, bug-eyed and open-beaked. So I picked the place that I'd gotten to know best. "New York, upstate."

"Yankee!"

Yeah, he was *the coolest.* I couldn't even imagine what it was like to have a pet like him. I'd never leave the house. But judging from the way he was watching at me, it seemed I had some work to do before I got into his good graces. The thing to do, I figured, was offer him some sort of olive branch, so I went for the nearest thing at hand—I took a thin slice of lemon from my glass. I bit off the sour pulp and offered him the rind.

He leaned back like he was offended. Then he leaned in slightly. "Potato?" he asked.

"Lemon."

Again with the head cock.

"Lehhh-mon," I repeated.

"Potaaaaay-to," he said, like *I* was the one who needed to learn a new word.

I tried a piece of the rind myself and made some exaggerated eating sounds so he'd know I wasn't trying to poison him or something. "Better than a potato."

He poked his dark beak out from between the bars. It reminded me of a mussel shell—black and bony. Very cautiously, he took a nibble of the rind. It seemed like he liked it, so I offered him a little more.

Progress, man. Progress.

But as soon as he seemed to warm up to me, he leaned back again. It reminded me of the way someone nearsighted would lean back from a book or a phone. "Suitor?" he asked.

I laughed a little, caught totally off guard by the question. Was I a suitor? If I wasn't, I definitely wanted to be. "Yeah, I guess I am."

He drew his head back and ruffled up his chest feathers. Then opened his mouth wide . . .

And shit got *crazy*.

He let loose with a sound unlike anything I had ever heard in my life—part yell, part scream, part siren. It went up and it went down, a god-awful, deafening shriek that made my glass of lemonade shiver in my hand. One floor below, I heard Lily's nephew start screaming, followed by the menacing *thump-thump-thump* of a mop or broom handle on the ceiling below. "You're blowing my cover, man! Easy! Easy!" I said, ducking down.

The bastard stared me in the eye and upped the ante, screeching even louder. It was a yodel from the gates of hell, so fucking loud that it gave me vertigo. *"Christ!"*

Lily's footsteps cut through the racket, and in an instant, she was standing beside me. She wore a pink dress that she hadn't even gotten all the way zipped up. "General!" she boomed. "General! I have a message from Lee! Stand down! Union forces are in full retreat!"

Instantly, and I mean *instantly*, the Noise stopped. The change in decibels made my ears ring, like I'd stepped out of a dance club onto a silent street at midnight. As if nothing had happened, the General went back to eating his veggie medley. I stared at him in total astonishment. "How the hell can something so *small* be so *loud*?"

Lily held the front of her dress up with her palm and repositioned the cover of the cage. She lifted her eyebrow at me. "Couldn't resist?" she asked.

"What *was* that?" I whispered.

"I have absolutely no idea. I call it the Noise. All I do know is that the only way to get him to stop is to tell him that the U-n-i-o-n is in s-u-r-r-e-n-d-e-r." Lily sighed. "He's wonderful. But he's a bit complicated. Anyway! Would you mind?" She twirled around. "I can never get this dress on by myself."

With one hand she held the sides of the open zipper together. Just beneath her hand I could see the lacy edge of her bra. Below that was the small of her bare back. And below *that* was the very, very top of her panties, black with red accents, and the silky lingerie tag poking out from beneath. "Jesus," I growled.

She inhaled and gasped, like she'd only just realized what she was doing to me. She straightened her shoulders and tightened her grip on the gap between the sides of the zipper. "What was I thinking? I'll have my sister do it."

Fuck that. "No you won't." I took the delicate zipper between my fingers and drew it up, up, up, hiding all that magnificent skin and making her bra disappear. It made me ache to see it vanish. And ache even harder to think what that zipper would sound like when it was coming back down.

8

LILY

It was turning into a stormy night. Even though I lived just down the street from So Fondue for You, Gabe insisted on calling an Uber for us because it was beginning to rain. The ride felt gloriously longer than it actually was; every detail about him was fresh and exciting. The cut of his pants, the place where his sideburns met his stubble, the way his dress shirt accentuated the contours of his shoulders.

And, of course, the bulge. Oh, the bulge.

When we pulled up in front of the restaurant, I reached for my door handle, but he squeezed my other hand to stop me.

"Not while I'm around," he said and made his way around the front of the car, eyeing me all the time. Our driver was a rather spiffy older lady with turquoise glasses, and she glanced over her shoulder at me.

"Now *there's* a gentleman, hon," she said.

"And how!" I gasped as Gabe opened my door for me. He offered his hand like he was an old-fashioned hero helping a lady from a carriage.

"Thank you . . . sir!" I said as I smoothed my dress.

"Very welcome, *madam*," he said, with a delightful doff of an imaginary hat. Side by side, we headed inside, as dark clouds had filled the sky overhead and little droplets of rain spattered onto my bare shoulders and the blue fabric of his shirt, reminding me of the speckles on a robin's egg. We waited at the hostess stand for just a moment and were seated at a little table for two near the back.

He held my chair out for me and then took the seat across from me. But as the hostess handed him his menu, she froze with it perched dangerously close to the votive candle. "Hang on," she gasped. "Are you . . ."

I watched Gabe wince—a barely noticeable instantaneous reaction that I was positive the waitress hadn't noticed. But I had. It was the merest tightening of his eyes, as if to say, *Not this again.*

He nodded. "I'm Gabe Powers, yeah."

"Oh my *God*," the hostess said and steadied herself on the table. I stared at her and suddenly felt quite out of place with this man who made unknown ladies gasp out loud. I'd had my fair share of boyfriends over the years, ranging from mediocre to awkward to downright dreadful, but the closest I'd ever come to dating someone *famous* was a blind date with my sister's dentist, and that was because he paid to have his face plastered all over every city bus in a thirty-mile radius. I'd never been with a man whose very presence made women act so . . .

Wait, though. What was she doing? I didn't really know, because I'd never seen anything like it before. She was biting her lip. She was slowly tracing the edge of the table. She was moving her eyes all over him. Now she was sensuously caressing her collarbone! Hussy! "Loved that Borneo episode," she said, all seductively, like she was actually saying, *Wanna get a room?* "Where they had to pixel out your—"

I cleared my throat and snatched the menus from her hands. "Yes, thank you! Thanks! Hello! Hi. I'm Lily. Hello."

She shook it off like she was coming out of a trance. "Sorry!"

"That's fine! Thank you!" I said in an edgy little clip. "Off you go!"

She breathed out a long breath as she blinked at me a handful of times. "Your waiter will be right over."

I gave her a thin-lipped smile and a flare of my nostrils, the way ladies at the Universalist church did when they found old buttons in their donation basket. *Bless your heart!* in action.

When she walked away, I leaned against my menu, sandwiching the page between my boobs and its hard leather backing. "Are you really *that* famous? Am I an idiot for not recognizing you?"

Gabe coughed in a very gentlemanly way into his clenched fist. "I don't know about *famous*. But it's weird. Every time, it's weird."

"I'll bet!" I leaned in and dropped my voice to a hush. "I can imagine ladies shoving Sharpies into your hand for autographs!"

He nodded slowly, like he couldn't believe it himself. "Sometimes they even ask me to sign"—he came closer, making the candle flame between us quiver—"*their skin.*"

"No!"

"Lily, there's a Facebook fan group. With, like, thousands and thousands of members. Plus a YouTube channel."

My mouth dropped open. *My* biggest claim to digital fame was that one of my Yelp reviews had been marked *helpful* nineteen times. "Shut the front door."

He shook his head. "I never actually expect anybody to recognize me. The fact that you didn't recognize me at first was a *huge* relief."

I didn't know if he was joshing me or not, but it didn't seem like it. Hunky *and* modest. If he could give a decent massage, he'd be my trifecta. "So you don't mind that I have the viewing habits of an eighty-year-old woman?"

"Not at all. To you, I'm just a guy." He smiled. "A very grateful guy, on a beautiful night, in a beautiful place, with a beautiful woman. Who I can't stop thinking about kissing."

"Really?" I asked in barely a whisper. I realized I'd been clutching my menu to my chest so hard that the paper had crumpled up against my boobs. I tried to smooth it, but my hands were a little bit sweaty and it wrinkled under my palms. Some women got more graceful and self-assured as they aged. I was not one of those women.

Mercifully, the waiter appeared, and I paused trying to hide the boob wrinkles. He, at least, had the good taste not to start fondling himself as soon as he looked at Gabe. "Hello, you two. Welcome to So Fondue for You. What can I get you to start?"

"I'd like a lemonade," I said, now trying to reposition the corners of my menu into their little holders. "With extra lemons."

Over the top of my menu, Gabe's face caught my eye. He cocked his head slightly. "Not much of a drinker?"

I stopped with my menu fussing. "I'm as fond of a mango margarita as the next girl, but I've got audio to do for you. And I don't want to mess it up."

Gabe stared at me as if to say, *I'll tell you what I'd like to mess up . . .* And suddenly I found myself fondling *my* collarbone.

Gabe told the waiter, "Lemonade for me too, then. For dinner, we'll do . . ." He leaned conspiratorially toward the waiter and pointed to something on the menu. Judging from where he was pointing—three-quarters of the way down—he was asking for the full So Very, Very Fondue for You for Two prix fixe menu. It was the one I always eyed enviously, with its luxurious bold font and special box to make it stand out. The full spread. The works. The five-star treatment. An assortment of cheese fondues, a salad, an entree, and white, milk, and dark dipping chocolates for dessert. His leg pressed against mine under the table, a firm and manly quadriceps warming the side of my bare thigh. So fondue for you *indeed!*

"Excellent choice, sir," said the waiter, tucking his pen into his pocket with a smile.

"Good." Gabe handed over our menus. And then he turned to me, reaching under the table to give my leg a squeeze. In that instant, a flash of lightning lit up the room. Followed by a heart-rattling rumble of thunder.

The lights flickered and seemed to become half again as bright, casting everything into extra-sharp focus. Gabe and I locked eyes for a seemingly never-ending second. The lights got so bright that they seemed to buzz. His cheekbones caught the light, and his deep-set eyes became doubly dreamy and alluring. Then all at once, the music went silent and restaurant went dark, and everybody let out what felt like a single "Ooooooh!"

The power had gone out, but the electricity between us *definitely* had not. Gabe pushed aside the votive candle and knitted his fingers into mine across the table. He pressed his leg against mine a touch more firmly, and I gave his hand a squeeze. It was as if we were the only two people in the place somehow. The waiters had hopped into action, and votive candles were added to every table, filling the room with golden light. The world bustled and hustled around us, but I hardly noticed—it was like being in the center of a snow globe.

But then the waiter reappeared, frazzled and shadowy above a tray full of candles. His slight comb-over had come undone in the chaos and floated wispily above his head, carried higher by the warmth of the small flames. "I'm so sorry, you two. I hadn't even gotten a chance to get your order in before the power went out. We've phoned the power company. It's not going to be on anytime soon." He let out a big sigh, one so forceful that his nostrils whistled and a few of the candles on the tray blew out. "If you'd like to stay and wait it out, I'd be delighted to bring around your drinks. And bread, if you'd like."

I tightened my grip on Gabe's hand. Underneath the table, his other hand moved an inch higher up my leg, and his thumb pressed into my thigh. It sent a wave of desire prickling through me, and my own breath came out in a shudder that made the candles dance.

"What do you want to do?" he asked me.

Aside from going back to the Willows and frantically ripping off every piece of clothing on his body, I did actually have a rather romantic idea for us. He'd said it himself—we were here on a beautiful night in a beautiful place. In *my* hometown. Which meant I had a couple of tricks up my sleeve for how to make this night last and last. "Are you up for a little adventure?" I asked Gabe.

"Might as well be my middle name," he said.

"It's hardly monster hunting," I teased.

He gave me that glorious up-and-down stare, like he was tugging my dress off in his mind. "Maybe not. But I've got a couple of mysteries I'd like to solve myself."

Mmmm! Somehow, I managed to turn politely, if red-faced, to the waiter. "I think we'll come back another time, if that's OK."

"Absolutely," he said and hustled off to distribute his candles around the room.

Gabe stood and came around to pull back my chair for me and offered his hand as I rose to standing in my kitten heels. Rather than letting him guide me toward the front door, I led him out the back door, onto a deserted cobblestone alley. The air was cool and fresh, like the summer heat had broken for the night. I held out my hand for him and he grabbed it, and together we ran across the Dayton Ramp footbridge while the thunder rumbled above.

9

GABE

She led me to a storefront with sparkling plate-glass windows that said
SAVANNAH DRY GOODS AND GROCERY, EST. 1817 on the
door in gold leaf. Underneath that was a handwritten sign on a piece
of cardboard. The handwriting was an old-fashioned cursive, written
in a spidery, shaky hand, that said **CLOSED. NO POWER.** With a
frowny face.

Lily rapped on the window and glanced up at me mischievously.
"Just as a warning, she swears. A lot. Brace yourself. Also, she has no
filter whatsoever."

Within a few seconds, a face appeared on the other side of the door.
It belonged to a friendly-looking older woman with white hair, rosy
cheeks, and kind eyes. When she saw me, she scowled and pointed at
the sign. But when she saw Lily, her face lit up with a huge, welcoming
smile. "My darling girl!" said the woman as she flung open the door.

She wrapped her arms around Lily, kissing her twice on each cheek.
A smell of old-fashioned perfume filled the air. The older lady bellowed,
"The goddamned power grid, honey! It's gonna be the death of me!
Such bullshit!"

Lily laughed into the old woman's shoulder as she hugged her. When she let her go, she said, "Auntie Jennifer, I'd like you to meet Gabe. Gabe, this is Great-Aunt Jennifer."

The old lady looked me up and down with a serious face. Almost a sassy pout. "Aren't you a dashing young buck!"

Lily snickered. "Jennifer."

"Well, he is, honey! You get to my age and there's no point in beating round the bush!" She reached up and gave my cheek a pinch with her cool hand. Suddenly, I felt like I was a kid again. I hadn't had my cheek pinched in more than thirty years. And now here I was, in a two-hundred-year-old grocery, on a cobblestone street, with a lady who swore like a sailor and looked like everybody's ideal grandma. Next to me was a gorgeous woman whom I'd kissed once already today, and I was making plans to do a hell of a lot more than that.

I wasn't sure whose life this was, but I sure wasn't complaining.

Auntie Jennifer shuffled around to the other side of the polished wood counter. Behind her were rows of old-fashioned jars with equally old-fashioned candies. Colorful lollipops. Caramels in wax paper. Enormous gumdrops. Off to the right there was what looked to me like a nice selection of wine. A bottle of wine by candlelight during a thunderstorm? First-date *win*.

Auntie Jennifer struck a match and lit a brass oil lamp on one end of the register. She adjusted the knob, and the shop was bathed in warm light. She clasped her hands together. "What brings you by?"

"Well, we were just about to sit down to eat when the lights went out." Lily reached over the counter to grab a few paper bags. "I know how you hate for things to go to waste. We have to run to do some work, so I thought we could put together a little picnic."

"Thank heavens for you, my dear. Got all sorts of stuff that won't survive the night without power." Jennifer looked up toward the ceiling like she was scrolling through a grocery list; it was exactly the same thing Lily had done when she'd been trying to think of the right words to use when asking me about my show. Aunt Jennifer said, "I'm up to my neck in homemade peach ice cream, coconut Popsicles, and herbed rotisserie chickens. Got a nice Greek pasta salad that's going to need eating too. Darling little tortellini stuffed with pesto and feta." She kissed her fingers. "How'll that suit you?"

Lily glanced at me for approval. So did Aunt Jennifer.

I ran my hand down my jaw. "So this is it, right? This is heaven?"

Both of them erupted in laughter that filled up the shop from floor to ceiling.

"A face like that and he's a good eater!" cooed Aunt Jennifer. "You got yourself a keeper, hon! A real keeper!"

For one fantastic instant, I caught Lily's eye. Before she looked away.

We took her van back to the Willows on Abercorn, and I carried the groceries in behind her. It was the mother of all picnics. We had a roasted chicken, a nice pinot gris, pasta salad, fresh figs, three different kinds of ice cream, and a wax-paper bag full of pear candies. We arranged the spread on the big old wooden kitchen table. She found a few candles in a drawer, and she stuck them into a houseplant as a centerpiece.

"But no matches." She riffled through the drawers again. She bent down to check in the bottom drawer, accentuating the curve of her hips, her ass, and the soft creaminess of her inner thighs.

"It's a good thing I'm your date then, isn't it?" I said, and she whirled around. "I might not be able to make roast chickens materialize in a power outage, but I can *definitely* promise that no matter what, no matter when, I can get a fire started." I grabbed my bag and pulled out my trusty pack of waterproof strike-anywhere matches. I slid one out and lit it on the edge of the box and then lit the candles. Light spread out from the houseplant and revealed a smiling Lily.

Together we got all the dishes and glasses we needed from the cupboards. I set to work carving the chicken, and she arranged the other takeout containers. In the reflection of the window over the sink, I watched her secretly spear a few tortellini with a fork and pop them into her mouth. I loved watching her get so much pleasure from something so small. When I was in Serbia, I'd learned a word that I'd never been able to use for anybody before. *Merak.* Bliss from the simplest of pleasures. She was full of that. It radiated from her like light.

There we sat, across from one another in the candlelight, eating and talking. She told me all about her business and how much she liked her job. She told me about her sister's work at the Living History Museum. She glowed when she talked about her nephew. She also told me about her parents, who were retired—like mine—and who were right then traveling on a cruise through Alaska. "They own the grocery along with Auntie Jennifer. It gives them all something to do. And *I* get to be the sampler for the new cheeses."

"It must be nice to live in a place where everybody knows you. Where you've got such deep roots."

She delicately wiped her lips off on the back of her hand, somehow elegant even without a napkin. "It is, yes. Absolutely. Sometimes it's a little . . ." She shifted her lips off to one side and wrinkled up her nose as she chewed. "Cozy, maybe?"

I was betting everybody knew her business, whether she wanted them to or not. But with the way I'd been living for the last however many years, *cozy* sounded pretty damned good. "I don't even have a houseplant back in LA."

She nibbled on her chicken leg, getting the last bite of meat off the bone. "Your life must be so exciting, though." She dropped it into the paper bag we were using for the trash. "Seeing so many new places. Having so many adventures. I'll bet you travel a heck of a lot!"

A heck of a lot was an understatement. I was always on the move; one way or another, that had always been part of my life. "I'm only in LA about four months of the year, tops. And never for more than a few weeks at a stretch. I'm used to that, though. We bounced from Fort Belvoir to Fort Bliss to Fort Carson. And that was just in grade school. I got used to not having one single place to call home."

She frowned. "That must have been hard," she said, watching me closely, wrinkling up her eyebrows a little bit. "I don't know who I'd be if I didn't live here. Savannah is such a part of who I am. I'd be lost without it."

"It was tough. But I suppose I never knew any different. Maybe that's why I don't mind traveling so much for my job."

She nodded and took a fig from the box and bit into it, letting her eyes flutter shut. She made this little moan that fucking killed me. If she moaned like that over a fig, I couldn't wait to find out what she sounded like when I . . .

I forced myself back to reality. "So tell me about the General."

Lily laughed softly. "His full name, if you want to know, is General Fuss and Feathers."

I actually snorted. There was a first time for everything. "No way."

"Yeah!" She laughed. "If you'd like a little history nugget, that was a real person! Winfield Scott. The longest-serving active-duty general in the US military, *ever*. Grandma started calling the General *Fuss and Feathers* because," she snickered, "if the shoe fits! One thing I can tell you is that I can't have rotisserie chicken in the house. You'd think I was some kind of cannibal. Once I tried to make a chicken pot pie and it was like the world was ending. *Murderer!*" she squawked in the General's voice. *"How dare you!"*

I dug into the pasta salad. "Where did he learn all of it?"

"I don't know," she said, blinking thoughtfully. "Some of it he's learned from me, I guess." She leaned in and cupped her hand to her mouth to say, "I swear a lot when I knit! But occasionally he'll come out with something brand new. Like *Jaws*? We've never seen *Jaws*. But all of a sudden, daaaa-dun!" She sniffed and shook her head, laughing. "He's lovely, though. He's very good company. Mostly." She took a tiny sip of the wine I poured her and eyed me over the lip of the delicate antique glass. "OK. My turn to ask a question. How is it possible that a man with a Facebook fan group doesn't have a girlfriend?"

"I do like a woman who cuts to the chase," I said. But I didn't want her to think I was some sort of insufferable Hollywood manwhore. I hated those dudes. Yeah, I'd dated, but never seriously and never for very long. "I'm married to my job. That's what Markowitz says."

She tsked me, same as the General had when I was snooping around the gratitude jar. "Don't tell me you're too busy for love."

It sounded like a lame-ass excuse, because that's exactly what it was. I wasn't too busy. The truth was that just like I'd been hunting for urban legends all these years, I'd also been trying to find *the one*. And Christ almighty, I'd looked for her. I'd become a serial first-dater of the first order. I believed, in my gut, that there was one woman out there for me. The one who would make me crazy with need. The one who made the world make sense. The one who would make me whole. Finding that woman, if she existed at all, was proving harder than tracking down all the urban legends put together. "I could ask you the same, you know. I'll bet they're after you like a pack of hounds."

She drew back from the table slightly. She nibbled on her top lip; when she let it go, it caught the light with a shimmer. "I've never been that girl."

You're about to be, beautiful. Just you wait.

The tension between us was heavy; I loved coming up against the edges of what made her comfortable. But even though I wanted to push her and see her laid bare, I'd be an idiot to push too hard, too fast. Everything in its own time. I finished off the last of the pasta salad and asked, "You think we're going to be able to pick up any audio tonight? Without power?"

Lily nodded. "Oh yes, for sure. I have a whole handful of handheld recorders in my van. There's no need for power at all. But let me ask you . . ." She put her elbows on the table and nestled her chin between her hands. "Do you *really* think we're going to find any ghosts in here?"

"Nah. I go into all these things a skeptic. As far as I'm concerned, the abominable snowman is some dude in a snowsuit, the chupacabra is a coyote with mange, and ghosts are nothing but faulty wires and bad plumbing. But at the same time, who the hell am I to say?" I looked her up and down, zeroing in on the milky edge of a tan line peeking out from her cleavage. "Sometimes the thing you've been looking for shows up when you least expect it."

She flipped the up-and-down around on me, nodding and nibbling her lip. She didn't actually say anything, but she didn't have to. I felt it like I was touching an ungrounded wire.

I slid one of the pints of ice cream over to her and opened one of my own. "So I say we finish this up and then roll tape. Then see where the night takes us."

She took a big scoop of ice cream on her spoon and paused with it almost to her lips. Keeping her eyes on me all the time, she turned the spoon over and slowly, sensuously, took a lick of her peach ice cream. The cream on her tongue made me think of some dirty fucking things. I could see it—she knew it too. She had me right where she wanted me. And finally she hit me with a knockout triple combination—one more lick, one more twirl of her spoon, and finally, "You got it, boss."

Christ almighty.

10

LILY

We sat together on the small parlor love seat, waiting for the ghosts. Next to me, Gabe jotted down notes in a notebook that he had balanced on his leg. I listened for any thumps or creaks but heard nothing except the scratching of his mechanical pencil on the paper. I made a mental catalog of the mics on the various floors, and I was confident that if a mouse so much as licked his whiskers, we'd get it in full stereo. I took a tiny sip of my wine and turned my attention back to Gabe once again. He glanced up from his notebook as soon as I looked at him and paused writing midword. I felt a blush warm my cheeks and neck. "Hi," I whispered. He inhaled, long and slow, growled a little when he glanced down at my cleavage, and then went back to his notes.

The tiny details about him really intrigued me. Surely he made a fortune, but the notebook was the kind they sold for fifty cents at any old drugstore. It was made of greenish paper with a spiral at the top and a line down the middle. Same as I used to use in school to learn my vocabulary words for beginning French. At his feet, leaning against the delicately carved love seat legs, was his backpack. It wasn't some high-tech, newfangled thing like I'd seen at the chic outdoorsy shops on Broughton Street. Instead, it was a faded old rucksack that probably hadn't been fancy even when it was brand new. On the top, above where the straps met the back, was a distinctive square orange patch with careful stitching all around the edges. "Is this your handiwork?" I asked and ran my fingertip over the tidy stitches.

He stopped writing and glanced up, then at his bag. "Yep. Had to teach myself. YouTube is super helpful," he said with a wink and went back to writing.

I imagined him stitching it on, and it made my heart hurt a little. Him, all on his own, with nobody to even help mend his bag. I also felt a little envious; his stitching was *fab*.

As he jotted down his notes and sketched out what I thought must be storyboards, I thought about what his bag really meant in the bigger scheme of things. All the places he had traveled with it and what kind of life he must lead. My whole world, everything—from where I got my groceries to where I went for barbecue—was some version of *home*. But his home was right there on the floor: faded, patched, and portable. On the table sat his cell phone, in a waterproof case, and an old Swiss Army knife with his initials engraved in the handle. It seemed that the things he kept close to him were all slightly broken-in and well worn. If I'd had to live like he did, I supposed I'd have made a little home around me in the same way. But I couldn't really imagine it. And I was glad I didn't have to.

He quietly closed his notebook and placed it on the table. Then he gave my knee a gentle squeeze. From his bag he produced a small handheld video camera—bigger than what my sister had bought when Ivan was born, but still very compact. He switched it on, popped the viewfinder from its little slot, and flipped it around so he could see what he was filming. "This is Gabe Powers, coming at you from the house where I was earlier on Abercorn. I'm here with my audio tech. This is Lily." He began to pan toward me. I tried to lean out of the frame, but he caught me, and I stared at myself on the screen.

That morning, I'd seen him talking to a river guide in Africa who waved him off with a *"No camera! No camera!"* before hurling himself headlong into a nearby stand of bushes. I suddenly understood the feeling. I was also feeling a whole new level of simpatico with deer caught in headlights. "Is this going on TV?" I whispered. And blinked.

He panned back to himself. "She's a little camera shy, but we're working on it. We're going to see if we can summon up someone from the other side. Be right back." He hit the record button again to stop the video. He placed his phone on the table and then unzipped the largest compartment of his backpack, from which he produced something black, white, and rectangular. A brand-spanking-new Ouija board. Still wrapped in shrink-wrap.

Oh *no*.

I'd never used a Ouija board, but I had a healthy fear of them, just like people who live in the bayous know to beware of alligators under the waterline. Everything I knew about Ouija could be summed up in what my grandma had taught me about them: *"Stick to Monopoly, hon! Better safe than sorry."*

Rain lashed the windows and pinged off the old panes. Gabe snagged the edge of the plastic wrap with his fingertip and let the staticky film fall to the Oriental rug. I stared at the letters and the old-fashioned logo and fonts that were somehow both wholesome *and* sinister.

Gabe placed the board on the coffee table in front of us and scooted closer to me. Close enough to depress the cushions of the love seat and make me lean into him. "I have no idea what I'm doing. Do you?" He set the planchette on the letters, upside down.

I pressed my fingers into my lap. "I've never used one."

"Want me to ask Google?" he asked.

"No," I said, pushing down my worry. "I know how. They outsell Cards Against Humanity down here ten to one." I righted the planchette and positioned the pointer end in front of the letter *A*.

Gabe leaned in close. "Attagirl."

A sudden gust of wind made one of the old willow trees outside tap the window, and I gasped. Gabe put one arm around me. It did, I had to admit, have a rather marvelous calming effect. Like being doused in chamomile tea.

"All right," Gabe said. "Let's see what we can do."

From his bag he grabbed a small tripod. With a few expert moves, adjusting the telescopic arms, he positioned the camera above the board. In the center of the frame was the planchette with my fingers on it. His hand joined mine, and I found myself a more than a little captivated by how our hands looked together. Next to his, mine was so delicate, even though I'd never thought so before.

And there we sat, staring at the unmoving planchette. There were no knocks or thumps. There were no sudden and unexplained drafts. Everything was A-OK. With each passing minute, I felt more and more relieved. As I'd suspected, this place was no more haunted than my own house. Gabe didn't seem ready to throw in the towel just yet, though, and he opened the booklet that came with the board. He read over it and then put it aside. He cleared his throat. "We're here to get in touch with the residents of 19 Abercorn Street."

Eeeek! Again, the rain lashed the windows, suddenly louder and with more force. I didn't like this. Not one little bitty bit. Desperate not to let Gabe see that I was probably shaking, I gripped the sofa cushion like a life preserver.

After a moment, I made myself look at Gabe in an effort to try to calm my nerves. It worked *marvelously*. When I stared at him, all other thoughts seemed to drain out of my mind like soapy water from the sink. I admired his scruff. I flashed back to the way his mouth had felt on mine, the way my skin had stung afterward. And I imagined how good he'd look, naked, in those high-thread-count sheets one floor above.

But before *I* could even think about making a move of my own, the planchette started to move.

I repeat. The planchette. Started. To move.

"Holy shit," said Gabe.

I was so astonished, I couldn't even talk. I could barely even think. My hand glided along with the pointer as it slid across the shiny surface of the board. It landed on *I* and paused.

Gabe and I sat there, frozen. "Did you do that?" I asked him. Now I wasn't just hanging on to the sofa—I was squeezing it so hard that feathers had begun to poke out of the upholstery.

"Fuck no," he said.

It began moving again, and it slid over to *W*. And then *A*. And then *N*. And finally *T*.

"I want," Gabe said.

God and Elvis help us, we had opened the gates of Ouija and I had no idea how we were supposed to close them. "Gabe!"

"I want," he repeated.

I pressed my free hand to my mouth. I held my breath and glanced at Gabe. He didn't seem the least bit freaked out. But of course he didn't. He'd spent his career chasing things like frogmen and dog-men and abominable snowmen. But me? The scariest thing I'd gotten involved in lately was a homemade curry recipe with sixty-seven spices, with each measurement written in grams! I didn't know how to deal with urban legends, I didn't know how to deal with haunted houses, I didn't know how to deal with . . .

"Y," Gabe said as the planchette skidded wildly around the board. It didn't even feel like gravity was holding it down; it felt like an air-hockey puck on the move.

Goose bumps gave me prickles all over. Gabe turned to me without taking his fingers off the planchette as it shuttled around the board, like it couldn't find the right letter. "Are you moving it? Tell me you're moving it."

"I'm not!" I gasped. "I swear!"

The planchette skidded to a stop, and he looked at me for a long second, like he was trying to find a lie on my face. He was so dead serious that I burst out with a little giggle and then clapped my hand over my mouth so that it didn't mess up the audio. "I'm not!" I whispered. "Promise!" I grabbed Gabe's notebook off the coffee table and flipped it over to write on the cardboard back. *I WANTY*, I wrote out.

"Lily, it's moving again," Gabe said as it moved from the *O* to the *U*. I placed my fingers next to his and felt it move along beneath our hands. Then it landed on *S*, and then *O*. With my other hand I scribbled down the message. My hand was shaking so hard that my writing was squiggly and enormous.

For one second, it stayed in the middle of the board. *Monopoly from now on, I promise!* But it wasn't over. It was on the move again, and moving fast. It darted over to *B*. Then to *A*. Then to *D*. And finally it slid down to *Goodbye* on the bottom of the board. There it stayed. Gabe inhaled and drew back from the board, blowing a long breath into his massive fist. "What the fuck was that?"

An absolutely terrible idea! With my hands shaking, I quickly jotted down the rest of the letters. And realized I'd been had. *I WANT YOU SO BAD.* "Oh, you *stinker!*" I swatted him with his notebook. "You terrible man!"

He roared with laughter, a sexy and deep baritone laugh that filled the room. He grabbed my hands first and my hips second, rolling back onto the sofa and pulling me on top of him. He tossed his head back, laughing silently now as the thick columns of his neck muscles pulled tight. "You really thought it was moving? *Really?*"

I hooked my legs around him and scissored him as tight as I could. I planted my hands on his chest and tried to give him a shove. "Of course I did! If your middle name is Adventure, then mine is Total Sucker."

He wrapped his arms around me, sliding one hand up along the back of my neck to keep me close. Running his thumb down my cheek, he held my hair back from my face. The laughter and playfulness were gone. Now he was back where I'd seen him in the bedroom. Greedy and serious. His palm grasped my tush in a delightfully possessive way. "Ouija speaks the truth. I do want you. So bad."

"Me too," I whispered back, but then I realized how confusing that sounded. "I mean, I want *you*. Not I want—"

He kissed me to shut me up. His hands gripped my body, and his tongue swept mine aside. Straddling him on my knees on the sofa, I felt him hard underneath me. I tipped my hips into him, with nothing but my panties and his chinos between us. This kiss was different than the one in the bedroom earlier. This was like a slow drizzle of caramel all through me. Just as the room began to spin, and just as I started to reach for his belt, he broke us apart, pulling my head back slightly with his fingers knotted into my hair. He nudged my cheek with his nose and said, "I'm gonna take you upstairs, Lily. And rock your fucking world."

11

GABE

Halfway up the steps, I slid my hand around her waist from behind. She stopped and I took one more step up so my hips were even with hers. I was rock hard in my pants, and I let her feel it between her ass cheeks. She groaned and held on to the railing more tightly. White knuckles. Fuck yes.

"You're going to need to keep doing that," I told her as I sheltered her with my body, the curve of my abs and chest pressed against her back. I slid my hand up to her tits and pinched her nipple through her dress.

"Keep doing what?" she asked. Her voice was thick with heat and desire. Not so soft and gentle anymore.

I placed my hand over hers on the banister. "Keep hanging on tight."

She let her head drop down, and I swept her hair over one shoulder. I placed my lips at the curve where her neck met her shoulder and looked down into her cleavage. I was torn—part of me wanted to ravage her, part of me wanted to worship her.

There was plenty of time for both.

I undid her delicate zipper tooth by tooth. It sounded every bit as good as I'd imagined it would. She was holding her breath as I did it, tipping her head to the side to get me to keep kissing her. Fuck knew I wanted to. But I needed her to know that this wasn't going to be all tenderness either, and I needed there to be no doubt that no matter how bad I wanted her, I was the one running this show. Once I had her zipper undone, I hiked her dress up and yanked her hips back into mine, making her gasp. The ripples of the impact made her ass tremble. She bent forward as her dress slid from her shoulders. She supported herself with her palms on the stairs, her fingertips on the edge of the step. Her dress slid off her into a flowery circle at her feet, revealing a black thong. With a tiny red bow that I hadn't been able to see earlier.

"I'm keeping these." I traced the edge of the thong over the topography of her curves. I slid my index finger underneath the lace, over the handle of her hip, and onto the soft skin above her pussy. Close enough to the bull's-eye to make her moan for it. She inhaled when I touched her there, drawing her stomach in. Whatever self-consciousness she had just made me want to break her walls down faster. I pressed my palm into her lower belly, keeping her steady. With the first two fingers of my other hand, I traced the line of her thong in the other direction. Over her ass and down between her legs from behind, teasing the edges of her lips.

She was soaked already—I felt it right through her panties. Her wetness sent a pulse through my cock, and a sheer primal need in me said, *Fuck her here. Fuck her now.*

But she deserved better than being fucked from behind on a staircase. This time, anyway.

I kept on teasing her—one finger outside her panties, one finger underneath. She was slick, hot, and ready. Exactly like I needed her to be.

I pushed her down to make her bend deeper at the hips. When I had her where I wanted her, I tucked my hand back against her abdomen. I kissed a line down her ass, making sure I scratched her with my stubble as I went. She moaned a little, and I felt her stomach begin to relax. With my teeth, I pulled her thong down and drew it back from her body, letting it snap against her flesh. Then I slid both fingers along her slit, slowly pressing them in and drawing them back out.

"You always this wet?" I asked as I sank my teeth gently into the milky smoothness of her perfect ass.

She responded with a low "Nun-hnnnn." I drew my face away from her skin to get a look at her pussy in all its magnificent glory. Swollen, pink, and wet. I made a V of my fingers to open her up. When I entered her, one of her knees went out from under her, but I kept her steady, supporting her body with my hand.

"How do you want it?" I asked her. I slid my tongue down her thigh and then into that wet, hot silk. Her taste was like a shot of Jack and a hit of weed—exactly what I needed. The best high of all.

"Every way you want to give it to me."

Shit yes. "That's the right fucking answer." With the tip of my finger, I teased the edge of her clit. As I did, she whimpered, a helpless little whine that echoed through the foyer. I moved down the stairs one more step so my face was level with her pussy from behind. As my tongue touched her clit, she grabbed my hand. "Oh God, Gabe."

With my first two fingers I teased her G-spot as I slid my tongue into her, which made her knees shake. I could've stayed like that all god-damned night, feeling her thighs tremble against my shoulders, feeling her wetness intensify as I worked on her clit. Once I'd gotten enough of her to hold me over, I pulled away from her and inhaled her scent. Like seawater, heady and salty. I pulled her up to standing and helped her step out of her dress.

Again I placed my lips to that place where her neck met her shoulder, this time giving her a sucking kiss hard enough to pull her flesh into my mouth. I penetrated her again with my fingers, getting the measure of her, the curve of her, imagining my cock inside her. I bit down, gently but firmly, and she hissed. "Bedroom," I growled against her, keeping her flesh between my teeth.

She nodded, but she didn't move. He toes curled up on the hardwood as I hooked into her more deeply. I leaned back from her and studied every inch of her—her feet, her ankles, the soft skin at the backs of her knees. Her inner thighs. The way her hair fell in ringlets on the step below her. And that ass. Her ass was a vision. Grabbable, kissable, fuckable . . . and even more slappable than I'd thought at first. So sexy it deserved a handprint.

I slowly pulled out of her, my fingers slick and wet. And then wound up and gave her a flat-handed smack that left a red welt and a smudge of her own wetness on her skin. I rubbed in the sting, pulled her back into me, and told her again, "Bedroom. Right now."

She was going to be a fantastic fuck. When I pushed her backward across the bedroom, she shoved me in return. I went at her harder, and she gave as good as she got, laughing all the time. Fire in those pretty eyes. Risk and reward. She was feisty, and I fucking loved that.

"Getting inside you cannot happen fast enough," I told her as I shoved her onto the bed. She landed with a cushy thump on the mattress, giggling as she was enveloped in the sheets. I dropped my pants, and the clasp of my belt pinged as it hit the ground. She got up on her knees and started to undo my shirt buttons. But I stopped her. "Put your hand on my cock where it belongs."

She looked up at me, full of challenge in the moonlight. Instead of going straight for me, she undid the button at the opening of my boxers and drew her fingertip up the shaft. I pulled my shirt off and tossed it aside. With the heel of my hand to her sternum, I got her on her back. She planted her arms on either side of her and pressed her foot against my chest, arching her body up in a tantalizing curve. Using me as an anchor, she reached behind herself and undid her bra with one hand. Her breasts came free, and I saw them both in all their perfection in the moonlight. Still arched off the bed, she hooked her toe over the edge of my boxers. I took hold of her ankle and kissed the underside of her left foot. As I did, her toes curled and she arched her foot—pure pleasure.

She pulled my boxers down farther with her toe. The elastic waist-band got caught on my cock, and she teased me with a few more tugs. When my cock finally sprang free from my boxers, she gasped. I stroked it for her, working the length. She rolled up and got onto her knees in front of me. Gently, almost reverently at first, she took my cock in her hands. She ran the pad of her thumb along the vein that zigzagged up the side and underneath the head. With her other hand, she cupped my balls. I loved the way she played with me. She let one slip between her fingers, and then she switched. She inched to the edge of the bed on her knees and dropped down onto her elbows so she could take my cock in her mouth. The bed was high, a mahogany four-poster that was just the right height for everything I wanted to do to her. And apparently, everything she wanted to do to me too.

Because whatever she was doing with her tongue was making me *crazy*. "Holy *fuck*, Lily." I held on to one of the bedposts and let my head fall back. With the flat of her tongue, she worked her way down the base. Then she went back up again, fisting my cock in her hand. Not some delicate bullshit, but hard and aggressive. Like she knew what she wanted and she was damned well going to take it.

She took me deeply into her mouth again. She grabbed my hand and placed it on her own cheek so I could feel what she was doing. She got messy about giving me head—lots of saliva and teeth. Just the way I liked it. Every so often, she looked up at me with my cock in her mouth. She looked sweet, but she was fucking *dirty*. And I couldn't get enough. As she went back up, she turned slightly to let me feel my own cock through her cheek, pressing into my palm.

"Jesus," I growled. But as much as I wanted to stay there and watch my cock stretch those creamy cheeks, I'd been waiting since last night to have my way with her, and now I was just plain greedy. I shifted my hand to her throat and pushed her backward onto the bed. I stroked myself in front of her, and she parted her legs for me. Kneeling between her thighs, I lubed up with her wetness.

Never looking away from her, I put myself at her opening. Her hips rose to meet me. Everything about that move said *yes* and *now* and *please*. But even as her body begged me, I took my time. Even though I wanted to fuck her until the bed busted, I teased her opening with my cock. Even though I wanted to fill her with my cum, I savored the way her pussy opened to take me. Even though I wanted to fuck her until she roared, I inched my way inside her. I made myself go slow. Because I didn't want this to end.

God*damn* did she feel like heaven. But halfway in, her hips bucked and she gripped the covers. She turned away and closed her eyes. She sucked in a hissing breath between gritted teeth. I stopped exactly where I was, because for all the things I wanted to do to her, the last thing I wanted was to hurt her. Unless it was on purpose. "You good?"

She smiled with her cheek against the sheets. "You're just . . . huge."

Awww, yeah. Now we're fucking talking. "Think you can handle it?"

She snapped her head toward me and opened her eyes wide. All that fire. All that heat. She reminded me of one of those goddamned chocolate lava cakes. Tempting and cool on the outside, molten hot and dangerous inside—you'd burn the shit out of yourself if you weren't careful.

But tonight was gonna be a lot of things, and *careful* wasn't one of them. "Answer me," I said, giving her another inch. "Can you take it?"

And that was when she did it. She squeezed. Squeezed until my knees buckled and my eyes rolled right the fuck back into my head.

"Jesus *Christ*," I said as I drove into her. I was halfway between control and total surrender. Who was I kidding, though; control was an illusion anyway. With the way my balls were throbbing, that pussy owned me already.

She spread her legs and hooked her ankles around me, pulling me on top of her. She raked her fingernails down my back and licked up the edge of my ear. "I can handle you," she whispered. "But can you handle me?"

Fuuuuuuuck.

12

LILY

Yep. He could handle me. Like a boss. Every thrust sent a wave of pleasure radiating through me—not like ripples on a pond, but like breakers crashing and fizzing against the rocks. He slowed a little and slipped his forearms beneath me, cradling me against him, like he was protecting me from himself.

There was no awkward negotiation—no *Is that how you like it?* Or *Is that too hard?* Listen, boys: if you have to ask, you're doing it wrong. And Gabe did *not* have to ask. Everything he did was juuuuust right. My moans sounded lurid and lewd, like some other version of myself was making them—some deep-down vixen that I had never known I'd been keeping caged. Each drive was deeper, each thrust harder, and each growl more aggressive. Buried deeply inside me, he lowered his head so our foreheads were pressed together. "Your pussy is fucking magic," he said with another ruthless drive.

Then came the undeniable, sudden, and *very* unexpected shiver. The butterfly batting its wings before Hurricane Orgasm.

I didn't even know how it was possible. We'd only just started. He wasn't touching my clit, and neither was I, but I zeroed in on the sensation and realized that with every drive he was hitting my clit with his pelvis. He was going to make me come. And my vibrator was on the other side of town. *"Gabe,"* I said as I drove my nails into his skin. I inhaled hard against his body, my nose near the hollow of his throat. His cologne was so yummy. His body was so yummy. *He* was so yummy. And from that place of yummy warmness, where I wasn't thinking or worrying about if he was doing it right or if I was going to be able to come, it began to happen. Everything inside me went still. I felt myself fluttering against him. The world was starting to shiver, starting to tremble. "I'm going to . . ."

In response, he gave me an insane thrust that made the headboard slam against the wall, and then . . . he pulled out.

All the way.

". . . come *on!*" I growled.

And he said, "If you think I'm going to let you come that fast, you better think again."

I sucked in a desperate breath and writhed against the sheets. I tried to hook my legs together behind him to get him back inside me, but he came up to sitting on his knees and slowed things down. He stroked himself slowly; he wet two fingers inside me. He tasted me and groaned again, and then wet them some more. And let me have a taste. I bit down on his fingers as I sucked my wetness off him.

"I'm going to learn you." He began to tease my clit with his middle finger, a featherlight touch on the edge. "I'm going to find out *exactly* what you like." He moved his finger counterclockwise, and the tension spiraled out into pleasure. I arched my neck so I was looking back at the mahogany headboard, upside down. He slid into me with two fingers and ground his palm into my clit.

I gripped his thigh hard and groaned. "Oh my *God*, what is happening?"

"Me and you is what's happening," he said, now slipping out of me and coming at my clit from the opposite direction. I felt his cock, warm and hard, lying on my thigh. With the hand he'd been using to stroke himself, he slipped inside me again and now it was his turn to groan.

He changed tactics and compressed my clit between his fingers. He wasn't touching it at all, and it became extra sensitive as he teased it away from my pelvis. He rolled his fingers side to side, and it sent me whirling. I grabbed the sheets hard and felt a cramp in my feet. He planted his hand beside my head and looked down at me. "Talk dirty to me," he said, tugging my bottom lip down with his thumb. "Let me hear something filthy from that pretty mouth."

It surprised me, and I suddenly felt shy and vulnerable. "I don't really know how," I said softly. "I've never done it before."

"That's the whole idea." He pressed into me one more millimeter. "You want this dick? Fucking earn it."

What a cocky bastard. *He* was the one who needed to be begging me. He was the one who needed to be earning *me*. The red streak of anger inside me blew up into a warning flare. My sister once told me every woman is sitting on a fortune. He might be one gorgeous buck, but I was the one with the pot of gold. "Don't be an asshole, Mr. Powers."

"Yeahhhh," he growled and gave me the head. He was thick, and just the tip made me slap the sheets and paw at his chest. But he swatted my hand away. We faced off in the moonlight for I don't know how long. He didn't soften at all. Nor did he let me have any more of him. "Go on," he said. "Do it. Let me hear you."

The words didn't come easily. How could I give him what he needed if I didn't even know what to say? There were things I wanted to say, of course—*You feel incredible. I need you to be back inside me.* But none of those things felt dirty enough. Those were one chili pepper on the hotness scale. But if he wanted dirty? I could get dirty. I could give him five chili peppers at a time. All I had to do was tell him exactly what I wanted. And that's exactly what I did. "Fuck me. Hard."

His eyes flashed in the moonlight, and I felt his cock pulse inside me. "I'll do *anything* to hear you talk like that."

Power. I felt it then, in a crazy wild rush. Here was this beast of a man who responded like that to just my words. I pulled his face down to mine and dug my fingers into the back of his neck. "Fuck me until I come, and don't stop even then."

"Natural beauty, natural filth," he said and gave me another thrust. The more I felt him give in to me, the easier it was for me to get out of my nice Southern girl ways.

If he wanted me to be rude, he was going to get me being rude. "Get inside me, you . . ."

"You *what*," he growled, pinching my cheeks.

I could do this. I was a Jameson, for God's sake. Even though I didn't swear much out loud, I sure as hell knew how. So I looked straight at him. His intensity and fury gave me courage, and my inhibitions vanished all at once. Prim and proper had its place. But this wasn't it. "Get inside me, you motherfucker."

"Atta-fuckin'-girl," he said with a visceral roll of his body and a powerful drive into me. All his control, all his resolve vanished, and he thrust into me with a primal fury that made me roar. His hips slammed into my clit. His fingers dug into my thighs. Within seconds, I was right back there in that place again. About to come, about to be lost. He'd made me wait, and my senses were heightened.

"Let go for me," he said into my ear. "Show me what you're made of and come on this cock."

Like he'd pushed me off a cliff, I was falling. Down, down, down, roaring his name. I hung on to him and dug my nails into him and bit down on his shoulder. And came.

Oh God.

How I came.

13

GABE

I fucked her through her orgasm and back again. Every contraction made me want to bust my load deep inside her, but I fought off the urge, making sure I gave her exactly what she needed and more. Once I felt her come back to me—when her breathing went back to normal and her roars quieted down into panting gasps—I asked, "Are we going to screw around with condoms, or are you going to let me come inside you?"

She looped one arm around my shoulders, narrowing her stare. Thinking. Considering. Deciding where my cum was gonna go. Fuck yeah. "It is safe?" she asked.

Her innocence was adorable, but she didn't get it. "I'm not about to put this perfect pussy in danger."

Her laugh was coy and soft. She pulled me closer and ran her fingertips through my hair. "I don't know if you've earned it."

That was my sweet spot right there—that place between respect and disrespect. The fire burned hottest right on that line. "Think I earned it right when your *oh God* turned into *oh Gabe.*"

She didn't answer with a word, but with another squeeze of her pussy, one so intense that it made a wave of precum spill out of me.

Mother. Of. *Fucks.* Once I could actually speak again, I said, "I'll take that as a yes."

Another squeeze, even harder. "A definite yes."

I eased back into the rhythm I'd found with her before, addicted to the new thickness of her wetness. Astroglide had nothing on her postorgasm liquid silk.

As she dripped out onto my balls, I gave it to her hard, I gave it to her wild, I gave it to her until I felt her walls begin to pulse for me again. But it felt less intense than the time before, so I pulled out of her, tucked my arm under her, and rolled her over. "Get on your knees. Come for me again."

She hesitated and looked back over her shoulder at me. I rammed into her so hard that she dropped her cheek to the mattress and roared. I slowed down enough to let her answer, and she said, "I don't know if I can."

There was some vulnerability in there that was hard for me to rail against, but I wanted what I wanted and she was going to give it to me. "Don't fucking argue with me," I said, going slow on the withdrawal, until only my head was still inside her. And until her toes curled up and she gripped the sheets in her fist. "I know you can do it. So do it."

She listened that time, and as soon as her fingers met her clit, I felt the flutters intensify. I held on to her hips, digging my fingers into her muscles, feeling her every curve and valley. Her long hair slid off her back over one shoulder, and she supported herself with one arm. I felt her fingertips against the sides of my cock as I powered into her. I aimed for her G-spot, and I hit it again and again. I knitted my hand into her sweaty hair and pulled back, drawing her jaw upward. She made a long, dirty "Nnn-hnn-nnnn" and began to touch herself faster.

I gave her everything I had, and she took it. More, more, *more.*

"Oh *God*," she gasped. "Please come with me. Please."

"Don't be so fucking polite," I told her as I drove into her even harder.

She let out this angry roar that blew my mind. I was fully ready to let her have it, but then she doubled down on me. "Come inside me. Right fucking now."

That was *that*. She had me before I even knew I was gone. Hanging on to her hips so hard I knew I'd leave bruises, I came in three hard waves, shooting my cum deep inside her heaven-sent cunt.

Both of us were spent, and she fell asleep in my arms with sweaty ringlets framing her face. The moonlight inched across her body and the messy sheets all around us. I pressed a kiss to the top of her head, her silky hair cool against my lips. Through the musky, salty smells of the two of us together, I could still smell her sweetness. Sweeter now because I knew how fucking dirty she could be.

But right as I was falling asleep with her in my arms, the power came back on. The room was bathed in light from the hallway, shining in through the door and the window she'd crawled through earlier. She made little sleepy moans of protest, rolling over and curling up against my chest. The air-conditioning kicked on, and I felt cool air begin to fill the room. I wanted to stay exactly where I was, with her nestled up against me, but if I didn't get the quilt from the floor and shut off the lights, odds were pretty good that one or the other would wake her up. No way was I going to let that happen.

Very gently, I slipped my arm out from under her and placed a pillow under her head. I got out of bed, careful not to let the old wooden frame squeak, and pulled the sheet up over her, as well as the quilt. I went out into the hallway and switched off the lights, then carefully made my way down the staircase and switched off the foyer light as well. I picked her dress up off the stairs and laid it over the banister and then headed back up to bed. But halfway up I heard a sound. A faint, unfamiliar sound. Like breathing but not quite. I froze and turned to look down the steps behind me.

The noise got louder, and I realized what it was. It was Lily. And she was snoring. Smiling to myself in the darkness, I made my way back to the bedroom, closed the door behind me, and got back in bed beside her. I pulled her close against my body and placed my chin against her shoulder. Last night, I'd fallen asleep thinking about her. Tonight, I had her in my arms. Sometimes shit didn't work out like you hoped. But sometimes it most definitely did.

14

GABE

I was alone when I woke up. For a second, bleary-eyed and half-awake, I thought last night might have all been a dream. But right in front of me was proof she was real. She'd left me a note on the bedside table. It was the receipt from her aunt's grocery store, and on the back she'd written:

> Gabe,
> Had to go help my sister doing a thing for her work!
>   I didn't want to wake you. oxoxox
>   PS: Last night! OMG.

Maximum cuteness. I rolled out of bed and grabbed my boxers from the floor. Hanging on the bedpost, I found her panties. She'd left them for me. *Mine, all fucking mine.* I ran the delicate lace edge between my fingertips. But if her panties were here, it meant that she wasn't wearing them. Which meant she'd left the house naked under her dress. And *that* idea . . .

I pulled my boxers over my raging morning wood, did my best to get the stallion in the barn, and wandered downstairs into the kitchen. I turned on the coffee pot and splashed my face with a handful of water.

Through the window above the sink, I looked out at the backyard, with its tire swing and overgrown garden. The place was lush and private, with an old, high fence running around the perimeter of the property. Big oaks, velvety green grass. Like paradise. It had to be a quarter acre at least. I'd noticed a lot of houseplants at Lily's place, and for one awesome second, I imagined her out there—in a sun hat, with pruning shears, and a dog running around her feet.

Once I got my coffee squared away, I set up my laptop on the dining table to check my email and got my day started. Even though last night had been a huge success personally, professionally it had yielded exactly *fuck all*. Which was totally fine. It was another day, and God knew there were plenty of alleged ghosts in Savannah. But just as I was sitting down, something caught my eye. There on the buffet by the wall was one of Lily's audio recorders. The digital display said *Memory Full*.

Holy shit. In the heat of the moment, I'd completely forgotten that they were everywhere around us. Did that mean . . . I cycled through the display info and saw it had almost ten hours recorded on it. That meant it had been recording all night. That meant it had recorded us. Together.

Having mind-blowingly excellent sex.

If I couldn't have her with me now, at least I could get some of last night to tide me over. Coffee and recorder in hand, I got situated at the big wooden table. I got my laptop booted up and connected to the Wi-Fi. I grabbed my headphones from my bag and put them into my ears. Then I stuck the USB stick end of the audio recorder into the slot on the side of my computer.

Expecting to hear me coming on to her via Ouija board, I turned up the volume. But the mic seemed to have only picked up the audio from the dining room itself. Very faintly, I could hear her laughing, but it sounded far away. Still, though, cute as hell—it sounded like a distant wind chime, and it made me feel so fucking good. If I hadn't known what I was hearing, it wouldn't have been obvious. But I'd lived every fantastic second of it, and as I listened I replayed every touch and sensation. I heard us going up the stairs and very faint breathy whispers. No actual words, but I remembered it all in vivid detail. It was me talking to her. Me eating her out from behind on the steps.

I turned up the volume, and I was almost certain I heard my hand slapping her ass. Then came the sound of footsteps and then silence for a while. A few seconds later, the *thump-thump-thump* of us pushing one another across the bedroom. More silence, which would've been when we were teasing each other, talking dirty. Getting rude. And then came the very definite sound of me fucking her, as the headboard *ka-whump-ka-whumped* the wall. I pressed my fist to my mouth and groaned.

Leaning back in the massive old dining chair, I listened to myself having my way with her. The dining room was directly below the bedroom, and the recorder had gotten every last bang and roar. There were no clear words, only ferociously sexy sounds. Hearing her come got me painfully hard, so hard that I thought I was going to have to do something about it. But I didn't. I was going to let that feeling build and build; I'd be taking it out on her—in her—soon enough. Once the recording went silent, once we'd gone to bed, I rewound and listened again. The second time was even better, even hotter, and I remembered new details. The way she'd arched up off the mattress with her heel to my sternum, the way she'd squeezed. The way *motherfucker* sounded on those full pink lips. But right as I was starting to hear her give me her gritted-teeth roar . . . my phone started to ring.

Lily. It had to be Lily. I needed it to be Lily. I was so high on that sound of the two of us together, so distracted, I didn't even look to see who was calling. Until it was too goddamned late.

Panting. Grunting. "Powers! Where the hell is my pilot?"

The guy would interrupt his own funeral. I smacked the space bar to pause the recording. "You have the *worst* timing."

"Morning to you too, sunshine!" he bellowed.

On the screen were the peaks and valleys of the audio WAV file. Coming up there was a big spike. It was her first orgasm of the night. Magnificent. "Go back to your spin class, man. I'm *really* busy."

"No spin today!" he panted. "I'm on the elliptical! Really working those glutes!"

I winced. The image of Lily in bed was replaced by Markowitz in his home gym-office setup. He'd rigged a laptop to his elliptical machine with bungee cords and carpentry clamps so he could work while he burned "mega calories." He'd given me a demo the last time I was over at his house. Every time he took a step, he clenched his ass. Hard. Made the spandex pucker and everything.

"So where's my pilot? I got bigwigs breathing down my neck! Gettin' real hot in here!" His breathing got louder and more like a crank call.

In the background I could hear the whooshing of the pedals and tried to unremember those godforsaken spandex shorts. He weighed like 160 pounds. Nothing good about any of it at all. I rubbed my temples and then ran my hand over my jaw. "I'm working on it. Seriously. When was the last time I let you down, man?"

"Well, there's always a first time for everything, Powers." I heard him take a swig of water on the other end of the line, and then what sounded like some static. "Goddamn it. Got another call. Hold on," he said, and the *whoosh-whoosh* of the elliptical went silent.

While I waited I moved my mouse around on my desktop. When I minimized the audio window, a new window popped up asking if I'd like to download the file from the digital recorder. I hesitated with my arrow over the yes button.

Jesus. Should I? Would that be weird? Would I be *that guy*? I really didn't want to be *that guy*. But what if some crazy shit happened with the file? What if . . . I looked at my cup of coffee and then at my computer. What if I knocked my coffee over and the file got erased? What if . . . it got corrupted? What if some awful shit happened and I never got to hear it again?

It'd be a goddamned tragedy. All I had to do to prevent it was click my mouse.

I put the call with Markowitz on speaker and opened the text conversation with Lily.

Hey beautiful

Your digital recorder in the dining room picked us up last night.

                                                        Hi!

                                                OMG. Really?

Thumps and groans.

                                                Aaaah!

Listened 1.5 times already. Just want your permission to download.

Or I can just listen off the recorder. Whatever you want.

                                        Yeah! Download for sure!

                                        Maybe we can listen together!

Which she followed up with a kissy face. Well, shiiiiiit. She was hitting every kink I never knew I had. I found myself smiling like a goddamned idiot at my screen while I thought up a reply. Best to keep it simple, especially since I was getting exactly zero blood to my brain.

So get over here

Soon soon!

Call you later, k?

Can't wait

I moved the file off the digital recorder onto my desktop, and the progress ribbon went from 0 percent to 100 percent. Markowitz came back on the line a second later. "First things first. I'm thinking Brazil next. What do you think?"

Well, shit yes, I wanted to go to Brazil, but the last goddamned thing I wanted to do right now was talk about the next place I was headed. I had an audio file to listen to. I had a woman to ravage. "Sounds great. Man, I gotta go."

"Powers!" he said as his breathing got less frenzied and the sound of his elliptical in the background slowed down. "Thought you said you had nothing from the haunted house. But I'm looking at an audio file!"

I froze. I stared at my screen.

Shit, shit, shit, shit, shit. The file had automatically downloaded to the folder I shared with Markowitz. Usually, that was fine—I didn't give two shits if he saw my outtakes and rough cuts. But this, *this* . . . As fast as I could, I tried to drag it out of the shared folder.

It was too late. On the other end of the line, I was almost sure I heard the file playing. I said, "It's raw audio. Don't listen yet. Let me clean it up."

Yet again, the son of a bitch ignored the thing he didn't want to hear. I could just see him in my mind's eye, skipping forward with manic pokes of his trackpad. I heard a thump and possibly a growl. "Whoa! Sounds spooky! Call you right back!"

And *click* went the line.

Fuck.

15

Lily

My sister, Daisy, was the curator and only full-time employee of the Savannah Living History Museum. She often recruited me to help her with her special exhibitions, which started unpleasantly early on Sunday mornings. This morning was no exception. While Aunt Jennifer looked after Ivan, Daisy and I manned the museum. According to the calendar on the museum's website, today was "A Demonstration of Textile Coloring Techniques of the Antebellum South." In other words, beet juice tie-dye. Hooray.

My sister loved her job, but I quietly filed the Living History Museum on the Bummer List, right alongside taxes and Pap smears—a bit of a drag, but what could a girl do? Like everything else on the Bummer List, living history didn't give two shakes that I had wobbly thighs and dreamy thoughts, or that I was hiding a hickey for the first time since I was sixteen. Living history didn't care that I would much rather have been in bed with Gabe, verifying that he had, in fact, not just a six-pack but an eight-pack. Oh no. All living history cared about was me, dressed up in my petticoats, smiling at confused tourists who wandered in thinking that we were part of the Starbucks next door.

I was hiding in the butler's pantry with my phone, which was class-A contraband for museum volunteers. I touched my ringlet curls, piled high in a style that was apparently all the rage when General Grant was still in diapers. Mercifully, my dress was from the same era and featured an uncomfortable—but hickey-hiding—lace collar. As I checked my curls and adjusted some bobby pins with one hand, I flipped through Gabe's YouTube channel with the other. Thumbnail after glorious thumbnail of his smiling face flashed back at me. Borneo. South Africa. Myanmar. One hundred thousand views. Two hundred sixty-eight thousand views. One particularly astounding number whizzed past, and I flicked my thumb down to go back to the video. One *million* views. The title was "Cliff Diving in Mexico." The thumbnail for that one was him, in midair, about to plunge into the water. Even looking at him through my cracked and smudgy phone screen, one thing was very clear: I now knew exactly where my loins were.

Like a prisoner watching for the warden, I leaned out of the pantry to do a quick double check for Daisy, made sure my volume was all the way down, and hit play. He was up close to the camera at first, a tight shot that featured his chiseled jawline and his scratchy stubble. I ran my fingertip over my neck, over the lace frill above my hickey that was in the shape of that delicious mouth.

He adjusted the focus, and his broad shoulder appeared in the corner of the frame. Then he stepped back, revealing a wide shot of a heavenly blue lagoon rimmed with palms, like a huge, sparkling sapphire set in emeralds. I imagined the tripod I'd seen him using last night nestled in between exotic jungle flowers to film the panorama behind him. He ripped off his shirt, and I squeaked out a close-lipped "Meep!" He extended his arms above him, drawing out the contrast between his waist and his sculpted back and shoulders. He looked back once to wink at the camera and dived into the water, his rippling body and glistening muscles catching the tropical light. He slipped into the blue depths with hardly a splash. A few seconds later, he resurfaced. He swung his head side to side like he was doing a cologne ad and swept his dark, dripping hair back from his tanned forehead. And then he smiled up at the camera.

Mercy!

I scrolled down to the comments. Top one, with one thousand up votes, said, "Kaboom go my ovaries."

"You said it, girl!" I whispered at my phone.

"Lily," my sister whisper-barked from around the corner. "Get your bustle over here and help me dye this tablecloth!"

I stashed my phone into the pocket of my dress and trotted out into the kitchen area. A few people milled around, looking at the displays and period dishware. A lady in pink Crocs and pink cargo shorts said, "This isn't Starbucks, is it?" to her husband.

He came around the corner, wearing a complementary baby-blue Crocs-and-shorts ensemble, and replied, "I don't think so. But come in here, Marge. This mattress is stuffed with horsehair! It smells like a farm!" And off they wandered, with their Crocs squelching.

I took my place next to Daisy in the kitchen. Our shtick was that we were sisters; her husband had left her to raise her baby alone while he struck out for gold in California, never to be heard from again. I was a spinster with no prospects who was trying to learn to knit. Truth in advertising.

With my sleeves rolled up, I plunged my hands into the basin of beet juice and warm water. I squeezed the sheet of linen in the basin and gazed down into the purply-red water, as well as my now purply-red hands and forearms. Beet juice was *really* gruesome if you didn't know what it was. When the visitors ambled off into the dining room, set with period china and silverware we'd found at a flea market, I whispered to Daisy, "Why do we have to do this? All anybody wants is your peach preserves and my lemon curd. And that doesn't make us look like ax murderers for four days either. Am I right?"

In response, Daisy gave me the Glare. Oooh, she was good at the Glare. It was especially effective when she was in all black like she was now, complete with a cameo choker on a wide black velvet ribbon. Antebellum resting bitch face—the original. She pursed her lips into a ferocious line when she did it. She'd really gotten that expression down to a science. It was more than possible that the Glare was what had sent Boris scurrying back to Moscow. "It's educational," Daisy said as she squeezed the linen. "And sustainable!"

I pulled my hand out of the beet water to push aside my bangs. A red droplet landed on my replica gown, which was off-white with tiny cornflowers. It was one of three dresses I was allowed to wear at the museum; the fabric had come from Joann, but it wasn't cheap to have a reproduction gown made by a seamstress—so many pleats!—and Daisy was *very* protective. Her eyes locked onto the splotch of red. Cut to Lady Macbeth saying, *Out, damned spot!* "Lily!"

"Daisy!" I tried to fling the Glare back at her. I was a total amateur. I was pretty sure it just made me look like I was doing an advertisement for Excedrin, but still. Same general idea. Same squint and purse. She doubled down. I hissed and turned away. *All hail the queen!* She'd undoubtedly perfected it by side-eyeing Boris for all those miserable years when he'd graced us with his presence like an incurable rash. I, on the other hand, had never spent a sustained period of time staring at any one single man. Or really feeling much of anything for one single man. Except . . .

The thought of last night plopped me back in the house on Abercorn. And the way Gabe had looked all sprawled out in bed when I'd left.

But for as wonderful as it had been, it also made my heart ache. Like a combination of joy and sadness. Soy. Jadness. Something. As I squeezed and twisted and rubbed the linen to get the beet juice to soak into the fibers, I preworried my way through what might or might not happen next. I knew that he wouldn't be around for long. And I knew that this feeling inside—this buzzing, electric excitement—was just temporary. I couldn't float on butterflies forever. We were worlds apart: a million people had watched him cliff dive on YouTube—or ten thousand ladies, over and over again. But still! Ten thousand! Women looked at him and their ovaries went *wa-whump*; men looked at me and said, *Awww*. He had a television show; I had a one-employee business. His passport was probably stamped on every page; I didn't even have one. He lived a jet-set life; I lived with a parrot. We were worlds apart. It really was that simple. The hometown girl and the television star?

Pshaw, as we said in the museum. Impossible.

He'd have to be like the last slice of peach pie. Wonderful while it lasted, but not something that I could have forever. And that was OK. At least, that's what I kept telling myself as I squeezed the linen over and over again.

One splotchy red tablecloth later, my phone began vibrating in my dress pocket. A lot. Like my skirt was full of bees.

This time Daisy didn't give me the Glare. Instead she let out an exasperated snort-sigh, and she shook her head at the water and at the napkins that now floated on the surface. She was hard-line about the museum, but she was even more hard-line about her coffee. "Go ahead. Get me a soy latte while you're out."

"'Kay!" I pulled my hands out of the purple water. I grabbed our secret roll of paper towels from their hiding place underneath the counter, well out of view of the visitors, and dried my hands, leaving behind a clump of paper towels that would've fit right into any grisly murder scene. Then I trotted out the back door into the alley. Once I got myself and my puffy skirt out the door, I pulled out my phone again. The lock screen was covered in message alerts and phone calls from Gabe. At the bottom was a text message from early in the flurry.

I accidentally shared the file.

Oh boy.

Before I could even start to reply, my phone started to ring again. But it wasn't Gabe this time. It was the 323 area code from last night. His producer.

It had to be a dreaded Shared File Disaster. I was no stranger to digital snafus myself; I was the queen of the Reply-All Catastrophe. Once, I'd been included on an email from my sister about how to make the Living History Museum "more authentic." I'd meant to reply only to Daisy but had instead replied to the entire museum staff and board—including the mayor!—with the message:

> Hi,
>
> I'm all for authenticity, but can't we get some two-ply toilet paper?
>
> Regards,
> My vagina

Winner, winner, chicken dinner. And so, bracing for anything, I hit the answer button and said, "Sounds Good, this is Lily."

"Ms. Jameson?" he panted.

"Yes, hello!" I said as my phone continued to buzz against my cheek with little staccato bursts of texts. I briefly pulled it away from my ear and saw more messages from Gabe streaming through.

It's just thumps. No names or anything. But here's the thing . . .

I pressed the phone back to my ear just in time to hear Markowitz say, ". . . the raw audio from last night, sent it along to the bigwigs."

Oopsies! It certainly explained why my phone was hot with all the buzzing. But what was done could not be undone. What was sent could not be unsent. So I rolled with it. "Oh! Very good!" I said in my most chipper voice, desperately trying not to let the surprise seep in. "Was it . . ." I searched for the word. Something neutral. Something G-rated. Something on-brand. "Does it sound good?"

"Shit, yes! Sounds *great*! The Savannah episodes are a go!"

I let out a hoot of laughter and tried to stifle the ensuing giggle. Our wild night of bed-shaking sex had been mistaken for a houseful of ghosts. Powers of Suggestion *indeed!* "We noticed quite a bit of . . ." I cleared my throat. "Action?" I was smiling so hard that my cheeks burned. "I'm not sure of the word."

"Me neither, but the suits upstairs loved it! I'm emailing through some employment documents for you. We'll take care of all the tax forms and whatever. You'll get a thank-you after each episode in the credits. Blah, blah, blah. There's money for you in the budget already, and plenty of it. Should offset anything you might have to cancel. That all right?"

There's a budget? I'm in the budget? I'd spent the last five years feeling like I was playing some quasi-grown-up version of store, like my sister and I used to play when we were girls, selling each other stubby pencils and incomplete Barbie outfits. Sure, I had an LLC, but my logo was a microphone flower that I'd designed in PowerPoint! To be hired to work on a real live television show made me feel incredibly legit. I was also positively thrilled at the prospect of not having to say goodbye to Gabe so very soon. "That would be fantastic!"

"Just sent the docs. Take a look real quick; make sure I spelled your name right. All that good stuff."

"OK!" I opened my email while Mr. Markowitz waited on the line. The document was very official looking and had my name and company placed in all the relevant blanks. I scrolled through with my heart pitter-pattering along. This wasn't a contract with the Universalist church for Sunday bingo; this was the big time. The pay was generous. The requirements were reasonable. It was a huge break for me. *And* it meant that I'd get to work with Gabe on a steady, well-funded project. So it was all just Georgia-peachy keen . . .

. . . until I got to the section labeled *Conduct.* In my head, I heard the scratchy squeak of a needle coming off a record.

> By signing this document, all parties agree that for the term of the dates listed under Section 2, Employment Terms, there shall be no sexual contact of any kind between employees. For the purposes of this document, "sexual contact" includes but is not limited to: comments of a sexual or flirtatious nature, "petting" (heavy or light), kissing, touching, "coitus," intercourse of any type, so-called hanky-panky, so-called business time, and all other euphemisms not mentioned herein. Failure to adhere to the rules of conduct set forth in this section will result in immediate termination of this contract.

I felt my face flush, and I broke out in a sweat that had nothing whatsoever to do with the sweltering July heat. I looked blankly down the alley. A tourist on the street stared at me and my beet-red hands. A small, plump little boy hung on to her leg and smashed his face into her thigh. But I wasn't really there, in that moment, ensuring that some poor child was destined for talk therapy because he'd been scared half to death in Savannah. I was still very much in the Land of the Suggestive Fine Print.

No touching. No kissing. No hanky *or* panky? It would be like getting the peanut butter away from the chocolate in a peanut butter cup. I pressed the speaker button on my phone. "Umm, Mr. Markowitz? About this *Conduct* section . . ."

"If you're worried, don't be! That's got nothing to do with Powers! He's as honest as they come. But we have to have it in there. It's the Age of the Asshole, you know? Boilerplate stuff."

Reading over the document again, it didn't feel particularly boiler-plate. It felt like an overview of what we'd done last night. Minus the dirty talk. God, how I'd *loved* the dirty talk.

"You on board, Ms. Jameson?" hollered Mr. Markowitz.

Reality check: even if he was here to do a series, Gabe wasn't here to stay. Maybe the conduct clause was just that little shot of common sense that I needed—a reminder that this was a job, just a job, and nothing more. And as for the job itself, I couldn't say no. That would be crazy. That would be a huge mistake. I had to say yes. I just had to. And I could figure out what to do with Gabe when I saw him. Provided I *seriously* expanded my personal bubble. By twenty to thirty feet.

"I'm on board." I pressed my pink hand to my forehead. "Yep. Absolutely." I shut my eyes and leaned against the warm brick wall of the museum. Oh God. What was I going to do? And where the heck were my manners? "Thank you so much!"

"My pleasure!" panted Mr. Markowitz. "Welcome to *The Powers of Suggestion!*"

I wandered into Starbucks, feeling totally dazed. The girl behind the counter was new; I didn't recognize her, and she was understandably confused at what *my* deal was. She looked at my hair. At my outfit. And finally at my red arms and hands. And blinked.

"Beet juice," I explained.

She cocked her head. "We don't have that here, hon. This is Starbucks. Not Whole Foods."

I stared at her and then inhaled hard, trying to get myself to crash-land back in the real world. I dragged myself out of the finer points of hanky and panky and thudded down into grandes and ventis. "Sorry. A soy latte and an iced black tea, four sugars. Venti for both," I said and ran my phone over the little payment cube. As I did, the Facebook app caught my attention, and I remembered he'd told me that he had a Facebook fan club in addition to the YouTube channel.

I wedged myself between the bathroom and a display rack of sale-priced mugs and travel cups. I went to Facebook, and within a few keystrokes, I'd found his fan group, naughtily named "Powerfully Gushing for Gabe Powers," with thirty *thousand* members. The description of the group was short and right to the point: "This is a group devoted to Gabe Powers. If you aren't a fan, we don't understand you!"

At the top of the page was a pinned announcement asking the group members to vote in a competition called "Superlative Hunks" from *People* magazine. I clicked through to the competition and saw it was set up like a high school yearbook, with graphics made to replicate embossed book covers and "Most Likely To" pages. The idea was that fans would vote for their favorite man, and the results would be published in the next edition of the magazine. The categories included Most Likely to Make You Swoon, Most Likely to Make You Binge-Watch, Most Likely to Get You to Ask Your Husband to Install a Television in the Kitchen.

Gabe was miles and miles ahead of all the competitors in every category. Ninety-eight percent for the swoon, 98 percent for the binge-watch, and 100 percent for the kitchen TV.

I felt a sinking dread welling up in me. The yearbook thing happened to hit a very raw nerve. One of my most raw, without a doubt. So raw that I hadn't really let myself think about it in fifteen years. But now it all came flooding back.

When I'd been in high school, I had been passionately in young love with a boy named Matt Fransen. He had been my first everything. He was the captain of our football team, and for some reason that I neither understood nor questioned, he had become very, very smitten with me. Oh, how I'd loved him, with that blurry, hormonal teenage love when anything and everything is possible. But after just a few wildly passionate months of sneaking kisses behind the lockers between art and math and Friday-night dates that started in a movie theater and ended in his steamed-up Bronco, the yearbook had come out.

He had been voted Most Likely to Star in an Action Film. And I had been voted Most Likely to Have Thirteen Cats.

I'd gotten dumped so fast it had made me feel carsick.

I felt the pinch and nausea of that memory all over again. Even though I'd put it behind me, I could still feel that old and terrible sting. A vivid memory of sitting in a bathroom stall between class periods while tears slid down my cheeks.

Once again, here I was. The eccentric girl in the eccentric life, swooning over a man so popular it made me wonder how he could even see me.

It wouldn't work. It would never work. The job might, but not the romance. Maybe I didn't have any cats, but I was still that girl. And he was definitely that guy. So I took a deep breath, tried to cheer myself up with a little *chin up, buttercup*, and gave him a ring.

He didn't answer with a hello. Instead he answered with, "There she is."

His words made my whole body tighten. It was unbelievable. It was like I was a rubber band, and from all the way across town, he was pulling me tight. But I held my ground. No matter how he made me feel with three tiny syllables, there was still a conversation that needed to be had. Rules were rules. Yearbooks were yearbooks. "So. A little birdie told me that Savannah is a go."

He sort of groan-laughed. "We knocked it out of the park last night. They agreed to the Savannah episodes based on the audio alone. But I'm not using that audio in the show. That's mine. All fucking mine."

I clapped my hand over my mouth from stop myself from moaning and bumped into the display of mugs. That voice was going to be the end of me. "We have to be good. Haven't you seen the contract?"

Gabe growled. "Haven't you seen *yourself*?"

"Gabe!" I said, running my fingers along one of the mug handles.

"Lily," he shot back.

Just my name on his lips made my knees wobble. "I'm serious."

He let out a long, gruff breath. "You really think you're going to be good?"

I nodded at a huge photo of a scone on the wall. I felt a ribbon of warmth unspool through me. It wasn't going to be easy, but it had to be done. "Yes. I am."

"So then meet me this afternoon at two. At Uncle Jimmy's Secret Ingredient BBQ."

The mention of Jimmy's Secret Ingredient made me salivate immediately. Gabe's gravelly and sexy voice was hard enough to resist, but now he was pulling my favorite barbecue out of his sleeve? *So* unfair.

I stepped aside to make room for some tourists, nestling my petticoats next to the cream and sugar table. I brought the receiver close to my lips and tried to get serious. "We can't be going out for barbecue, Gabe. Work. Not play."

He cleared his throat. "We're going to work. I just hung up with a medium who asked us to meet her there."

See? It's gonna be fine! "Oh." I straightened my bodice. "Right. OK. Good, then! Work it is."

"Because let's get one thing straight. When I play with you, you're gonna fucking know it."

Or not! The way he talked made me involuntarily clench my thighs together. No apologies, no explanation—just pure masculine desire. But I would have to resist him. I would. Like the last Oreo in the package. Like the last chip in the bag. In the name of unpopular girls everywhere. "We're going to be good."

"Speak for yourself, beautiful," he said, all growly and dark. "Speak for yourself."

16

Gabe

Uncle Jimmy's Secret Ingredient BBQ was a squatty white building on the outskirts of town with rows of painted red picnic tables under massive cypresses. Sitting in my truck with the AC blasting, I could smell the smoker going full throttle. Holy shit, did it smell good. But as soon as I saw Lily's van rumble in behind me, all thoughts of mouthwatering barbecue left my head. Nothing sounded better to eat than her.

I cut the engine on my truck and watched her touch up her lipstick. She pouted at her reflection in her rearview mirror and rubbed her lips together. Then she flung open her door, and I saw a pair of pink Converse land on the gravel. I got out of my truck and turned to face her. I gave her a hey-baby flick of my chin. Today it was black leggings that accentuated the Y between her legs and a pink T-shirt that said PUMP UP THE VOLUME! She straightened her shoulders and gave me a polite smile. "Hello, Mr. Powers."

Here we go. Full names? Bring it on. I knew exactly what the contract said, but I'd never worked with anybody who made me want to break it until now. And I didn't just want to break it with her—I wanted to light the goddamned thing on fire. Yet it didn't surprise me that she wanted to follow the rules. She'd gone doe-eyed when I asked her to get filthy in bed, when I'd pushed her to go past what she was used to doing. If she wanted us to be good, I could roll with that. For a while. So I gave her a respectful nod. "Ms. Jameson."

She turned away for a second, pressing her fist to her mouth and hanging on to her fender.

Closing my truck door behind me, I took a few steps toward her. Cicadas screeched, and the wind rustled the trees. But all that seemed far away, like it was in another world. Another place. My whole focus zeroed in to just her—her beautiful face, the lovely way she had about her. And the fact that clearly she *thought* she was going to be able to keep me at bay.

Not a chance.

In the dappled sunshine, something caught my eye. Something very distinctive on her neck, in exactly the place that I'd gone for her as she came. Proof that I'd already breached her walls. "Holy shit." I took a few more steps toward her. "That's a hickey, isn't it?"

She slapped her hand to her throat like she was trying to squash a mosquito. "I have no idea what you're talking about." She shook her head, and her curls bounced. "Small blemish. Heat rash."

She hadn't covered it the whole way, and I saw the telltale bruising just past her pinkie. "I marked you. Admit it."

Pursing her lips, she pulled a delicate scarf out of her purse, pink and white to match her shirt. She tied it around her neck and shifted the knot to hide the damage I'd done to her. And had every intention of doing again.

I put one hand on the side of her van to cage her in, giving her no place to go but straight into me. "Don't tell me you haven't been think-ing about last night all goddamned day."

She placed her fingertip on my chest and pushed me back. "Conduct clause, Mr. Powers. I'm going to follow it. Full stop."

Fuck that. There wasn't going to be a full stop until I had my way with her again. Repeatedly. "Chemistry, Ms. Jameson. I want you. Full stop."

For a second I thought I'd won. Her eyelashes fluttered, she rocked back on her heels, and her chest rose and fell. But as soon as she'd started to give in to me, she got a handle on herself again. She wiggled her finger at me. "Nope."

Yep. Before I could make another move, like hoisting her up on her fender and saying, *I'll show you what bad conduct really looks like,* the noise of a screen door being flung open cut through the air and a man boomed, "Are you shitting me? Goddamned celery seeds? What kinda operation you think we're running here? *Celery seeds!*"

The man stormed out of the back door of the restaurant. He was dressed in a barbecue sauce–stained apron, a Hawaiian shirt, and khaki shorts. On his apron was the word *AWESOMESAUCE.* I watched him plunge his hand into his pocket, from which he produced something small and square. He peeled the back off it and slapped it on his massive biceps. At first I thought it was a bandage, but then I realized, nope. Definitely a nicotine patch. "Celery seeds!" he roared as he chased one of the patch wrappers across the grass. It fluttered away, and he circled back toward the restaurant. He produced a box of what looked like nicotine gum from his apron pocket, popped a bunch of pieces from the blister pack, and shoved the whole handful in his mouth.

I turned to Lily. She glanced up at me and asked, "What are we actually doing here, anyway?"

Her eyes were even prettier today than they had been yesterday. For a second, I got caught up in the way the sunshine brought out hints of green near the center of her irises, which made me think of how they looked when I had her right on the edge of . . .

She put her hand on her hip. "Gabe!"

"Sorry." I shook it off, inhaling hard and looking away for a second. "Sorry. We're going to record a séance. I got in touch with one of the mediums from town, and she told me to meet her out here. Apparently Uncle Jimmy has, you know"—I lifted my eyebrow and lowered my voice—"passed on."

Lily pressed her hand to her heart. Her small, soft fingers fanned out over her breastbone. She wasn't playing it up; she was genuinely shocked. "Oh my God. Not Uncle Jimmy."

I forced myself to look at her face—*just* her face. And what a face it was, especially the slight dryness on her chin from my scruff. "Worse still, it seems he took the secret ingredient of the legendary sauce with him."

Now her mouth dropped open. The hand that had been on her chest extended to press again *my* chest. *Awww, yeah.*

"Are you serious? *The* ingredient?"

I leaned into her hand, letting her get a sense of what she was really up against. "Come on. Just one kiss."

"Nope!" She spun on the toe of her Converse, grinding the gravel as she pivoted away. I stepped back to let her do her thing. As she gathered up her recording equipment, I watched her every move. Every curve, every line, every hill and valley. Sassy and confident, she slammed her van doors and marched off toward the entrance of Uncle Jimmy's. Her steps were purposeful and forceful. Each one sent a ripple up through her thighs and ass.

"I like you coming," I told her, loud enough for her to hear, "but I like you going too."

She turned back over her shoulder to face me and shook her head as if to say, *Oh no you didn't.* "C'mon, Mr. Powers. We've got work to do," she said with a lift of her shoulder and a pout and set off again, walking faster. Not quite a strut and not quite a march. Maybe that was what they called a sashay.

I grabbed my bag and locked my truck. In a few strides, I caught up with her, and I made it to the restaurant door before she did, stepping in front of her to grab the handle. I opened it for her, and as she passed under my arm, I leaned in close. "Know what's *not* mentioned in the conduct clause?"

She turned around to face me. Her stance was defiant, with her hands on her hips. But her face was flushed, and her lips quivered before she pursed them tight. "What doesn't it mention?"

"Checking you out. I triple-checked."

Normally when I arrived at a filming location, *someone* recognized me. But not this time. This time, it was *all* about Lily. As the bell on the door clanged to announce our entrance, what I assumed was Uncle Jimmy's family spilled out of the kitchen with booming cheers of "Miss Lily!" and "Lily Marie!" and "Well, would you look who it is!" They gathered around her in a circle asking her how she was doing, and how her sister was doing, and how business had been. Meanwhile, I stood off in the corner holding my backpack and watching her. Behind every beautiful woman, there's a dude just happy to be there.

Seeing her in her element confirmed what I'd known already—she was a sweetheart, holding hands, kissing cheeks, and being wrapped in warm embraces. Just as fast as they volleyed questions at her, she asked them all manner of things back—about a cat named Francis and a dog named Lulabell, something about some hydrangeas and a tomato patch, and finally, she asked about Jimmy, who had passed away. When she brought him up, the family went quiet. I noticed that on every wall there were big photographs of a man who looked jovial and content in every image. He wore a Hawaiian lei in one, and in another he had a rack of ribs and cheeks smudged with barbecue sauce. Lily held the woman who I guessed was his daughter in a loving, heartfelt hug. "I'm so sorry to hear it." She clasped the woman's hands in hers. I could hear the emotion in her voice, that kindhearted frankness of someone opening their heart without hesitation. "He was the biggest love. He will be missed so much."

And echoes of "Mmm-hmmm" and "Yes, indeed" filled the room.

The big guy in the apron trundled out of the kitchen last, looking as pissed off as a grizzly bear woken up from hibernation. But when he saw Lily, his face lit up into the biggest, widest smile. A 180-degree transformation. He opened his arms, and Lily ran to him. He scooped her right off the floor and twirled her around as she laughed into his burly shoulder. She lifted up her feet and crossed her ankles as she spun through the air.

"Gabe!" she said when he finally set her down. "This is Jimmy Jr. He's known me since I was . . ." She raised her face to him, shifting her lips off to one side. "I can't even remember."

"This big," Jimmy Jr. boomed, lowering his hand to about knee height. "Maybe this big." He lowered his hand even more. "Always a ray of sunshine, though! Even when you were baby and a little . . . gassy!"

The whole room roared with laughter, Lily's loudest of them all. Once the laughter died down, she took Jimmy by one massive hand and dragged him over to me. "This is Gabe! He's the one that's going to be doing some filming. I'm doing his audio."

"Jimmy Jr.," said the big guy in the apron. He gave my hand a shake so firm that it made his nicotine patches ripple. "Real pleasure to meet you, Mr. . . ." He trailed off, squinting. "Powell?"

"Powers," I said. Lily was clearly suppressing a giggle. It was the flip side of the hostess falling all over herself last night. I was on Lily's turf now, and it felt pretty damned good. Weird, but good. I added, "Thanks for letting me—us—come and do some filming."

"Real glad to have you," Jimmy Jr. said. He turned more toward Lily than me to add, "But listen, we got ourselves a big problem. The secret ingredient?" He rubbed his wrinkled forehead and scratched his close-cropped hair. "I'm hosed without it!"

Lily patted his massive arm and gave it a reassuring squeeze. "One way or another, we'll figure it out. If this doesn't work today, then we'll try something else."

"Or we'll have to start buying some factory-made shit in plastic bottles by the case from Costco," Jimmy Jr. said and headed for the kitchen. "What a week to stop smoking, Christ almighty."

From there, Lily and I settled into a smooth and effortless professional routine, like we'd worked together a hundred times. One of the reasons I liked working on my own was that it was so much easier than having to tell someone what to do and how. But it was different with her. She took charge of her stuff, and she left me to mine. And every chance I got, I sneaked a glance at her.

Once she moved off into the kitchen, I flipped on my camera and held it out to film myself. Behind me was a specially set table in the middle of the main dining room. All the other tables were raw wood with benches, but this one was set with a checkered tablecloth and surrounded by folding metal chairs. "We're here at Uncle Jimmy's Secret Ingredient BBQ," I said, walking backward through the empty dining area. "They've shut the place down for the afternoon for a séance. Uncle Jimmy passed away last month at the age of ninety-three. Unfortunately, he didn't pass along *the secret ingredient* to anybody. So we're here today to see if we can figure out what that is."

I panned toward the kitchen and caught Lily in the frame, zooming in on her tight. She got up on her tiptoes to adjust a microphone that she'd stuck near the big industrial fridge and then lowered herself back down, straightening her leggings. Her eyes connected with the lens and she stopped. "Mr. Powers. Are you filming me?"

"Checking the light levels."

She placed her hand on her hip. "Are you really?"

I looked at her over the camera and shook my head. She tsked up at the ceiling and went on about her business.

Outside, I heard the crunching gravel of a car pulling up in the parking lot, where I saw a lady getting out of a little hatchback who was . . . *really* familiar. Like *really* familiar. Like my grandma. Or my seventh-grade English teacher. Or . . . I signaled to Lily and pointed outside. "That the medium, you think?"

Lily peered outside. "I don't know. She could moonlight as a Jessica Fletcher impersonator, though, couldn't she? Like from *Murder, She Wrote*? Got the same purse and everything! And the gingham shirt!"

Exactly. "Nailed it." Down to the pleated jeans, the hairdo, and the glasses on a chain.

As Jessica Fletcher came around to the back of the restaurant, Lily and I made some last-minute adjustments to the audio and visual. From the kitchen, we heard Jimmy's family introducing themselves to the medium, and each of them gave their two cents about the secret ingredient. Jimmy Jr. was betting molasses. His sister voted for liquid smoke. The cousin said cayenne. And Jimmy's older brother, an old man with a cane named Cletus, insisted on celery seeds. Had to be celery seeds. "Just has to be!"

"Goddamn it!" boomed Jimmy Jr. "I love you, Uncle Cletus, but can we stop right now with the celery seeds? I don't even know what a celery seed looks like!"

"Like a mouse turd, except it's a seed!" roared the old man, his hearing aids squealing. "Mark my words, Junior! Mark 'em! When was the last time I was wrong, tell me that!"

I heard the sister mutter, "Ten minutes ago when you thought I was the maid?"

Jimmy Jr. shoved another handful of nicotine gum in his mouth, like a palmful of Chiclets. Next to me, I watched Lily stifle another giggle. She found a little bit of joy in even the tensest family feud. I wanted to know how that felt—what it was like to be in that mind of hers. Fortunately, I realized, there might be a way to see the world from her perspective. From my bag, I grabbed my spare camera, booted it up, and handed it to her. She gasped a little and smiled at me with such beautiful happy delight. "Really? For me?" she asked.

I wanted to give her a whole lot more than a filming credit. But for now, it'd have to do. "Ready?"

Lily beamed. "Ready!"

17

LILY

Uncle Jimmy's family joined hands around the table, which was set with votive candles on top of jars of the sauce. The lights were low, the blinds were drawn, and Jessica Fletcher was all business. She adjusted her bifocals and looked around the room. She took one of the glass jars and unscrewed it. The seal broke with a sucking sound and a *snap*. She placed the open bottle in the center of the table, like an offering to the smokehouse gods. Then she rolled up her starched gingham shirtsleeves, placed her hands flat on the table, and closed her eyes.

Except for the seven thousand home videos of Ivan that I had on my phone, I had never done any filming before, so I followed Gabe's lead. He'd positioned three stationary cameras around the room, and from their blinking red lights I knew they were rolling. With his hand-held camera, he circled Jimmy Jr.'s family. But he was respectful about it—he never got too close, never invaded their space. He was, after all, a total stranger, so that made sense. I, on the other hand, had known everybody in the room since before I could talk. When I got close to Jimmy's sister, Jimmy Jr., or Uncle Cletus, they glanced at me and smiled. It was really exciting, moving in and out of the group, getting to be right in the middle of everything. I crouched right down in front of Jimmy Jr. and focused in on the medium.

She lowered her head. "We are gathered today to speak with James LeRoy Waters of Savannah. First I'm going to take the overall temperature of the room. I want all of you to take a deep breath, relax. Focus on where you are and your immediate surroundings. Because we're trying to summon up someone very near and dear to all of you, I want you to focus on your most recent good, happy memory of Uncle Jimmy. Or, if you're someone who didn't know him as well"—here, she glanced at Gabe and me—"then please bring to mind the most recent happy memory you have had. Really happy. Doesn't have to be anything big, but I need this room to buzz with joy."

Even though I was filming, I still wanted to help. *Happy memory, Lily. Happy memory.* In spite of what I had decided about him, the first thing that popped to mind was Gabe and me together, last night at the kitchen table. It was before everything had gotten oh so sexy, when it was still just oh so sweet. The whole night had been wonderful, but there was one particular moment, after we'd finished eating the chicken and had moved on to the ice cream. We were sitting there, in the quiet and the candlelight, and I thought, *I will never forget this, never. Not as long as I live.* That was where I returned to, and I felt my heart patter away in my chest. Everybody else in the room had their eyes closed except Gabe and me, and I glanced at him over the camera.

I found him looking right back at me, smiling a little. I wondered, *Is he thinking about last night too?*

And he nodded, very gently but clearly, a few times.

It made my toes curl right up in my sneakers.

The medium cleared her voice. "I'm getting a reading coming through from some of you in this room. Uncle Jimmy isn't in touch yet, but I'm sifting through the energy here." Even though her eyes were shut, I got her on camera pushing her glasses back up her nose. "I'm seeing . . . some of you gathered together. I believe it was last night. I think you were . . . here, perhaps?"

Next to me, Jimmy's daughter said, "Mmm-hmmm!"

The medium cocked her head slightly, like she was trying to make something out in the distance. "At dinner?"

"Yes, we were," said one of the other brothers. "Right here last night. Talking about Jimmy."

"God bless him!" said the cousin.

"Amen," rumbled Jimmy Jr. from behind me.

The medium exhaled long and slow. "It was a very happy occasion, I think?"

Surprisingly, that question yielded total silence. Crickets. Until the sister next to me said, "Don't know about that, girl!" with an exaggerated roll of her neck. "Don't know about that at all!"

The medium wrinkled up her face like she was squinting, even though her eyes were still closed. "It was a quiet, pleasant evening," said the medium, more insistent this time. "It was very happy. There was . . . a meal of some sort . . ." She leaned forward like she was trying to see a little farther. "Dinner, during the power outage, perhaps?"

Gabe and I looked at one another again. He slowly lifted one of his thick eyebrows. But I shook my head the teensiest bit. There was no way. Everybody in this room had dinner last night. It was probably the only thing that each and every one of us had in common.

I suddenly felt more than a little skeptical of Jessica Fletcher. I wondered what her hourly fee was. I wondered if maybe this was nothing but a big racket. It *had* to be a racket, didn't it? Just had to be! But *then* she said, "Ice cream, I think. Maybe a roast chicken?"

Holy *smokes*. Gabe had moved off to my left, and I peeked back at him past Jimmy's arm. I was met with an expression that could only be described as *Fuck!*

The medium said, "There was a lot of laughter. A lot of . . . it's very flirtatious."

Oh my *God*. I kept hold of the camera with one hand and pressed my palm to my lips with the other. Across the table, Uncle Cletus boomed, "Don't know what dinner *you're* visiting, lady! Sure as hell wasn't here!"

"Hell no, it wasn't!" echoed the sister.

"We were busy yelling at each other!" added Jimmy Jr.

"Celery seeds!" hollered Uncle Cletus.

"Christ almighty," grumbled Jimmy Jr.

But I couldn't hold it anymore and made a noise that was a cross between a snort, a cough, and a laugh.

The medium turned to me. "Oh, *I* see. It's you two, isn't it?"

I nodded, almost sheepishly. "Yes. Definitely us."

"First date," Gabe said, smiling hard. So hard I could see his dimple in the candlelight.

The medium adjusted her hands again and shook her head, halfway between humored and annoyed. She pointed at me and Gabe. "One of you. Out."

The rest of the family boomed with laughter. When it died down, Gabe said, "We'll be good, promise."

But the medium was undeterred. She straightened her bifocals and smiled at us. "Not a question of good or bad, hon. New love is like a black hole. I can't see past it. So leave your cameras, but give me some space."

New *love*! I crouched down a bit, and my shoe squeaked on the linoleum floor. I didn't know if I was embarrassed or shocked or happy or all three. But one thing was for sure, it was a darned good thing the lights were so low, because I was pretty sure my face was cherry red all over.

Gabe mouthed, *I'll go*, but I shook my head. The show wasn't called *The Jameson of Suggestion*, for heaven's sake. It was his show, and he was the one who had to stay. So I slipped out from the circle and handed my camera over to him. It was close quarters, though, and I had to scoot between two chairs to get to him and out of the room. My legs brushed against his. He felt so rugged and warm against me.

"I'll be outside," I whispered into his ear, bracing myself on his shoulder as I scooched past.

"Don't leave," he whispered to me.

I was having lusty thoughts about the fabric of his pants; I wasn't going *anywhere*. "OK," I whispered back.

Just as I was about to leave the kitchen and go outside, I heard footsteps behind me. I spun around and felt my heart sink when I realized it wasn't Gabe. But in an instant my heart rebounded, because it was Jimmy Jr. with that great big smile.

He held up one finger to tell me to wait. From one of the warming ovens, he pulled out a covered dish. When he opened the lid, I saw that it contained heaps of chicken tenders. My absolute favorite. He used a pair of tongs and put half a dozen in a red plastic basket lined with wax paper. Then, from the top shelf of the nearest fridge, he took a small to-go container of barbecue sauce and nestled it between the tenders.

I clutched my basket in my hands, savoring the peppery, steamy deliciousness that wafted up to my nose. Behind Jimmy Jr. were racks and racks of spices—at the bottom was a row of small glass bottles of herbs and spices, and at the top was a rack of commercial-size powders in rectangular plastic jugs. "You have no idea what the secret ingredient is?" I asked in a whisper.

Jimmy Jr. shook his head glumly but then grinned as he glanced back at the dining room. I followed his gaze and found Gabe watching me, smiling a little. Jimmy Jr. laughed softly and tightened his apron bow. "All my dad ever said was it was good old-fashioned l-o-v-e *love*."

18

GABE

I should've been totally focused on the séance, but I was totally focused on Lily instead. Through a gap in the blinds I saw her lying on the grass outside next to the picnic tables under the massive old trees. One of her legs was bent at the knee, and it cast a long and sexy shadow beside her in the afternoon sun. The curve of her breast gave way to the dip of her stomach and the slight rise of her pelvis. She kicked off her shoes and ate her chicken strips while looking up at the sky. A tiny bird hopped along the picnic table nearest to her, and I watched her turn to say something to the bird, smiling as it cocked its head. She rolled over onto her side with her head propped in her hand. When the bird flew off, she nestled herself back into the thick green blades, revealing a strip of her stomach between her leggings and her T-shirt.

"I really need *everybody* to focus now," said the medium. *"Everybody."*

I forced myself to turn away from the window and zoomed in on the medium. Her eyes were locked on me to say, *That means you, buddy!*

I nodded to confirm it was a 10-4 and gave her my full attention. I'd doubted her at first, but when she pulled the roast chicken out of the air, I became a believer. She made everybody in the circle join hands. There were rustles and squeaks as the family scooted their chairs closer and formed a circle. "Now, I need you all to create a welcoming atmosphere. Imagine a time when you were really happy to see Jimmy. A time when you saw him here, or when you picked him up at the airport, a time when he came to help you. A time when you came around a corner and saw him and felt happy in that moment. Bring forward that joy, that intense delight at seeing him. That happiness at feeling his presence near you after a time away."

Around the room, I saw smiles and nods. One of his sisters wrinkled up her nose, raised her shoulders, and beamed. It was so awesome to imagine having that reaction at just the *thought* of seeing someone—all that love, all that warmth. It had been a long time since I'd felt that, but I felt it nice and strong in that room. It was so powerful and palpable that I couldn't stop myself from smiling too. "*Really* welcome him now. Really feel that joy. That joy at knowing Jimmy has arrived. Big breath in." The medium inhaled through her mouth and held the breath. "And ouuuuuut," she said and exhaled it with such force that the candles on the table flickered.

It was fascinating because I could actually feel the energy in the room change. The seriousness somehow eased up—the tension over the celery seeds fell away. It was like there was an invisible light that changed the feel of things completely. Something very real was happening. But I had no idea what it was.

"Jimmy, is that you?" asked the medium. "Everybody here has been missing you terribly. And they need your help."

At first, there was nothing. But then across the room, I saw the spotlight flicker on the big portrait of Uncle Jimmy. A very definite, very obvious flicker. Holy *fuck*. I froze with my camera on the portrait, zooming in close. The medium had everybody breathe in and out once again. On the outbreath, the bulb flickered even more. For an instant, it even went dark. The fact that Lily wasn't there to see it annoyed me. What I would have given to see her eyes get wide and her mouth drop open. But as it was, I was the only one who had seen it. "Spotlight on the portrait," I said under my breath. Most of the family turned to see what had happened, but the medium kept on with total focus.

With careful steps backward, I moved around the room, placing each foot cautiously before letting it take my weight. But the change in position also put me up against a window near the kitchen, and this one had a bigger gap between the blinds and the window frame. Through that gap I caught another glimpse of Lily. This time she was sitting up in the grass with her hair scooped over one shoulder. I could see her in profile, and she very delicately dipped her finger into the barbecue sauce. Her eyes closed with pleasure as she sucked it off her finger.

I turned away, focusing on a stack of menus. But the image of her puckered lips got stuck in my mind on a loop. Those lips. The way she kissed. The way she moaned.

The way I wanted her.

The more I tried not to think about her, the more I *had* to think about her. Her keeping me at arm's length was going to make me crazy, and I knew it. Her hiding behind the conduct clause was going to make me tear apart that contract with my teeth. I sneaked one more peek at her outside, one last hit. Now she sat cross-legged with her back to me. Her shirt had inched up and it revealed the tiniest strip of the pink lace of her thong above her leggings. She had her earbuds in, and I could tell she was talking to someone on her phone. I saw her body shake with a laugh, and she leaned back with the biggest smile on her face and then flopped down into the grass, wiggling her toes.

When I turned my attention back to the medium, she was staring right at me. "Unfortunately, I've lost him. We almost had him." She flared her nostrils but then smiled. "But then there was what you might call a tremor in the force."

19

LILY

I ended the call with my sister, lay back down in the comfy and cool grass, and recommenced my quest for the secret ingredient. I dipped my finger into the little container of sauce and put a small drop on my tongue. Then I closed my eyes and focused. There was something unexpected in there, something very familiar . . . and yet just out of reach. It was a taste that I couldn't quite pinpoint. I kept losing it right before I had it. Same thing happened to me when I watched British dramas and I knew I recognized everybody from everywhere but couldn't remember how. The flavor was like that. So familiar, so obvious, but not quite . . .

Cumin. No. Coriander. No. Cinnamon. No. But close, and yet spicier than that, more like . . . I wiggled my tongue in my mouth the way people did when they were tasting wine.

"Fuck, you really are so cute."

I opened my eyes and found him standing above me. Towering over me, really. The wind rustled the cypresses and magnolias behind him. A leaf fluttered down and landed on his shoulder. He plucked it off with a muscular veined hand and smoothed it between his fingers. I rolled up to a sitting position, placed the container of sauce in the grass, and shielded my face from the sunshine. "Any luck in there?" I asked.

Gabe tipped his hand side to side. "Something happened with the lights."

A wave of excitement made my skin tingle. So much for trying to interpret Grandpa's "knocking" on the radiator! "Really?"

He seemed more amazed than skeptical. "Got it on video. It could've been a fluke, but"—he glanced back at the restaurant—"I wish you'd felt it." He offered his hand to me and I stood up, brushing the leaves of grass off my legs. I sat down beside him on the picnic bench, keeping a sensible distance between us. Like employer and employee. Not lovers.

It was agony. But it was the way it had to be.

"Did she figure anything out?" I asked. "Aside from our date? Which was capital-*C* crazy!"

Gabe shook his head and smiled. "No recipe. *Tremor in the force,* she said." He rested his elbows on his knees. He was a bit of a manspreader . . . but I liked it. I liked the way he took up the space around him—the way he exuded that aura of confidence and strength. Just because I couldn't have that manspread didn't mean I couldn't admire it.

He let his head hang down slightly and looked at me from the side. His hands rested between his legs, and I traced the edge of the seam of his pants with my eyes. "Listen, about that conduct clause."

I made myself look at something neutral. His abs. No. His chest. No. His face. No. I focused on the ground, where a ladybug was fluttering her wings in the grass. "What about it?"

He hesitated for a second, looking out at the big grassy expanse, dotted all over with dandelions. "I get that you don't want to put us in a bad spot."

Part of me was relieved that he was getting it—that he at least understood where I was coming from. But the other part, the bigger part, was so disappointed. I loved that animal desire of his. Even if it was awfully dangerous.

"But we only live once. I'd rather break the rules and fuck you every night than follow the rules and never get the chance to feel you again."

Oh *God*. His words made me feel like I was standing in a warm shower on a cold morning. Clutching my legs, I pressed my thighs together. "Gabe."

"Lily." He shifted his leg slightly so that it was pressing against mine, and when our bodies touched, a shiver ran through me and came out as a shaky breath.

He had such power over my thoughts, over my breathing, over my body. Just his eyes on me gave me a warm rush, and I felt my panties cool between my legs. He was making me wet. With his eyes. In semi-public. He moved his left hand onto my knee and gave it a possessive squeeze. "You say the word. And I'm yours." Gabe stood up from the picnic table and faced me. "Got it?"

I managed a tiny nod. Somehow I knew that if I tempted fate too far, I'd be making grabby hands and yanking him to the picnic table before I knew it. So I wedged my hands under my legs and said, "Got it."

His belt was at eye level, and his bulge was undeniable. He leaned into me, and instinctively I raised my face to him. He came in close enough for me to feel his breath on my cheek and drummed his fingers on the wooden table. "Good," he said gruffly. Then he gathered the trash up from my chicken tenders and headed back toward Uncle Jimmy's.

His body was incredible. His buns were scrumptious. He was, from top to bottom, delish. And as he walked away, I remembered what he'd told me earlier. That he liked me going *and* coming.

"Me too," I whispered into the breeze.

But in spite of what I *wanted* to do, the termination warning from the contract kept scrolling along in front of me like a breaking-news headline as I packed up my mics. Even if I took myself out of the equation, the undeniable fact remained that it was *his* show. It was *his* reputation on the line. So what if someone did find out? He was a famous man. What if someone had a grudge? What if someone saw impropriety where there wasn't any? What if that producer of his caught wind of it and had some reason to make things difficult for Gabe? It wouldn't matter *at all* what had actually happened between us. A whiff of wrongdoing could torpedo him. I imagined his beautiful face splashed all over some slow-to-load gossip site with popups saying, *Poof Goes Powers!* And it would all be my fault.

I would not let that happen. Not on behalf of myself—or his adoring fans with their exploded ovaries either. I would not tarnish his name or his reputation. I would not get him in trouble. Never.

Once I had all my things packed up, I said my goodbyes to Uncle Jimmy's family and made my promises to Jimmy Jr. that I'd be back soon with Daisy and Ivan. All the while, Gabe watched me, stealing sexy glances that made my heart speed up like crazy.

Exhausted from resisting so much temptation, I trundled out to my van. I heard Gabe's heavy footsteps crunching the gravel behind me—one of his for every two of mine. Just the sound of his footsteps made me woozy. I was in desperate need of something high calorie and comforting to keep my resolve high; all this "doing the right thing" was wearing me the heck *out*.

I flung open the back doors of my van and shoved my equipment inside. I could feel his presence behind me, like a lion ready to pounce. Slamming the doors, I scurried around to the driver's side. But as I jumped in, just about to close my door, he grabbed the edge and stopped it midswing.

The way I'd parked meant that nobody could see us from inside the restaurant. Something in his eyes told me exactly what he was thinking. *Just one kiss.*

Maybe nobody else would see us, but *I* would know. And that was the only judge and jury I really had. Back during the yearbook snafu, I'd learned that I was a close contender for Most Likely to Do the Right Thing. That, at least, was a description that fit me. So I stuck my key in the ignition and my van roared to life, with the AC blowing hot air full blast. Gabe pressed the button to roll down my window and closed my door softly, resting his huge forearms on the frame of my van.

"You're sticking to your guns, aren't you?" he asked.

I didn't turn toward him. I adjusted the air-conditioning and buckled my seat belt. If I didn't get lost in those eyes, I still had a chance. Gripping the wheel like my grandma used to, I looked straight ahead. Above the whoosh of the AC, I heard his phone buzzing in his pocket. Out of the corner of my eye, I watched him silence it without looking to see who was calling. And that solidified my resolve to stick to the conduct clause even more. My phone rang so rarely that when it did, it was stop, drop, and answer. When his rang, it didn't even merit a glance at the screen. It was the perfect metaphor. His life was big and buzzy and full of important things that interrupted private moments. Mine was small and safe and almost totally buzz-free. Mind-blowing passion aside, none of this made any sense *at all*. "I told you. Conduct clause. Full stop. So I'll see you tomorrow."

In response, I saw a flash of disappointment on his face. It set off a visceral wave that went up from between my legs, into my stomach, and caught my breath in my throat. I turned to face him and saw the anger dissolve into something more measured and respectful. He stepped back without looking away from me. "Suit yourself, gorgeous."

With my whole body tingling, I put the van in gear and lurched out of the parking lot. He slipped his hands into his pockets and watched me go. I rolled to a stop at the cross street and felt that buzzing desire fizzle out into dismay. I wanted him so much that it ached. But my sister was living proof that making romantic decisions based on *the ache* was a recipe for a broken heart.

With Madonna making my van speakers buzz, I made a beeline for the drive-through of my therapists, Drs. Fries and Root Beer Float. I placed my order, paid, and pulled into the parking spaces reserved for those of us with a passion for eating in our cars. I slurped up my float and jammed curly fries into my mouth, reassuring myself over and over again that I had, in fact, made the right choice. One of us *had* to be sensible. Apparently, it was going to have to be me. Because that man was a hound on my heels. An animal. A primal, carnal, unstoppably alpha male who seemed to want nothing more than little old . . . me.

Me? I thought as I looked at myself in the rearview mirror with a curly fry hanging out of my mouth.

Me.

My therapists didn't help even one teensy bit. I arrived back home resigned to the fact that my night would be spent binge-watching episodes of Gabe doing adventurous things in romantic corners of the world while I moaned pathetically into my sofa cushions. Before I knew it, it would be two in the morning and I would be three bags of microwave popcorn and a whole pint of rocky road into this thing, and there'd be no turning back.

I caught a glimpse of my hickey scarf in the glass on my front door. *As if there was any turning back anyway.*

Just as I began to run up the steps to my apartment, though, Ivan let out a roaring wail. I did a 180 on my heel and knocked on my sister's door. I heard her footfalls, and Ivan's crying got louder. She flung open the door, and I was hit with a wave of baby screams. He was red-faced and his cheeks were tearstained. She was covered in something green and pureed, along with some splatters of what I desperately hoped was gravy.

"I love this child with my whole heart," she said from behind gritted teeth, "but he's learned to throw, Lily. I will never be clean again. There are peas on the ceiling. There are peas in my hair. There are peas *everywhere.*"

I scooped up Ivan from her arms, and he clung to me. She wasn't kidding about the peas. They were all over him like the sugar crust on a churro. He yanked on my hair, hard enough to make me hiss. But also hard enough to pull the plug on my Gabe Jacuzzi. Reality wasn't a hunky television host—it was a diaper that needed changing. "I've got him. I'll give him a bath and put him down for a nap. You sit. Rest. Have a shower. Relax. Put some Welch's in a fancy glass and pretend it's cabernet."

My sister leaned on the doorjamb for support and wiped a glop of peas off her cheek. "Really?" she asked, and then studied me more carefully. "You OK? You look kind of . . . frazzled. And since when do you wear scarves?"

Daisy and I didn't have much reason to have heart-to-hearts these days, but right then, on our shared landing, with Ivan screaming his lungs out, I desperately wanted sit down and spill the beans. About Gabe. About these feelings. About how impossible, silly, and ridiculous it was. My heart was so full, and yet I was so conflicted. But Daisy was exhausted, and I was pretty sure the very last thing on earth she wanted to hear was about me falling all over myself trying to stay *away* from a perfectly eligible bachelor.

"Scarves are *all* the rage this summer," I said as I bounced Ivan against my hip. I grabbed his hand and gave him a raspberry on the palm, and he screamed in delight. "You go. Take it easy. I've got him."

My sister let out a big breath and let her head fall slightly. She peered at me through her bangs. "Thank you. I love you. I don't know what I would do without you."

Something about those tiny words made my heart hurt a bit. She didn't say them often, and right then I needed to hear them a lot. "I love you too," I said as I carried Ivan up the steps. "Might want to do two shampoos if you do take a shower. Those peas are *really* in there."

Daisy sighed. She plucked at her crusty hair and closed the door.

I pulled my keys from my purse and jingled them for Ivan. He grabbed them and gave them a shake. Once I pried them out of his plump fingers, I let us inside.

Ivan pointed at the cage and started calling out, "Ba-ba!"

"Bird, I know!" I said to Ivan. "It's your favorite birdie!"

The General leaped from bar to bar, making happy squawks. He puffed up his feathers and shimmied his little body as he danced around. There was only one person on the planet that the General liked more than me. And that was Ivan.

Ivan clapped and squealed, and the General bobbed his beak in joy. The two of them picked up right where they'd left off, in an unintelligible single-syllable conversation. Babbles and warbles forever. I got a snack prepared for each of them, carrying Ivan around in the kitchen with me while I cut up a banana into thin slices and distributed it on two plastic plates. One was decorated with blue trains. The other was a badly battered Hello Kitty plate that the General loved with an almost inappropriate passion.

"Potato?" said the General.

"Pa-paaa!" replied Ivan.

"Pa-paaaaaaaa!" echoed the General.

I got Ivan situated in his high chair, facing the General's cage. Ivan grabbed a piece of banana and smashed it between his hands, making him giggle. Then the General giggled. And Ivan giggled some more.

Once everybody was laughing hysterically into their bananas, I flopped down on my couch and picked up the remote. During my brief and half-hearted commitment to low-carb dieting, I'd learned that willpower is a finite resource; I was running on Gabe Powers willpower fumes, and something had to give. In this case, I could do better than eating kale chips and pretending they were Pringles. If I couldn't have

Gabe in person, at least I could watch him. So I pressed the power button, searched for *The Powers of Suggestion* on Netflix, and braced for sexiness.

When he appeared on the TV, the General's happy noises ceased immediately. I'd done my earlier binge-watching in my sister's half of the house. That meant the General was seeing him again for the first time. "Suitor!" he screamed.

"No, not a suitor," I said frantically. "Not a suitor!"

But the General was on the warpath. He opened his mouth with his leathery tongue extended.

"Don't you dare," I warned, pointing at him as a warning. "Don't you . . ."

He *did* dare, and the Noise filled up the apartment at full volume. Ivan screamed in terror. Above all the racket, I hollered, "The Union cavalry is in retreat, General! Grant has asked you to draft the terms for a Union surrender!"

No effect. Whatsoever.

As the Noise went into a whole new set of decibels, I leaped off the couch and tried to comfort Ivan, who had been instantly spurred into full-scale meltdown. He banged his hands on his high-chair tray, and bananas slices went flying.

"Yankees are in retreat, General! Beauregard has secured the gates! Fort Sumter is ours!" I bellowed. But he was glued to the screen, cawing out his awful siren at Gabe.

I rushed over to television and pawed for the power button on the side of the screen. For one horrible instant, I turned the volume *way* up and the room was filled with Gabe's booming voice, saying, "So we have to ask ourselves, is the abominable snowman real or is it just *The Powers of*—" I hit the mute button and turned the screen away from the General.

As Gabe went silent, so too did the Noise. Ivan looked around like he couldn't remember why he'd been so upset, and then he returned his attention his snack, as the General did the same, saying, "Nom-nom-nom!" as he ate.

Standing there stunned, with my ears popping and ringing, I really only knew one thing for sure. The General had ratified the conduct clause. Gabe and I were absolutely not meant to be.

Once everybody was settled again, I sat on my sofa and stared at the angled and muted TV from the side. But I could still see him. Gabe was still there. He was in winter clothes now—a parka, neck warmer, and gloves. A graphic appeared at the bottom of the screen in the same font and style as his opening sequence: *Search for the Abominable Snowman: Day 2.* He was marching through deep snowdrifts, talking to the camera, with his cheekbones slightly windburned and a big smile glinting in the winter sun.

The very sight of him sent a prickle of warmth through me. I knew I should switch to something else. I *knew* I should look away. But I couldn't bring myself to hit the back button. In spite of my common sense, and much like the time I had polished off not just one but two bags of kale chips, I slid off my couch and scooted closer to the screen. He was talking to some cute little old lady who wore a huge puffer coat with fur around the hood. The bit of her face that I could see reminded me of a wrinkled apple. Gabe wore black snow pants that did amazing things for his already-amazing thighs. She gestured at the tree line with a gnarled finger. He lowered his head so he was very close to her, listening intently and nodding as she explained something to him. He pointed at the trees, and she turned to him and said something with her old eyes twinkling. When she burst out laughing, so did he, and she clapped her hands together and touched him lovingly on the arm.

I knew how that biceps felt under my fingertips. I knew how that forearm felt as a pillow. I knew how that shoulder felt . . . between my teeth.

Mesmerized and on autopilot, I reached for my knitting as I always did when I watched TV. But as I watched him, I went into a sort of knitting catalepsy. His face made it so I wasn't even paying attention as I tried to purl. His buns in his snow pants made me lose all interest in checking whether I was yarning over. He put me in a sort of dreamy happy place, where nothing made much sense and yet everything somehow lined up just right. Like that moment right before falling asleep when everything makes perfect sense.

When he went to commercial break, I looked at my knitting, expecting to see a knotted mess that was headed for the trash. But that wasn't what I'd done at all. As I'd been watching him, thinking about nothing but him, I hadn't just managed to cast on correctly. I'd also knitted three not-so-bad rows. Miracle of miracles.

20

GABE

In spite of the fact that all I wanted to do was Lily, I still had to do my show. Back at the Willows, I sat down on the sofa with a beer to run through the footage from that afternoon. After she left Uncle Jimmy's Secret Ingredient, I stayed to shoot some extra scenes to send over to Markowitz. We worked piecemeal like that, making order out of chaos. I went over some shots of the ribs as they rotated through the smokers and the ovens. I'd gotten a nice pan-through of the kitchen and some close-ups of the herbs and spices over the stove. I'd done a few interviews with Jimmy Jr., the medium, and some of the family. But all my favorite shots had Lily, right in the center.

Once I had the rough cuts of an episode put together, I carried my laptop upstairs to the master bedroom, the sheets still rumpled and messy from the two of us. I got in bed and pulled the comforter over my head. I was plunged into darkness, except for my computer screen. Beneath the covers, it smelled exactly like Lily. I inhaled hard. She was the sweetest goddamned thing.

Surrounded by her, I focused on the images on the screen. I hit play on the rough cut and narrated the script I'd put together in my head. Markowitz would slice and dice, and so would our production editors, but this at least would give them an idea of what I was thinking for the segment. Thirty minutes and a handful of audio files later, I shut my laptop and pulled the comforter off my head. Outside, I heard the faint *kish-kish-kish* of a nearby sprinkler. I lay down and rolled over, pressing my face into the pillow where she'd lain. I ran my eyes over the headboard that she'd hung on to as I fucked her. And I worked her panties on the bedpost into a knot around my fingers. The lace was sexy, but the hottest part of all was the triangle of cotton that showed just how wet I'd made her. That, right there, was my Kryptonite.

On one hand, I respected her boundaries. I respected that she took this job seriously and that she wasn't going to screw around when it came to fine print. That was sensible, logical, and responsible. But on the other hand, I could feel it in the way she looked at me, the way she'd hung on to the picnic table when I'd gotten close to her: we both wanted it and we wanted it *bad*.

I thought about what she might be doing in that cute place of hers. Painting her toenails, maybe. Or taking a shower. The image of her all sudsy with shower gel filled my head. Bubbles sliding over her nipples and down between her legs.

My original plan for that night had been to shoot some footage at the Moon River Brewing Company, but I had a way better idea for what the two of us could do together instead. All I could do was set the scene and open the door between logic and instinct, between responsibility and desire; it was up to her to walk through it. So I shot her a text to say:

We've got some more work to do tonight, Ms. Jameson.

Dots appeared to show that she was typing a response. When I saw them, I felt my goddamned heart start pounding in my chest. Three months ago, I was swimming in a Costa Rican lagoon with crocodiles and I hadn't even been particularly nervous. Now, typing-in-progress dots were making my heart rate speed up. She got my gears grinding, no doubt about it. In a second, she replied with:

OK, Mr. Powers.

Just tell me where and when.

Pick you up at 7

I'll bring dinner

A few hours later, I was showered and changed and walking back into Savannah Dry Goods and Grocery. Lily's aunt spun around when she heard the bell ding as I came through the door. When she saw me, her face lit up with delight. "Well, hello again, young man!" She sprayed some furniture polish on the gleaming wooden counter and wiped it off with a towel. "Gabe, wasn't it?"

"That's me." I didn't even have to force a showbiz smile onto my face. This one was instant and genuine. I was going to treat Lily, and I was going to treat her right. I stood at the counter and took a deep breath as I scanned the old-fashioned rows of candies, the racks of fresh bread, and the cooler of fancy cheeses. The place was epic. "So it's probably no surprise that I'm *really* interested in your niece."

She beamed up at me. "Not hard to imagine. She's the sweetest thing this side of sweet tea, after all."

Sweet tea had nothing on her. Nothing. "I'm picking her up tonight, and I want to surprise her with *all* her favorite stuff."

The delicate skin around Jennifer's eyes formed into well-worn smile wrinkles. I could see a bit of Lily in her—that same full-hearted joy. "Oooh. How romantic. And thoughtful!"

"I mean *everything*. Flowers, favorite candies, perfumes, whatever she likes. Money doesn't matter. If I need to spend the next two hours driving around town to get what she likes best, then that's what I'll do. But I figured you'd probably be the place to start."

She gave me a series of quick, happy claps. "I know a thing or two about what she likes! How's this strike you for a start?" she asked and hoisted a big picnic basket up onto the table.

It was dark wicker with leather buckles. She opened it, and I saw that the inside was rigged up with all the basics—plates, champagne glasses, forks and knives, and bright-white napkins. I pulled out my wallet and put my credit card on the table. "Let's do this thing, Auntie Jennifer."

She reached up and patted my cheeks with her soft, plump hands. "Oooooh. I like you, young man! I like you *a lot*!"

21

LILY

Ivan was asleep in his nursery, and I was in my sister's bedroom, where she was helping me put the finishing touches on *her* choice for my outfit for the evening. Normally, I wouldn't let her weigh in on these things— I was all about boatneck tees and cute shorts and floral sundresses. But my sister had different ideas about what to wear; ever since Boris had left her high and dry, Daisy had gotten *seriously* into dressing for herself and herself alone. It meant mom jeans and passive-aggressive feminist T-shirts. It meant no makeup and topknots. It worked like man DEET. Lord knew that tonight, I was going to need it.

I hadn't explained who I was going out with or why, except to say, "I am doing some audio work for a guy from out of town. Things between us are a little . . ." I'd swallowed hard and searched for the word. If I'd ever known it, it had been permanently erased when I watched him dive into an icy Alaskan pond to save a sled dog from drowning, followed by an all-night Inuit celebration that made him an honorary tribe member. So instead of filling in the blank, I fanned my face to say *hotcha-hotcha* and added, "But I don't want him to get the wrong idea."

She'd peered at me like she was trying to read the second-to-the-bottom line on an eye test. "So we like him, but we know we shouldn't have him. The last third in a pint of Cherry Garcia."

Birds of a feather are sisters together. "Already leveled with the spoon and everything."

Daisy had nodded once and flung open her meticulously organized closet. As a pair of ancient stonewashed jeans flew from her closet onto the bed, she'd said, "Makeup remover is in the bathroom. Get to it!"

Now I looked at myself in the antique oblong mirror that sat in the corner of her bedroom. I wore the high-cut jeans that she'd picked out, rolled once at the ankle. I wore a T-shirt that said I MAY BE WRONG BUT IT'S VERY UNLIKELY, and I had my hair in a high ponytail, secured with a bright-pink scrunchie that I was *almost* positive she'd stolen from me in 1991. No makeup, no perfume. And on my feet were a pair of blindingly white Keds.

"I didn't even know they made this style anymore." I lifted my toes. The rubber and canvas groaned as I did.

"They don't. I bought five pairs online from eBay. Mint condition. Very collectible. Now, let's try these." She stood between me and the mirror and situated a pair of leopard-print reading glasses on the bridge of my nose. They were so thick that they made the world wobble, and I felt slightly nauseous. When she stepped away from the mirror, I was just a series of hazy smudges through the thick lenses.

"Excellent," Daisy said. "You look like a lady who is in a committed relationship with her collection of leather-bound Jane Austens. If he tries to get fresh, tell him your sister will come deflate his tires. Every day."

The outfit was just what I'd been hoping for, but the glasses and the hair tie were combining to give me the mother of all headaches. I just wanted to be unalluring tonight, not dizzy and miserable. So I yanked off the glasses, pulled the scrunchie from my hair, and roughed up my roots.

My sister put her hands on her hips. "I'm questioning your commitment to this! And we haven't even gotten to purses!" From her bed she grabbed a fanny pack and one of those very unfortunate chintzy drawstring backpacks—two nylon ropes attached to a shiny square pouch. "I vote for this one"—she jiggled the fanny pack—"but I'm willing to negotiate."

But before we could take *that* trip down fashion horror lane, a honk outside made my heart leap into my chest. I hurried out of her bedroom and sidled up to the dining room window to peek out without letting him see me. There he was, sitting in his big black pickup. He held the steering wheel with one hand at the very top. The other was casually slung over the bench seats where I'd be sitting.

I stepped away from the window and centered myself. I could do this. I could do this! On the wall in front of me I saw the cross-stitch that I had made and framed for Daisy for her birthday. It was of a cartoonish smiling uterus with the caption *Don't cramp my style!*

Yes! I was a strong, proud woman! I didn't need some hunk of burning love derailing my life plan or cramping my style either! I could handle this thing! Armed with that uterine solidarity, I caught one final glimpse of myself in the mirror by her front door. I looked . . . *awful.* Pale, bland, and shiny. Instinctively I reached for my little makeup bag in my purse but realized that wouldn't fly with Daisy. "Is there an approved lipstick?"

She placed a tub of Carmex in my palm. "Voilà."

I stared at the white-and-yellow container. I was about to face Gabe looking like I was ready for my eighth-grade school portrait and wielding nothing but mentholated petroleum jelly. But I was willing to do whatever it took. "All right." I gave her a kiss. "Wish me luck."

"I wish you the combined simmering fury of two hundred years of women awaiting compensation for their infinite hours of free childcare!" she said and closed the door behind me.

Steadying myself, I took a deep breath in the front entryway and then marched outside with my plastic suitcase of audio equipment in hand. When Gabe saw me, he leaned across the seats and popped open my door.

Maybe he had gotten the message after all. Yesterday he'd come around to get my door and doffed an imaginary hat. Now I got a flick of a handle while the engine was running.

Yay? I guess?

Bracing myself for his electric energy and preparing to pull my eyes away from his thighs and bulge when I got in the truck, I was surprised to find something sitting on the seat between us. It was a big wicker basket that took up the entire center seat and even a little bit of my seat too.

A not-so-tiny part of my heart whispered that I might have overshot the mark on all this. I'd actually *loved* being pampered and fussed over. But I'd stood firm by the conduct clause, and now I had to share my seat with a wicker basket. Wonderful.

Gabe gave me that same sexy glance that he'd given me at Uncle Jimmy's. He didn't say anything about the fact that I was makeupless. He didn't say anything about my shirt or my ridiculously unflattering pants. It was like he didn't see any of it. Or didn't care even if he did. "This is for you," he said, and patted the basket as he put the truck in drive.

Very gingerly, I lifted the lid with one finger. The wicker and leather creaked as I peeked inside. On the top was a bouquet of at least a dozen of the paper-thin ceramic lilies that one of the galleries downtown sold for fifty dollars a stem. I often thought of buying just *one* for myself but could never justify the expense. Next to that was a box from my favorite chocolatier, with its gold-embossed foil seal on top. I pulled back the seal and the flap and saw half a dozen dark chocolate truffles inside, surrounded by chocolate-dipped gooseberries with their papery leaves. Beside that were two full-size clamshells of plump raspberries, dewy and ripe. Next to that, a huge bag of Sour Patch Kids. A box of rosemary and olive oil Triscuits. A loaf of fresh French bread and my favorite brie. Some of it I recognized as having come from my aunt's store. But the rest of it . . . the candies, the chocolates, the lilies . . . he must have spent the entire afternoon going from store to store. He must have spent a fortune. All on me. "How did you know about all of this?" I shifted the box of truffles aside. Underneath that was a wooden box of ripe Bartlett pears, halfway wrapped in gold foil. *Be still, my heart!*

"Your aunt." He hit the turn signal to head out of town. "She knows your weak spots. What she didn't know, I asked about, like at the chocolatier."

I opened the basket a bit more, as much to see farther inside as to steal a moment for myself behind the lid. It was all so . . . *nice.* And so kind. And thoughtful. I was utterly flabbergasted. There I'd been trying to put on man DEET, and he'd spent the afternoon tracking down all my favorite things.

But even in the face of delectable goodies and extreme thoughtfulness, I resolved to remain strong. *Snacks, shmacks; lilies, schmillies,* I thought as I rubbed together my Carmexy lips. No matter how yummy this whole situation was to me, I wasn't going to be seduced by a picnic basket, thank you very much.

So I closed the lid with a creak and straightened up in my seat, glancing over at Gabe. "Are you going to tell me where we're going?"

Again he smiled at the road and tightened his grip on the steering wheel. He glanced over without turning his face toward me and said, "Lovers' Lane."

Of course we were. And right on cue, a baseball game that was playing over the radio erupted into cheers as the announcer said, "Going, going, *gone!*"

22

GABE

I drove us out to a spot overlooking the Skidaway River and the Isle of Hope. I backed the truck into a parking space so we'd have a view of the water from the tailgate and popped open my door. Not going around to open her door for her rubbed me the wrong way—chivalry isn't dead yet—but I knew I was already pushing it. The picnic basket full of all her favorites had been a gamble, and I didn't want to go over the top. If we were going to get back to the way things had been before she saw the contract, it was going to be on her terms. Mostly.

She joined me by the tailgate, where I hoisted the basket up onto the truck bed. She wasn't wearing any makeup tonight, and it let me see her eyes in a new, more vivid way. Her skin was flawless, and in the evening light her handful of freckles was even more pronounced. She had a timeless beauty and grace that made me wonder why she wore makeup at all. I held her stare for a second, but she looked away first. She ran her fingers over the wicker. "Thank you for all this," she said softly. She straightened out her T-shirt and lifted the toes of her sneakers, and then she glanced at me and my dress shirt. "I just feel a bit underdressed."

The last thing I wanted was for her to be uncomfortable. So while I had her eyes on me, I began to undo my buttons. She gave me a stare that said, *Gabe!* But I kept going. She gripped the edge of the truck bed, her pink nail polish a beautiful contrast against the black paint. I undid my last button and slipped my shirt off, revealing one of my trusty old cotton tees below. This one was one of my favorites. It had a faded *ThunderCats* logo in the center, ancient silk-screening that had almost disappeared from so many washes in so many laundromats all over the world. "Now neither one of us is overdressed."

"Pum-raaaaa," Lily said, and swiped the air like a tigress.

All that and *ThunderCats* too. I balled up my shirt and tossed it into the corner of the bed and then patted the tailgate. Lily stood beside me, and the breeze let me have a hit of something sweet—her lotion, maybe. She planted her hands on the tailgate and tried to hoist herself up. But the truck wasn't some little F-150. It was a serious piece of American engineering—the biggest truck I'd ever gotten to rent. She was way too short to get up on her own. She tried, though. A lot. Huffing and puffing and struggling so hard that it brought a blush up into her cheeks.

"Need a hand?" I asked her.

"Or a step stool!" she growled as she gave it another shot.

So I put my hands on her hips and turned her around to face me.

We had a moment—a serious fucking moment with energy and heat pinging between us. But I didn't push it—not yet. She placed her hands on the tailgate for support, and I gave her a boost. I was in the perfect position to kiss her, but I stopped myself. She didn't lean in to me, but instead, as her chest rose and fell with quickening breaths, she leaned back slightly to create some distance between us.

Message received. I took my hands off her and turned my attention to getting the champagne poured and everything else squared away. Chivalry wasn't dead and never would be. All I could do was wait at her drawbridge and hope like hell she'd lower it down far enough to let me back inside.

♥ ♥ ♥

Once we made a dent in the picnic, I grabbed one of my cameras from the truck. In the dying light, I took my chance to get a few minutes of footage. I hit the record button, with the lens focused on my face. Out of the corner of my eye I saw Lily nibbling on a gooseberry, the stem pinched between her fingers. *Three, two, one, action.* "So we're out here on Bluff Drive. The story about this place is a pretty classic lovers' lane legend. In 1861, at the start of the Civil War, a young woman named Mary Goodwin came out here with her lover, William Hackett. It was to be their very last night before he went off to fight for the South."

Next to me, Lily coughed delicately and whispered, "The Confederacy."

I panned over to her. When she realized I'd gotten her on camera, she froze. Then she smiled, a cute and polite smile. Not the vixen but the sweetheart. It was more proof that nobody should *ever* believe what they see on television.

"I'm with my assistant again, as you can tell. She's from around here, aren't you, Lily?"

She stared at the camera. "Born and raised."

"Which is good, because I clearly need to get schooled in the local lingo. So what I call the South, you call . . . the Confederacy."

She nodded with more certainty this time. "Right." She looked away from the camera and straight at me, which seemed easier for her. I sure as shit wasn't complaining. She went on, "When you're talking about that era, it's the Confederacy. And it's not the Civil War down here. It's the War between the States."

I panned back to myself. "*This* is why it's good to have someone local, right? Just think of the emails I'd be getting from you guys."

"All y'all," Lily said.

"From all y'all," I echoed back.

Lily snickered beside me. "You're doing fine, though!" In the viewfinder, her eyes sparkled, and the deep-blue water glittered behind her. She got some sass going for the camera—hamming it up like only a gorgeous goddess could. Then she said, "He's doing fine . . . bless his heart."

"Ohhhh! Boom! The classic Southern shut-down, right?"

"Kinda!" she said. She talked right to the audience now. "Y'all know what I mean, though." Now she'd put on her accent, thick and rich. Fucking sexy as *hell*. "He's all right, though. For a Yankee!"

My belly laugh filled the air along with her giggle. She was a natural on camera. Totally herself, and just as she'd been the first time I saw her. Unselfconscious. Authentic. Beautiful.

"All right, so chime in here whenever." I zoomed out so we were both in frame but kept the angle high so the picnic stayed our secret. "In 1861, at the start of the War between the States," I said as Lily nodded approvingly, like a teacher giving the go-ahead to her student, "Confederate soldier William Hackett came out here to the road now known as Bluff Drive to spend an evening with the woman he loved." Lily made a circle of her thumb and forefinger to give me the A-OK sign, so I went on. "He proposed to her that night, and she said yes. But Hackett was killed at the Battle of Antietam—"

"Also known as Sharpsburg," Lily added.

Rather than stopping to acknowledge what she'd said, I rolled with it like we'd written this whole thing out. "Mary Goodwin never married and never stopped pining for him. They say that if you come out here on a quiet night like this one, with your lover . . ." Lily's eyes met mine for a millisecond before darting away. "They say you can still hear Mary singing to William. Apparently, there's one she likes most of all. 'The Darling of My Heart.'"

"Just 'Darling of My Heart,'" Lily corrected.

Sometimes, in this strange-ass business of mine, life handed you a great scene on a silver platter. This was one of those moments. If she knew the song, that was a million times better than my having to find some recording. I panned over to her fast and captured the expression on her face when she realized what she'd said.

"It's all you. Go for it," I told her.

She shook her head. "Oh no." She waved me off. "Nope. I don't. Nope." She looked up at the sky. "No idea. Nope. Never heard the song before in my life."

Bullshit. "Come on now."

Lily gave me a sidelong warning stare.

I watched her over the top of the camera. "If you don't like how it sounds, I won't use it. Just let me hear you. I'd love to hear you sing."

She shook her head again and plunged her hand into the picnic basket. But I kept the camera right on her and waited until she glanced at me again. I mouthed *Please* to her. She bit the inside of her lip, watching me all the time.

"Come on. Please. For me."

She sighed, glanced away, and wet her lips. "Lemme see." She ran her fingertips along the rippled liner of the truck bed. She began to hum very softly. It was such a beautiful sound—like a lullaby but sadder. Her voice was lovely, just like her. The more she got into the melody, the more confident she became. I watched her, captivated by her beautiful face as much as the lilt and emotion in her voice. It felt as though time stood still as she sang to me about the darling of her heart . . . and the home he would be leaving.

23

Lily

We watched the sun set and then rigged up some audio recorders around and inside his truck. As the sky turned from dark blue to black, Gabe helped me back up onto the tailgate where we sat, waiting to see if anything happened that we might be able to say was Mary Goodwin. I kept the picnic basket between us in an effort to maintain a somewhat professional distance. But the facts were the facts: drinking champagne with him under the stars on Lovers' Lane didn't make me feel like being very professional, and I felt my resolve slowly start to flag.

Out over the ocean, a shooting star whizzed across the darkness from left to right, and I gasped a little. I'd have taken one shooting star for all the fireworks in the world. There was something so magical to me about that—a little sign in the sky. "That's good luck, you know," I said.

He added, "They also say that when you see one, you get to ask a question. And whoever you ask has to tell the truth."

I turned to him and narrowed my eyes. I was very much up on my shooting star lore; that sounded a bit like baloney. "Did you just make that up?"

He clicked his tongue and looked out at the water, smiling. "Possibly. But you can't blame a guy for trying."

I'd been smiling so much that now my face actually hurt, and I lay down on the truck bed, still warm from the heat of the day. I looked up at the North Star and then glanced at him. His broad shoulders drew his T-shirt tight over his back, each muscle and ridge accentuated by the light of the moon. "All right then. Go ahead."

Gabe lay down too, and though the basket was between our hips, our shoulders were roughly in line and there was nothing to stop us from turning to look at one another. But we both lay on our backs, like we were at a planetarium. "OK. I've got one for you. How'd you learn to sing like that? Your voice is just beautiful."

I wasn't even sure about *somewhat OK*, let alone *beautiful*. But it was awfully nice of him to say so. I turned to face him, pressing my cheek to the plastic liner. A lock of my hair fell into my eyes, and I blew it out of the way. "I practice a lot," I said, and then added in a whisper, "with the General!"

Gabe laughed, stretching out a bit and making the truck rock slightly. "Now that's something I'd kill to hear." He tucked his forearm behind his head, and his clenched biceps accentuated the magnificent size of his arms. The rippling and untanned skin on the inside of his arms was somehow even sexier than the tanned and rugged outsides. "Your turn," he said. "Ask me whatever you want."

This all felt a little bit like playing cards with my sister—*rules* were just a mere suggestion. "So, wait . . . we get unlimited questions per star?" I asked.

He nodded at the sky. "Made-up star games are the best games."

I couldn't argue with him on that because there was, in fact, something about him that I was dying to know. I'd been wondering about it since the first time I saw him on TV, and since I'd begun thinking about what his life must really be like—different in every single way from mine, I was sure. "Did you always want to host your own show?"

"Hell no," he said quickly. "I had no plans to be in show business. I went out to LA to go to graduate school."

I didn't know what I'd expected him to say—that maybe he'd planned to be an actor or a model. And yet, what he'd said rang much truer. Except he'd left out the really good part, so I asked, "Grad school for . . ."

He scoffed a little. "Archaeology. I wanted to teach it and take students around the world on digs. Ridiculous, right?"

Oh Lord. The very last word I'd have used was *ridiculous.* Him as a professor? Tweed, maybe? Blazers with patches? Or wait, wait . . . like Indiana Jones! Tanned and dusty in some faraway place, uncovering ancient secrets? Mmm-hmmm! "Hardly!" I rolled onto my side and propped my cheek on my palm. "You still investigate mysteries in faraway places. Makes sense to me."

His eyes locked on to me for a long moment—a very intense few seconds when he stared deep into my eyes. And finally he said, "Nobody understands that about me, Lily. Not even my own family."

"I definitely understand it." I ran my fingertip over the corrugated ridges of the truck bed. "I can see it now—Archaeology 210: Ancient Civilizations and Their Legends with Professor Powers."

He laughed to himself again and ran his hand down over his scrumptious stubble. "God, if only. But what happened was that I was playing a game of pickup basketball and some talent agency scout insisted on introducing me to Markowitz. I wasn't really interested, but Markowitz is persistent as hell. He pitched this idea about an adventuring legend hunter; he said he'd been looking for a guy to do it and asked what I thought. At first, it sounded nuts. But I warmed up to it. Eventually, we came up with *The Powers of Suggestion.* Gave up grad school, got some capital saved up to do the first few seasons, and here I am."

The wind caught the willows, and far away the sound of a freighter blowing its horn cut through the air. In barely more than a whisper, I told him, "I'm glad you're here."

Rolling over to face me, he reached across the gap between us and pushed that same pesky lock of hair away, tucking it behind my ear. "I am too. You've got no idea."

He didn't take his hand away, and I let my cheek rest against his palm. As I savored the warmth of his skin against mine, I found that the things that had worried me earlier—the yearbook factor, the buzzy phone, the fan club, the General's strong opinions on him—began to feel less and less important. Each moment I spent with him showed me that he was much more than a celebrity studmuffin; the more I learned about him, the more he went from *out there* among the collarbone-fondling fans to *right here*. With me.

Looking into his eyes, I knew how utterly unlikely it was that this thing happening between us could be anything more than a fling. Our lives were too different, our worlds too far apart. We'd never be celebrating silver and gold anniversaries together, I was certain of that. But in twenty-five or fifty years, or even tomorrow, I didn't want to look back on this moment with regret. I didn't want to see him on television one day in the future and think to myself, *Oh, Lily, if only you'd had the guts* . . .

So I took a deep breath and asked the question that had been in the back of my mind since I'd read the contract. "If we did decide to . . ." I searched his face, like maybe I'd find the word there. "To . . . *ignore* the conduct clause . . ." I swallowed hard and let the rest of what I hadn't quite known how to ask hang in the air unsaid.

Gabe's expression got more serious, and he gently ran his thumb over my cheek. "Whatever happens here stays between us. I promise you that."

I blinked a few times, purely out of nervous awkwardness, and couldn't quite settle on which of his irises I should focus on. "And you won't get in trouble?"

He shook his head. "If it's what we both want, then neither of us will. I'll make sure of that."

A cool breeze off the water made me shudder. Gabe rolled up to sitting and grabbed his dress shirt from where he'd thrown it in the corner of the truck bed. He pushed the picnic basket back and helped me up to sitting, draping his shirt around my shoulders. "What do you say we wait for 'Mary' in the cab?" He offset her name with air quotes. "But I won't push you. I promise."

I laughed a little and pulled my hair out from under his shirt collar, letting it fall loose around my shoulders. My curls slipped across the starched fabric. There was something oh so sexy about feeling his shirt against my skin. His cologne. Him, so close to me. Him, enveloping me. "I think waiting in the cab sounds perfect."

24

GABE

Closing up the tailgate, I made sure all the stuff I had bought her was safely inside the picnic basket. The cab doors had locked automatically, so I decided to take a chance on being a gentleman again and didn't press the unlock button until I had my hand on her door. I helped her inside and shut the door for her, taking one second to hold her stare through the window before I went around to my side. Once we were in, I reached behind her and unzipped my bag. I grabbed an old hardback book that I'd found at the library: *The Haunted Cypress: Ghost Tales of Savannah*. I flipped to a chapter I'd marked with a scrap of paper. I tapped on the page and handed it to her. She angled the book slightly to catch the light of a nearby streetlamp. "'Chapter Seven. Mary Goodwin, the Ghost of Bluff Drive,'" she read aloud.

"Keep going," I said, watching her closely. "Find the part where it says what you have to do to get her to show herself."

She cleared her throat and read, "'In 1861, William Hackett, a cooper from Savannah, brought his beloved . . .'" Lily made a little *pa-pa-pa* with her lips as she skimmed on, picking out key phrases. "She says yes. He goes off to war. Antietam, right, right. Here it is." She put her fingertip on the old-fashioned typeface on the heavy paper. "'Legend has it that if Mary Goodwin doesn't sing for you, it's possible to lure her out of hiding. With a kiss.'"

"I'll be damned."

Lily put the book down in her lap and gave me a sternly playful glare, as if to say, *Oh no you didn't!*

I liked her when she was being soft, I liked her when she was being wild, and I even liked her when she was being slightly indignant. She pushed all my buttons in exactly the right way. "Just one kiss." I held up my finger to my cheek to show her where I wanted it. "Tiny. You won't even feel it."

"Pffft!" She tossed her head back and slapped the book shut. "Have you kissed you lately? I'd *definitely* feel it."

"Speak for yourself—you're the one who's going to be doing the kissing. But I *think* I can take it." I tapped my cheek even more firmly and leaned toward her. "I won't even cop a feel. Scout's honor." I gave her the Scout salute. "You have my word. One peck."

She placed her hands to her mouth, giggling softly into her palms, and then peeked over her fingers at me. "I can't give you a *peck*. If there is one thing we established last night, it's that you and I are way past pecks."

You're goddamned right about that. "All right, I'll meet you halfway. If you won't give me a peck, at least hold my hand." I put it palm up on the bench seat between us. For a long second, I thought she wasn't going to give me even that. Just because she'd asked about the conduct clause didn't necessarily mean she intended to break it. That would be one hell of a bummer. But the ball would always be in her court.

She let her hands slide down her cheeks and into her lap. She knitted her own fingers together, twisting them nervously. She gave me a glance and looked out the window. "I know that you're not here to stay."

"That's true," I said.

"And I don't want to get my heart broken."

"Lily," I said, being as serious as I felt like I could be without going too far. "Look at me."

Her posture stiffened, and she shook her head. "I melt when I look at you. I can't melt right now."

That was it *exactly*. Right then, I didn't want to wreck her, I didn't want to ruin her. I didn't even want to be especially dirty. I just wanted to very slowly, very carefully, warm up that sensible shell until it dissolved in my hands. "You have to know that I want to melt you. So fucking badly."

She let out a little gasp, and I watched her close her eyes while she pursed her lips.

I left it there. I kept my hand palm up on the seat. I watched the rise and fall of her chest, the curve of her neck as she turned even farther away.

But then, very slowly, without turning to face me, she let her left hand slide across the upholstery toward me.

I didn't move a muscle until we were palm to palm. As soon as our skin touched, I felt that wave of desire tear right through me—through my chest, my stomach, my head, my cock—and I took her hand in mine. When I squeezed her hand, she took a deep breath. Still, she didn't turn to face me and looked out into the darkness with her hand pressed to her chest. Ladylike and demure. For the moment.

I ran my thumb over the back of her hand, again and again. I watched her shoulders relax, and she leaned against the window. I tightened my grip. "Want me to beg you?" I asked. "One kiss, Lily. Please."

Very slowly, very cautiously, she turned to look at me, her eyes sparkling by the light of the streetlamp. I wanted to pin her right up against her window and kiss her breathless. But this was her call. "You're doing the kissing. You set the pace."

The wait felt fucking endless. We stared at each other in the low light as her chest rose and fell with more and more intensity. Finally, she tentatively placed her other hand on the bench seat and began to lean into me. Even though I didn't want to look away from her, I held up my end of the bargain and turned my face forward to give her my cheek. I savored every second of her getting closer. The way she smelled, the sound of her breath, the sound of her jeans sliding against the uphol-stery, the way her nose brushed against my cheek just before the kiss.

When her lips touched my skin, I tried to hang on to that feeling forever. Because if she was really going to stick to the contract, this might be all I was ever going to get.

But the peck lingered. She stayed there with her lips grazing my cheek and her forehead resting gently against my temple. She was so close that when she blinked, I felt her eyelashes brush against my cheek.

"You know how much I want you," I told her. "You *know* how much I need to feel you again."

Her breath came out as a shudder and I turned to face her, bringing my left hand up to caress her face. I let my fingers slide into her thick, dark hair, holding her jaw steady with my thumb. "I can't be around you unless I get to have all of you, Lily. I'll go out of my goddamned mind."

At first she didn't say anything, and I didn't even know if she would. But finally, fucking finally, she took a breath, and said, "Kiss me. Right now."

Christ almighty, did I kiss her. I'd been a gentleman long enough; it was time to get wild. As soon as our tongues met, we were off to the races, and we went for each other in a teeth-clashing kiss that left zero room for her to doubt how badly she and I needed to be one again. As the kiss intensified and we both got more aggressive, I brought my hands down her body and gripped her by the hips. I pulled her into me and she hooked one knee over my body, slipping herself between me and the steering wheel. With one hand, she gripped my T-shirt. And with the other, she pulled the lever to make my seat recline all the way. God*damn*, how I loved a woman who understood the fine art of mak-ing out in a pickup.

She dropped her weight onto me more firmly, and I growled as she compressed my cock between my thigh and her pelvis. She looped her arms around my shoulders, and I slid my hands under her shirt, feeling the smallness of her waist, the ripples of her rib cage, the lace-wrapped underwire of her bra.

When she came up for a breath, her eyes were glassy with desire and her lips were red around the edges from my stubble. Damn, I needed to be back inside her. "Let's get the fuck outta here."

She ground into me more deeply. "What about Mary Goodwin?" she said, all coy and sassy. "What about the show, *Mister* Powers?"

"To hell with the show." I pulled her down into me to let her know what she was in for. She gasped a little and her hips bucked, making her pelvis drive almost painfully against my cock. Her hair brushed against my forearms and swept along the steering wheel. The hickey that I'd given her was now far less visible, and I didn't like that one fucking bit, so I pulled her back down toward me and kissed her there, a sucking, biting kiss to show her that I'd marked her once and I'd mark her again.

She sank down onto me even more deeply and whispered up at the ceiling of the cab, "And to hell with the conduct clause."

"Fuck *yes.*"

25

GABE

For the ten-minute drive, she doubled down on me with the dirty talk. Last night she'd been shy about it, but not anymore. She got up on her knees beside me, whispering into my ear as I drove. "I want your cock inside me" made the stoplights blurry. "I want you to fuck me all night" damn near made me drive off the road.

Somehow, I managed to get us back to the Willows. I pulled into the driveway and threw the truck in park. I flung open the door and dragged her out of my side by her hips. Her knees parted for me and I envisioned fucking her right there, just like that, out in the open. Give a fuck who saw us. But as tempting as that was, I had other plans. I pressed into her spread legs. "Some other night, this'll be enough. But not tonight."

I scooped her into me and put her in a fireman's hold over my shoulder. She giggled and drummed on my back, but I wasn't letting her win this one. With my arm wrapped around her thighs, I carried her toward the back door. Halfway there one of her sneakers slid off. Didn't fucking matter—she'd be buck naked within the minute. I reached into my pocket, grabbed the keys, and unlocked the door. The kitchen was cool, dark, and quiet. I tossed my keys aside, wrapped my arms around her body, and laid her down on the marble island in the middle of the kitchen. "Don't move," I told her.

She tucked her arms behind her head. There was some fear in her expression—playful but cautious. Obedient. Such a good fucking girl.

Playing with fire was fine. Having control over that fire was what real power was all about.

I closed the blinds over the sink. I shut the swinging door that went into the dining room and the door that went into the walk-through pantry. I pulled off her remaining sneaker and tossed it aside.

"As soon you walked in here with me," I said as I undid my belt, "I wanted to fuck you on this marble slab." I unzipped her fly and peeled her jeans off her, yanking them off her ankles inside out. I pulled her top off and tossed it into the dark. I bent over her and took her breasts in my hands, pinching both nipples at the same time. She hissed and came up off the marble just far enough for me to reach behind her and undo her bra. And then I kissed a line down her stomach, took her panties in my teeth, and looked up the length of her body at her. From my back pocket, I took my Swiss Army knife. I flipped it open, and it glinted in the dim moonlight. I pulled the fabric away from her body. Then I placed my knife against the front panel . . . and cut those lacy little suckers right off her.

She sucked in a surprised breath, which made her stomach contract in the most ball-busting way.

With her panties cut away, I tossed my knife onto the counter and dropped my pants and boxers. I leaned down over her again, feeling the chill of the marble against my balls. I took her left nipple in my mouth and sucked it until it was hard and firm. It left my mouth with a *pop*, and I straightened up above her, fisting my cock in my hand. "Let me film you."

Her eyes sparkled in the dim light, and she came up on her elbows. "Now?"

Slowly I worked my length, with my head at her opening. "Yeah. Now." I could tell what she was thinking—about *trust* and *risk*. "We can use your phone. You keep it. Show me if you want, or not. But I just wanna capture this." I ran my hand down her breastbone. "All of it."

I pressed into her half an inch, far enough to feel her body resist . . . and relent. But no farther. Her eyes shut slowly, and she rolled her head back on the marble, moaning.

Only an inch into her and I felt my balls tighten up. Give a shit about stamina—I wanted to put everything I had inside her, and I didn't want to wait to do it.

She studied me for a second once she'd gotten used to me inside her again. I gave her another inch, and her neck arched back. Her silhouette appeared in shadow on the cabinets across the kitchen.

"My phone, my file," she said as she wrapped her legs around me. "That's the deal?"

"That's the deal." For a couple of long, deep, slow thrusts, I stayed inside her. The deeper I went, the wetter she got. It was so addictive— that wetness, the way she felt, the way she squeezed, the way her ass slapped the marble when I gave it to her hard. I eased up on her, though, and watched her, waiting for her answer. To make fantasy into reality.

"Outside pocket," she said finally.

"You drive me fucking crazy." Keeping one hand on her body, I grabbed her purse and found her phone. I flipped over to the camera and made sure her face was in frame. "You're on," I told her.

"Oh yeah?" She looked right at the camera. "You're getting this?" She slid her fingers down her body, into her pussy. And then licked herself off her fingertips.

"Jesus *Christ*," I growled as I filmed every inch of her, tilting the camera so I didn't miss a thing. "How'd you get so sexy?"

"Born this way," she teased and tried to push my back with her heel like she had last night. But I didn't let her and pinned her leg between my arm and my body. With the camera in my left hand, I fisted my cock with my right and went tight on me entering her. Amateur POV porn, the best kind of all. At first I went slow, until I was halfway in. And then I gave the rest of it to her in one savage drive. She gripped the edge of the marble, groaning as I hit her cervix. She let her head fall to the side, and her hair spilled back over her shoulders, fanning out behind her. As slow as I could stand it, I pulled out, almost leaving her, and caught her watching me. I moved the camera up her body and onto her face. She looked disappointed and pouty. One more time I powered into her, and in the frame I watched that pleasure overtake her. Buried deep inside her, I ran the camera over her creamy white breasts, and like she was in my goddamned head, she took one of them between her fingertips and pinched it. Not the nipple, but the breast itself, and her fingers made deep indentations that made me wild. For as long as I could hold out, I filmed her as I fucked her. But after a few more deep thrusts, just holding the camera was too much distraction. To make her roar, I was going to need both my hands.

Time for the closing shot. "Tell me something dirty," I said as I brought the camera back in close.

She turned her cheek away, all sass and sparkle. She reminded me of one of those sexy dark-eyed vamps that they put in the silent films—so animated they didn't need to say a goddamned word. "Not on camera." She tried to push the camera away, smiling and laughing, like she was embarrassed. Like I was bringing her right to her limit.

That's where I wanted to take her—and push her right over the edge. "Don't you hide from me. Don't you start being coy now."

I drove into her again, slow and steady. I envisioned my cock sliding into her. Flesh to flesh. Head to G-spot. Cell to motherfucking cell. Her expression got serious and focused. I watched those pretty lips and finally she said, "Please just take me, Gabe. Please."

It wasn't dirty, but it was fucking *hot*. As she said it, I felt my precum pulse into her. She had me by the balls and she knew it, which made her exponentially more powerful. I killed her phone and tossed it over into the pile of our clothes. I pulled her into me so that her ass was slightly off the edge of the countertop. Using my shoulders, I bent her knees back, revealing the mouthwatering lines of her pink pussy. I got a mouthful of saliva and let it trickle down onto her clit. Then I took her hand, put her fingers where they fucking belonged, and I gave it to her. For real.

26

LILY

He felt so good inside me that I kept forgetting to touch myself like he'd shown me he wanted me to do. I got lost in his strength and his ferocious and unbridled desire. I let him take over. I let him do whatever he wanted, however he wanted to do it.

Each drive into me was accompanied by a slap of his hips against the backs of my thighs, and I felt a sheen of sweat begin to cover my body, making the marble slick. Again and again he drove into me, with his eyes trained on me and his teeth set. Sometimes he'd slow down a bit and tease me with a tantalizing near withdrawal. As soon as he got close to leaving me, I realized I *needed* that pressure inside me. Not just wanted. *Needed.* Needed the pressure and the release that was coming. *Oh God, it was coming.* Then he'd drive into me with everything he had again, making me let out a porn-star growl. As I felt that undeniable flutter deep in my hips, I grabbed his hand.

He gripped my hand tight in his, our fingers interlaced. His face softened, not so intense and primal now as much as cautious and atten-tive. Laser focused on me and what I needed. He tensed up his abs, revealing new sexy muscles in new sexy places. As he tensed, he changed the way he was driving into me—the angle, the depth, the intensity all shifted. Everything went into overdrive. "What are you . . ." I rolled my neck back, the back of my head against the marble edge. "Oh my God."

"Tell me," he said, hitting that spot again. And again. And again.

Every pound brought me closer. This pleasure wave wasn't coming from my fingers. It wasn't coming from his hips hitting my clit as it had last night. *This* was coming from inside. Deep inside, and every drive got me that much . . .

"*Closer,*" I gasped.

Every time he drove into me, my walls constricted around him involuntarily.

"Let go." His voice was gruff and serious. He yanked me farther off the edge of the island and rammed into me harder than he ever had before. "I've got you."

He's got you. He does. I focused on that pressure inside me, on the way he was making me feel, on the way he made my body pulse and throb and flutter.

The whole world got blurry and faraway with pleasure. Halfway through it, somewhere halfway down, I heard him grind out a long, dirty "Fuuuuuuuck" as he took me even harder. My screams came from deep inside my chest, noises I'd never made before. I didn't try to be quiet. I didn't try to be polite. I just let go, exactly like he said.

It went on and on and on, one wave right on the heels of another. I didn't know if it was multiple orgasms or maybe just one epically long one. But really, it didn't matter. Nothing mattered but him and the things he was doing to me. Things I had never even imagined before.

When the waves of pleasure began to let me go and I came back to earth, I let my knees drop to the side so I was in a ball on the pastry island, with him still inside me. With the back of his forearm, he wiped some sweat from his forehead. "Now *that* is what I'm talking about."

I nodded, my chin grazing my shoulder. I felt faraway and dreamy, like the time my sister and I had shared a joint. He was still hard inside me, and he didn't slip out of me even when he bent down over me to give me a row of kisses up my shoulder.

He moved my arm aside and took my right nipple in his mouth. Again his eyes closed in that pure bliss. Total peace. I let him stay there for a while and savored the way his tongue felt running over my nipple, the way his stubble felt against the soft skin of the underside of my breast.

Figuring out what he liked wasn't about to be a process of trial and error. Oh no. I knew what got him revving. He'd shown me already. "Hand me my phone."

He let my nipple slip from his mouth and looked up at me, like he was searching to see if I was serious. "You're shitting me."

I shook my head, feeling the pinch of my pinned hair tugging on my scalp. "You filmed me. Now I film you."

He drew his head back slightly, turning his cheek. It reminded me of a boxer squaring up in the ring. *Think you can handle this?* "Give it to me." I wiggled my fingers. "Right now."

He pulled out of me, and my hips rolled back involuntarily. Keeping one hand possessively on my thigh, he knelt down and grabbed my phone from our pile of stuff. Then he handed it over. I woke it up and went to the camera. I saw myself in blurry streaks and hit play. My recorded moans filled the kitchen. Seeing myself in that state of total surrender turned me on *intensely*. I felt the warmth rush through my body, and he echoed it with a growl as he placed himself at my opening. "You just got so wet."

I started filming him, full frame, full torso. I got up on my elbow and brought the camera in close on both of us together as he entered me. "Look at that," I whispered as he pushed inside me. I leaned back, my whole body quivering with so much sensitivity from what he'd just

done to me. I drove my heels into the edges of the countertop for support. As he pushed into me, I zoomed in on his face. I panned down
over his chest, his abs, and back up again. Using two fingers, I made a
V around his cock and made them slick with my wetness. I reached up
and pressed them to his lips, and he licked them clean. "Yeahhhh," I
said softly as I watched in the frame.

"Jesus Christ, you feel so fucking good."

I gave him a little squeeze and watched his lower abs tighten as I
did. Having him on camera magnified all the hotness, knowing that he
was doing this for me and to me. Knowing that it wasn't fleeting—I
wouldn't have to imagine this. I could relieve it. As many times as I
wanted.

He furrowed his eyebrows slightly, and his thrusts got more intense.
I felt his balls slapping my ass and I had to focus, *really* focus, on keeping the camera trained on him. The more I focused, the more intense
it all became. Because this wasn't about me, not now. This was about
him and what I could do to him—with a word or a glance or a shift
of my body.

He took me. *Hard.* Hard enough to make my hip bones ache, hard
enough to work me right back up into a furious frenzy.

I could tell he was close. His eyes fluttered shut, and he inhaled
hard. He ran his hands down my body and gripped my hips. I let my
legs part slightly, and he pulled me closer so my skin squeaked on the
marble.

On the next deep drive, I relaxed inside but then tensed up as he
was pulling out. "Holy *shiiiit.*" He let his head fall back so he was looking up at the ceiling. "Fuck," he said. "Lily. Fuck."

"Now it's your turn to let go," I said, egging him on. "Let me film
you doing it."

"You gonna send that file to me?" he asked, his voice gruff and
heavy with desire.

"Maybe," I said, sucking in a breath to keep myself focused on him. "If you're good. And if you give me what I want."

"I'll fucking give it to you," he said with a new edge and new tension in his voice. I liked that about him, the way he sometimes let me peek down there between the cracks. Like the red-hot, churning heat underneath a dark lava field.

I leaned back a little farther with my elbow locked. I let my hair spill over my shoulder and waited until he was looking at me again. He powered into me with that same intensity that made me come before. "Shit, Lily," he said, with closed eyes and that sexy, dreamy expression on his face. "You're going to make me . . ."

"Look at me," I told him.

He opened his eyes, almost icy with desire. He was tough, but I could be tougher. "So now stop fucking around. And come for me."

"Where the hell have you been all my life?" he snarled. "Shit. *Shit.*" He let his head fall back and roared at the ceiling, *"Holy* shit." With one more squeeze, I had him. That beautiful man coming inside me.

He stayed inside me for a long time after he finished. When he left me, I rolled up to sitting and wrapped my legs around him. He drew me into him and smoothed my hair with rough strokes down my back. "Bed?" I asked with my cheek pressed against his sweaty chest.

"I got a better idea," he said and slipped out of my grasp. He offered his hand to me, and I slid off the island. When I did, though, my knees almost went right out from under me and I stumbled.

He was there to catch me, and I hung on to him for support. "You OK?"

I looked up at him. My thighs were both rubbery and tight. "I think so."

"Did I fuck you until you can't walk?"

I felt like a newborn foal on one of the General's favorite nature shows. "You sure did."

"Goddamn. This night gets better and better," he said and scooped me up into his arms, newlywed style. I squealed when he did it. I wasn't very big, but I wasn't small either, and I most definitely wasn't used to being carried around like this. Twice, just tonight! Like I weighed nothing at all, he carried me up the steps and into the big, spacious bathroom. He paused by the light switch and I turned it on, dimming the lights to their lowest point. I'd seen the bathroom that morning, but I'd been in such a rush I hadn't taken the time to really appreciate it. The wainscoting was old-fashioned tile hexagons, no bigger than quarters. And the floor was hexagons too, but bigger, in a checkerboard pattern of black and white. He gently let me slip from his arms, so I stood on the bathmat. Then he turned on the water in the majestic, beautiful old fairy-tale claw-foot tub. He turned to look over his shoulder as he plugged the drain and winked at me.

"A bath? Together?" I gasped.

"Told you I was going to treat you right. But I gotta do one thing. You stay here, OK?" He grabbed two huge terry-cloth towels from the rack behind me. One of them he wrapped around me like a cloak. The other he wrapped around his waist, working the edge into a knot against his rock-hard stomach.

"OK," I said, dragging my eyes off his abs.

"Be right back." He let himself out of the bathroom, closing the door behind him. For a second, I listened and watched the water slowly filling up the tub. But when I heard his footsteps get softer, so soft that I couldn't hear them anymore, I turned off the faucet to figure out what he might be up to. In the silence, I heard the creak of the screen door in the kitchen. Cinching my towel around me, I padded to the big window at the end of the upstairs hallway and looked out over the backyard, where I saw him heading to his truck. He opened the passenger-side door and flipped the seat forward. When he leaned inside, his yummy buns in their fuzzy terry-cloth wrapping caught the moonlight, highlighting the slight concave curvature on the side of each one.

Lord have mercy on me and those beautifully sculpted buns.

He slammed the door shut, and in his hand I saw a small paper gift bag. Just like Aunt Jennifer used at her store. He grabbed the picnic basket and made his way back to the house, stopping to pick up my sneaker on the way. I sprinted back to the bathroom and turned the water back on. I closed the lid of the toilet and waited. He reappeared just a few minutes later, still holding the gift bag.

"That's for you."

"I think I've had enough gifts for a lifetime."

He lifted his eyebrow and shook his head. "Tough. You better get used to it. Now open that."

I took the bag from him and pulled the rattan ribbon off the handle. Inside was a full set of my most favorite, favorite, favorite bath supplies, the ones I *never* splurged on. "Bubble bath. Salt scrub. And massage oil!" I clutched all three fancy glass bottles and pressed their cold edges to my bare chest.

Beaming, he took the bubble bath from me and drizzled an oh-so-generous amount into the water. The suds foamed up and filled the room with the scents of lemongrass, ginger, and rosemary. He offered his hand to me and helped me into the warm water. I lowered myself into a crouch at the front of the tub, and he climbed in behind me. He was a big guy, and the water level rose a lot when he got in, covering me with warmth and suds, sloshing from side to side. He pulled me back into him, making my tush squeak on the porcelain. He wrapped his arms around me and placed his lips to my shoulder. I melted back into him, with my arms tangled up around his.

His Dopp kit on the counter caught my eye, and I studied the small travel containers with a pinch in my heart. I bought my shampoo by the family-size bottle at Costco. He barely had enough for a week. It was concrete proof that he wasn't here to stay. But it was no use worrying about that, not now. Not yet, I told myself, as the bubbles all around us whispered, *"Hushhhhhh."*

27

Gabe

I woke up facing her in bed, with the sunshine illuminating her from behind as she slept. I blinked hard to clear the sleep from my eyes. Once, in the Sahara, I'd seen a mirage. Looking at her was exactly like that—like you thought your mind was playing a trick on you, like whatever you saw was too good to be real. Except this mirage didn't dissolve into the sands. This one got clearer and clearer, down to every freckle on her cheeks and every ringlet curl.

Looking at her made one word come to mind. I'd learned it in Germany when I was filming there. *Fernweh.* The feeling of being homesick for a place—or a person—that you had not yet called home. When I'd learned about it, I thought it was for other people. But maybe not.

Moving slowly and carefully so that I didn't shake the bed, I slipped out from between the sheets and pulled my boxers on. I headed into the bathroom to take a leak and got a look at myself in the mirror. I almost didn't recognize the face staring back at me. I didn't look haggard. I didn't look tired. I didn't look jet-lagged or run-down. I looked . . . *happy*. Which was exactly how I felt.

Quietly, I made my way downstairs and got the coffee started. Normally, I'd check my email or text Markowitz, sketch out some plan for the next segment, or try to figure out a way to make Lovers' Lane seem spooky when all it had been was red-hot. But instead, I just stood there, utterly spaced out, listening to the coffee sputter through the filter, content knowing that she was sleeping safe and sound right above me.

I took two china cups from the cabinet and put them on a tray. I put the small container of half-and-half beside it, as well as a few sugar cubes and two spoons. Next to the mugs, I found a high and thin vase into which I put two of the handmade lilies. From the fridge, I took the raspberries I'd stashed before our bath last night and placed them on the tray. And then I headed upstairs. When I got to the bedroom, I savored the way she looked—all curled up in a ball in bed—before knocking on the jamb and finally saying, "Room service."

She inhaled hard and rolled over, stretching her arms above her and giving me a magnificent yawn. "Hi!" she said, her voice squeaky with sleep. I set the tray on the bed beside her, and she rolled up to sitting. "Oh my gosh, who *are* you!" Her toes peeked out from under the sheet, and I saw them curl down into the mattress as she stretched again. She tucked her knees up slightly, and her breasts rested on her thighs.

To her coffee cup she added three sugar cubes and so much cream that it turned khaki. I got back in bed next to her, making sure I didn't knock anything over as the bed shifted slightly under my weight. She sipped her coffee and placed the warm mug in her lap, nestled in the sheets. For a second she studied me with her chin tucked against her arm. "Thank you," she murmured. "Nobody has ever taken care of me like this."

I slipped my arm around her and put a kiss to the side of her head. "The pleasure is all mine."

She bent her neck from side to side, catlike almost, elegant and comfortable in her skin. "So what's on the docket for today?"

I took a berry from the bowl and brought it to her mouth. She sucked it off my finger. What I really wanted to be on the docket were those lips on every inch of my body. But life was life. Goddamn it.

"Brace yourself, beautiful. I've got to do some production work and cut some segments together for Markowitz. Boring, I know. But necessary."

She smiled and rolled her eyes in an adorably dramatic way. "Suppose it had to happen eventually." She took a tiny sip and nestled the mug back in her lap. She looked down at her coffee, and her expression became more serious as she furrowed her eyebrows. "How long are you going to be in Savannah?" she asked as she traced the rim of her mug.

I wanted to talk about beginnings, not endings, but I knew it was a conversation we needed to have. "A week, I'm guessing," I said.

Her fingertip froze on the edge of the porcelain. "Just a week?" she whispered. Her eyes sparkled with emotion. I understood just exactly what she was feeling. It hadn't been long, but that didn't matter. Something was happening here between us. Something intense and undeniable.

I took the mug from her lap, setting it on the bedside table, and straddled her as she nestled down into the pillows. Her hair spilled out behind her, shimmering in a ray of sunshine. She placed her fingertips on my chest and dragged them down my pecs and abs. "I don't want to say goodbye to you yet, Gabe."

I pushed her hair away from her face and cradled her cheek in my hand. "I gotta be honest. I don't think I want to say goodbye to you at all."

She smiled and turned away, pressing her cheek to the pillow as a breathy laugh escaped from her nose. "You're crazy."

"Crazy for you, yeah." From the breakfast tray, I took the bowl of raspberries. "You got a problem with that?"

Lily shook her head, and her curls slipped along the pillowcase. "No problem at all."

"Good," I said.

And I took two raspberries from the bowl. One for each of her nipples.

An orgasm apiece and all the raspberries later, I dropped her at her place, giving her a filthy, possessive kiss before she got out of my truck. When we finally parted, she wiped her mouth with the back of her hand and growled, "A week, Gabe. A week is *not* enough."

Tell me about it. But far as I was concerned, life was only complicated if you made it that way. The other option was to make it really goddamned simple, and that's exactly what I was going to do. "I'm going to Brazil next. Come with me."

The ferocious desire I'd seen on her face after the kiss was replaced with an almost innocent surprise. She drew her chin back into her neck and let her purse slide from her shoulder. "Wait. Brazil . . . the country?"

For a split second, I did wonder what other Brazil there was, but I didn't push it. I'd surprised her, and I dug the way that felt. "Shit, we'd have so much fun. Even if you didn't want to do the audio for the show, I could fly you down with me. All expenses paid."

Her lips parted slightly. She swallowed hard and crossed her arms. "I . . . I've got so many . . . ," she stammered, blinking like she had dust in her eyes. "But what about . . . what about . . . the jobs I've already got lined up here? And the General? And . . . my nephew . . . And I mean . . ." She took a deep breath and gasped, *"When?"*

Jesus, I liked making her babble. I wanted to whisk her right off her feet. I wanted to see her drink daiquiris out of halved coconuts. I wanted to samba with her in Rio until the sun came up. But none of this could be figured out with her halfway out of my truck with the engine running. "I'm not asking you to run away with me . . . *yet*," I said, only half teasing. "I'm talking about a week or two. How about we talk about it tonight?"

Still with wide eyes, she slipped out of the passenger's seat. Again she swallowed hard, gripping her purse tightly in one hand, and nodded.

"OK," she said in barely a whisper. "I'm babysitting my nephew tonight, but I'd love to make you dinner. Then we can . . . talk. Some more. About all this."

"You're on," I said, revving my engine.

"See you at seven thirty, then," she said slowly and closed the door. I put the truck in drive and rolled down the street, watching her in my rearview mirror. But she didn't turn toward her house. She didn't move at all. Instead she just stood there, with her fingers pressed to her lips, and watched me drive away.

Something about her posture made me think that she looked almost . . . scared. But that couldn't be right, I thought, as I rounded the corner to go back to the Willows. Had to be surprise. Yeah. Had to be.

Back at the Willows, I took a shower so long I used up all the hot water. Full disclosure: I got involved in using the girly bath and shower stuff that I bought for her.

Verdict: absolutely awesome. Especially the salt scrub.

I toweled off and got dressed and then headed downstairs. I flipped my computer open and lined up the rough cuts to send to Markowitz. I put in some good hours working on the barbecue segment, patched together some rough stuff for the Mary Goodwin segment, and sketched out some new ideas for the episodes that remained. I'd planned on a total of three, but there had to be ways to stretch it out—I had to be able to stay for longer than a week. We could go out to Tybee Island or drive up to Hilton Head. Five episodes, maybe. Or six. But even twenty episodes wouldn't give me enough time with her. Wherever I went next, I really did want her with me. It was fast, it was a bit crazy, but it was really that simple. Brazil would be a fucking blast.

My phone began to buzz and cut into my thoughts. I'd personalized the vibrate setting for Markowitz to be one solid and annoying thrum.

Like a tornado warning from the National Weather Service. I pulled my phone from my pocket and read the text from him.

Gimme the goods, Powers!

How are the glutes?

I tucked my phone back between the couch cushions while it buzzed away. Markowitz was a rapid-fire texter, but I'd learned from a whole lot of experience that really only the first text mattered. The rest of them were almost always irrelevant updates on chia smoothies, his last trip to the gym, and his feeling on his newest pair of bike shorts. In my head I heard Lily cooing, *Bless his heart!*

Yes indeed.

So I ignored Markowitz and refocused on the Lovers' Lane segment. Looking back at me was Lily's beautiful face. I hit play and heard her correcting me, schooling me in Southern Lingo 101. The camera loved her, and I decided to keep all the footage I had of her because I couldn't stand the idea of cutting any of it. I put each of the segments into the video editor and patched them together. All the rough cuts would go to our editors in LA, but first I liked to run it by Markowitz so he could see where the episodes were headed. I put placeholder spots in at the opening and the end, which I marked with the subtitle *Drone pan in/Drone pan out*. Then I saved the file, compressed it, and shared it with Markowitz.

Within half an hour, he was calling. This time, he was FaceTiming me. It was about fifty-fifty that he actually hit the phone icon. The rest of the time, it was video. Sweaty video.

I hit the answer button, and his wet and jostling face appeared on the screen. "Powers! Just saw the rough cut! Is that the audio engineer? Is *that* Ms. Jameson?"

"That's her." I glanced at her on my computer screen. I'd paused it midgiggle. It might've been my favorite still frame of her. For now. Once I saw the video of us from last night, I was pretty sure I was going to have some new favorites. X-rated ones.

"What a cutie!" Markowitz panted, beaming at me through the screen. "She's terrific! Such a good idea to put her in the show! Ten out of ten! Love that Southern charm!"

"She's a natural, right?"

"Absolutely! As your producer, I'm contractually obliged to say don't fall in love, but as your friend, I'm contractually obliged to say that you look happy! And I'm happy about that!" he said, panting the whole damned time. Smiling and head bobbing around, he reminded me of a super excited yellow Lab.

Markowitz and I were hardly the types of dudes who went out for beers and wings on Friday nights—not least because he was a hard-core gluten-free vegan. But all his eccentricities aside, he was, effectively, my work wife. Or work husband. Whatever. He'd been my date to more red carpet events than I could possibly count. There was nobody I was in contact with more often than him. When it came down to it, there was no point in lying to him. There was no point in pretending that all this didn't matter, or that it was all for the sake of the show. It wasn't. It was more than that. I felt it in my gut.

My own smiling face reflected back at me from the thumbnail in the corner of the FaceTime feed. Other guys felt this way, never me. Until now. Like I was watching some other guy in some other life, I watched myself run my hand over my scruff and say, "I *am* happy, man. I really am."

"Which gives me an idea!" He gave me some jazz hands. "One word. Cohost!"

It was a classic Markowitz Idea Fart: presumptuous, half-baked, and over the top. She hadn't even said yes to Brazil yet, and here Markowitz was putting her name before mine on the credits—permanently. "How many shots of espresso have you had today? Did you double up on your Adderall?"

"Four triple shots and very likely!" He sped up on the elliptical and the video feed got stuck in blocky pixels, but the audio was still coming through. "Think of the male demographic! Those boys will be falling all over themselves! Her fan group will break the internet! She'll be America's sweetheart!"

I rubbed my face with my hand and shook my head at the camera. "Take your Rescue Remedy and call me later," I said and ended the call. I slumped back on the couch and looked up at the ceiling, laughing to myself. But I did have to admit, I fucking loved the idea. Not of her as America's sweetheart, no. But the idea of her as *my* sweetheart and cohost. The idea of her by my side, the two of us cruising at thirty thousand feet, flying off into the sunset to have endless adventures together. Champagne in first class and making the world our own. Yeah. That. Goddamn, I *loved* the sound of that.

28

LILY

Aviophobia is the overwhelming fear of flying. About 20 percent of the total population has some version of it because, obviously, humans do not belong in the sky! Of that 20 percent, about 1 percent has an acute and paralyzing case that does not seem to respond to treatment, that gets worse with age, and that makes air travel not just uncomfortable . . . but utterly impossible.

Hello. My name is Lily. I am the poster child for the land-bound 1 percent.

I really and truly had tried to overcome it, with talk therapy and virtual reality visualizations, with Xanax and horrible kava teas, with essential oils and Valium. I'd tried exposure therapy and hypnosis and mindfulness. Everything. But none of it worked, and even after something as innocuous as a ride on the kiddie Ferris wheel at the fair, I ended up with my head between my legs, panting into a paper bag while my sister did Lamaze breathing next to me and stroked my hair.

Sexy!

Like phobias tend to do, mine had shaped who I was and the way I lived. Every responsibility I had—the General, my sister and Ivan, our house, my job—was one more tethered stake that kept me grounded, one more reason I couldn't leave, even if I'd wanted to . . . which I didn't. I was cozy and safe in my happy little bubble. Everything I needed and everybody I loved was inside it with me, which meant that there was no need—ever!—for me to even *look* at an airplane.

Until Gabe Powers sauntered into my life and asked me to go forty-five hundred miles away with him like it was no big deal at all.

"Lily!" snapped my sister, accompanied by a series of actual snaps by my ear. "Earth to Lily. I'm giving you some pro baby tips!" she said as she lurched into a parking space. Even though she was only going to be away for the night—buying secondhand antiques off Craigslist was a *very* quick and dirty affair—she had insisted on taking me grocery shopping with her to make sure I had everything I needed for Ivan. "I was saying that you don't wanna know what happens when you run out of diapers during a blowout! The joys of motherhood!"

Desperately trying not to get stuck on the thought of flaming airplanes cartwheeling through the sky, I helped Daisy get Ivan out of his car seat, freeing his chubby little legs from the nylon straps. I tried to take comfort in his baby goodness and carried him through the rolling doors, watching his three hairs blow in the gust of air-conditioning that greeted us. We grabbed one of the kid-friendly carts, with a big red plastic booster seat in the front, and I buckled him in.

But as we approached the bananas, Daisy came to a screeching halt. She dug through her purse and patted herself down. With each pat, her face got more and more angry. "Don't tell me I did it again . . ."

I didn't even have to ask what *it* was. My sister had a whole lot of very admirable qualities, but keeping track of her keys wasn't one of them. When Ivan was born, Daisy bought a hybrid minivan . . . with a push-button ignition. As we had learned from a lot of experience, it was entirely possible to start and drive it while the keys were still hanging on the key hook. And not be able to start it again whenever you got to wherever you were going. Fortunately, we had figured out a fail-safe for this. She had two key fobs, and I always kept one with me. I patted my purse. "Gotcha covered, as usual," I said as I gripped the bar on the cart and stared at a Mylar balloon in the shape of cartoon airplane in the floral department. It was slightly deflated, not unlike the *Hindenburg* before it burst into a ball of flames.

Daisy let out a sigh of relief, reached into my purse, and double-checked for my keys. As soon as she jingled them, Ivan started making grabby hands and she handed them over. He gummed my frequent shopper card and pressed my van key into his chubby, drooly cheek.

On we went through floral to produce. "I think there might be a coupon for apples," Daisy said. "I better check."

Then she did something that had never, ever been a problem before. Everything we had was pretty much interchangeable, including our phones. As she had a hundred times, she grabbed mine from the outside pocket of my purse. She typed in the code, which she knew, same as I knew hers. But as she hit the last digit, I realized that there was a very real possibility that she was in for a surprise. I hadn't closed out my apps when I jammed my phone into my purse before we left for the store. That meant that she was about to be met with something that was a whole lot naughtier than BOGO apple coupons: the video I'd taken of Gabe. I'd been watching it when she came banging on my door to go grocery shopping in a desperate attempt to get myself to think of something, *anything*, besides enormous and rickety tubes of metal whizzing through the upper atmosphere at five hundred miles an hour. How could they be sure the wings would stay on? *How?*

"Lily!" she gasped, her eyes wide and her mouth gaping. She didn't seem shocked as much as *amazed*. She clapped my phone to her chest and gave me a little shove. "Lily!"

I pressed my hands to my mouth. "Sorry," I said into my palm. "Should have warned you."

She steadied herself on the side of the grocery cart. "What have you been up to!"

I considered some dusty-looking grapes, but through my fog of sudden embarrassment, they felt really far away. I had encountered quite a number of awkward situations with Daisy over the years—her tendency to lose keys also applied to the key for a pair of handcuffs she'd once used on Boris, and she'd had to call me for help—but never, not *ever*, had they involved nude videos of me and a famous television host. Or anybody else. Clearly!

"I've been . . ." What in the world was I planning to say here? *Having a torrid romance with the sexiest man on the planet?* She'd think I was delusional! Best to keep it simple. One step at a time. "Do you know that show *The Powers of Suggestion?*" I said as we headed toward the kale.

She gave me another shove. "I *knew* it!" she whisper-barked. "It's him, isn't it! It's him!"

I tried to get busy with a bunch of broccoli, but I was so flustered and my hands were still so sweaty from the thought of airplanes that it was a bit difficult for me to get the bag open. So I clutched the broccoli to my chest like a bouquet. "It is. And he's . . ." I looked out at the produce somewhat dreamily, thinking about him as I gazed from fruit to fruit. Tasty. Delicious. Hard. "He's wonderful. But Daisy. He's asked me to go on a trip with him. To Brazil."

"Oh sh . . ." Daisy stopped herself before she dropped the S-bomb on Ivan. "Oh, salamander!"

"I know."

She cringed. "What the helllll . . . man's mayonnaise are you going to do?"

"I have absolutely no idea," I said and maneuvered the cart toward the baby aisle, jostling along with one stuck wheel honking on the linoleum.

When I got home from the grocery store, I tried to keep myself and my swirling thoughts occupied as I tidied up my apartment and prepared dinner for my date with Gabe. The problem was that with his invitation, he hadn't just gotten me worrying about planes—he'd also catapulted whatever was happening between us to the next level, and it made my head whirl like a cheap tabletop globe spun by a sticky-fingered toddler. Brazil. *Brazil.* Never had such a pretty word sounded so stinking terrifying.

The problem with fear and anxiety was that it didn't behave in any predictable way; one stray what-if attracted other stray what-ifs, and soon enough I was in the What-If Whirlwind. It reminded me of being in a vacuum canister when you sucked up something really noisy that banged around in there like crazy. Rice or lentils or couscous.

Of course, I could just give him a big fat no. But I didn't want him to think I wasn't interested. I was *very* interested. And yet what if I was just reading too much into this? What if he hadn't really meant it? Or what if *Brazil* or wherever else was what he suggested to all the girls? And speaking of which, what if there were other girls? What if there were *lots* of other girls? What if there were lots of other girls he'd met on lots of other shoots and who had been working themselves up into tizzies over international travel, only to get their poor fangirl hearts split apart like cheap Valentine's Day lollipops?

Except that wasn't the Gabe I was getting to know. He didn't have a constantly buzzing cell phone that made me think he had twenty girls named Lauren sniffing around him like fluffy little terriers with pink ribbons in their hair. The Gabe I knew seemed both genuine and genuinely interested in *me*, which meant that his offer to me—however off the cuff—was heartfelt.

But even if it was heartfelt, what if I was just being silly about this whole thing? What if I was putting the cart miles and miles before the horse? What if he had some bummer of a habit that would end up being a deal breaker for me, like correcting people's grammar when they spoke or talking during movies? What if we ended up being *totally* incompatible and I eventually looked back on these hazy, lusty days with a chuckle as I thought, *Oh, if only he hadn't been such a dreadful asshat?*

That wasn't the Gabe I was getting to know either. He wasn't an asshat. He was lovely, and I was . . . smitten. Definitely smitten. If there was one thing that the last few days had made abundantly clear, it was that we had a special sort of spark between us—the sort of thing that can't be learned or practiced. Already I could see that our personalities and our passion made sense together . . . even if he did lack my encyclopedic knowledge of air-travel accidents. *Twenty-two in Brazilian airspace since 1939!*

Once I got dinner prepared—yellow-beet salad with gorgonzola and pecans, salmon on puff pastry with pesto, and peach tartlets à la mode for dessert—I took a shower, dried my hair, and put on my favorite summer dress. I went downstairs to get Ivan and saw my sister off on her trip. I played with Ivan and put him down for a nap. Still, it was only four thirty.

Scratch that—4:31.

That was the other thing about anxiety. It made time *crawl* by.

I grabbed my needles and yarn. Even the knitting obsession was phobia related; it had been suggested to me by a therapist who was big on both dopamine reuptake and also hats and scarves. In the past, when I'd gotten myself worked up over the thought of flying or when I got a news alert that yet *another* plane had tumbled out of the sky, knitting hadn't been nearly enough to calm me down. This time, though, the knitting actually did help a little bit, and I was at least able to get my mind back on a more even keel. Knit, purl, knit, purl. Calming breaths. Calming thoughts. The hat was far too big for Ivan, but I thought it might be just perfect for Gabe.

A photograph on my mantel caught my eye. It was my sister on her wedding day. She'd been so very happy when that photo had been taken; even now, I could almost feel her joy when I'd hugged her before walking down the aisle in front of her. She'd been brimming over with possibility and hope. But it hadn't lasted. And now Boris was only barely visible at the left edge of the frame. Or, more precisely, his elbow.

When he vamoosed without so much as a *do svidaniya*, Daisy had ripped all her wedding photographs in half in a ritual ceremony at my kitchen table that was heavy on boxed chardonnay and light on sentimentality. I remembered that day just as well as her wedding day. Better even, because of the swearing and never-ending pints of ice cream. And as I had with quite a number of things—from overzealous home bang trims to accidentally using the diesel pump at the gas station—I'd learned my lesson through her. She had been down this road of falling for a man who shot into our world like a meteor into a swimming pool. It had ended with heartbreak, complications, and chaos. On the day I'd written *ABSENT* on the line on the divorce papers where Boris's signature should have been, I'd promised myself that I would never get entangled with a man who wasn't firmly, fully, and permanently rooted in Savannah. I would not get involved with a man would eventually become nothing but an elbow in the frame.

And now here I was.

Was I getting ahead of myself? Probably. But even still, Brazil was a big problem. The issue wasn't that I'd fall to pieces if he jetted off to Brazil for two weeks. Of course not. The issue was that he'd suggested traveling together as a *solution*. But for me it was *the problem*. I couldn't go away with him. Not to do the audio for him for his show or for anything else. Not even to visit him in LA.

If that was what he wanted—some easy, breezy girl who could hop on a plane at the drop of a hat, who didn't have responsibilities and family and reasons she had to stay put—well, then, I definitely was not the girl for him. But if he'd be willing to settle for a girl who could, with ample prior advanced scheduling notice, go on short trips to any location within driving distance of Savannah, then maybe I was.

Riiiight, Lily, I thought, as my needles ticked along. *You might be cute. But you're not* that *cute.*

When my hands started to feel crampy, I checked the time on the cable box. I'd gotten so used to focusing on the yarn up close that it took me a second to make out the fuzzy numbers. But when I did see the time, I couldn't believe it. It was 6:46.

"Oh my God," I gasped and stashed my needles and yarn in my knitting basket. Gabe would be here in fourteen minutes. Or maybe even less. Without meaning to, I had let Ivan nap all the way through his normal nap time and straight into cranky-baby territory. He was just waking up in my bedroom, and his yawns and murmurs spilled out of the video monitor. I scurried to the bedroom and scooped him up from his crib, a warm ball of sweaty baby wonderfulness. I bounced him in my arms and brought him to his high chair in the kitchen. In record time, I got him fed and the General too. I put an apron over my head and preheated the oven. I made sure everything was set on the table, and I heard a door slam outside.

I peeked out between the curtains. It was him. And he looked so handsome in his crisp gray shirt, sleeves rolled up his tanned forearms. In his hand was a bouquet of red roses, long stemmed and lush, with glossy leaves. He was on the phone, pacing in my driveway. He looked impatient, like he was trying to wrap up the call. His voice, low and strong, carried through the single-paned windows. That was when the room was filled with a low and throaty growl.

Fear of airplanes was one thing, but I had another airborne object to deal with at the moment. The General. We'd tried having Gabe walk right into the apartment, and it had ended in the Noise. So I decided to go for a more drastic approach: removing the General from the battlefield for a while. I placed my hands on the sides of his cage, which I had fastened to an old metal bar cart that I'd never used. With my foot I undid the wheel brake and began to push him out of the main room.

"Aaaaaah!" he shrieked.

"It's OK!" I said, as reassuringly as possible. "We're not going to the vet!"

"Noooooo!" he screamed, because obviously he was a parrot—his brain was the size of a shelled walnut—and the only thing he'd understood from that entire sentence was *vet*.

"No vet!" I repeated as I maneuvered him down the hallway and into my spare bedroom. I felt like a television doctor hurrying down a hallway as I pushed a rattling gurney. "No vet!"

There was a crazy panic in his eyes, and he plucked a feather from his chest, letting it dangle from his beak as he stared at me. There were whole chapters in my parrot books dedicated to understanding the complexity of feather plucking. All I really knew for sure about it was that it foreshadowed a total meltdown that would end in either my having to replace pretty much everything in his cage, or a round of squawks and shrieks that would positively ruin Ivan for the evening. And maybe bring the police knocking. But for the moment, he was silent. Worryingly silent.

In the silence, I heard the sound of Gabe coming up my stairway. It was time to pull out the heavy artillery.

It was a strategy that I only resorted to in times of total parrot-soothing emergency. It was a vinyl record that my grandma had played for him when she found herself in dire General straits, which she had purchased from the same estate sale where she'd found the General himself. *Twenty-Six Civil War Favorites for Slide Guitar and Ukulele*. Blowing the dust off the record, I opened the turntable. I placed the record on the spindle, dropped the needle, and turned to check on the General.

As the ukulele filled the room, he dropped his feather and began gently swaying side to side.

I crept out of the bedroom and closed the door just as Gabe gave a few firm knocks on the door. Manly knocks, even.

Oh boy. I was really in trouble here. Even his knocks were making me quiver.

I smoothed my dress, put on my sandals, flung open the door, and smiled. "Hi!"

He looked freshly showered—his thick hair still slightly damp. As soon as he saw me, he blew out a *whoa* breath, giving me a slow up-and-down. "Hey there." He leaned in for a kiss, and the floral plastic on the big bouquet of roses crinkled between us. "These are for you," he said and handed over the flowers with their satinlike petals and rich scent. He slid his bag off his shoulder and set it down next to my purse on the floor.

I clutched the flowers to me, feeling a touch like Miss America. "I just preheated the oven. It might be a little while. And Ivan slept longer than I'd planned. So we might have to have some company for dinner."

Gabe didn't seem the least bit bothered by the change in plans or the fact that I'd begun to babble. It was almost as if he didn't notice what I'd said at all—he seemed utterly mesmerized by Ivan and went right over to him. "Hey, little man!" He crouched to bring himself down to Ivan's level.

Ivan tried to clap his hands but ended up throwing Cheerios all over Gabe's shoes. Much to my utter amazement, Gabe knelt down, picked up a few of the Cheerios from the floor . . . and ate them. Which made Ivan shove a few in his mouth too.

Oh my God, who *was* this man?

I didn't have a vase big enough for the roses, so I used the beautiful old china washbasin pitcher that my grandma had left me. As I filled it with water, Gabe came up behind me and wrapped his arms around me, pulling my hips into his. It made my knees wobble, and I held on to the sink for support as the pitcher overflowed with water. He brushed my hair aside from the nape of my neck and kissed me there as he slid his hand down past my lower belly, holding me possessively by the thigh. He reached past me and turned off the water and then turned me in his arms. He nudged my cheek with his nose, and I looped my arms around his neck. Then he slid his hands down my hips, onto my ass, and hoisted me up onto the edge of the sink. He dipped me as he kissed me, and I wrapped my legs around him.

How I loved his lips on mine. But before I let myself get carried away, I put my hand on Gabe's chest. He pulled away with that fire in his eyes, and I wiped my lips on the back of my hand. "Listen," I said, trying to approach this whole issue in the most straightforward way that I could—not with my very convincing litany of reasons about why *nobody* should ever set foot on an airplane but rather simply why *I* would never be able to. "I need to tell you something."

"Anything," he said, holding me firmly by the shoulders. "You can tell me anything."

He looked so patient and so understanding. I inhaled slowly for a count of eight and took as much strength as possible from his grip. I steadied myself and quieted my thoughts, focusing on the way my feet felt in my sandals, the way my dress straps felt against my shoulders. The way he really did make me feel safe in his arms. "The thing is . . ." I inhaled deeply through my nose. "It probably sounds crazy but . . ." *And exhaaaaale.* "But see, I'm, I've always been . . ."

Just as I began to find the words, there was the sharp *raa-raa-raa* of my phone buzzing on the counter. I ignored it. "It's that I'm absolutely . . ."

Yet again, *Raa-raa-raa. RAA-RAA-RAA.*

I eyed my phone. I could have *sworn* I put it on Do Not Disturb, but there it was, rattling away. "Let me get that." I slid off the counter and scurried across the kitchen, grabbing my phone from its charger.

My sister was calling. My sister, who had left hours ago. My sister, who knew I was having dinner with Gabe and who wouldn't be calling unless it was urgent. Which gave me a sinking feeling that my explaining the finer points of aviophobia was going to have to wait.

I clenched my eyes shut and answered. "Don't tell me."

"Why, though? Why?" she growled. I was pretty sure I could hear her pounding on the steering wheel. "Would it be so freaking hard for there to be some *system*? Like, I don't know, a goddamned keyhole? Fuckers!"

Daisy hardly ever swore since Ivan had been born. But when she did, she let loose like a seventeenth-century schooner captain after three helpings of grog.

"How far?" I asked, wincing and envisioning a GPS driving map in my head. The longer the little blue line of her route was, the less time I'd have with Gabe.

"I'd been on the road for two hours. I stopped at Cinnabon, turned off the car, and now I'm up shit creek! Before you ask, yes. I have called everybody else in creation. Aunt Jennifer is at the shop. My friends from yoga are out having a girls' night. Mom and Dad are still on that goddamned interminable Alaskan cruise—how many polar bears does *anybody* need to see? So it's just you, Lily. I'm so sorry."

I scrunched my knuckle into my eye but then realized I had makeup on—idiot! I rubbed my knuckle into my palm and did some cursory under-the-eye cleanup. Probably looked like an NFL linebacker now. Fabulous.

Glancing over my shoulder, I saw Gabe was once again engrossed in Ivan. He held a stuffed penguin by the little loop on its head while Ivan batted at it like a piñata.

The problem was that Ivan had just eaten *and* he had just gotten up from a really long nap. One plus one equaled the obvious: poops. I'd been so eager to talk about real life with Gabe, but this was all a slightly larger helping of real life than I'd planned on serving.

Gabe unbuckled Ivan from his high chair and scooped him up into the air, blowing a kiss on his belly. In my head, I envisioned the

comments section under his cliff-diving video and saw myself responding to the lady whose ovaries exploded. *You have no idea, sister!*

That was when I remembered that way back after I almost poked
out his eye at the Willows, he'd said he loved to look after his nieces.
It was worth a try. I placed my hand over the lower part of my phone.
"Do you think, by any chance, you'd be willing to do a little . . . light
babysitting? Just for a bit? My sister forgot her keys. She's two hours
from here." As soon as I said it, I realized how absolutely ridiculous it
sounded. Which of course, it was! "See, she drives . . ."

Gabe hoisted Ivan up in the air, with his sexy biceps pulling his
shirt tight. From between Ivan's parted, kicking legs, Gabe asked,
"Push-button ignition? I always wondered if that could happen."

"It can. And does. Often."

"Lily!" roared my sister into my ear. "Don't key-fob shame me! I
haven't even met him yet!"

Gabe bounced Ivan in his arms, and Ivan pressed a chubby hand
into Gabe's chiseled cheekbone. *Kaboom!* "I'd love to watch him."

But a tubby baby was only half the battle. Less than half. The
journey of a thousand miles begins with a single step and also a one-
pound parrot. "And the General?" I asked, slapping a grimace-smile on
my face.

"*And* the General," Gabe added, without hesitation, glancing
meaningfully at the back bedroom, where the General was now cawing
along to the "Battle Hymn of the Republic" in the style of "Aloha Oe."

Before I could even gasp out a thank-you, my sister let out a long
swoon in my ear and said, "Marry him, Lily. ASAP. We'll figure out the
airplane thing. I'll pay the city hall fees. I'll make the cake. Just don't
you dare let go of that man."

29

GABE

Everything was all good . . . until the music stopped. I was bouncing Ivan on my knee on the couch, cleaning some spit-up off his chin, when I heard that telltale *tick-tick-tick* of an LP that has finished the last song.

I looked Ivan in the clear blue eyes, and I swear to God the little guy opened them up wider. "Not good," I said.

But as soon as I spoke, I realized I'd gotten myself even deeper into the shit. The General chimed in with, "Suitor? Suuuuuuuitor?"

I didn't say a goddamned word. Ivan wriggled in my hands, shaking his fists and blowing bubbles with his drool. Maybe I could pretend I wasn't even in the apartment. I could whisper to Ivan. I could build a sheet fort with the couch cushions and the General would never know we were here.

Don't be chickenshit, Powers. It's a parrot in a cage. It's a bird in a box. Man the hell up. Facts were facts: Damn right I was a suitor. And I was proud of it. No need to hide it. No need to take cover in a blanket fort and pretend I wasn't feeling the feels. Anyway, all I needed to do was restart the damned record. In, out, and back to babysitting. "We'll get him squared away and then we can watch *Peppa Pig*. How's that sound?" I asked Ivan.

He answered with a drooly, gummy smile. Babies. The *best*.

I wanted to have two hands ready for the General, just in case. Carrying Ivan on my hip, I went over to grab the BabyBjörn from a row of hooks on the wall by the front door. Lined up on every peg was a jacket or a sweater of Lily's. Each one was cuter than the last. For a second I imagined my stuff mixed up with hers—my backpack next to her purse. Her sandals on top of my shoes. Our rain jackets side by side.

Man, oh man. What a thought that was.

I carried Ivan back to the sofa. I considered laying him on the cushions, but that seemed pretty risky because he liked to wriggle, so instead I laid his blanket on the ground and put him there while I got the baby carrier strapped on. Extending the loops on the straps, I tightened it to my body and hoisted him back up. I got him situated in the carrier, facing out from my chest. His head was snug against my body and his arms and legs could move freely. We were ready to roll. I gently held his arms out in front of him like Superman and added a *"zoooooooom!"* in his ear. Together, we airplaned our way down the hall toward the *click-click-click*. At the door of the spare bedroom, I paused. And knocked. Because . . . I don't know why. Because the General was a semi-sentient creature who wasn't too hot on me and barging in seemed like a *really* bad idea. "Enter!" he cawed when I knocked. Very slowly, I opened the door.

There he was, waiting. He had one wing slightly up and his beak tucked down into it. Over the ridge of his gray feathers, he gave me the stink eye.

Ivan erupted in *baa-baa-baas*, and the General cooed back at him. But the poor bird was *clearly* pretty conflicted about this whole situation, because the one he loved was strapped to the one he hated.

Apparently, he wasn't going to stand for that shit. Because he puffed up his feathers, fanned his tail, opened his mouth, and let loose with that horrendous goddamned noise yet again. But even louder this time.

"Why!" I ducked down, like that would make shit for difference. "Jesus, man! Why?"

No answer on that. What I got instead was the Noise on 'roids. It went up into this crazy *whoo-whoop* and then went down again into a throaty scream. Up and down, again and again. As he did it, he thrust his chest out like an opera singer belting the chorus to the rafters, with his leathery tongue extended and his beak open all the way.

Fighting the mind-numbing decibels that made me feel off balance— I'd once been in a small earthquake in Japan and it felt *just* like that—I managed to get my brain to go back to what Lily had done when it first happened. The Union was supposed to be in surrender. "General! Hold position! The Yankees are in retreat!"

There was a blissful pause. But it was just a break for the General to get his breath, because he fired back at me with, "Inadequate Yankee suitor!" and started up with the Noise all over again.

In response, Ivan began screaming and crying and kicking his surprisingly strong legs, landing a glancing blow to my balls with each kick. But that wasn't even close to the biggest of my worries, because against my stomach I began to feel a telltale rumbling. A somewhat concerning tremor. It was forceful enough to make Ivan's diaper vibrate and crackle. It filled the air with a whoopee cushion sound effect, accompanied by a smell so spectacularly awful that even the General ceased and desisted. There was a moment of total calm, eerie quiet. In the stillness, I looked at the General and he looked at me.

Then Ivan took a deep breath, tightened up his little body, made some huffs and puffs . . .

And literally, epically, and spectacularly *lost his shit*.

Only my boxers survived the blowout unscathed. Everything else within a four-foot radius—my shirt, my pants, the BabyBjörn, Ivan's clothes, and *both* of our pairs of socks—went into the washer with a double measure of detergent on *sanitize*. My shoes got a good rinse in the laundry sink, and I put them upside down in the basin to dry. I cracked the window in the guest bedroom just an inch so that the General didn't pass out from the smell as he whispered, "The horror, the horror!" like Marlon Brando in *Apocalypse Now*. Finally I grabbed Ivan's essentials from the pile of baby stuff that Lily had left for me and carried Ivan to the kitchen, him naked and me in just my boxers. With him hanging on to me, I filled the kitchen sink with some warm water to heat up the basin so it wasn't uncomfortable for him. I used some baby shampoo as shower gel and cleaned him off with handfuls of suds and water. I used the spray nozzle set to a trickle to rinse him off and then refilled the sink and plugged it so he could have a nice little soak.

The kid was *incredibly* cute, and I recognized Lily in his nose and his splash of freckles. There was just enough of her in him to make me fall for his chubby self even more. "That was pretty awesome." I ran clean water over his head, dampening his downy blond hair.

Ivan *ka-ka-kaed*, smacking the water with his fists.

"Epic, even," I added as I soaped him up.

"Da-da-da!"

But from down the hallway, over Ivan's babbles, I heard a very ominous sound: a rattle followed by a metallic creak. A very distinctive creak. As in, possibly, from the door to the General's cage. I paused with a handful of water trickling out of my palm. In the mess and chaos, I hadn't thought to restart the record. The General had gone silent, and I figured we were in the clear.

We weren't. Half a second later he swooped through the living area with his wings spread wide. I ducked, shielding Ivan's head with my hand. "Holy shit," I said as he leered at me from the edge of the sofa. "How the hell did you do that?"

The General parroted my own voice back at me: *"How the hell did you do that? How the hell did you do that?"*

Ivan looked back over his pudgy shoulder, squealed and bounced in the water, and then let out a long buzz with duck lips. The General hobbled back and forth on the back of the sofa, happily dancing along as he snagged threads from the upholstery.

Lily was going to kill me. In a matter of twenty minutes, I had managed to turn her guest bedroom into a hazmat scene, and now her parrot was destroying her couch. *Great.*

A certain professional instinct kicked in. In all unexpected wild-life situations, I'd found that acting without thinking was a terrible goddamned idea. The smarter the animal, the calmer you had to stay. Parrots weren't like docile dairy cows. Parrots were intelligent. Parrots made *plans*. Like Komodo dragons. Those bastards conferred like NFL refs, and I could just tell that the General was made of the same pre-historic stuff.

So I decided to use something I'd learned on Komodo, because that felt about right. I gave the General a confident lift of my chin. "You good, man?"

Which he answered with a sound that sounded *a lot* like a chain saw.

But I ignored it. I had a baby in the sink and I was almost buck naked—I was in exactly no position to be bargaining with a creature who could, at any moment, go straight Hitchcock on my ass. Or face. Or whatever. So I focused 100 percent on Ivan, ignoring the General's stares and occasional growls. When Ivan was warm and clean, I put him on a bath towel on the counter and dried him off. I laid out the fresh diaper I'd gotten for him while he kicked at the sky and tucked his chin into his neck, giggling and cooing.

Midway through getting Ivan's diaper on, the General came in closer, using the kitchen faucet as a perch. There was no doubt that he was supervising me, checking to make sure I did it right. He craned his neck and leaned in close. Apparently, I did fine. He didn't make the Noise when I put on the baby powder and didn't even growl out a "stupid Yankee" under his breath when I had some trouble getting the Velcro tabs to fasten under Ivan's belly. The General flew over my shoulder and landed on the top of the fridge, watching me as I got Ivan situated in a onesie—blue-and-white-striped with a bee on the front— and then carried him to his crib in Lily's room. I laid him down, made sure the video monitor was on, and quietly shut the door behind me.

When I rounded the corner to the kitchen, the General was still there, staring right at me as he poked his talons into the black rubber seal of the freezer, each clench of his toes accompanied by a sticky, plasticky *snap*.

My stomach let out a serious growl, and the General stared at me with one foot up in the air. I was hungry, and all of Lily's delicious food was right inside the fridge. The oven was preheated, and all I had to do was put the salmon in. She'd made me dinner, and not even an angry parrot was going to stop me from getting it. I crossed my arms over my chest and squared off with him. "Listen, Fuss and Feathers. You gonna let me in there or not?"

In response, he whistled the opening riff from *The Good, the Bad and the Ugly*.

But I wasn't a dude to be swayed by a couple of nasty stares and some heckling. I was in showbiz, for God's sake. I took a step toward the fridge and opened the door. The salad was in a big bowl on the top shelf. But as I grabbed it, the General made his move. He hopped down onto my shoulder. His sharp talons pinched my skin, and he waddled in an awkward circle so he was facing forward. Like a proper parrot on a pirate's shoulder. It was worrisome. But it was also . . .

I glanced at him. He leered at me.

. . . pretty fucking awesome.

As slowly and carefully as I could, I straightened up, being cautious not to tighten my delts or make any sudden movements. He kept his balance by pitching his body and adjusting his stance, as if he were riding a skateboard. When I was stationary, he leaned forward and side-eyed me, puffing up his feathers as he did. I set the salad bowl on the counter and grabbed my phone off the counter, more grateful than I'd ever been for my waterproof and babyproof case. I opened my camera and held my phone out at filming distance. As soon as the General came into the frame, he let out a long, soft "Ooooooooooh!"

He bobbed his head at himself, preening his feathers in a new way. A proud way, so they were more fluffy than threatening. Like he was . . . *happy*.

"That's you," I said, bringing the camera slightly closer.

He leaned back in surprise when he got bigger on the screen. I shifted my grip on the phone, flipped over to the video, and hit the record button.

He weaved side to side, chattering nonsense at himself.

"What's your name?" I asked.

"The General!" he squawked.

"Where are you from?"

"Savannah!" he said.

I played it back for him. When he saw himself on the screen, his beak dropped open. *Whoa!* His eyes got wider. He watched himself talking to me and let out what sounded *a lot* like a good old-fashioned and totally human gasp.

"Cool, right? Video is awesome." I hit the play button again, and out of the corner of my eye I watched him. I didn't know if parrots could smile. But if they could, he most *definitely* was.

"Again!" he cawed when it ended. So I played it back. Once. Twice. Three more times. I grabbed a glass from the cabinet and put my phone inside it. When I hit play, the sound of the video was amplified—an instant portable speaker. Trick of the trade. The increase in volume made the General even happier. I placed the glass with my phone on top of the freezer so he could see it. While he watched himself, I put the salmon in the oven and ate the whole salad right out of the bowl—it was *fantastic*—and played the video again and again and again. Once I polished the salad off, I put the bowl in the dishwasher and grabbed my phone. I patted my shoulder, and the General took his place. This time he used a way less menacing grip. Progress. I'd take it.

The salmon was even better than the salad, and the peach tart? *Christ.* Once I did my dishes and put the kitchen back the way I'd found it, I hit the record button again. "What's your favorite color?" I asked him.

"Yellow!" he said into the camera.

"Who do you love?"

"Lily!"

I nodded at him. "I like her too. Because I'm a suitor. Like you said."

He turned to me, now ignoring the camera. "Suitor?" he asked softly, this time in a *very* different tone. Like now he was the one doing the wooing.

"Definitely."

He blinked his strange lids. He adjusted his powerful claws. And then he leaned in close, nuzzled my ear with his bony head, and whispered, "Good suitor. Goooood suitor."

While Ivan slept, I put in some time getting rough cuts lined up and sent to Markowitz and our production editors. The General watched over my shoulder, perched on the back of the couch, occasionally adding some running commentary whenever Lily appeared on the screen. *Love you!* And *Hello!* And *Pretty!*

When the washer buzzed to announce it had finished its cycle, Ivan woke up with a cry. The General and I headed into Lily's room to get him out of his crib. I bounced him in my arms as I got the dryer going and hung up his BabyBjörn to dry, but he was fighting sleep and fighting it hard. I grabbed a blanket off Lily's bed, a quilt that was threadbare in spots, well loved, and antique. From the guest bedroom, now mercifully free of the lingering smell of the blowout, I wheeled out the General's cage. I put it where it had been when I first came to visit, with a view of the street. I left the door open for him; there was exactly zero chance of my coaxing him into the cage, but at least it'd be there for him if he wanted it. As we approached the couch, the General flew from my shoulder to take his place on the back of the sofa. This time, though, he didn't knead his talons into the upholstery. He shuffled side to side, looking expectantly at the TV. When I switched it on, I saw my own face staring back at me.

As fast as I could, I changed channels. I hated seeing my own show. There was no better way to screw up a perfectly nice night than to get in the *I should've done that differently* loop. I flipped through the channels and landed on a nature show about some tiny multicolored crab. Ivan quieted down in my arms, and within what seemed like about one second, he fell sound asleep against my bare chest.

I glanced at the General, who was transfixed by the crabs running sideways on the screen. I rubbed my face with my hand and surprised myself with a huge yawn. It might've been barely after sunset, but I was exhausted; I'd spent the last few nights all over Lily and probably hadn't slept more than a few hours total. Not that I was complaining. But now, it was like the bottom had dropped out from under me. I was worn the hell out. Her place was comfortable, quiet, and peaceful. Even though she wasn't there with me, I sensed her in all the touches and the details. It felt like the one place that had never quite been within reach for me . . .

Like home.

Sitting on the coffee table was a notepad. I recognized the paper as the same as the notes that were inside the gratitude jar. On the top sheet, I saw the indentations of a word. I angled it toward the light.

And saw my own name. *GABE* in swirly feminine letters.

Holy, holy shit.

With some *intense* warm fuzzies, I lay down on her sofa and pulled the quilt up over me and Ivan. Keeping my hand securely on Ivan's back, I stretched out my legs and put a throw pillow behind my head as another yawn hit me. The General mimicked my yawn and I told him, "I'm going to close my eyes for a minute. Wake me up if you need me. OK?"

He nodded. "OK!" he said and turned his attention back to the crabs.

I inhaled and relaxed. Tension I had no idea I was carrying around with me seemed to melt out of my shoulders. Lily was grateful for me, and I was damned grateful for her too. But then my mind drifted back to the way she'd looked right after I kissed her in the kitchen. She'd looked pretty terrified as she searched for the words for whatever it was she'd been planning to tell me.

Terrified of what, I didn't really know. But she'd seemed worried long before I walked in the door for dinner. In fact, she'd looked pretty spooked even when I'd dropped her off at her house earlier that day.

The idea of her worrying that pretty little head of hers didn't sit well with me. But whatever it was, I was positive we'd be able to sort it out.

We'll be able to sort it out, I thought as I began to drift off to sleep. Not just *me* anymore. *We.*

30

LILY

When I opened my apartment door, I was greeted by the cool blue light of the television and that was *it*. No baby crying, no bird screaming, no desperately shouted bungled rewrites of history to silence the General. All was quiet except for the murmurs from the TV. I switched on the lamp in the front entryway, and that was when I saw Gabe. He was passed out on the couch. He was bare chested and holding Ivan tight to him. The General was sound asleep in his cage, which had the door wide open.

I was hardly Agatha Christie, but I could piece together what had happened: *The Case of the Nine-Month-Old on Solid Foods*. There had been a poop incident, but it seemed as though Gabe had handled it like an absolute pro. It also looked as though the General had escaped—something he *never* did when I was home—but Gabe had handled that too without even a phone call or a panicked text to make me worry. What a love. I crept across the apartment and carefully closed the door of the General's cage. I slipped the sheet over it and slid my phone from my purse pocket. I snapped a picture of Ivan in Gabe's arms and sent it to Daisy. Within one second, she had replied.

Wake him up.

Why?

So you can go elope!

I tiptoed around my apartment so as not to wake Gabe. I moved his huge and muscular hand off Ivan's chubby back and put Ivan down in his crib for the night. Changing out of my dress in the dark, I grabbed my stretched-out old cotton nightie with faded butterflies without thinking, but then I opted for a slightly nicer pink one that I had bought on an impulse but had never worn before. Slipping it over my head, I looked at myself in my bedroom mirror. It barely came down over my rear end, and the place where my thighs met my tush was hardly hidden by the lacy hem. It was a bit over-the-top, but too sexy *had* to be better than too frumpy. Using a trickle of water, I wet my toothbrush and brushed my teeth, keeping my lips tight around the brush to stay as quiet as possible. But all my creeping around was for nothing because just as I was rinsing, Gabe appeared in the doorway. Sleepy faced, hair sticking up every which way, in only his boxers.

In other words, absolutely *delish*.

"Hi!" I said around my toothbrush.

"Hey," he answered, his voice about two octaves lower than usual. Morning voice at bedtime. Lordy.

He scratched his stubble and blinked against the bright bulbs of the bathroom. "You done in here?" he asked.

I wiped some minty foam off my mouth and nodded. I set my toothbrush down and turned off the faucet.

"Good." He tugged me by my nightie into the bedroom. It pulled tight around my body, and I barely managed to switch the light off before he dragged me from the bathroom. He grabbed my hand, led me to bed, and crawled in beside me. As I was getting my pillow situated, he scooped me into him, spooning me from behind. I felt him hard against me, between my legs. He slipped his forearm between us and pulled down his boxers. I reached behind me and bunched up my nightie to get it out of the way, and he slid himself along my opening. I hadn't been particularly turned on before, but now the floodgates were open, and he groaned when he felt me. With a small adjustment of his hips, he pushed into me, and I curled up instinctively, but he didn't let me curl up all the way. He stayed as close as possible to me, the curve of his chest right against my spine and his strong hand cupping my breasts. He reached around me with his other arm and found his way to my clit.

We had been wild and noisy. We had been risqué and intense. But this time we were soft and quiet, and I loved that. I love the way he touched me, the way he held me, and the way he made me feel so cherished.

When I felt myself getting close, I gripped his hand to tell him where I was. He drove into me and stayed there, nestled his mouth against my ear, bit down on my earlobe, and whispered, "Come for me."

I slid my hands over his and held on tight as I began to let go. I saw shimmering water and dappled light. As I was coming, I had this vision of a string that linked our hearts. Something bound us together that I felt but just didn't quite understand yet. He came as I did, not with savage thrusts but with one deep drive and a rumbling groan.

As we finished, he pulled me into him even deeper. I snuggled down into him, my chest against his back, and our slowing breaths fell into rhythm.

I didn't want to ruin this moment. But I didn't want to stay mum and keep things from him either. And so, into the darkness of my bedroom, I whispered, "Gabe. I have my life here. I have my responsibilities here . . ." I swallowed hard and clamped my eyes shut. "Our lives are so, *so* different."

His embrace tightened, and he pressed his lips to the crown of my head. "Is that a bad thing or a good one?"

I truly didn't know how to begin to answer him. The feeling in my heart was indescribable—*infatuation* with a twist of *uh-oh*. But how was I going to explain that? By rattling off a series of hypothetical bullet points about things that he hadn't even broached yet and that we might not even be headed for at all? By saying something like, *All right, so think of an iceberg. Above the waterline is my fear of flying! Below, we have all other unknowns that could sink this ship too! Lemme start by telling you a cautionary tale about a turdmuffin named Boris . . .*

He'd think I was out of my freaking mind.

So I decided to keep it simple and address the most pressing issue— the only thing he'd *actually* asked me about so far. "The thing is . . . about Brazil . . ."

He adjusted his embrace so that his forearm was diagonally across my chest, and his hand gripped my shoulder, making me feel tiny and safe. "Say yes. It'll be fantastic. I promise."

Oh, how I wanted to say yes. With all my heart, I wished I was stronger than my fears. But honesty mattered to me, and I was not about to pretend that we didn't have something very real, and very scary, that might come between us. Yet again, I took courage from his strength and stared at the clock as the second hand ticked past. "I want to say yes, but I have to say no. Because I am absolutely *petrified* of flying."

I braced for his reaction—disappointment, disbelief, incredulity. *But it's the safest mode of transportation* and all those logical things to say. Instead, I was met by nothing but the sound of his steady, calm breathing. Very slowly, I turned my head, being careful not to move too much in his arms. His face was peaceful and his eyes were closed. He had already fallen asleep.

31

GABE

Even though I'd been right on the brink of falling asleep, I'd heard her. My first thought as I'd been drifting off was *Well, shiiiit.* But when I woke up, I was in Action Jackson problem-solver mode.

She'd obviously been worried about telling me, which made it clear that it wasn't some small-potatoes thing. It wasn't like Markowitz and his ridiculous flailing afraid-of-bees dance that turned a lunch meeting on the patio at Chipotle into total pandemonium. This sounded legit. The word she'd used was *petrified*, and I'd heard her voice shake when she said it.

It sounded serious, and I took it seriously. I was falling for her hard, and I sure as hell didn't need to take her to Brazil to prove it.

With as much stealth as a guy my size could have in an old house with seriously creaky floorboards, I crept out into the main living area. When the General saw me, he hopped up one rung in his cage, making the bars rattle. I pressed my index finger to my lips and said, "Shhh."

"Whisper?" he whispered.

"Whisper," I whispered back.

"OK!" he replied and then tucked his beak back into his chest feathers, lifted one foot, and closed his eyes.

I took a stack of blank paper from the shelf by her printer and sat down at her kitchen table. Using the notes I had on my phone as well as some searches online, I worked my way through all the places we could go for a start. Her role in the show, if she wanted to go with me, would be up to her. I wasn't about to Idea Fart *cohost* into the situation first thing in the damned morning. If she wanted to cohost, that'd be awesome. If she had some cameos, that'd be great too. If not, and she wanted to be in charge of sound on the other side of the camera, that was also just great. Whatever she wanted was fine by me as long as I got to be with her. I wouldn't be able to avoid planes forever, but at least for now—at least as we really developed a foundation—this would give us a chance to spend some more time together.

Because Savannah was about ghosts, Markowitz and I had decided the next few episodes needed to be about monsters, so I drew up five different options to share with Lily. Just as I was putting the finishing touches on the fifth one, I heard the floorboards creak way more softly than they had under my footsteps, and she came into the kitchen. Her hair was all tangled, one strap of her lacy nightie had fallen down her shoulder, and I could still see a hint of the hickey. It didn't get any hotter than her.

I stood up and pulled her chair out for her. "Welcome to the pitch presentation for the next story line on *The Powers of Suggestion*."

She rubbed her lips together and glanced around, looking coy, cute, and slightly confused. "Thank you?"

"Have a seat. Can I get you anything?" I gestured to the coffee maker. "Coffee? Tea? Leftover peach tart?"

She rubbed her eyes and snickered. "I think . . . I'm OK for now. But thank you!"

"Excellent. So given our travel limitations . . ." I paused here for effect, and she cringed when it registered what I was saying. "I've put together several ideas. All of them are in the US. No planes necessary."

"Gabe." She reached out one hand as if to stop me. But she didn't look panicked. More like embarrassed. So I decided to keep at it. "We'll have some Q&A time afterward. Lemme just get my presentation squared away." I took my stack of pitches to the fridge and stuck them down with magnets shaped like slices of citrus fruits, blocking the fridge with my body. I heard her snickering behind me, and I smiled hard at the freezer. From the small ceramic crock by her stove, I grabbed a wooden spoon to use as a pointer and stepped to the side of the fridge.

She tucked herself up into a ball on the kitchen chair and watched me expectantly with her chin resting on her knee.

"Now, the first thing for you to consider is that Markowitz has suggested you become my cohost."

Lily's mouth dropped open. "Your *what*?"

"Just marinate on that awhile," I said. "And forget about Brazil. Instead, here are some ideas that are a bit closer to home. First option is the Mothman, in Point Pleasant, West Virginia." Here I pointed to the page I'd illustrated. I'd written down some info about the legend, the rough mileage, and the number of days it would take us. I'd done the same for all five. "Second option is the Wampus Cat in eastern Tennessee. Third, the Pukewudgie in Massachusetts. Fourth, the Beast of Busco in Indiana. And finally, the Ozark Howler. In the Ozarks. Obviously."

With big and innocent eyes, I watched her scan the options, and then she glanced at me. "You're serious?"

Serious as a goddamned lightning strike. I cupped my hand to my mouth and whispered, "I'm putting in a word for the Ozark Howler right now."

Lily shook her head, laughing a little like she just couldn't believe me. "Gabe. This is all very kind and very thoughtful. But I have all sorts of stuff that I'm responsible for here in Savannah." She gestured to a calendar on the wall, which had events written all over it. I saw *Ivan's birthday* and *Help out at the library* and all sorts of other things. Unlike my calendar, hers wasn't all about work. Her life was about *life*, as I wished mine was too. "I can't be going away with you all of a sudden, even if you *are* willing to drive to wherever it is we go."

I grabbed the other kitchen chair and turned it around so I sat down straddling it. I put the spoon on the table and took her hands in mine. "Just think about it. I'm not going to push. If the world is the oyster, then you're the pearl. And I want you to see that I'm willing to change my plans if that's what it's going to take."

She nodded, studying me closely. She shifted her hand so we were palm to palm. She interlaced her fingers with mine and gave my hand a squeeze. Finally she lifted her chin and gave me a decisive nod. "Then I shall take your pitches under consideration, Mr. Powers."

It was a relief, but I didn't want her to think that her fear was something that I was simply trying to fix or solve or work around. She'd opened herself up to me. And I really wanted her to know what whatever she shared would be safe. I cared about what she went through, whether or not it was a problem with an easy solution. I gently turned her other hand over, so it was palm up on the back of my chair, and traced her love line and her heart line. "Can I ask you something?" I asked. "About the mode of transportation that will remain unnamed?"

Lily nodded tentatively, tucking her knees up even closer to her chest. "Yes."

"Don't want to freak you out."

"It's OK. Go ahead." Her heels squeaked on the seat of the chair. "I'll tell you if it's too much. Safe word is *engine fire*."

I wasn't a guy who felt fear very often, but I'd been in a lot of situations that were dangerous as shit. I could understand how someone could develop a fear of just about *anything*. "Did something happen? Or have you always had it?"

"As a tiny kid I could fly," she explained. "But once I was able to understand what was going on, it was out of the question. By the time I was three years old, my parents were trying to fix it." She watched my finger as I traced her health line now, and then down along the soft skin on the inside of her wrist. "Spoiler alert. There is no fixing it."

"Let's get one thing straight. You definitely do not need *fixing*. I like you just like you are."

She didn't look convinced at all. "Well, that's very nice of you. But I have tried to fix it. Virtual reality simulators, drugs . . . exposure therapy, even. My sister used to take me to the municipal airport, and half the time I ended up losing my cookies in the bushes. And I've tried *lots* of meditation."

"Oh man," I said. "I love meditation."

"You?" She turned away slightly and smiled as she sized me up. "A big strapping buck of a guy like you? Counting breaths and *clearing your mind*? Don't know if I buy it," she said, laughing and tipping her head so her hair fell in a curtain beside her leg. "But maybe I do. You're full of surprises."

"Baby, I can *om shanti* with the best of them."

Lily burst out with that wonderful giggle of hers, and from the baby monitor came the sound of Ivan starting to babble himself awake.

The chaos of getting a baby and a bird set for the day swirled around us. We worked together like a couple who had danced this morning get-ready dance a thousand times. We got Ivan and the General fed and made breakfast together—I scrambled some eggs while Lily lined up English muffins in the toaster and got the coffee going. Together we sat down at her kitchen table with the sun streaming in. We caught up on emails, had our coffee, and read the news. We did all the things a couple would do. All the things I'd never done with any woman before.

"So," Lily said, slurping her hot coffee and tucking her feet against my thigh on my chair. "What's the plan for today?"

I dragged my eyes off her and refocused on what lay ahead of us for the day. I scrolled through the production calendar and landed on today's date. "At one thirty this afternoon, Markowitz got us booked on a VIP tour of the most famously haunted spots in Savannah." I took a sip of my coffee as I scrolled through the tour description. "The Marshall House, the Kehoe House, Sorrell-Weed, the Mercer Williams, Hamilton-Turner Inn, and the Davenport. Inside scoops, up-close access."

"Ooooh, fancy! I've never even gotten to go inside half those places!" She clasped her hands together, which made her cleavage compress and made me forget every goddamned thing I was about to say.

She lowered her head, slightly cockeyed, and adjusted the lace, tugging it up by an inch while also pulling the satin tight over her nipples. "Still with me?"

I cleared my throat. "Doing my best. Then tonight," I said, glancing down at the most recently arrived email message, which was, without a doubt, one of the weirdest things I'd ever received. "What do you say to this?" I spun my tablet around for her to get a look.

As she read, her face went from ordinary curiosity to *now hang on one second* to *shut the front door!* "Could that be . . . a prank?"

"Don't think so," I told her. Her eyes boggled a bit and she reread it, and I skimmed over it upside down.

To: Gabe Powers
From: Gen. Robert E. Lee

Dear Sir,

It has come to my attention through various official channels that you are a guest in our fair city of Savannah at this time. I thus humbly extend an invitation for you to visit our encampment at

20:00 this evening, upon which occasion we shall
be communing with the Confederate dead in an
effort to uncover a great mystery that has plagued
our forces for 150 years. If you are amenable, I shall
send you travel instructions via cellular telephone.

Your dutiful servant,
General Robert E. Lee
General in Chief of the Armies of the Confederate
States
GenRobertELee@ReenactmentSocietyofGeorgia.
org

Lily looked up from my tablet. She gave me a series of slow, deliberate blinks. "Pretty standard stuff for you? Receiving emails from the dead?"

I tipped my hand side to side. "Depends on the location. But I gotta say," I said, considering the email with its parchment-scroll background, "this is right up there with the weirdest. You game?"

"Absolutely!" Lily bit into a hot English muffin smeared with butter. "God, it's so fun to be with you." She delicately shielded her lips with her hand, smiling as she chewed. "I adore this." She wiggled her toes against my leg and tucked the last of her muffin in her mouth. "I adore every minute with you."

Adore was one word for it, I thought as I watched her dust muffin crumbs off her cleavage and then lean over to feed Ivan a slice of banana. But it wasn't the only word.

After we did the dishes and grabbed a shower together—so fucking sexy, goddamn—I heard Lily's sister downstairs. Lily darted out of the bathroom with a makeup brush in one hand and a hairbrush in the other, wearing nothing but her lingerie. Light pink with black trim today. Christ. Totally oblivious to her hotness, she listened to the footsteps and said, "I'll just put on my clothes and take him downstairs. I'm just about ready to go." She spun on her heel. Today's panties were lacy shorts. I was such a goner for that ass.

But there was no need for her to hurry her sexy self. I was dressed already, and I really dug playing airplane with the little guy. "You get dressed." I unbuckled Ivan from the high chair. "I'll take him down." I held him on my hip as he yanked at my earlobe. Together, we zoomed off through the door into the stairway.

As I headed down the stairs, Lily's sister opened her door. When she saw me, she let out a gasp and pressed her hand to her mouth. "I'm trying so hard not to fangirl all over myself," she said, and that same blush Lily sometimes got reddened her cheeks.

I held Ivan close to me with one arm and reached out to shake her hand. She made a little whimper and leaned against the doorjamb. We made the Ivan exchange and she said, "I heard there was a small situation last night." She added a Lily-like cringe. "A blowout?"

"It was no problem at all." I wiped a little glop of snot out from under Ivan's nose, and he giggled at me.

Daisy jiggled Ivan as he yanked mercilessly on her earring, and she glanced up the staircase at Lily's door. She pursed her lips and took a big breath. "OK, fangirling aside, *please* be good to her. She deserves happiness. Not some guy who's going to disappear. Because I can tell you from experience, that's a truly terrible feeling." She looked up at me with a mix of dismay and protectiveness. "There is hardly anything worse in the world. Believe me. I should know."

There was one definite difference between Daisy and Lily—the hope in their eyes. Lily had it, but Daisy didn't. It was special kind of sparkle that was hard to explain but easy to see. The very idea of Lily ever losing that glittering hope made me sick. "I won't hurt her," I said, not glancing away from Daisy's worried eyes for an instant.

"You promise me? I might be a fan of yours, but I'm her sister first and always."

The last thing on earth that I wanted to do was hurt Lily. Never. "I promise. You've got my word."

"Good," Daisy said. "Insert obligatory half-joking threat from older sister *here*," she added. And then nailed me with the mother of all glares.

Whoa, *shit*. The Glare had actual force, like a gust of wind. I gave her a nod. "Absolutely. Understood. But can I ask you something?"

Her glare softened one half of one percent. "What do you want to know?"

"This fear of flying. How can I help?"

Her ferocity lessened and was replaced with a more sisterly and protective concern. She blew out a long breath and let her shoulders go slack. "I was wondering if that would be an issue. She told me about Brazil."

"I proposed a change of itinerary on that one. But I still want to know what it is that she's going through."

"Well, she used to be pretty gung-ho about working on it. She even got a passport a while ago . . ." Daisy glance up the steps, like she was making sure the coast was still clear. "Never used it, though. Never even took it out of the envelope, I'm guessing. She's tried everything. And I honestly don't know that she can overcome it."

It wasn't what I'd wanted to hear, not so much because I was hell-bent on having her come with me on a plane, but because I could tell that the very idea scared her. And I didn't like that idea one goddamned bit. But intense emotions were strange. Once people got it into their heads that something was going to happen—good, bad, mysterious—things like logic didn't necessarily apply. "So I shouldn't push it?"

Daisy shook her head. "Not unless you want to lose her."

From behind me, I heard Lily trotting down the steps. I turned to find her in white shorts and a striped long-sleeved shirt with buttons on the shoulders. The shirt made her tits look incredible, even without a single hint of cleavage. She joined me on the steps and put her arm around me. "So you two met!"

Daisy nodded and gave Ivan a few kisses on his cheek, watching me over the top of his head. "Now I'm going to make a graceful exit before I make a fool out of myself. Very nice to meet you." She looked back and forth from Lily to me, lingering on my eyes just long enough to make her point one last time. *Kapow.*

It was important to me to leave no question in Daisy's mind about my intentions. There was no way in hell I could convey as much in a single glance as she had, so I just straight up said it. "Never," I told her. "I promise."

Lily peered up at me, clearly confused. "Never what?"

Daisy gave me a big warm smile at last. "Never *mind*," she said, laughing, and closed her apartment door.

Lily's mouth dropped open, and she barked out a *how dare she* sort of gasp. "Did she give you a speech?" Lily asked. "Did she give you the Glare?"

The General had the Noise. Daisy had the Glare. Seemed about right. "Oh yeah," I said, reaching for my keys. "She *sure* did."

32

LILY

We went into full *Powers of Suggestion* production mode. We drove around town, drinking sweet tea and getting what Gabe called transition shots, which, he explained, he would then send to his production editors to put in between the various segments. Determined to make Savannah shine like the gem that she was, I picked out her prettiest places—the tree-branch arches of Oak Avenue at Wormsloe, the orderly gardens at the Owens-Thomas House, the row houses of East Bryan Street with their pastel shutters. I took him to the offices of the Historical Society in Hodgson Hall, where we dug up photos of infamous haunted houses from their glory days, and then we got footage of each house in the here and now: the long-abandoned 12 West Oglethorpe with its Greek columns and its rumors of a man who leans on the building scaring the bejesus out of tourists; the Willink House on East Saint Julian, where neighbors say they hear the doors slamming at all hours; 432 Abercorn, which was dark somehow, even in the middle of the day. And it would have all been just perfect. Except for one thing, which bothered me like a price tag stuck to the bottom of my shoe.

Throughout our morning, his phone kept on buzzing constantly, either in his pocket or on the dash. It was a little reminder, each time, not only of how different our realities really were, but also that the outside world was trying to break into this little bit of heaven we were living inside. And I wondered how, in the midst of all those endless notifications, *my* little messages would ever be able to get through.

But I squashed worries as best I could and took him to get chicken salad from Back in the Day Bakery and ice cream from Leopold's. Then we headed out to Battlefield Park, where he set up his drone—no bigger than a liquor box—and taught me how to fly it while we sat in the shade under the big magnolias. Using the joystick to make it zoom around town brought back that pure joy of driving the pink radio-controlled Mustang around our yard when my sister and I were kids. Sitting together on the grass, I gave him a bird's-eye tour of the house where I grew up, the movie theater where I'd gotten my first kiss, and the parking lot where my sister had taught me to parallel park. Once we flew the drone back to us, we got snow cones and lay together in the grass. I looked up into the leaves with my head on his stomach. Heaven.

He said, "It was good to see all your important places. First kiss and all."

I turned to face him with a spoonful of strawberry ice almost to my mouth. "For the record, I'd like to see where *you* got your first kiss."

He chipped off a spoonful from his cone and glanced up into the trees. "I think the first kiss was in Texas. But it might've been Delaware."

"Broken hearts in every zip code, I'm sure," I teased. I rolled over onto my stomach in the grass so I could see him better and propped myself up on my elbows. "What about your parents? Where are they?"

His smile got so wide that his beautiful eyes were surrounded by lines of happiness. "They retired to a little town called Jasper, Arkansas, right on the border with Missouri. One of the prettiest places you've ever seen. I bought a cabin down there for when I visit. It's not Savannah, but it's my kind of paradise."

I was no geography ninja, but I had a pretty good idea where that might be. "So that explains your vote for the Ozark Howler? Finding a way for me to meet the parents?" Even though I was a little sassy when I said it, it made my heart sort of melt.

"You're onto me. But not just them, actually. My brother and his wife live there too. And so do these little treasures." Gabe grabbed his phone from the grass, opened it up, and went to his photos. He used the map view at first, and the whole globe seemed to be littered with tiny thumbnails. He zoomed in on the southeastern US and brought up one of him with two little girls in an enormous pile of leaves. The girl on the left was maybe two or three—chubby, towheaded, and rosy cheeked. "That's Lacy," he said, beaming with pride. "And that"—he pointed to the other girl, who was lanky and dark headed, and she had his hair and that same wonderful smile—"is Gabriela," he said, smiling even harder. I knew that feeling. I felt just the same with Ivan. Like my heart was about to burst. "They named her after me. Isn't that awesome? She's so smart. It's magic to watch her grow up. The last time I was there, she and I put the constellations on the ceiling of her room with those little glow-in-the-dark stars. You know the ones?"

Know them? "My mom is still peeling them off the walls of my room. And I'm thirty-five."

Gabe let out a wonderful laugh. "Gabby is a lot like you. Thoughtful, kind, and always thinking. Fantastic sense of humor." His eyes darted up from his phone, and he stopped himself. I knew that hesitation—I often had to stop myself from going on and on and on and on about Ivan. But the pride in Gabe's expression made me think not so much of him as an uncle, but of what he'd be like . . . as a dad. He'd be a natural. And the idea made me feel tingly in a way that made me very glad I'd kept a thought *inside* my head for once.

He put his phone aside and gently swept my hair from my cheek. The wind rustled the trees above us, making a cool breeze cut through the midday heat. Gabe seemed just as oblivious as I was to the other people in the park. I knew they were there, with their Frisbees and their dogs, but they seemed so far away. He tucked my hair behind my ear and finally said, "I like being with you, beautiful. A lot. When I'm with you . . ." He shook his head. "I don't know. It's crazy. It's like things make sense in a way they didn't before. Like maybe you're what I've been working toward and I didn't even know it."

I had looked for so long for someone who made me feel like he did, that wild and intense passion that overcame logic and common sense. I had never wanted some ordinary romance—what woman did? I had always wanted to be swept off my feet. And maybe that's why now I really did feel as though I was falling, falling, falling.

I balanced my chin on my palm and, with the other hand, dug my fingers into the place where the grass met the soil, as if to ground myself a little. "What I said to you yesterday, in your truck, I still mean it. I don't want to say goodbye to you either." I tugged on a blade of grass and pulled it out at the root, smoothing the dark-green leaves between my fingers as I plucked up my courage. "But surely you can't stay in North America . . . forever."

Oh jeez. *Forever.* I'd just said *forever.* Strong work, Lily. Way to take it one step at a time.

But Gabe didn't seem shocked at all. He blinked slowly and nodded again. "That is true. That will be a thing we'll need to deal with. For now, for the rest of this filming season, I can stay in the States. I *want* to stay in the States."

I felt my cheeks begin to redden. I wasn't used to this sort of thing *at all*—this take-charge, anything-for-me attitude. It was almost over-whelming. Who was I kidding? It was *totally* overwhelming. "You really, really don't need to do all for this for me."

"But I want to, Lily. For the first time, I have someone other than me to worry about. And I need that. I like my life, but I like it better when I think of you in it."

I tied my little blade of grass into a knot. "So do I."

"This . . . ," he said, caressing my cheek a bit more firmly, ". . . matters. We're just starting. I want us to be solid for whatever comes in the future. Leaving so soon would be like . . ."

I knew exactly what it was like, because I felt that way too. But until that moment, I hadn't quite pinned down the feeling. Now I finally had it. "Like poking dough before it's risen."

"Right." His eyes twinkled in the dappled sunshine. "So what do you say?"

Deep down, a part of me did worry that this was just a North American monsters–themed Band-Aid on a much bigger issue. I felt as though there was a bridge up ahead, and I had no idea how to cross it. He lived in Hollywood. I lived in Savannah. But he was willing to upend his plans for me, and the very least I could do was meet him halfway, with open arms and an open heart. And so I scooched closer to him, took his beautiful face in my hands, and whispered, "I say, Ozarks, here we come."

33

GABE

After a fantastic make-out session in the grass—her, me, the Ozarks, *hell yeah!*—we arrived downtown just in time for the VIP private ghost tour. It began at the edge of Colonial Park Cemetery, on the corner of Oglethorpe and Habersham. The tour guide was a big brute of a guy who could've been a stunt double for Mr. Clean, right down to the thick ridges of skin on the back of his bald head. I watched him dig around in his shirt pocket. From there he produced a pair of horn-rimmed Harry Potter bifocals and studiously checked some handwritten notes in a leather-bound journal. If there was one thing I'd learned in this business, it was to expect the unexpected.

I'd also learned to be careful with experts—they tended to get proprietary about being filmed. Of course, Markowitz always left the explaining to me. He said I had the showbiz face; I said he was the king of the semi-wuss move. But before I'd even begun to explain the situation to her, Lily walked right up to the guide, shook his hand, and explained who we were. If it had been me, I would have expected there to be a whole bunch of discussion about rights, credits, and even compensation. Might've even been a total nonstarter. But for her, he couldn't get the microphone on his shirt fast enough. She thanked him, shaking his hand with both of hers, and came back to me beaming.

"I like a woman who takes charge."

She gave me a wink. "Oh, I know you do."

Fuck. I pulled the two high-res GoPros from my bag, one for each of us, and we were off. As she watched through the viewfinder, smiling, laughing at the tour guide's legitimately awful punny jokes, she wrinkled up her nose and pinned her tongue between her teeth.

I could watch her do that forever.

Right as the walking tour advanced down another block toward Chippewa Square, my phone buzzed in my pocket. I checked to verify what I knew already. Markowitz. Just as I was about to power it off, Lily glanced at my phone and whispered, "Go ahead! I've got this!"

I nodded at her and fell back a ways. I watched her hips sway as she rounded a corner with the rest of the tour, and I answered the call. "Hey, man. Make it quick. I'm in the middle of something."

The elliptical whooshed in the background. "Just calling to see if I should change the Brazil ticket. Tell me you're both going, Powers. Throw me a bone!"

Aww, shit. Markowitz wasn't going to like this fear-of-flying thing one bit. "Change of plans. Brazil is out. We're doing the Ozark Howler next."

I heard his pace on the elliptical slow by at least half, which only ever happened when some serious shit was going down. "Hang on. You're going to pass up drinking caipirinhas in Rio and using machetes in the Amazon for . . . the Ozarks?"

The guy knew all my weak spots—I did love a decent drink and a chance to play Eagle Scout in the rain forest. It wasn't going to happen, though. It was a bummer, but I wasn't going to push her. We'd make the best of it. "You heard me. She's got a problem with flying."

Markowitz made a sort of strangled croak. "Well, that's going to *seriously* jam up the jimmer, Powers. A cohost . . . that can't fly? What are we gonna do? Skype her into the Congo? FaceTime her into the tundra? I don't want to be an asshole about this," he said, which was, as I knew full well, his announcement that he was about to be an asshole, "but are you thinking with . . . your head or your *head*?"

How about I come cut the bungee cords on your elliptical desk? "After we're done here, it's the Ozarks. Period."

"So that means the *taniwha* in New Zealand . . ."

Goddamn. I'd never get to see our footprints in the sand around the Moeraki Boulders. "Out."

"Thunderbirds in Alaska?"

Nor would I ever get to see our snowshoe tracks under the northern lights. "Out."

"Powers. Think about this. The next few months were going to be huge for you. Ha-uge!"

He was right; this filming season was when we'd expected to really put my career over the top. But that was the thing about expectations; they weren't always what you'd planned. I'd assumed my life was headed one way, but as my dad always told me, "*assume* makes an *ass* out of *u* and *me*." I certainly hadn't expected to meet Lily here, but I had. And there was no changing that. It wasn't like me to pull the *star of the show* card, but Markowitz needed to understand that this was non-negotiable. No matter how much I wished I could take her far away or scoop her up into my life without changing a thing, some shit was gonna have to change. Starting now. "Ozarks next. Got it?"

"All right," Markowitz said, blowing out a long breath with his lips flapping, like an exhausted horse. "You're the star."

We said our goodbyes, and I ended the call. I had to admit, there was part of me that was pretty bummed about not being able to go to all those spots with her. I loved my job, and I loved the places that it took me. But I also loved her.

Holy fuck.

There it was. The word. *Love.* When I was with her, nothing else mattered. When I wasn't, there was only one place I wanted to be. Since the minute I'd met her, she'd been the only thing on my mind. I wanted her, I adored her . . . and I loved her. And I needed her to know it.

The universe had done me a solid. I realized that right in front of me was the storefront of an antique jewelry shop. Rows of old-fashioned rings lined red velvet displays. Hatpins stuck out from a crystal glass filled with rice. At the bottom of the display was a row of lockets. Right in the middle, on its own velvet platform, was a gold locket with an enameled lily in the middle.

I knew the tour was moving on without me, but there was no way I was going to let anybody scoop me on that locket that I could already imagine hanging from her neck. So I pocketed my phone and stepped inside the jewelry shop. "I'd like to see that locket." I glanced at the window. "The one with the lily on it."

"Oh, very good choice, sir," said the shopkeeper. She slipped out from behind the register with her silver bracelets jangling. "I have it on good authority that this belonged to one of our most famous residents." She leaned over the velvet display and gently picked up the locket by its delicate chain. "Her name was Lucinda Abrahams. They say she still haunts these parts, embroidering hearts on handkerchiefs and searching for her lover, George."

The locket was delicate and beautifully made. I pressed on the mechanism, and it popped open in my hand. Inside below the jeweler's marks, there was a small engraving, clearly visible. I blinked at it as I ran my thumb over the old letters.

To L from G

Me falling in love with a hometown girl who was terrified of flying hadn't been in my five-year plan. But that didn't mean I wasn't going to jump in headfirst and backward, like a scuba diver in full gear.

34

LILY

"We'll be visiting the fourth floor, which is usually closed to visitors," said the tour guide as he led us up the curving double staircase of the Davenport House. The old white wooden door creaked as he opened it. "Please make sure you leave everything as you found it. No leaping out of closets at me either." The tour group let out a unified chuckle. "Big guys like me scare *really* bad."

I fell back from the group and looked up and down State Street for Gabe, but I didn't see him. I sent him a quick text to tell him where we were and then followed the tour group inside the majestic, spectacular old foyer. I'd been to a wedding at the Davenport once, and I'd also taken my sister there for high tea when she was the throes of her Boris fury. She always said that cucumber sandwiches and Earl Grey in the Davenport garden had helped her get back on her feet. But for all the memories I had of the house, I had never had the chance to go up to the fourth floor, where—rumor had it—the *real* ghosts were.

Whatever that means, Lily. Real ghosts. Pffft.

The members of the tour followed the guide up the curving, elegant stairs, every piece of wood carefully joined and polished. The treads creaked as everybody headed up the steps, and their whispers got quieter as they got to the second floor. Again, I hung back to get some shots of the empty foyer with its black-and-white floor tiles, inset with a circle that reminded me of a compass. Still no Gabe.

Following the tour upstairs, I heard the tour guide explain that we were free to explore as we wanted. "Even though it's daytime, there is still a chance you will feel a presence or a specter. Sometimes things happen when we least expect them, but never when we don't believe they will."

Most of the tour group ambled off toward the rooms on the left side of the hallway, but I found myself drawn to the rooms on the right, where the light was dimmer and the rooms slightly less welcoming—more frowsy, crowded, and dark. After wandering through two larger bedrooms, I found myself in an elegant and tidy bedroom with a single bed in the middle. It had a handmade quilt and yellowed lace curtains that filtered out most of the light from the dormer window. A doll sat on the bed, leaning up against the pillow. As I knew full well from my sister's efforts to furnish the museum accurately, antebellum dolls were a *really* long way from friendly and chubby-cheeked Cabbage Patch Kids. They were, in a word, *spooooooooky*. This one—with her porcelain face and black dress, her tattered shoes and stained cotton legs—was no exception. I went tight on her oddly adult features and her too-wide painted eyes, one of which had been rubbed off almost completely.

Maybe it was the doll giving me the heebie-jeebies, but something in the room gave me a shiver. "There is a sort of strange feeling here," I said to the camera as I filmed. "I'm not sure what it is, but it feels a bit odd." Turning away from the bed, I made my way through the bedroom, between the bed and the window, and I could have sworn I heard something behind me. When I spun around, though, I found I was still alone.

But something was different than when I walked in. The closet door, on the far end of room, was now slightly ajar. It had been closed tight when I walked in. I was *sure* of it.

Oh *no*. "That wasn't open when I walked in here." I swallowed hard and tried to get my heart to slow down. My breath got caught in my throat, and my fingertips went cold. "That definitely wasn't open a second ago."

I turned the camera to the bedroom door, hoping that Gabe would walk through. Or one of the other tour members. But nobody appeared.

I was all on my own for this one.

For the sake of the show and, more importantly, for Gabe, I swallowed my worry. Forcing one foot in front of the other, I approached the closet. "Let's see if we can find anything." I gripped the camera in one hand and, summoning every ounce of courage I had, reached out to open the door. Just as I touched the edge of it, a hand shot out and grabbed my wrist. I was so astonished, so terrified, that I couldn't even get a peep out of my mouth. In an instant, another hand shot out of the closet, a big, brawny forearm attached to an equally brawny biceps. Before I knew it, I was in the darkened closet in Gabe's strong arms. "Boo," he said into my ear, laughing softly.

"Meanie!" I whispered with a shove, unable to suppress my terrified and relieved breathy laughter. He pretended like I was a whole lot stronger than I was and staggered back, making the wooden hangers clatter behind him.

He pulled me close, and I let my purse slide from my shoulder. His hands moved down my body, gripping my tush tight. "Got you a present."

A thin strip of light spilled into the closet from underneath the bottom of the door. It was enough for me to see his beautiful smile. "If it's another picnic basket, I think we should probably go ahead and get married."

Oh, Lily. Inside thoughts. Inside thoughts!

But Gabe didn't seem the least bit shocked that I'd just said the *M*-word. He snickered into my ear, scooping me up into his arms as I hooked my legs around him. He walked us across the closet and pressed me up against the wall. He came in for a kiss, and I got lost in him all over again. Until I heard the sound of the tour entering the room where I'd just been standing.

I pulled away from the kiss and looked into his eyes. The floorboards outside squeaked under the feet of the tourists. I heard the beeps and shutter sound effects of phones and digital cameras.

"Now," said the tour guide, "I want everybody to try to get in touch with the feeling here. Really consider how you feel in this room, at this moment. Maybe you feel cold or warm or nervous or calm. Try to get in touch with that feeling if you would."

Gabe smiled down at me. Every time I looked at him, my heart melted a little more. The feeling he gave me, though, it wasn't just melty surrender. It was steadier than that, both more lasting and more peaceful. With my fingertips, I traced over the edges of his cheekbone, and he closed his eyes, pressing his cheek into my hand.

There were rustles and sniffles from the group outside the closet door. "It will be a feeling unlike anything you've ever felt before. Something new, something strange. Something wonderful." The guide paused and then asked, "Do you feel it?"

Gabe nodded against my palm. "I feel it."

I held him close. I squeezed him tight. And I whispered into his ear, "I do too."

35

GABE

All day I'd been trying to find the right time to give her the locket and tell her I was falling in love with her. But we'd been hustling and no time had felt quite right. Until now. It was a quarter to eight, and Lily and I were waiting at the rendezvous point that General Lee had sent by text. Of course, he didn't text like a normal guy. Instead, he sent me a message that might as well have been off a strip of telegraph tape: DEAR SIR/STOP/AWAIT ARRIVAL AT CHATHAM LAKE AT 20:00/STOP/ SNCRLY GEN. LEE

So there we were at Chatham Lake, which was overhung with mossy willows and littered with lily pads in bloom. All around us was thick Georgia forest. Lily grabbed a handful of stones from where the water lapped at the edge of the lake. I took the small jewelry box from my pocket and put it beside me, just out of her view. She came back and sat next to me. From her handful of stones she chose one that was round, smooth, and symmetrical. She glanced at me, smiled, and then skipped it across the water. It had three, four, five bounces before it slipped under the surface. Then she handed me an equally round and smooth stone and lifted her eyebrows. "Let me see what you've got."

I followed her lead. I'd never actually skipped a stone before, but it couldn't be that hard, I figured. I mimicked her throw, but mine sank immediately, and she tossed her head back, laughing softly. "Here." She chose another stone, positioned it in my hand, and parted my fingers. "Think of it like a Frisbee." She picked a rock for herself and in one smooth and graceful movement sent it skipping six times across the glassy surface of the water.

I tried again and had the same result as before. Plop. Sank like a stone, literally. She got up from her crouch and brushed some grass off her white shorts, giving me a powerful throb of desire. But I stayed the course. This wasn't the time for down and dirty—that would be for later. Now it was time to get serious. I took the jewelry box and placed it where she'd been sitting. When she turned back to me, her eyes lit up, sparkling in the setting sun. She lowered herself down onto her knees, and I placed it in her hands.

Very carefully, tugging at the satin with thumb and forefinger, she undid the ribbon. She slipped the lid off, glancing up at me and smiling a little. But she froze when she saw the black velvet box inside. It was exactly like a ring box, and I knew what she was thinking because I had been thinking the same goddamned thing all day. I studied her every expression, her every move. She slipped the velvet box out and placed it on her knee, holding the edges between two fingers. On her face was a kind of pure, honest surprise. Innocence. Maybe even uncertainty. "Gabe . . ."

"Open it up," I told her.

She flipped the top open. As she did, I saw something that made my heart fucking burst—disappointment. There was no question in my mind that she was disappointed that it wasn't a ring. Holy *shit*. That microexpression, that tiny tell, gave me more courage than anything ever could have.

Her disappointment vanished and was replaced with that same delight she'd had when she'd opened the picnic basket I'd put together for her. "Oh, Gabe." She slipped the locket out of the box, the chain dangling from her fingers. I took it from her and undid the clasp. She scooted around so her back was to me, scooped up her hair in her hand, and took off her microphone charm necklace. I fastened the tiny clasp at the back of her delicate neck, letting my fingers brush past the ringlet curls at her hairline. "There," I said, and her hand went to the locket on her chest.

"Isn't it *beautiful*." She carefully ran her fingertips over the lily and the vines that surrounded it. "I love it so much. I'll wear it always."

"Look at the engraving," I told her, reaching out to open it up for it. It butterflied apart, and she drew it back from her chest, crumpling her chin to read it.

Her mouth dropped open, and she traced the hand-carved letters with her fingertip. "This is *old*! But with our initials!"

"I know." I straightened out the chain. "The lady at the jewelry store said it might've belonged to a lady named Lucinda, who got it from her lover George."

She smiled so hard that I felt it right down in my bones. "I like Lucinda and George. But Lily and Gabe sounds much better." She looked back down at the locket, with her cheeks bright and flushed. It was absolutely beautiful on her, like it was made for her.

"But wait! I have something for you too." She grabbed her purse. "I got this when we went home to feed the General. When your back was turned," she said, smiling mischievously as she unzipped the inside pocket. "Close your eyes."

I pretended to close them but still kept her in view between my eyelashes. But she had me all figured out and clicked her tongue against the roof of her mouth. "All the way."

"Fine. But you don't make it easy." I squeezed them shut. I held out my hand and waited.

"So . . . ," she said. I heard her scoot closer toward me on the grass—Christ, that sexy sound of her thighs sliding together. "It's not fancy, but now whenever you come here, you'll have somewhere to stay."

In my palm, I felt something small and metallic. I opened my eyes and saw it was a key. A house key. *Her* house key.

"Lily," I said, gripping it hard in my palm. The wave of emotion that came up through my chest spilled into my voice.

"Well, don't get excited," she said, almost as if she were embarrassed. "It only cost me seventy cents, and I already had it in the drawer."

She could be nonchalant all she wanted, but the look in her eyes told me that this meant just as much to her as it meant to me. I tucked the key into my pocket and took her beautiful face in my hands. *Now or never, Powers. Do it. Tell her how you feel. Don't waste one more second.*

I took her hand in mine. I opened my mouth.

And the noise of a bugle cut the air, followed by the *boom-boom-boom* of cannon fire.

The rebel army had arrived. And I thought Markowitz had shitty timing.

36

LILY

The whole day had been a bit surreal and dreamy, and it was getting more surreal by the minute, because now Gabe and I seemed to be walking back in time. As a Savannahian, I was no stranger to men in homemade rebel uniforms. But as Gabe and I walked into camp, both of us with backpacks full of equipment, I realized that these weren't the ordinary, garden-variety actors who wandered around Forsyth Square with their plastic muskets and spray-painted gold buttons. These weren't the guys who traipsed into the Living History Museum, tipping their hats to us as they drank their caramel macchiatos. These weren't the guys who filled up the strip mall urgent care with toe injuries from dropped replica cannon balls. These guys were *the real deal*, from their battered uniforms to their waxed cotton tents, right down to their homemade boots and their gunpowder-blackened hands.

Except up ahead of us stood a woman who was decidedly not part of our time traveling back to the 1860s. She was a strikingly statuesque lady, wearing *lots* of flowing, elegant linen. As we got closer, I saw she had fabulously oversize earrings and a chic close-cropped white haircut. Around her neck was what looked at first like an antique amulet but was—on closer inspection—a stylized Ghostbusters insignia, made of brass, coral, and mother of pearl. She had this *way* about her. This sort of glorious postmenopausal *I've got this handled* attitude. May we all be so lucky.

She reached out her hand to me. "Elaine Corynn," she said, giving me a warm and welcoming smile. I recognized her immediately from Daisy's ghost shows. This lady was definitely somebody in the ghost world. She shook my hand, but she didn't let it go, and as she held it she looked from me to Gabe and back to me again. "Well, aren't you two a lovely couple. Better stand back, though, when we get down to business. The love waves are coming off you like signals from Sputnik."

I glanced up at Gabe, and he smiled at me. *Love waves!* Automatically my hand went to my new locket. "Don't worry. We know. I can go wait in the van."

But Elaine wasn't having it. She shook her head, pursing her lips and studying us. "Nope. Both of you are going to need to clear the area. I've got a job to do, kids, and I'm not going to muck through your lovestruck auras to do it."

Then from out of the dusky darkness emerged a face from another time. Thanks to my sister's insistence on watching literally *every* Civil War documentary ever made, I recognized him right away.

"General Robert E. Lee," he said as he tipped his hat at me. "Pleasure."

Whoa, *Nelly*. No wonder he had a dedicated email. It was *uncanny!* "Oh my God," I gasped, peering at him in the dim light. "That's amazing!"

General Lee gave me a wink.

Under his arm, I noticed a book that was about the same size as my grandma's large-print Bible. On closer inspection, I saw it was Ron Chernow's biography on Grant. The last time I'd checked, I was twentieth on the wait list for it at the library.

I tapped on the spine. "Is that why we're here? Making contact with You-Know-Who?"

General Lee scoffed. Or maybe that was a *guffaw*. "Good God, no. I know all I need to know about my old enemy. I must say, Chernow has a very accurate, thorough, and interdisciplinary historical approach," General Lee said thoughtfully. "My friend Grant was a truly complex man. I admire his struggles, both personal and professional. Shows a mighty fine level of character. How I do envy his horsemanship." He looked somewhat glumly at the portrait on the cover. He sighed and tucked it back under his arm. "Pardon me, my friends. I'm going to have a brief consult with my lieutenants about our battle plan for this evening. I bid you a fond adieu," he said with a slight bow.

And he ambled off with his saber rattling.

I turned to Elaine. "I mean . . ."

She snorted. "His real name is Jerry Slattery, and he sells real estate."

Gabe sniffed next to me, scratching his forehead. "So what exactly are we doing here?" he asked.

"As I understand it," she said, adjusting her earrings, "these guys are historically accurate down to how much coffee they put in their pan over the camp stove. But there is one important thing that nobody in this strange business of theirs really knows. It's called the Rebel Yell."

Thanks to Daisy, I had developed a knack for willfully forgetting historical trivia; the sheer volume that she berated me with meant I *had* to pick and choose. But this, at least, I knew I didn't know. Because nobody did. "It's a mystery, isn't it? Nobody *really* knows what it sounds like?"

She lifted an expertly pencil-shaded eyebrow at me. "Correct. There's a few short clips of it from some Civil War veterans' picnic when film was new and the veterans were old, but it's not enough to really hear it. These guys are telling me that when they come out here, to this battlefield, they *have* heard it." Elaine dropped her shoulders and lifted her chin, as if she were moving into a yoga pose. "We're here to try to see if we can make contact to hear the sound. You all are here to record it."

"Fantastic," Gabe said, smiling. He let his backpack slide to the ground and pulled out his low-light camera. "We'll get some shots around the camp. We'll set up the audio and visual. Then where do you want us?"

Elaine looked at the two of us, spinning her wedding ring on her finger. "As far away from me as possible, lovebirds," she said and twirled away, linen flapping.

As far away as possible put Gabe and me between the parking area and the so-called provisions tent, which I'd found to be stocked with enough danishes, sweet tea, coffee, and doughnuts to feed, literally, an army. Elaine, as the medium, was sitting on the other side of camp in the captain's tent, and we'd set up cameras to film her séance from every angle. Not even once had Gabe grumbled that our *love waves* had exiled us to the edge of camp, and now we sat together on a cooler behind the provisions tent in the cool summer darkness, listening to the drills and the shouted commands. A patch of light streamed out from a lantern inside the infirmary tent, and inside I watched a lady dressed up as a battlefield nurse wipe a glop of jelly off her crisp white apron.

Gunfire punctured the sound of the willows blowing in the breeze, and shouts and calls of *Fall in line* and *Hep-two-three-four* cut through the air.

"We're one violin solo away from being inside a Ken Burns documentary," I whispered.

Gabe snickered beside me. He leaned into me and put a kiss to my cheek.

I slipped my hand underneath his and gave it a squeeze. "OK. So forgive me for being such a noob, but if we don't know what it sounds like . . ." I trailed off, looking at Gabe.

He answered me with a knowing expression. "Then how the hell are we going to know it when we hear it?"

I nodded. "Ding-ding-ding!"

"Exactly what I was thinking." Gabe slipped his phone from his pocket, and I glanced around to make sure we were in the clear. Nobody had specifically told us phones weren't allowed, but getting the Glare from Daisy had taught me a thing or two about behaving appropriately in a rigorously accurate historical setting. Cell phones were tied with corn syrup on the list of no-no's.

Gabe boldly held his phone out in front of the two of us. *I like a man who knows how to take risks!* "Let's see what we can find." He pulled his earbuds from his bag and plugged them in. He gave me one to put in my ear, and he did the same with his. I watched him type "rebel yell" into his browser, and up popped the usual array of stuff that I'd expect with any vaguely historical internet search. Lord knew I was no stranger to those. Only the week before Daisy had tasked me with finding out "How did they get rid of ants in the 1800s?" Answer: they didn't.

On the screen was the usual array of hits—Wikipedia, history.com. But the third link was something from the Smithsonian that looked *very* interesting.

"Very promising." I tapped the edge of the screen.

Gabe clicked on the link, and up came an article explaining what the Rebel Yell was and what it sounded like, but none of the descriptions were particularly helpful. Colorful, yes! Helpful, no. "'The battle cry to rally the troops before a fight, the Rebel Yell is believed to be influenced by the war cry traditions of Native American and Scottish warriors. It is sometimes described as a cross between a rabbit's scream and a whoop, or wolf's howl and a cougar's scream.'"

It sounded just dreadful. Rabbits screaming? I felt like Clarice Starling trying to forget the sound of the crying lambs. *Pass!* "What does that even *mean*?"

"I've heard the wolf and the cougar, but the rabbit is beyond me. Look at this." Gabe highlighted a sentence to draw my attention to it. He read aloud, "'There are no audio recordings of the yell from the Civil War period. Archivists have, however, recently unearthed audio clips from the 1930s of veterans performing the yell at a Civil War reunion.'"

There, embedded in the middle, was a video from the Library of Congress. It had to be what Elaine mentioned earlier. The thumbnail was black-and-white and showed a positively ancient man in a uniform that was identical to the ones that the troops in the encampment wore. Gabe hit play on a very, very old digitized film. One Civil War veteran acted as a sort of impromptu emcee, standing in front of a microphone and introducing various other veterans, who each gave the Rebel Yell a try. The first one was hardly more than a single hoot—it was over in an instant. The second one was a little longer but certainly wasn't enough to get a sense of what the sound really was. It was clear to me that the old veterans, and their old lungs, weren't strong enough to sustain much of anything, and so in each case the yell was barely a second or two before they ran out of air.

Onto the stage hobbled a slightly more spry old fellow, thin and gangly. He stood in front of the microphone and gave it his best. This time it wasn't a matter of mere seconds. It was just enough to make me realize I had heard that sound before. *"Gabe!"* I gasped.

Gabe turned to me. "Holy shit. Is that . . . Lily, that's . . ."

All those years of bellowing about Vicksburg, all those shushes and bribes, all those endless fibs about the Union in surrender. It all made sense. It *all finally* made sense. *Hallelujah!* I clapped my hands on Gabe's shoulders and gave him a shake. "That's *the Noise*! The General's Noise!"

37

GABE

Whatever progress the General and I had made the night before was totally undone by the fact that he was now convinced I was trying to kidnap him. "Unhand me, swarthy villain!" he screamed as I loaded his cage into the back of Lily's van. The bars rattled, and the bottom banged. "Help! Police! Nine-one-one! Nine-one-one!" he said in a completely different voice followed by an eerily accurate *whoop-whoop* like a cop car making a traffic stop and the piercing *eee-ooo-eee-ooo* of an ambulance.

I hopped in the back of the van with the cage. A porch light from across the street popped on, and I heard the sound of a screen door squeaking open. "Everything all right, Lily?" someone called through the dark. "What's all that ruckus?"

"Everything's fine, Mrs. Weatherly!" Lily cooed. "Just doing some historical reenactment! Carry on! Nothing to see here!" she said and slammed the van doors.

Lily got into the driver's seat, muttering, "I'm going to have to make her some brownies so she doesn't call the ASPCA," and fired up the van. I turned on the dome light above me as she put the van in reverse and then peeled out down the street. The General's eyes were wide open, like stick-on googly eyes from a craft store, each with a clean white rim around them. "Bad suitor!" he screamed. "Bad suuuuuuuuuitooooooooor!"

"Have a potato." I grabbed the baggie that Lily had put together before we pulled the sheet off his cage and carried it downstairs. I broke off a piece and tried to feed it to him through the bars.

He recoiled from the potato, flapping his wings. "Live free or die, sir!" he screamed. "I say, live free or die!"

He locked on to the door of his cage, giving it a firm rattle with his beak. Lily had used two twisty ties to secure it for the drive, but I wasn't sure how long those were going to hold. He was putting together sentences, doing voices, and copying sirens. Two sandwich bag ties weren't going to make shit for difference. Reflected back at me in the rearview mirror, I saw Lily's panicked face. Time to get serious about this, I realized. Time to bring out the big guns. Abandoning the bag of potato slices, I pulled out my phone, made it so the camera was in the right direction, and started filming him.

The panic gave way to wide-eyed adoration as he stared at himself. "Hellooooo," he said.

"Is he OK?" Lily screeched to a stop and turned around to see what I was doing. "Why is he so quiet? Please don't tell me we've killed him."

I held up a finger to quiet her, and her mouth dropped open when she saw what we were doing. "I learned this last night," I whispered. "He loves it."

"Oh my God, that's brilliant," Lily said, marveling at him and at me. She placed her palm to her mouth and let out a muffled laugh. "You're a genius!" she whispered.

"Genius!" the General said to his reflection, with what looked a whole lot like a smile. "Hello, genius!"

Ten minutes and sixteen videos later, we arrived at the parking lot. Lily pulled into a spot and hopped out. I grabbed the front end of the cage, and Lily took the back. Together, we carried him through the camp like we were carrying an emperor in a sedan chair. As we walked, he made a low and ongoing "Aaaaah!" like kids do when they go over a washboard road. We carried the General to the captain's tent, and I stuck my head inside. Elaine Corynn was flipping over tarot cards, seeming somewhat peeved. General Lee sat across from her with his hands clasped in prayer over the Grant biography. One of Lee's lieutenants was eating a chocolate doughnut, reading a magazine with his feet up on the table. The whole thing had a low-budget carnival palmistry-tent feel. Not good television. At all.

But I knew how to fix that. In my head I heard one of Markowitz's Idea Farts from long ago. *Know what makes really good television, Powers? Talking animals!*

I cleared my throat. "Sorry, I don't want to interrupt, but I think we have someone you might want to meet."

Elaine paused with a card halfway off the table. I couldn't tell if she was relieved that I'd interrupted or annoyed. It made no difference to me at all. Lily and I knew the answer to the mystery, and we were damned well going to share it.

General Lee stood up from the captain's table and pushed past me into the clearing with his sword jangling. "A parrot. We don't need a goddamned parrot, son!"

Meanwhile, the General looked around at the men in gray uniforms who'd gathered around his cage. He puffed up his feathers like he did when he was on camera. The happy puff. "Hello." He hopped around in a circle, making an effort to greet everybody. "Hello, how do you do? Hello!"

As the crowd of men grew larger, Lily came closer to me and gave me a little elbow in the ribs. She held one of the GoPros in her hands, and I could tell from the red light that it was already rolling. "OK," she whispered. "Get him to do it."

I approached the cage and bent down so I was at eye level with him. The General turned away. "Villain," he snarled.

"Make the Noise, man," I told him. "This is your big moment. Go for it."

The General eyed me again and turned away. "Swarthy Yankee," he hissed.

I glanced at Lily. I think she probably *thought* she was smiling, but I saw on her face a painfully uncomfortable grimace as she glanced around at the quickly growing group of grumbling soldiers around us.

It was time to up the ante. I needed the General to make the Noise, and I knew exactly how to do it. But that said, I also thought it was *probably* better if Lily wasn't within earshot. This wasn't exactly *the moment* I'd been waiting for all day, that was for goddamned sure. "Give us some space, will you?" I asked her.

She wrinkled up her eyebrows and cocked her head at me in confusion. But instead of asking me what and why, she just nodded and stepped back slightly. As she did, the rest of the circle did the same. Like they were widening the ring for a bare-knuckle brawl. I leaned in close to the cage. The bird let out his angry growl, and I flicked my chin at him to egg him on. But he stopped short and turned his face away from me yet again.

So I cleared my throat, placed my hands on my quads, and got right up close to him, damn near nose to beak. "Who do you love?"

"Lily," he croaked angrily, refusing again to look at me. He snapped his head away, spoiled and snooty. "I love Lily."

When he said it, I saw Lily smile. That meant she was close enough to hear what I was about to say.

Well, fuck it. But there was no better time than *the now*. Even if I had to say it to her parrot first, at least she'd finally know.

"So do I." I glanced over the top of the cage at her. Her, who made my heart hurt. Her, who I wanted to be with so bad it ached. Her, who had begun to change everything for me.

Her eyes sparkled by the firelight. At that moment, it was just us. There was no battalion. There were no cameras. There was nothing else in the world besides Lily and me together.

Well. Except for the General. He puffed up his feathers, and then the growl got a little louder.

"I want her," I told him, and the growl ramped up. "I need her," I said, and the growl changed to a low roar. "And I love her," I said, looking right at her as I did. And that did it. The roar changed into a whoop, and the whoop into a cry, and then the General let loose with the Noise at the top of his tiny but insanely powerful lungs.

In response, the battalion erupted in full-throated *I'll be goddamned* cheers. And Lily mouthed *I love you too.*

Telling her how I felt made me feel possessive about her in a way I hadn't expected to feel. It almost pissed me off that the troops wanted to hear the General do the Yell again and again. History was fine and all, but right then I had a woman to make mine. A woman to undo. A woman who needed to hear I loved her as I made her come again and again.

Finally the General tuckered himself out, hoarse from doing his demo, and we packed up our gear. I drove her van and she sat shotgun, holding my hand the whole way back to her place. We didn't say much of anything as we drove, comfortable together even in silence.

Back at her house, Lily began to pull the cage out of the van, and I reached into my pocket for my truck keys. I could see her face by the dim light of the streetlamp above, and there I saw that flash of disappointment again. But I wouldn't make her feel it for long. "Aren't you coming in?" she asked.

I took a step into her and let my keys drop back into my pocket. Putting one hand on each of her hips, I pulled her into me. The cage rattled behind her as she pressed against it. "I'm not coming in. Because you're coming back to the house with me. Where you belong."

She let out a shuddering groan. Her cleavage compressed against my chest, and I felt that bolt of need through my cock again. That feeling might've been inside me, but it belonged to her. And her alone.

"I love the way you talk to me." She gritted her teeth and tugged on my belt. "Absolutely love it."

I let her feel me hard against her. "We better do something about that. But you're gonna make too much noise to stay here." I dragged my tongue up the side of her neck and over the curve of her ear. "You'll wake up half the block with what I've got planned."

She hooked her fingers around my belt loops and pulled me into her even closer. "What is it that you've got planned, Mr. Powers?" She ran her fingertips up the back of my neck and through my hair. She got up on her tiptoes and teased me, tempted me, taunted me.

But no amount of her sexiness was going to distract me. I knew what I wanted, and I was damn well going to get it. "We'll get him set, then I'm driving you back home."

"Home?" she said, exaggerating the bow of her lower back to press her body into mine.

"Yeah. Home." I slid my hand down her bare ass, under her shorts and panties. Then I leaned into her. "But I need you to get one thing from here first."

"Name it," she whispered.

"Your vibrator."

She was so close that I felt her smile more than I saw it. "Which one?"

That's my girl. "All of them."

38

LILY

He led me up the back staircase of the Willows, guiding me by the small of my back. The house was dark but for the moonlight. As he followed me, I felt all that masculine energy radiating off him, all that pent-up fury, ready to be unleashed. When we got to the top of the steps, he pulled me into him and kissed me as we walked backward into the bedroom. He pulled away from the kiss just long enough to yank my shirt off over my head. My hands went for his belt, his fly, his top button, but before I could get his pants off him, he pushed me back onto the bed. "Put your hands on the headboard, and don't you dare move them."

I felt a new fury from him, a new kind of urgency. I might've been full of moxie and spunk, but he turned me to warm goo inside instantly. I could not resist him like this. I couldn't even tease and play. I was his, completely, and he hadn't even touched me yet. I slid my hands up the sheets and took hold of the headboard behind me, with my elbows slightly bent on either side of my head. He stood over me, and I watched him grind his teeth, bite his lip, and growl out, "Fuck."

Tossing his shirt aside, he let his pants and boxers drop. Next came my shorts and my panties, which he tugged off me and threw into the darkness. He bent down over me, his strong arms depressing the mattress, and took one of my nipples in his mouth; he closed his eyes in pure and calm bliss, and I felt both my nipples tighten even though he was only teasing one. Instinctively, I let go of the headboard and tried to touch him, but he pulled away from me, shaking his head. "No touching. I'm running this fucking show."

I swallowed hard and felt my toes curl. "OK," I said, my voice honey thick and my whole body trembling.

Some men played at being an alpha. But not him. For him, it was effortless. Innate. Part of him. The essence of him. He crouched down beside the bed, and I heard him going through my bag. "Dirty girl," he said as he rummaged through all my favorites. In his big, rugged hands he held my sparkly bullets and a pastel-pink dildo. These he spread out on my stomach, and I felt myself get wetter still.

He tested them out on me. A bullet to my nipple made me gasp; the dildo to my clit made me writhe and tremble. One after another he tossed them aside until he landed on my favorite. The universal favorite. The Magic Wand, God bless it. "That's what I'm talking about." He shoved the bedside table away, and its legs squeaked along the floor. He wasn't gentle about anything now, and I heard him rip the lamp cord from the outlet, followed by the noise of him plugging my vibrator in.

"God," I said, up at the ceiling, gripping the hard wood in my palms. The familiar whir filled the air and I gasped, feeling my heartbeat quicken in my chest. He straddled me, pinning my body beneath his as his erection pressed into my leg. I felt the heat of his balls on my skin. As if my hand wasn't attached to my body, I reached out to touch him once again.

"You touch me and I stop," he snarled, leaning down into me and pinching my cheeks so I could see just how serious he was about what he wanted to do to me. "Got it?"

I felt the trickle of my own warmth spilling out of my body onto the sheets. I nodded, looking up at him and digging my fingers back into the carved edges of the headboard. "Yes."

He didn't answer but lowered his eyes back down onto my body. With two fingers, he parted my lips and teased me with the vibrator, using the lightest touch. I was so turned on that it was like an electric current. The pleasure made me drive my hips back, and I arched my neck. The pillow came up on either side of my head, muffling that familiar whir. He pulled it away from me just as quickly as he'd touched me. Using two fingers, he slipped inside me, groaning as he dipped into my wetness. "Christ almighty, Lily," he said, his voice low and greedy.

It was time for me to take some power back from the beast, but power didn't have to snarl. Power could also beg. Topping from the bottom was a very real thing. "Take me, please." I tipped my hips toward him, trying to get him to go for my G-spot. Again he touched the vibrator to my clit. It made me groan, and the room spun as my body responded. But again he took it away, and I let out a low whine.

With his free hand, he stroked himself. He wet his cock with me and rubbed it all over him. The vibrator hovered near me but still didn't touch me. *"Please."* I squirmed a little bit, writhing under his weight and rustling the sheets.

This time, he pressed the vibrator against me hard—hard enough to make it so that my pelvic bone was absorbing the vibrations, hard enough to flatten my clit and dull the sensations for a second. My hand flew out, and I dug my fingers into his thigh as my eyes rolled back in my head.

Instantaneously, the vibrations stopped, and I gasped for air.

He stared at me, hard and serious. "Lily." He pulled my hand off his leg, and I slid it back up to the headboard. And he started the vibrator again. Again and again he teased me. Taking me to the brink, pushing me back. Letting me think he was going to let me come but stopping me every time. He wound me up so tightly that I felt myself starting to get angry that he was denying me the thing I wanted and needed so much. On the next intense press of the vibrator to my clit, I grabbed hold of it, pressing his hand and the vibrator into me. His eyes flashed, that mix of anger and excitement. He tried to pull it off me, but I fought him and felt myself starting to come.

"Fuck that." He yanked it away hard, tossing it aside. The whirring went silent as the cord was pulled from the wall and the vibrator clattered to the floor. He dropped into a push-up over me, pinning my hands over my head, elbows against my cheeks, and we faced off in the moonlight, my chest heaving, my body writhing. I was so *mad* at being denied, so angry at getting so close over and over again, that I almost wanted to push him off me. But before I could show him how annoyed I was, he pressed into me and everything went . . .

. . . black. A noise came from my mouth that I had never heard myself make, a roaring scream, frenzied and *very* impolite. As he entered me, I was thrust into the most intense, insane, and inside-out orgasm I had ever had. With every drive that he gave me, I got more and more lost in mind-bending waves of pleasure that made me forget where I was. All I knew and all I needed to know was his body, the way he made me feel, and the way he made me think of *forever* even when I knew nothing else. "I love you and I never want to let you go," I roared as I came.

He pushed me back down again and scooped me into his body, one hand on each of my ass cheeks. Wave after wave of pleasure was still coursing through me, and my legs locked around his hips. "I love you too. That is where this *starts*. That is not where this ends."

39

GABE

The proof that she was a goddess was that being inside her was fucking heaven. I gave her three ball-busting thrusts and felt her toes curl against the backs of my thighs. She made long, ruthless scratches down my back that stung like a son of a bitch. Pain of the very best kind.

With every drive, I wanted her more. More. Fucking *more*. I didn't just want to fuck her because I loved her. I wanted to fuck her for keeps. I wanted her to be mine now and tomorrow and *forever*. I want to give her something that would bind us, now and always.

And the thing that would do that wasn't a goddamned locket.

The idea had never even crossed my mind—not with Lily and not with any other woman either. Not once. Now, though, it was like an obsession. With every drive and every smack of the headboard against the plaster, the idea possessed me more and more. Us, doing that. Me owning her, and her owning me.

Me knocking her up.

She arched her back and planted her palm against my chest on the next drive, pushing me away from her and creating space. Space that I didn't want to be there. "I'm not letting you go," I told her as I rammed into her yet again, this time changing my angle like I knew she liked, bringing my shaft along that inside curve of her pussy.

"Prove it," she said soft, sultry, naughty. Not a fucking Southern belle within miles and miles.

I took her old-school missionary. Good traditions die hard. "Guess what I really want, beautiful. Tell me. Say the words."

Her eyes met mine as she rolled her hips back. "You want my pussy."

Close. "Dirtier."

"You want your cum inside me."

Closer. "Filthier."

She searched my face, like she was trying to figure it out. And goddamn, the idea of her thinking so hard to give me what I wanted almost got me there by itself. Still, though, I needed her to say it. I needed to hear it from her lips. "Be *filthy*," I growled as I locked eyes with her, telling her, *Go there. Say it. Fucking say it.*

She set her teeth, lowered her chin, and dug her fingernails into me. I felt her squeeze my cock, and she ran her fingers up my flanks like a bitch in heat. And she said, "Put your baby into me right fucking now."

I was coming hard before she'd even finished the sentence. With brutal drives and ball-draining pumps, I was hers forever. I didn't need her key to find my way home. Because I was already there.

We lay tangled up together on the comedown, and I savored every minute with her. Every shift of her body, every breath, every sigh. There were a lot of mysteries in the world, but the way I felt about her wasn't one of them. She was the one I wanted. She was the one I had been looking for. *The one.* "Tell me what you want, beautiful. If you could have anything."

She rolled over in my arms onto her stomach. She traced a line up my chest, with her eyes following her fingertip, before finally looking at me. "Big dreams, you mean? Not picnic baskets."

I pulled her closer, making sure we were skin to skin—not even the sheets keeping us apart. "The biggest. What do you wish for, right now?"

She scooped her hair over one shoulder and paused with her fingertip just above my heart. "You really want to know?"

"I asked, didn't I?" I swept a stray curl off her back and my hand down her arm and back up again.

Lily nibbled gently on her lower lip. She searched my face for a second, like she was trying to find the right words, before finally pressing her palm to her chest and saying, "I wish, with my whole heart, that you lived here."

Here. With her. The only thing I'd ever known was constant forward motion—one army post to another, then California, the hustle, the grind, the next big thing. Now, though, it hit me—it was high time to start working to live. I wanted to make her happy, and I needed to know exactly what she had in mind. "Tell me more." I studied her body, each soft curve and valley. Like a map of paradise. "Don't be shy about it."

She opened her mouth slightly before closing it again. Her eyes darted back and forth between mine.

"You're not gonna scare me," I told her, touching my thumb to her cheek. Even as I said the words, though, I knew it really was a lie. It scared me shitless; it was like thinking of my world getting flipped upside down. But it was also the good kind of fear, like that moment before you jump off a high dive. "Promise."

She took a deep breath and turned away, placing her cheek to my chest, her ear right above my heart. "I wish we could stay here. In this house. Together. Christmas lights and Sunday roasts. Traditions. Kids and chaos. I would love that. I'd give anything for it to be that simple."

It wasn't simple. It was fucking beautiful. And lying there, with her in my arms, I had that feeling like when a compass finds true north.

40

LILY

The next morning, I was washing two pears in the kitchen sink when Gabe's phone began to buzz. Mr. Markowitz's name appeared on the screen, along with a photo of him in a novelty nose and glasses that made him look slightly like Mr. Potato Head. I glanced at the clock next to the pantry and did the time calculation as best I could. I was pretty sure Los Angeles was two or maybe even three hours behind Savannah time, which meant it was *awfully* early in California.

"Gabe!" I called over my shoulder. "It's Mr. Markowitz!"

"Christ," Gabe grumbled, and I heard his heavy footsteps thundering down the steps. "Grab it, will you?"

My hands were dripping wet, so I leaned over and tapped on the speaker button with my elbow. Before I had the chance to say *hello* or *It's Lily* or anything else, Mr. Markowitz launched right into the conversation. "Powers! It's me!" he panted. Gabe came around the corner in his boxers just in time to hear Mr. Markowitz say, "There's been a Nessie sighting. And the old guy who saw her wants *you* to come get the exclusive. Says he loves your show and wants to talk it over with you. ASAP! As in, fly over tonight!"

On Gabe's face I saw the purest and most instantaneous delight—like he'd just walked into a room full of people yelling, *Surprise!* Utter happiness from the bottom of his heart. He was, obviously, thrilled at the news. But as soon as his face lit up, it went dark again. He looked at me, and I saw a flicker of what I knew had to be disappointment. Disappointed *in* me or *because of* me or *with* me. Disappointed that he'd somehow found himself with a girl who made his life more difficult. Disappointed that he couldn't have everything he'd had before.

My stomach rolled at the thought that *I* could be the source of anything like that. I wanted to be the cherry on his sundae, not the pebble in his shoe. The whole sequence of emotions couldn't possibly have taken more than a few seconds, but it felt like an eternity. His delight and his disappointment. The high and the low. The possibilities of his great big world colliding with the limitations of the little one I had to stay inside.

My heart sank right down into my feet. I never, *ever* wanted him to feel that way when he looked at me, or because of me, or because of my stupid fears or *any* of it. Him being gallant made me feel like a queen; him giving up his aspirations for my sake made me feel cold all over. I might've been in a sexy lacy nightie, but I felt just like the old ball and chain. "You have to go," I said to Gabe. "Go! It's OK!"

But his expression didn't change back into sparkling delight. It stayed firm and focused, and he shook his head at the phone. "I told you yesterday, man. It's North America or nothing."

"For Chrissake, Powers! It's Nessie! It's the myths and legends mother lode!"

But Gabe was totally unmoved, and he ended the call without even telling Mr. Markowitz goodbye.

I stood there stunned, with a dripping pear in each hand and the faucet running. The idea of him rearranging things to make room for me in his life had been wonderfully romantic *in theory*. But the actual experience of seeing him turn down something that he so clearly would have loved to do made me feel just terrible. In the world there were penguins and there were eagles, both literally and figuratively. Some people were meant to soar. I wasn't one of them, but he most certainly was. "Call him back. You're going."

Gabe shook his head, and I watched the muscles in his jaw flutter. He slid his phone down the counter and said, "I told you, Lily. I want to take this time to build something with you. And I never go back on my word."

I knew that this was all much bigger than what was happening right now. Of course I would be absolutely fine if he went away for a while— I'd been fine all my life without him. If he went away for a week or two or even longer, I was hardly going to wither away like an unwatered plant in the summer sun. No, this was more than that. This was about the big picture. This was about him and me and how we could make all of this work.

The truth was, I was so very tired of the crushing weight of fear keeping me where I was. I was tired of seeing an earth full of *no* when I wanted so much to finally have the courage to say *yes*.

I could let fear stop my love. Or I could let love stop my fear. I had to try. I just had to. For him and me and us together. For the sake of big dreams and possibilities. "You're not going anywhere without me," I said as I set down the pears on the counter and turned to face him. "Because I'm going to come to Scotland with you."

41

GABE

Holy, holy shit. We were doing it. *She* was doing it. Markowitz—who might have even been more excited at her saying yes than I was—booked a direct flight for Lily and me from Atlanta to London that evening. The next morning, we'd take the train north to Scotland. We'd decided to drive to Atlanta and fly straight from there rather than making another connection; even though the drive was a hell of a hike, I was more than glad to do it, because it meant one less flight for her to worry about. As fast as I could, I packed my stuff and locked up the Willows, and we headed over to her apartment to get her packed up too.

She was a bit of a mess. An adorable mess. A lovely mess. But still, a mess. Totally understandable. I just wanted to do whatever I could to help her. I was so damned honored that she was even willing to *try* to go with me that I'd have done anything to make it easier. But helping her pack, as it turned out, really meant me just getting the hell out of the way; she whizzed around the apartment like a tiny tornado, leaving a mess of charging cords and ziplocks and rain jackets in her wake. Then she lugged an enormous suitcase out from the closet and asked, "What about this?"

It would've been just right if she were trying to get rid of a body in the ocean, but for a quick trip to Scotland it was, you know, kind of *big*. Still, though, I didn't want to burst her bubble. For as hard as she was trying, I'd have lugged the thing anywhere for her, even if I put my back out doing it. "Perfect."

"'K," she said, and gave it a two-handed shove back toward her bedroom, like she was moving a minifridge.

On her desk in the corner of the living area she'd placed the envelope that contained her passport. I slipped it into the outside pocket of my bag, where I kept mine, and looked outside at her sister playing with Ivan next to an old and faded plastic play set. From the bedroom I heard nervous huffs and puffs, followed by annoyed and frustrated grunts. I could solve a lot of problems, but helping her face down her fear wasn't like a fixing a stuck tent zipper. She was up against herself on this, and I was worried that whatever I did to help might end up hurting more than anything. I needed information, and I needed it quick.

"I'm going to go say hello to Ivan," I called out to her.

She popped out of the hallway with her hair in a high ponytail and rain galoshes on. "OK. Tell Daisy I need her to look after the General. Also, should I bring these?" She lifted her toes, and the soles made rubbery crackles as they came off the hardwood.

"Definitely. Any chance you've got fly-fishing waders?"

She gave me a big blink. "No chance whatsoever. Closest I've ever been to fishing is standing at the fish counter at the grocery," she said and squeaked off back into her bedroom.

Whatever she didn't have I'd buy for her when we got there. Her, me, a camping outfitter. Game *on*. But before any of that could happen, before I could get her geared up in Gore-Tex and beanies and buy us a sleeping bag for two, I needed to make sure I got her there with the least amount of trauma and upset possible. So I headed down her back steps into the yard, where I joined Daisy.

"Well, hello." She shaded her eyes with her hand. She glanced back behind me at the open door to the balcony, as if expecting to see Lily. When she realized she wasn't behind me, she asked, "Everything OK? I heard a lot of racket from downstairs."

"Sort of," I said, coming down into a crouch beside her. "She's decided she wants to try flying with me."

Daisy sucked in a breath between her teeth. "Oh *jeez.*"

Her reaction didn't exactly fill me with a ton of hope. I wasn't quite sure what I'd been expecting—a slightly more optimistic cringe, maybe. But Daisy looked *anything* but optimistic. It didn't dissuade me, though. "Two things. Can you look after the General?"

Daisy clicked her tongue against her teeth. "Are you kidding? He's a nanny, a music box, and *Sesame Street* rolled into one. Obviously that's a yes!"

"Second, I need to know what's helped her in the past. If anything."

Daisy squinted a little bit and took a second to answer. "If I remember right, it seemed like the virtual-reality stuff helped the most. When we did it, it was pretty new, pretty wonky, but she said it really helped. It takes a long time, though. Little doses." She hoisted Ivan up into her arms. "Baby steps, as they say."

We didn't really have time for baby steps. Lily was up there taking a giant leap with an equally giant suitcase. Time was not on our side. "Has she ever flown at all?"

She shook her head. "Almost, once. We were going to Philadelphia for a conference for my job about seven or eight years ago, maybe. It was bad, Gabe. We got onto the plane and they were just about to shut the doors, but she couldn't go through with it. She was absolutely exhausted afterward. We never tried it again." She sighed and glanced back at Lily's balcony. "It's really, really hard to watch someone you love be so terrified."

The very idea made me feel sick. But if she wanted to try it, I sure as hell wasn't going to stop her. All I could do was be there for her. I'd never been anyone's rock. Now might just be my chance. "I'll do everything I can to make sure she's OK."

"When are you leaving?" Daisy asked.

"Tonight. My producer booked us on a direct flight from Atlanta to London. Flight leaves at 5:53. She said she wants to get there by lunchtime—said she'd rather wait at the airport than wait here. We're leaving as soon as she's packed."

"*Yikes.*" Daisy pried her sunglasses from Ivan's hand. "The Philly flight was only going to be a few hours, and that was terrifying enough. Across the Atlantic is going to be really tough. But if you really do want to help, hold her hand. Tell her she's safe. Try to distract her."

"I will."

"She'll probably start asking about if all the bolts are going to fall out of the fuselage on takeoff. Completely normal. Just keep on holding that hand."

"Absolutely. Anything else?"

Daisy's eyebrows furrowed and she nodded. "Yes. There is something. She used to have a specialist who tried to come up with a treatment plan. He was super nice. Looked just like Mr. Rogers. He explained to me that it was important to *engage her* . . ." Daisy squinted again. "It's a long word. Kind of complicated. Some part of the brain."

I was no neuroscientist, but I did know a thing or two about how the brain dealt with suggestion, fear, and belief. Score one for having a made-up pseudoscientific job. "Amygdala," I said.

Daisy snapped and inhaled when I said the word. "That's it. *Engage her amygdala.*"

Armed with that little bit of key information, and Daisy's phone number, which she insisted I take in case there was anything we needed, I thanked her and headed back up to Lily's apartment. I woke up my phone and went over to Google Scholar, where I typed in "fear of flying" and "amygdala." Mindfulness, virtual reality, even knitting came up as possible activities that might help, but most of those citations were from papers that were a decade old at least. What I was looking for was cutting-edge info—anything that she might not have tried yet.

That was when I landed on a recent citation from earlier this year from the *New England Journal of Medicine*. The article was entitled "Mobile Gaming and Aviophobia: Breakthroughs in Amygdala Engagement and Fear Response."

I read through it. The particulars of the neuroscience were Greek to me, but I got the general idea. Researchers had discovered, much to their surprise, that those suffering from severe fear of flying were helped most not by medication, not by mindfulness, not by talk therapy, but instead by video games. Of all things. *Angry Birds* was good. *Tetris* was better. And *Bejeweled* was the gold standard.

For the first thirty minutes of the drive to Atlanta, she held on to my hand so hard that my fingers went completely numb. She hadn't said very much since we'd left, and the nervous energy radiated off her like heat from a sunburn. All my efforts at any sort of conversation were met by gulps and one-word answers. Occasionally, she'd break the whooshing air-conditioned silence with nuggets of admittedly terrifying airplane trivia such as, "Did you know that it only takes three full-grown geese to destroy the engine of a 747?"

Jesus. Enough facts like that and I'd be the one who needed the Valium. "Will you just give *Bejeweled* a try?"

"Did you know that jet fuel is the ideal ingredient to use for napalm?"

"Lily."

"Did you know that eighty percent of plane crashes occur within eleven minutes of takeoff?"

"Seriously."

She glanced at me, looking stern and skeptical, with her lips pursed. It was the closest she'd gotten to her sister's sternum-punching glare yet. "There is no way that a game on my phone is going to do what a maximum dose of tranquilizers cannot."

I lifted my eyebrow, taking my eyes off the road for just one second to glance at her. "Just try it. For me. It can't hurt."

"Finnnnne," she huffed and slipped her phone from her purse. She let go of my hand, and I flexed my fingers to get the blood to go back into them. She tried typing in her pass code, but her phone rejected it three times. Then she wiped her hands off on her leggings and tried again. I noticed her finger trembling over the screen before she clenched her hand into a fist.

For the first few rounds, she still sat ramrod straight with her toes slightly curled against her sandals. But as she got more and more into it, I watched her whole body begin to relax and her breathing become more and more regular. She was actually relaxing. Holy *shit*.

After a minute or two, I decided to test the waters. "It really is going to be fine. It's the safest way to travel."

I expected her to reply with something like, *Ninety percent of near midair collisions go unreported!* But she didn't answer me at all. Instead, she made a happy gasp as her phone made a series of celebratory dings and bings.

So I kept at it. "We'll have dinner, we can watch movies all night. It'll be like a sleepover. I downloaded all of *Westworld*. You're going to love it. You won't even know we're flying."

"Mmm-hmm," she answered, totally absently. "Oh *man!*" She tapped away at her phone. "I keep missing the rhinestones!" The game reset to another round, and she looked up from her phone. "Did you say something?"

"Nope," I said, smiling at the road. She was gonna be just fine. I hoped.

42

LILY

Even though *Bejeweled* had been marvelously helpful, approaching the ticket check-in desk made me feel like I was heading for the gallows. In my head, I heard the General cawing the funeral march like he always did when I took him to the vet to have his nails trimmed. It felt as though everything around me was too loud and too intense. Children's screams grated on my nerves, the noise of the automated PA system gave me a headache, and the exhaust of cars idling in the drop-off lane wafted inside and made me nauseous.

But Gabe's presence was amplified somehow too—his size, his quiet calm, his confidence. He seemed taller and more powerful beside me than he had before. I leaned against him as we waited, and he wrapped his arm around me, pulling me close and pressing a kiss to the crown of my head. The line inched forward in its rectangular serpentine way until finally we were the next to be called. I looked at all the check-in attendants and the little clumps of people, busily and excitedly getting ready to fly. They all seemed so calm and relaxed. I knew I should have been excited to go on this adventure with him, but instead I felt a swirling, heavy mix of terror and dread.

As Gabe got our passports and tickets organized, I gripped the little pole that held the ribbon of nylon tape to keep the crowd in shape. The rumble of a plane overhead made the building shake. A wave of pure terror passed through me, and I found I could not stop my violent trembling, no matter how hard I tried. The harder I tried, the worse it got. And the more the nylon rope wiggled.

Gabe turned to me and took my hand. "We do not have to do this, Lily. Honest to God. I won't be disappointed, I won't be upset. I don't want to put you through something that you don't *have* to do."

But he just didn't understand it. I was so tired of being hemmed in by my fear, and I felt in my heart that if the two of us were going to make a go of this thing, if we were really and truly going to try to build a life together, I *had* to meet him halfway. For my sake and for his. So I was going to take this thing by the horns—today, for him, for us, for me. "I want to." I clenched my hand into a fist to hide how violently I was shaking. "I really do."

Gabe opened his mouth to say something back but was cut short by one of the attendants barking out, "Next!"

We lugged our stuff over to the counter. Actually, Gabe did the lugging. But I did try to provide some helpful pushing from behind. The ticket attendant was a heavyset and friendly-looking lady with big glasses and a pin stuck to her uniform that said NONSENSE inside a red circle with a line through it.

She pecked away at her keyboard with her long acrylic nails clattering. "Passports," she said, holding out her hand without looking up.

Gabe placed them in her palm, mine on top of his. Mine was shiny and brand new, the blue cover as untouched as a new paperback fresh from the shelf. Gabe's, on the other hand, was covered in stickers and noticeably thicker than mine, with rippled pages, surely covered all over with stamps and initials and visas.

Visas. Oh God. "Do I need a visa?" I whispered to Gabe.

He looked down at me with a knowing twinkle in his eye. "Not for the UK."

I gripped his hand harder and stared past the ticket attendant, at a promotional video that was running behind her on the wall underneath the Delta sign. Airplanes whizzed through the air, to and fro, glinting in the sun. There was a shot of a lush tropical island, the Eiffel Tower, the Colosseum. All the places I had never thought I would be able to go . . . but that I still couldn't imagine seeing for myself.

The flight attendant put Gabe's passport back on the counter and opened mine, bending the cover along the spine to make it stay open. She got back to work at the computer, but then the clattering of her nails on the keyboard came to a sudden halt.

She looked over her glasses at me. "This the only passport you've got?"

I stared at her and nodded slowly. From the corner of my eye, I caught Gabe's expression of alarm. And the attendant's glasses chain swung like a pendulum. *Tick-tock. Tick-tock.*

"Then I'm sorry to say you're not getting on a plane to London today, hon," she said, snapping her gum. "Because this document is expired."

We dragged our bags out of the ticketing line, and Gabe made a flurry of phone calls to Markowitz and then to the US passport office in Atlanta to see how quickly we could get an expedited renewal appointment. He paced slowly but purposefully back and forth along the concourse, getting slightly farther away from me with each lap. Talking on the phone, he seemed so authoritative and confident—and so oblivious to the female passersby whom he turned into unapologetic collarbone fondlers. He was also equally oblivious to the hurricane of emotions that was spinning inside me: Relief that I didn't have to fly. Foolishness that I thought I could. Dread that I'd been kidding myself all along and that the ticket attendant had saved me from my own idiotic naïveté.

My adrenaline was nose-diving, and I felt like I was trying to slog through quicksand. I shoved our luggage into a quiet corner, near a bank of now-empty cubbies that used to hold pay phones but didn't anymore. I slumped down onto my suitcase with a view of the underside of the old phone bank, dotted all over with ancient wads of gum. Like an explosion of tragic confetti.

I rested my forehead against the thick window, which thrummed with all the activity inside the airport. Closing my eyes, I felt the throb of a headache coming in both temples. Earlier everything had seemed too loud and intense; now everything seemed muted and far away, as if I was looking at the world through the wrong end of a pair of binoculars.

Saying yes to Scotland had been a split-second decision. Seeing that disappointment on Gabe's face had made me stop, drop, and do something *crazy*. It felt as though some other me had made that choice—some version of me that was full of moxie and courage. I had no idea where she'd gone, but she wasn't here anymore. In her place was the me that I knew oh so well. The one who liked her little bubble and stayed inside it, firmly rooted to the ground. Now I felt silly for imagining that I belonged with Gabe in Scotland. Or anywhere else, for that matter. Even our luggage underneath me was proof: my enormous suitcase was like a bench. His compact roller bag was like a footstool. He was cut out for this life. And I was not.

I wondered about how or even *if* I should say anything to Gabe—was swallowed fear the same as bravery?—when a sudden noise nearby made me open my eyes. Someone had tried to toss a magazine in a nearby recycling bin but had overshot it. Near my feet I saw a shiny copy of *People* magazine. Even though the cover was upside down, I knew that chiseled jawline. I knew that bare chest. I knew that heart-stopping smile. It was Gabe's picture with the headline AMERICA'S MOST ELIGIBLE BACHELOR.

Oh my God. I slid the magazine across the carpet and spun it so it was right side up. I cough-choked as I studied him. In the photograph, he was standing on a beach with sugar-white sand, wearing nothing but red swim trunks. Huge green cliffs came up behind him on one side, and to the right sprawled endless blue water. For one wonderful and unfiltered instant, I thought, *He's mine.* And yet just as quickly, my hazy possessive lusty thinking gave way to cold, hard reality. He was on the cover of *People.* I was about to have a meltdown over getting on an airplane.

This was all just . . .

Glancing up, I saw he was pacing back toward me, still with his earbuds in. I picked the magazine up off the ground and hid it behind my bent thighs. He gave me a wink, and I smiled at him, doing my best to keep up a brave face. But as he walked past, I let my smile drop and flipped to the lengthy center spread that featured images of him looking flashy, snazzy, and famous at red-carpet events interspersed with photos of him at locations around the world. There was one of him in a forest with trees that looked prehistoric and impossibly strange. There was one of him underwater, glistening with bubbles like diamonds and pointing at a huge turtle that was swimming past.

. . . impossible.

Each moment of the last few days had brought me closer to him. But now each word and image made me feel farther and farther away. Paragraph after paragraph described his life, his show, and his work, and I tried desperately to imagine how I'd be able to fit between those lines, between *production schedules* and *filming seasons.* I couldn't imagine fitting into that world of his. And I certainly couldn't imagine him shoehorning himself into mine either. Using Georgia as a home base and trying to stay in North America as much as possible? Even if he'd done all that, the guilt at making him give up so much would've squished me under its weight.

As it was, everything felt as though it was crashing down on me anyway. Near the end of the article were the results of the Superlative Hunks competition. He'd been the hands-down winner, and on the page was an image of him when *he* was in high school, in full football gear, standing on top of a bank of lockers with his biceps curled and his Prince Charming smile sparkling. I groaned as I moved my eyes over the image. Me and the football star. I knew how that movie ended already.

But it got even worse when I turned the page. Because there, on the last page of the article, was a Q&A with him. It was formatted like the transcript of an interview. There was maybe a tiny chance that the rest of the article could all be chalked up to PR and tabloid spin. But there, in black-and-white, were his own words telling me in no uncertain terms that the one thing I *couldn't* do was what he loved most of all. And between those lines I read what I should've known all along—that no matter what half measures we tried in order to be able to meet in the middle, I could never, *ever* be part of the world where he felt most at home.

What can't you live without? Travel.

Favorite place to eat? Tsuta Ramen in Tokyo.

Where is your favorite place to go? The Red Center of Australia.

Where do you want to go but haven't been yet? Iceland. Madagascar. Easter Island. Anywhere and everywhere.

What about a girlfriend? Ever going to settle down? Maybe one day. But definitely not yet.

We're betting she'll need to have the travel bug, right? For sure. I'd want to share the whole world with her.

I felt the sting of tears as I let the magazine drop into my lap. It had been such a beautiful dream. And it would have to stay that way. Because he belonged out there in the great beyond—anywhere and everywhere. But there was no way that he belonged with little old me.

43

GABE

As the passport office put me on hold *again*, I watched Lily put her hands on either side of her face. She hung her head, rubbing her temples with her fingers.

The Lily I'd come to know was bubbling with joy and excitement; seeing her look tired and defeated made me feel so fucking guilty. I'd never wanted to see her look so worn down, and I certainly hadn't wanted to be the one who pushed her to that point. But I was. And felt terrible about it. I also remembered what her sister had told me earlier—that all this stuff to do with the planes was exhausting for her. Walking back toward her, I realized that I'd swooped in to fix the passport issue without even asking her if that was what she wanted or not. I'd been shooting for Action Jackson again, but I realized I might have come off as Presumptuous Jackass. So I came down into a crouch in front of where she sat in a ball on her suitcase. I swept her hair gently to the side and asked, "Want to go home?"

She nodded with her lips quivering. "I'm sorry."

"Don't you dare apologize," I said as I ended the call with the passport office. "We'll go back to Savannah and get it all sorted it out."

She tried to force a smile, but it looked just that—uncomfortable, pretend, not *her* at all. "Or maybe . . ." She trailed off, searching my face. "Maybe you should just go on your own."

Out of the goddamned question. "No way," I said and loaded up our luggage. She kept slowing down and trailing behind me, so I adjusted my pace again and again. Together, we slowly retraced our steps and went back to the car rental place. The truck I'd rented hadn't even been checked in to the system yet, and before long we were headed back to Savannah.

Not even that seemed to cheer her up. I couldn't get a smile out of her or a laugh or anything. She wouldn't even really look at me and sat with her cheek pressed to the glass as green swaths of central Georgia streaked past.

Somehow I just knew that filling up the silence with plans and ideas would make her feel even worse, so I let the silence go on. I tried my very best to imagine what she was feeling. At the airport, she'd been right on the brink of facing her biggest fear. Real or imagined, there was some very significant part of her that believed setting foot on a plane would be the last thing she'd ever do. She'd been willing to do it for *me*, which was just incredible. Just because she hadn't actually gotten on the plane didn't mean that her mind hadn't run away with her, though. That, at least, was a feeling I'd experienced. Once I'd been cave diving in Puerto Rico. I'd been with a local guide, but we'd gotten separated. I was a pretty experienced diver, but every set of gear is different, and my tank had started to malfunction when I was way, way down deep—no light from above, no sense of up or down, and no idea how to escape. I remembered a moment of pure terror when I'd really believed that I wasn't going to get out of there alive. The local guide had found his way back to me and dragged me up to the surface. I'd been so thrown off balance by it that when I'd caught my breath, I'd called my brother so that I could talk to my nieces—just so I knew, for sure, that everything was going to be OK. It wasn't rational. But fear never is.

I glanced at Lily. She'd wrapped her arms around herself like she was cold. "You OK?" I asked and turned the AC way down.

She turned back to me with tear-sparkling eyes, and my heart fucking sank. I never wanted to see her cry. Never, ever. "I'm OK," she said with a sniffle. "I just really want to go back to my house," she added and turned away.

There had been a time not so long ago when I hadn't known what I wanted at all. But then I'd met her. Like some kind of crazy, life-changing, one-in-a-million accident, I'd found myself in her arms. And I knew nothing would ever be the same.

On the next long straightaway on the highway, I found myself looking at her ring finger. At first it wasn't even a fully conscious thought. Then it became the most obvious thing in the world. Yeah, it was crazy. Yeah, it was fast. But goddamn, it sure felt right.

I thought it through, mile by mile, and the more I thought about it, the more right it felt. The more I needed to take that wild chance on her and me and us together.

We pulled up to her house and began to unload our luggage from the back of the truck. But just as I started to pull my duffel from the bed, she stopped me dead in my tracks with five words I'd hoped I'd never hear her say.

"Gabe, we need to talk."

44

LILY

I sat down on my porch steps. My heart was in my throat, but I steeled myself. I pulled a dead flower from my potted petunia and waited for him to join me.

There was an intensity on his face as he walked toward me that made a shiver of desire—of unthinking, deep-down *want*—rumble through me. But I had to be stronger than *want*. And I had to be stronger than *need*. Now, more than ever, I had to be sensible and logical. Life changes could not be made on the basis of a few days of wild passion and happiness. Fears could not be conquered by hope alone. We had been inside a fairy tale for the last little while. I loved a fairy tale as much any girl. But every fairy tale came to an end.

He sat next to me on the steps, and I took his hand in mine. I'd felt strong before that moment, but as his palm touched mine, my strength began to falter, and the tears started to trickle down my cheeks. "I can't do this."

"Hey, hey, hey." He wrapped his arm around me. "Don't give Scotland another thought. I love that you tried, but it really and truly doesn't matter."

I shook my head, sniffling and wiping my nose with my palm. "I don't mean Scotland. I mean you and me. It'll never work."

Even through my tears I saw a flash of dismay and anger rumple his features—ferocious and intense. This wasn't the gallant and calm Gabe I'd seen out in the world; this was the Gabe I'd seen in the bedroom, the version of him that seemed like maybe it was for me alone. "The fuck it won't, Lily," he said.

I gripped his hand harder, trying to memorize how it felt so that I never, ever forgot. I looked out at the street, at the way the wheat-like weeds that grew up from the cracks in the pavement bowed in the breeze. "I need to be honest with you. When my passport was denied, I felt so . . ." I turned to look him in the eye. ". . . relieved." When I said the word, I saw him begin to search my face, like he just couldn't understand. "I was relieved that I didn't have to fly. But also that I didn't have to go with you."

He growled a little when I said the words, grunting almost. "*Have* to?"

I focused on my breathing. I had never been one for confrontation or hard conversations. I was all fizzle and no bang. This was a language I didn't know how to speak, but I blundered ahead. "If I did travel with you, every trip would be pure terror."

"Then you don't fucking *have* to." His voice was sharp and deep, certain and clear. "That was your choice. I would never have pushed you that far. Don't give up on me before we've even started to try. What about the Ozarks? What about what you wished for at the Willows?"

I didn't answer right away, and he stared at me with such hope and expectation. But I knew better. It was all so painfully clear to me. Where he saw solutions, I saw only problems and complications. Where he saw yes, I saw no.

Right on cue, his stupid freaking phone began to buzz *again*. He didn't look away from me. He didn't flinch. He was oblivious. But I was at the end of my tether—I felt like I'd managed to keep my cool for a whole movie of someone whispering behind me, but now I just wanted to let out a great big angry "Shhhhhhhhh!" The world would come between us soon enough, but not now, not *yet*. So I plunged my hand into his pants pocket, grabbed his phone, yanked it out, and pressed the power button so hard that it made my thumb bone ache. Finally, his phone went dark. Silent. Quiet. I thrust his phone across the porch steps at him, angry at what it represented, with its fancy case and its extra battery. And angry at myself too, for ever letting myself get too foolishly attached to a man who I'd known was not here to stay. "Our lives are too different. No matter what, you'd only ever be halfway here."

I'd stunned him, I could see that. He'd made such an effort to figure out a way for us to make it work, but in my heart I knew it was all a fool's errand. And I was embarrassed to be the fool in the middle of it. I said, "Even if we did take a stab at it, it would always come down to me. That I couldn't go with you. Or that maybe I could. Maybe, maybe, maybe. I can't live in *maybe*."

He didn't say anything at first. He looked so stern, so frustrated, I wasn't sure that he would. But finally he asked, "How do you know it's *maybe*? And how can you possibly assume I'm only going to be halfway here?" He leaned into me, pushing me up against the porch post. "Want me to give it all up for you? The show? The travel? Just say it, Lily. Just *say it*."

"Don't be ridiculous," I snapped. I would not ask him to give up his great big life to come live here with me inside my little one. I would not ask him to leave his flashy Hollywood reality for the world I'd built around myself. "I am not going to let my wagon drag down your star."

"That's *my* decision to make," he said, looking deep into my eyes. "Maybe I want you to do just that. Ever think of that? Maybe I just want to belong to you." He hooked my chin with his fingertip to make me look up at him. "Maybe I don't want any of it except for you."

It felt to me like he had to be talking about some other woman. I slid the copy of *People* out of my purse and pressed my hand to his beautiful body on the cover. When he saw it, he flared his nostrils and glared. "Is *that* what this is about? Some shallow article in a magazine that I've never read? I was a bachelor when they shot those photos. But I am not a bachelor anymore."

I pressed my lips together as a wave of grief stole my words. After a second I was able to say, "This isn't about being a bachelor. It's about *anywhere and everywhere*," I said, with my voice shaking. A handful of tears splattered onto his image like raindrops on his tanned skin. "You deserve so much more than I could ever give you. You deserve someone who can share the world with you, just like you said," I told him, finding a little more strength. "I will not let you settle for a woman who is terrified to experience that world with you."

His face showed a deep and undeniable hurt. "You are not just *a woman*. I am not *settling*." He slipped his hand behind my head and drew me into him so we were nearly cheek to cheek. I let the magazine slide off my lap and wrapped my arms around him. I inhaled hard so I wouldn't forget his scent, and I tried to memorize the way his stubble felt against my cheek. "You deserve to be loved senseless, Lily. And I want to be the man to give you that. I never knew what I wanted. And then I met you."

No matter what he said, I felt as though I'd gotten X-ray vision into the future; I could never make him happy enough to stay here with me, and I had to stop him from trying. And I knew too that his life would drive me out of my mind with worry and longing. I imagined endless nights refreshing my browser, willing his plane across oceans and continents. I imagined the dread at waiting to hear where he was headed next. I imagined secretly hoping that his show would become less popular instead of more so, just so I could keep him closer. That was no way to live and certainly no way to love. "Thank you for everything," I whispered as I reached up for the locket to find the clasp.

He pulled away with that fire in his eyes. "Enough," he growled, engulfing my hand with his to stop me from taking off the necklace. "I will not let you push me away because you have some bullshit notion of what's best for me. What's best for me, Lily, is you. And you cannot argue with me on that."

I wanted so badly to believe him. But I couldn't. I just couldn't. If it didn't end now, it would end eventually. Our lives and our worlds were just too far apart. "I can't do this, Gabe," I whispered. "I need you to go."

Now his eyes glinted with tears too, and he shook his head. "When we were driving back, you know what I was thinking about? I wasn't thinking about flying or trips or jobs or any of the seemingly immovable bullshit of life." He gripped my left hand in his right one, squeezing tight. "I was wondering about your ring size."

The dam began to break, and I let my tears tumble down my cheeks onto his shoulder as I shook my head. "Please stop."

"*You* stop. I love you. I want to marry you. I want to make a life with you. Fuck *fear*. Fuck the unknown. I have never felt anything like what I feel for you."

Every word he said hit me in the chest like a tiny poisoned dart, and I stifled a sob against his shoulder, holding on to him so tight that it made my muscles ache. I adored him. I adored his spirit and laughter, the way he looked at me and the way he made me feel. I adored his unchecked love and his unstoppable passion. But that didn't change a thing. It didn't change that we had been swept up in a handful of days of pure madness. How we felt didn't change who we were or where we came from. "Give me my key back, please," I said in barely a whisper.

Gabe drew away from me, looking hurt and stunned. He shook his head slowly, and the muscles in his jaw fluttered. His eyes never left mine. "Fuck no. I will not let you take away my home."

My heart sank even farther, like an anchor cut from its line. I looked away, focusing on the fuzzy petunia petals. And at the dried, lifeless buds that littered the soil in the pot.

"You've made this world for yourself," Gabe went on. "Maybe because you feel like you can't leave, you've made a little paradise around you. And my paradise is you. So don't fucking push me away."

I was a lot of things, but I could not believe that I was anybody's paradise. Let alone his.

I couldn't stand this anymore. It hurt too, too much. I stood up, wiping my nose on the back of my hand. I shoved my key into the lock and turned my back on him. But as I began to step through the door, he put his hand on my shoulder and spun me around, pressing me up against the hard edges of my mailbox.

This kiss was different than all the others because of our tears. He kissed me like we were just starting all over again. But I kissed him to say goodbye. I knew then that I would never love another man the way I loved him. He was my be-all and end-all. Never again would I get a chance to feel what I felt right then in his arms. I wanted to swim in those warm waters forever. But it was time to go back to shore.

When I pulled away from the kiss, he caged me in against my front door. He looked frustrated now, and when he spoke, he sounded stronger and more aggressive than ever before. "There's a big difference between playing it safe and playing it scared, Lily," he said. "I will do anything to keep you safe. But it's up to you to stop living in fear. And I don't mean just the fucking planes. I mean *everything*. It is up to you to think bigger and to realize that you deserve more."

I reached up and placed my fingertips to his damp cheek, admiring those beautiful eyes of his for what I knew would be the very last time. "You have this bravery about you, like anything is possible," I said, with my chin trembling. "But I don't have that, Gabe. I'm not brave like you and I never will be."

His eyes sparkled with new tears. As he wiped them away, I looked up at him one last time. He was all the things I never knew I'd wanted. And all the things I would never have. "I am in the palm of your hand, Lily. You turn your back on me and you'll fucking crush me."

I clapped my hand to my mouth to stifle my sob. And then I did it. I turned away and pulled the door shut behind me. Trudging upstairs, I knew he was still standing on the porch from the way his shadow darkened the steps in front of me.

"Lily," he said, his voice muffled by the door but still strong and clear. "Look at me."

I froze with both feet on the third step. I closed my eyes, willing him to walk away.

"Goddamn it," he growled and smacked the door. "*Lily.* Look at me."

I took a deep breath and looked back over my shoulder. I could see the hurt and the agony he was feeling. And I felt it too. I was responsible for all of it, which made it so much more painful. He held my stare for a second, blinking back tears before finally saying, "If I had a gratitude jar, the only thing in it would be your name."

Everything in me told me to go back to him—to take a step into that vast and magical unknown. But I didn't have the courage. I didn't have the guts. And so once again I turned away and made my way slowly up the stairs with a self-inflicted broken heart, back to my small, safe, and lonely little life.

45

GABE

I stood on her porch, stunned and reeling. I rang her doorbell again and again, but she wouldn't answer, and I finally walked back to my truck in a daze. She'd drawn the blinds in her apartment and closed them tight. I wanted to drop to my goddamned knees right there on her front lawn, but instead I slipped my keys from my pocket, got in my truck, and sat there with the engine off.

"Mother*fucker*," I growled as I whacked the steering wheel hard with my palm. I'd lost her before I'd even really had her. God*damn* it.

The pain I'd seen in her eyes was what really wrecked me. Seeing her cry, seeing her hurt, seeing her decide that she wouldn't take a chance on us was what split me right in two. I had fuckall experience with rejection and even less with this kind of pain. It both devastated me and pissed me off; I'd put it all on the table for her and she'd pushed me away.

I turned over the ignition and looked at her door one last time, like I was willing it to open—willing her to run out to me. To come to her senses. But she didn't. Instead, the mailman trundled up with sagging pants and stuffed her mailbox full of junk and then shuffled off.

Peeling out with the engine damn near redlining, I found myself heading back to the Willows. If she wouldn't let me be with her, at least

I could go back to where I'd gotten so close to her. We'd been in such a hurry that morning, I hadn't even bothered to shorten the reservation, so the house was still mine to use. It was a far cry from actually being with her—her touch, her smell, her laughter—but it was *something*, at least.

But when I walked into the kitchen, I felt a gut punch of anguish that knocked the wind out of me. I slammed the kitchen door and braced myself on the countertop. I tried my damnedest to man up, but it was no use. Ten minutes away from her and I was a fucking *mess*.

What I'd said to her was the goddamned truth. If she'd asked, I'd have given it all up for her. The show, the travel, *anything* she wanted. But I couldn't give it up if she wouldn't be waiting for me on the other side. I couldn't jump from that cliff without knowing that she was going to be there at the end of the dive.

I couldn't face this, not here—maybe not ever. Before she'd come along, the thing that defined me was my work. And with her gone, it was the thing that defined me still. So I grabbed my phone, turned it back on, and called Markowitz.

"Powers? What's the hell is going on? Been getting alerts up the yin-yang to tell you to check in for your flight!"

I looked out at the yard, where I'd imagined her with a garden and a dog. I looked at the island where I'd taken her. I looked at the kitchen table where we'd eaten together for the first time. "Get me the hell out of here."

For once, he didn't launch into a bunch of bullshit questions. I heard the sound of him typing and he asked, "One ticket . . . or two?"

I hung my head over the sink and shut my eyes, blocking out the light from the window and all the fucking memories. The ones we had. And the ones we'd never have. "One."

He let out a groan. "I'm awfully sorry to hear that, buddy."

Christ almighty, I loved her. I didn't want to let her go, but I wouldn't fucking stay where I wasn't wanted either. "So am I," I said as I pushed my tears away from my eyes.

There was a little more typing on the other end of the line, before Markowitz finally said, "Savannah to JFK, JFK to Edinburgh. Seven thirty tonight. Gives you two hours before you gotta be at the airport. That good with you?"

I braced myself on the kitchen table and stared at the houseplant that she'd used as a makeshift candelabra on that first night we spent together. "It'll have to be," I said to Markowitz and ended the call.

For a few ticks of the grandfather clock, I didn't move a muscle. I had that feeling like this just all had to be a nightmare, like I'd wake up any second with Lily in my arms. But this was real. It had happened. And another red-hot flash of anger came over me. Without even thinking, I shoved the potted plant off the table, sending it flying onto the floor. Shards of terra-cotta poked out from the dirt and flowers scattered all around the kitchen.

Wreckage from beauty. Misery from happiness.

Whoever said it was better to have loved and lost than never to have loved at all was completely full of shit.

46

LILY

I curled up into a snotty, tearful mess on my couch and let old episodes of *The Powers of Suggestion* play back at me from my computer. Every time I looked at him, my entire body ached, right down to my bones. I was sobbing over an episode of him in Hawaii—taking a break from searching for some sort of enormous bat to learn to surf—when finally I just couldn't take it anymore. It hurt too much. Every smile, every wink at the camera, every adjustment of his wet suit made me love him—and miss him—that much more. Slamming my laptop shut, I buried my face in the pillows. I had made my choice, and I knew logically that it was the best thing. For me, maybe not. For him, *definitely*. Because the last thing he needed was me tying him down. I was not going to be the woman to clip his wings.

I drifted in and out of sleep, but I was so stuffed up from all the crying that I couldn't breathe through my nose. Every once in a while, I would startle myself awake with a snort, only to find my face stuck to the cushions with snot and tears and drool. Lovely.

"Love you?" said the General. I poked my head up from the couch and saw him watching me, cocking his head side to side.

The General was obviously mystified at the full-blown wallow that was unfolding in front of him. He'd seen me in all sorts of states of happiness and not so happiness. He'd seen me frustrated with men. He'd seen me angry with men. Lord knew he'd seen me disappointed in men. He'd even seen me briefly go on a furious Google quest over "can nuns have birds in a convent?" But he'd *never* seen me break down into a weeping mess over anybody or anything.

"Love you too." I wiped my nose and tried to sniffle. It made a painful sucking sensation in my ears, like I was underwater or had a bad cold. I rolled off the couch and shuffled into the kitchen, where I prepared him a pathetic plate of the only easy-to-prepare vegetable I had in the house—frozen peas. Just like I'd recommended Gabe use for his face when I almost knocked him out. Even peas hurt now.

After microwaving them for ten seconds, I slid the General's dinner through the flap in his cage. He stared at his wrinkly peas and then at me. "Sad."

"Very," I sniffled. I sank back down on the couch and stared at the nearly finished hat I had been working on for Gabe. It was so close to being done. I held the work in my hands, getting ready to tear it apart. But I could not bring myself to do it. I could not get myself to destroy it, not because it was one OK-ish thing that I had made so far but because it was for him. And I didn't want to wreck it, even if he was gone. Or maybe especially because he was gone.

I fought through the waves of tears and finished the hat as best I could. Right as I was casting off, I heard footsteps on my staircase. My heart somersaulted and cartwheeled, and I turned expectantly, hopefully, toward the door. It was him. It had to be him.

It wasn't. It was my sister in costume, wearing her heavy-soled Victorian boots that made her clomp up the steps like she weighed 250 pounds. "Lily?" she said, bursting in without knocking, "I thought you'd be on your way to Scot—" She stopped midword. She blinked. "Oh my God, what happened?"

I turned away, looking at the hat in my hands. "I don't want to talk about it."

Daisy closed the door and came inside, sitting down next to me, with her petticoats rustling. "Is it Gabe?"

At the mention of his name, my lips began to quiver. "It's all over."

Daisy seemed shocked for a millisecond before settling into a *very* scary version of the Glare. "What did he . . ." She set her teeth. "Where is he? How about I go find him and wipe that Crest-sponsored smile right off his stupid—"

I shook my head. "Stop. Just stop." I pulled the magazine out from under the couch cushions and handed it to her. Even though it was the thing that had brought it all crashing down, I still somehow needed it near me. The thought of it getting ruined in a summer storm or blowing down the street into the gutter was more than I could stand. "It's not what he *did*," I said as the tears slid down my cheeks all over again. "It's what he *is*. And what I am."

Daisy still looked pretty mad. "What you *are* is wonderful, Lily. You're caring, you're kind, you're funny, you're smart. And he'd be damned lucky to have you."

I felt like I was none of those things. Or that even if I were, it wasn't enough. We weren't chocolate and peanut butter—we were oil and vinegar. I took the magazine from her, and it fell open to the centerfold. It was him at some sort of animal sanctuary, learning to shear a sheep. Then I turned the page, and he looked back at us in a sharp and expensive tux, beaming at the camera. Turning the page again, I showed her the yearbook photo, and Daisy groaned. But then I pointed to the interview, pressing my fingertip to the word *travel*.

"See? It would never work. You and Boris were doomed. Imagine *us*." I held the cover up next to my face.

Daisy took a deep breath and nodded as she held my hand. Her palm felt warm and comforting against mine. All the sadness seemed to drain out of me, and I felt nothing but pure exhaustion. I leaned against her, closing my burning eyes. She wrapped her arm around me and rocked me gently side to side. "How about we get you cleaned up, I get changed out of this ridiculous dress, and then you, me, and Ivan go get something to eat?"

"Not hungry," I said against her puffy starched sleeve.

"Don't care." Daisy gripped me a little tighter. "I'll take you to get your favorite, how about that?"

I flopped back on the couch and rubbed my face as my sinuses made a sort of worrisome spongy squelching sound. I blinked hard and looked at the clock on the cable box. It felt fuzzy and far away, just as it had on the day when I'd planned to make him dinner. I took the hat from the coffee table and smoothed it on my knee. "What if he comes back? I don't know when he's leaving."

My sister ran her fingers over the stitches. "Do you want to see him?"

Another geyser of grief sputtered up through me, and I struggled to keep it down. Of course I wanted to see him. Always. Now and forever. But I knew it would be the worst thing for me, and I managed a blubbered "Bad idea."

Daisy wrapped her arm around me again. "Well, then, we can leave his hat for him on the porch, maybe. How about that?"

"OK," I said, crumpling against her in surrender, wrapping my arms around her and sinking into her starched pleats. "Where are we going? Drs. Fries and Root Beer?" I asked, my voice muffled by her arm.

"Better," she said and gave me a kiss on the crown of my head.

It wasn't *better*; it was Uncle Jimmy's Secret Ingredient. But I was so busy half-heartedly making Ivan's baby giraffe dance for him on his car seat while I tried to keep my mind off Gabe that I didn't even realize where we were until we'd arrived.

"Oh God," I said as I locked automatically onto the picnic table where Gabe and I had sat. Where he'd pressed his leg against mine. Where I'd felt that warmth and joy inside me—which I'd never feel again. Maybe I really was destined to be a spinster, just like I played at the history museum.

"Told you!" Daisy said. "Better!" She leaped out of the driver's seat and came around to get Ivan from his car seat. She seemed so proud of herself, so happy, that I just didn't have the heart to say that anywhere, literally, *anywhere* would have been less painful for me. Except maybe Auntie Jennifer's grocery store, which, obviously, I would never be able to enter again without ugly crying so hard that I scared away all her customers. Fantastic.

I pressed the back door open with my shoulder, slumping out with heavy, flat-footed stomps. I followed behind Daisy and Ivan as they headed for the entrance. Jimmy Jr. was still outside pacing, but this time with a huge cigar between his teeth. "Lily!" he boomed.

My wave was a wet-noodle wave, and it actually hurt to smile, like I was wearing an egg-white mask. But I did my best. "Still haven't figured it out?" I asked. My voice sounded far away, like it belonged to someone else. Someone who had pinched her nostrils with a clothespin.

"Nope." He placed his cigar on a window ledge. He grabbed a few sauce-splattered menus and led us toward the picnic tables out back. As we got nearer to the tables, he looked over his shoulder at me. He nodded knowingly, with a slow lift of his massive shoulders, like somehow, he just understood. Granted, it was hardly rocket science. There was a very real possibility I still had snot dripping from my nose. But I appreciated his not asking about it, and I was grateful when he led us to the table farthest from where Gabe and I had sat together.

I tried to read the menu, running my eyes over all the usually mouthwatering things, but I felt pretty much nothing. No hunger. No delight. No interest even in barbecue.

"Boy, you are *really* feeling the feels," my sister said. She gave Ivan a pacifier and let him crawl on the grass, crouching beside him and looking up at me. I dropped my menu and nodded at her and then let my head rest between my palms. My elbows dug into the raw wood of the tabletop, and two tears splatted down onto the menu's plastic sleeve.

Within a few moments, Jimmy Jr. brought out my usual tenders with a side order of the sauce. He raised one of his bushy dark eyebrows at me. "That's the last of it," he said quietly. "Lord and Uncle Jimmy help us."

As Jimmy Jr. trundled off, I stared at the table where Gabe and I had sat, and the sadness welled up inside me all over again. Tears tumbled off my cheeks, and my sister grabbed a stack of paper napkins out from underneath their dedicated rock in the center of the table. I pressed them into my eyes so hard that I saw flashes.

"It's going to be OK," Daisy said. "I promise. It will."

I wadded up my napkins and looked at her as the world came back into focus. She dipped one of the chicken tenders in the sauce and held it out to me, same as she would have done to feed Ivan. She was a natural as a mom, and I was so grateful to have her with me. She held her palm underneath it to catch any drips of sauce and held it to my lips.

Biting into the chicken tender, I sniffled hard and was rewarded once again with that sucking thing in my ears. And since my nose was out of commission, I had to breathe through my mouth as I chewed. Like a Clydesdale at the feed bag. I was nothing if not elegant.

But then, between the stuffy nose and the plugged ears, something unexpected happened. I tasted something in the sauce that I hadn't been able to taste before. It was spicy yet sweet—exotic yet familiar. Star anise, no. Cloves, no . . . On the next big sniffle and openmouthed chew, I had it. Ginger. It was ginger. Not powered ginger. *Fresh* ginger. That same spiciness that was in my lemonade. And in the fancy bath supplies that Gabe had gotten for me too.

I dropped the tender into the basket and pressed my hands to my face. A noise came out of my mouth that was a rather dreadful combo of a hiccup, a snort, a cough, and a sob.

My sister's mouth dropped open. "Are you OK?"

Into my tearful palms, I shook my head. I was not OK. I was never going to be OK. In just a matter of days, he'd changed my life. Nothing would ever be the same—not even ginger.

I felt a big hand on my back and turned to see Jimmy Jr.'s concerned face. "Lily?"

"Fresh ginger," I blubbered into my hands.

"Shut the front door." He snatched up a chicken tender and tested it for himself. "You're sure?"

I tried to muster up a smile. But it didn't last, and within just a few seconds, I was weeping into my stack of soggy napkins once more.

47

GABE

I should've been halfway to the airport, but I'd gone back to her house
to try to reason with her. Everything about her was perfect to me, except
for this decision. Because this decision was bullshit.

The street and the neighborhood had that lazy summer afternoon
feel, like people were off doing better things with the people they loved.
And fuck knew I wished I was doing that same thing with Lily. I wished
that this whole day had never happened. Scotland had been her call,
her leap of faith, not mine. But I was paying the price. Maybe that was
exactly what dipshits who believed in *the one* deserved.

She wasn't home. Her van was parked in the driveway, but her sister's minivan was gone. And the only thing ringing the doorbell again
and again did was get the General to mimic the doorbell from one floor
above. Like some kind of hellish doorbell echo chamber.

Next to the door, there was a small package wrapped in white tissue
paper. There was no note on the outside, but I saw a few splotches on
the paper. Lily's tears. With my heart in my throat, I picked it up from
the porch step and folded back the paper. It was a beanie, knitted from
soft gray yarn. Inside it was a Post-it note that said *I'm so sorry.*

Seeing her handwriting and her words made me feel sick to my stomach—sick for what I was losing without being given a chance to save it. I pulled my phone from my pocket and gave her a call, but it went straight to voice mail. She'd turned off her goddamned phone. Stonewalling me at every turn.

I listened to half her message, "Hi! You've reached Sounds Good LL—" before I couldn't take hearing her sweet voice anymore and ended the call. None of this was fucking necessary, but there was nothing I could do about it—not if she wouldn't talk to me. I clenched my hand into a fist and braced myself against her doorjamb. I closed my eyes, lowered my head, and let the anger roll right through me. Anger wasn't something I felt very often—I didn't get attached to people, because I never gave myself the chance. To be angry like this, you had to give a shit about someone. And about Lily Jameson, I definitely gave a shit.

I was angry that she had decided all this without me, angry that she had crushed me out of fear, and angry that she wouldn't even fucking fight for what I knew, in my bones, was right. Us. Her and me, together.

But if she wanted to see the back of me, that's exactly what she was going to get. I wasn't gonna hang around to get crushed twice in one day, so I took her house key from my wallet, shoved it through the mail slot, and got back in my truck. I tore out of town toward the airport, hauling ass away from Savannah. And away from her.

My meditation mantra had always been, "Fuck *that*." But today it was something different. Fuck *this*. Fuck this pain. Fuck this hurt. Fuck it all.

48

LILY

Seeing my house key on my doormat brought the reality of what I'd done into too-bright focus, like when a flashbulb lights up a darkened room. I crouched down to grab my key, feeling as though everything was now too harsh and raw. The scratchiness of the sisal mat, the coldness of the metal, the sharpness of the teeth—they were tiny reminders of the heart-pinching truth: he was gone and I had only myself to blame. He'd opened himself up to me, and I'd crushed him. And crushed myself too.

"Come on," Daisy said, unlocking her door, "I'll make some popcorn and we can watch some house-flipping shows. We can heckle their paint choices and second-guess the wisdom of their countertops."

I pressed the key into my palm and shook my head. This day had worn me right out, and I felt deliriously tired as well as desperate to be back in the place where he'd held me in his arms. "I just want to lie down, I think."

Daisy narrowed her eyes and studied me. "I'm your sister. Let me wallow with you. It's the least I can do."

But again I shook my head. I gave her a kiss, and Ivan too, and began to head up the steps.

"I'll be here, Lily," she said softly. "I'm always here for you. *We* are," she added, jiggling Ivan and making him blow laughter bubbles from his drool.

I sniffled and nodded as I hauled myself upstairs. "I know," I said without turning to face her. I didn't want her to see more of my sadness, but more than that I didn't want her to see the sudden wave of jealousy that I was feeling toward her. Yes, Boris had made a truly spectacular mess of her life, but at least she'd had the courage to love him against all reason—at least she had been brave enough to step out into the love hurricane, consequences be damned. And now, even in his wake, at least she had Ivan. Like a morning glory after a nuclear blast. Not me, though. There would be no morning glories for me.

When I stepped into my apartment, I could tell that the General was in full parrot-polygraph mode. There was no point in slapping some painful fake smile on my face; he'd see right through it. So I opened his cage, offered him my finger as a perch, and let him sit on my shoulder. He nuzzled my cheek with his forehead. "OK?" he asked.

I shook my head. "Not really."

He clucked at me and puffed up his feathers and quietly chattered, "Not really? Not really. *Not* really," as he tried to perfect the sounds.

I lowered myself down onto my living room rug, sitting cross-legged with my computer in my lap. The General oversaw my every click and keystroke as I took a guess at the flight path that Gabe must have taken to Scotland. Without me and my absurdity to complicate everything, I guessed he'd fly right out of Savannah. On the screen appeared a flight-tracking map, showing an arching semicircle north to New York City, and then another across the ocean to Edinburgh. Each time I refreshed the page, the little plane icon got farther and farther away from where I sat. Each moment increased the distance between us, which I had put there. I'd been the one to fire that arrow, and I felt so full of regret about it that I could hardly see through the tears.

His life had him always moving forward. But mine had me fixed like a pin in the map. And that was just how it had to be.

I slid my computer off my lap and unfolded myself from the floor, awkwardly shuffling across my living room with pinprickly sleeping feet. Picking up my gratitude jar, I unscrewed the lid. I dug through the papers on top until I found the page on which I'd written Gabe's name. I stared at the letters and ran my fingers over each one.

I felt so bad for what I had done. Hurting him, rejecting him . . . and that pain his eyes. God, I would never forget the way he'd looked at me, not as long as I lived. And the mention of me being the only thing in his own personal gratitude jar made me almost weak in the knees. But I still felt that the two of us together was an absolute impossibility.

And maybe something best forgotten altogether.

Walking into the kitchen, I folded up the paper with his name, doubling it over itself. I put my foot on the lever of the garbage can and held my closed palm over the bin, hovering over the coffee grounds and banana peels.

But I couldn't bring myself to open my hand. I couldn't bring myself to throw the paper or what it represented away. I couldn't bring myself to let go.

There's a big difference between playing it safe and playing it scared, he'd said. He was on to something. I knew that. And even though I had no idea what to do about it, it made me very certain of something else. Once my bubble had felt like a cushion. Now it was starting to feel an awful lot like a cage.

49

GABE

I tried to skip a stone on the surface of Loch Ness, but I overthrew it and it plunged into the water with a *plop*. The air was thick with fog and misty with fine rain. I was there waiting for the guy who'd seen Nessie, but I gave zero fucks about the interview I was supposed to do with him. Zero fucks about exclusive interviews. Zero fucks about monsters. Zero fucks about anything. Except for Lily.

I pulled the hat she'd knitted from my jacket pocket and put it on. Or tried to, anyway. I had to pull on it pretty hard to get it to fit—I suspected it might have been intended for Ivan, but whatever. Even as broken up as I was, I still wanted to wear it. She'd made it, and it was mine, and that was what mattered. Even if it did fit me like a damned yarmulke.

Rubbing my eyes, I looked out at the dark water, rimmed with green. I was in one of the most beautiful places on earth, and I should've been enjoying myself. I should've been taking photos, making notes, recording clips. But instead I just stood there and stared out at the water, like a jackass who had lost the one good thing he ever had. I felt like utter, total, and complete shit. I had gotten a glimpse of what life could be like with her, and now it was just a slowly vanishing point in my rearview mirror.

"That's a lovely wee cap, my lad," said a voice behind me in a singsong Scottish burr. I spun around and saw an old man hobbling out of the mist. He wore a green rain slicker and huge muddy boots. He walked with a cane, and each time he planted it, he jiggled the handle, making sure it wouldn't slip. He hobbled closer. "I'm Malcolm MacGregor. I'm the one who saw Nessie. So I'm guessing that makes you Gabriel, then?"

Gabriel. Nobody had called me Gabriel in thirty-five years, not since my grandmother passed away. The word took me right back to being in her kitchen—pound cake on the good china and 7Up from the matching teacups. "Yeah. I'm Gabriel. You can call me Gabe. Pleasure to meet you." I shook his hand. It was a good handshake, firmer than I expected. A fisherman's handshake, maybe.

He was still peering up at me, smiling. Tickled. "It's really just a suggestion of a hat." He worked his mouth around his dentures and furrowed his bushy eyebrows. "A hint of a hat, perhaps!"

I yanked it down harder, barely getting the edges to touch my ears. The old man's eyes twinkled. His rain slicker was unbuttoned, and underneath I saw he wore a sweater that was all manner of screwed up—holes and knots and loose threads. Yarns that didn't match. A completely random pattern that looked like it might have been a snowflake until it turned into a flower and then a star. "I like that sweater," I said.

He snickered and nodded. "Aye! I'm blessed to be married to a terrible knitter myself." He reached out for my arm to steady himself, planting his cane and leaning on me. Arm in arm, we made our way over to a bench on the edge of the loch, surrounded by a carpet of moss. I helped him sit down, and he winced and groaned. Studying my hat again, he smoothed his sweater. "God bless the terrible knitters. Could I interest you in some misshapen slippers, perhaps? Or a curiously small scarf? A single mitten, even?" He beamed, sniffing and laughing. "Bless her soul." He sighed. "But I don't suppose you came all this way to talk to me about haphazard knitting."

True. But the fact was that I needed to talk to someone about Lily. And badly. Thanks to the time change, it couldn't be Markowitz. So it looked as though it was going to have to be old Mr. MacGregor. Because my heart was fucking blown apart, and not even the mother of all monster legends was going to put it back together. I needed to make sense of the pain or I was going to lose my mind. "How long have you been married to this terrible knitter of yours?" I asked.

Mr. MacGregor leaned back on the bench. He closed his eyes and smiled. "Seventy-two years this March. To tell you the truth, I don't much count the years before her. I don't know what I was doing, but I wasn't living, that's for certain." From his pocket he produced a small paper bag, wrinkled at the top. Inside were some jelly beans, and he offered me one, taking one for himself. "And your terrible knitter? How long have you been married to her?"

My jelly bean got lodged in my throat, and I coughed hard to stop myself from choking. Mr. MacGregor slapped my back, and I waved him off. Finally, I managed to say, "I'm not."

He drew back, startled. "But you're wearing her hat!"

"Right," I said, coughing a bit still. "But we aren't . . . we're not married. We aren't anything."

Mr. MacGregor gaped at me in disbelief. "But why not? You young people. Always thinking and planning and this and that. Doing your important jobs. Going to your important places. Saying you're so busy. But do you know what happens, lad?"

I waited for the answer. Apparently, judging by the wriggle of his huge white eyebrows, he was waiting for me to answer first, so I asked, "What happens?"

"You get old! Like me. With nothing to do. One day, you find yourself sitting beside a lake." He opened his arm, sweeping it out toward the loch. "You're just sitting. You're doing nothing. You're enjoying living your life. And then you see a monster. With your own eyes, you see lumps in the water, going past. You clean your glasses, you squint. And it's still there. Do you know who the first person you tell is?"

"Your terrible knitter?"

He slapped my leg. "Now you're onto it, lad! The terrible knitter herself! Do you know what? She *believes you*! Because she's been with you since the beginning of time and she knows you're not gonna come home and be telling bollocks tales. Aye? That's the point!" he said. "You find someone who believes in you, no matter what. And you believe in them! It's that simple, my lad. Take it from an old man like me. Marry that terrible knitter of yours. Don't waste a moment. Not a moment!"

I slipped the hat off and sighed as I ran my fingers over the yarn, over each stitch she'd done for me. Just me. All for me. I wanted to give her everything, if only she'd give me the chance. "Not going to happen."

He crumpled the bag of jelly beans. "What a load of hooey. She gave you her hat, didn't she?" He said it like it was, I didn't even know, *pledged her undying love to you* or *moved mountains to be with you* or *begged you to stay with her forever*.

I ran my thumb over the stitches and looked out into the mist. My heart fucking ached. My soul groaned. The idea of losing her forever made me feel a kind of pain I'd never felt before. The Welsh called it *hiraeth*. In Ethiopia it was *tizita*. In Portugal they called it *saudade*. So many words for one thing: the gut-wrenching longing for lost love. "She broke my heart. Pushed me away right when I laid it on the line for her."

Mr. MacGregor nodded and thoughtfully plucked a yellow jelly bean from the bag. "Aye, mine did the same a time or two. Are you in the mood for a story, lad? So I can share with you what I know about life and love?"

If Yoda himself had appeared to offer some wisdom, I don't think I could have been more grateful. I took another jelly bean from the bag and nodded. "Definitely."

He placed the bag of candy between us and clasped his hands together in his lap. "In 1944, the Second World War was on. I thought she was going to marry someone else. I don't know why I was surprised—I didn't have the nerve to ask her. *Pffuff!* Hardly had the nerve to even look at her! So when another fella asked her, why . . . she said yes. Like any sensible girl would! But Jesus, Mary, and Joseph, when I heard that news . . . I was *so* angry with her." Mr. MacGregor paused and looked out at the water. "Angry that she couldn't see how I felt, angry she couldn't see what I saw. And so what did I do? Seventeen years old, I joined up with Royal Air Force. I thought I was such a hero in my uniform with my anger and my broken heart and my righteous indignation. I was a right tragic poor sod. I had my mission. I'd lost my love. But you know who didn't care about any of that?" he said, beginning to chuckle. "The Nazis!" His laughter echoed out over the water, and his whole body shook. "Bastards! I got myself shot down over the Rhineland. And there I was," he said with a clap of his hands, "careening toward the earth, for the sake of love."

He pursed his lips, closing his eyes and shaking his head. "Such dramatic shenanigans. I thought I was teaching her a lesson, would you believe? But really, I was teaching myself one instead. I loved her as much the first time I saw her as when my plane was plummeting to the ground." He sighed and sniffed and then began to smile. "I got picked up by Allied troops and shipped to London. Word got back to her, and she wrote to me in hospital. Three lines, short and sweet." He extended his hand, counting off the lines, starting with his thumb. *"You idiot. I love you. Come home."* He chuckled to himself. "So I did. And I forgave her as soon as I saw her face." He pulled off his glasses, cleaning them with a small soft cloth before putting them back on. "But they do have the right to do it, son. The women do."

I glanced at him sideways. "To break our hearts?"

He shook his head. "Heavens, no. Merely to make mistakes. Men are mortals. A woman is a goddess. But I'll tell you from experience that sometimes even goddesses end up with shit on their shoes."

The last thing I felt like doing was laughing, but I couldn't help it. It was just the dose of old-man wisdom I'd needed, the kind of no-nonsense truth bomb that finally let me take a deep breath and get some distance from my own thoughts.

Mr. MacGregor went on, laughing too until his eyes sparkled with tears. "They don't always recognize it in the moment, though!" he said, wagging his finger and smiling. "You've just got to let them figure it out for themselves. At first they'll blame you. They'll say *you* brought the shit into the house. But eventually, with time, they'll see their mistakes if they've made them. And then they'll make them right." He smiled again. "I don't believe in God, lad. But I do believe in the way my wife loves me. And in the way your lady loves you as well."

This guy didn't know me, but love was universal. And he was right about a whole hell of a lot of things. About the anger, especially. And the lesson learned. Lily and I had been full bore and all cylinders on a high-speed burn into what had felt to *me* like the biggest adventure I'd ever had. But what had felt to her like pure terror. I'd needed a bit of time to get my head back on straight, and maybe she did too. She wasn't perfect; she was a human as flawed as me. And made me love her just that much more.

Like the mists clearing in front of me, I felt my anger start to lighten. I was still busted up inside, but the color of it changed somehow. And I started to see it all a little more clearly. "I love her," I said. I looked out at the water, imagining the two of us out there together in a kayak. I could almost hear her laugh. Jesus, how I loved her laugh. "I just love her so goddamned much."

"Then go back to her, if you're able. *She* is what matters." He patted my leg again and said softly, "Take it from an old man, Gabriel. Everything else will come and go. But love will change your world if you let it."

♥ ♥ ♥

After the interview with Mr. MacGregor, I went by myself to a pub called the Olive and Dove in Inverness. The bartender was a friendly older lady who put a heart in the foam on my pint of Guinness, which slowly separated into two halves split right down the center.

I sat alone in a booth in the corner by a window and opened the chat window with Lily. Since my anger had subsided, I'd texted her three times:

Talk to me.

I haven't given up.

I love you.

But she hadn't replied. According to my phone, she hadn't even read them.

I rubbed my temples and pulled out my production notebook. I tried to focus, but it wasn't any use. Work was a distant second to what really mattered now. Staring out into the night, I let myself sink down into how empty I felt without her, empty in a way I'd never felt before I met her. Like she'd opened a trapdoor and I'd fallen right through.

Way in the distance, there was a glimmer of the northern lights, a psychedelic ribbon cutting across the sky. Hell yeah, I'd wanted to share the world with her. Hell yeah, I wanted to take her to beautiful places like this to see the northern lights or the midnight sun or go dancing with me in Rio. I definitely wanted adventures with her, but falling in love with her had been my favorite adventure yet. There was no reason that our adventures couldn't be in English muffins on Sunday mornings and sweet tea every afternoon. If there was one thing I now knew for sure, other than this ache in my heart, it was that one tiny memory with her would mean more to me than all the other memories without her. No question about it at all.

And yet here I was. All by my damned self, half a world away.

I woke up my phone again and stared at the chat window where I'd been trying to talk to her but instead was just talking to myself. I thought about what I could say to tell her I wanted to make this work and I needed her in my life. I just didn't even know how to start. And then I realized I might not have to. Because suddenly, all three of my messages showed as being read, like maybe they'd only just arrived on her end. And then there they were. The dots.

Holy fuck, the dots. The typing dots. Lily was responding. Lily was *back*. She hit me with a rapid-fire one-two-three, each message making me even happier than the last.

Your messages arrived all at once just now!

I love you too.

And I miss you so much.

In my total surprise at hearing from her, I fumbled for my phone and managed to pull a Markowitz: I hit the video-call button by accident. I stared at the screen with my mouth open as I read the words *Video-calling Lily.*

"Fuck," I said, not sure if I should abort mission and end the call or pretend like I'd meant to, or maybe just . . .

Didn't matter. Because there she was. Her smiling, beautiful face filled my screen. But the connection was shitty, and just as soon as she came into focus, she dissolved into blocky pixels again. Glitchy bits of audio came through, but I could only make out half of her words as the signal cut in and out. I snatched up my phone and stepped out onto the back patio of the pub. "Lily? Are you there?" I asked as I shifted and tipped my phone to try to get a better signal. I also tried to get some light on my own face so she could see me, but it was dark as hell out, and I couldn't see myself in the thumbnail. But moving my phone around did help—though I couldn't see her, at least I could hear her.

"Gabe," she said, "I don't know if you can hear me. I hope you can. I just want you to know that I am so sorry. And you were right about everything. I just hope you can . . ."

The audio cut out again. *For Christ's sake.* If I didn't know how she ended that sentence, I'd go out of my goddamned mind. *I hope you can . . . forget about me? Move on?* Not a fucking chance.

But then the words I needed to hear came through my phone, cutting through the quiet night.

". . . I hope you can forgive me."

The call got cut off one second later, but I'd heard everything I needed to hear. My emptiness and heartbreak disappeared like dust blown off a table. Of *course* I would forgive her. She was what I wanted and she was what I needed. All my life, I'd been adrift. Not anymore. The sound of her voice gave me back all the hope I felt I'd lost, and endless possibilities of the future unspooled out there in front of me, same as the northern lights.

On our last night at the Willows, she'd talked about Sunday roasts and Christmas lights. Now that I'd heard from her, now that I knew it wasn't over after all, I had the courage to add new things to that list. Her in a wedding dress. Me putting together a trike at three o'clock on Christmas morning. Looking into those beautiful eyes of hers today and tomorrow and forty years from now.

I wasn't halfway in. I was all in. And it was time to prove it to her.

So I went back into the pub, slapped a handful of bills on table, and headed across the street to the B&B where I was staying. Since the minute she'd pushed me away, I'd felt out of balance, like my internal compass had gone completely haywire. But not anymore.

Lily Jameson was my true north . . . and I was going back home.

50

LILY

The next morning, I was at the Living History Museum to help with *The Savannah Yellow Fever Epidemic: A Day in the Life*. Gabe's texts had arrived late yesterday afternoon—since then, I hadn't heard a peep from him. I'd spent a restless evening pacing around my apartment and an even more restless night awake, anxiously trying to get back in touch with him. None of my calls went through, and he hadn't answered any of my texts, nor did I know if he'd received the ones I sent. The not knowing drove me bonkers, and around three in the morning, as I lay staring at my ceiling, it occurred to me that maybe the video call had actually been an accident. His side of the call had been pitch-black, and I hadn't heard him say anything. All signs pointed to one conclusion, cringe-worthy in its obviousness: his phone had been in his pants the whole time. I'd asked his pocket for forgiveness. Fabulous. One hundred percent Lily right there.

Ivan and I were crammed into the upstairs bathroom together getting ready for the museum to open. I dabbed little smudges of dark-purple eye shadow under his eyes, blending them into the base of green I had already applied. He looked absolutely *awful*. But not nearly as awful as I felt and looked. All the crying from the day before had made my skin oily and puffy, and my now eyes were bloodshot and dry. My sister had said we were going for *exhausted and unwell.* And boy, was I nailing it.

The bathroom door creaked open, and my sister's face appeared in the crack. Today she was dressed as a nurse, complete with a high starched white hat, a baby-blue dress, and an apron that looked like she'd been cutting sides of beef at the grocery store all morning.

"Why are you wearing your battlefield uniform?" I asked as I applied some purple shadow under my own already raccoonlike eyes.

"Because the clean one is covered in an unfortunate mixture of digested turnips and bananas. Whatever. It'll be fine. If any of the tourists ask, I'll give the party line. *The yellow fever is a terrible disease!*" She leaned into the bathroom a bit more. "But before things get crazy, I wanted to bring you a treat." She slipped me a little parcel wrapped in a flour-sack towel.

I stared at it warily. "Treats" from the second half of the nineteenth century tended to be the sorts of things that made a girl really happy about large-scale industrial white-sugar production. "Please don't tell me they're those pine-tar candies. My gums are still burning."

"Pine *sap,* and no, they aren't." She slid the corner of the cloth aside. Inside was a package of Twizzlers—the peely kind that come apart in little strands. They were one of my favorites, and normally I'd have been ripping those suckers apart with my teeth and wolfing them down, *Lady and the Tramp* style. But not today. Today I gave her a very tragic-sounding "Thanks" and handed Ivan over to her.

"Remember, team!" Daisy said as we headed down the staircase. "Exhausted and unwell!"

"I knowwww," I moaned as I followed behind her, clumping along in my painfully tight ankle boots. If I ever had to have bunion surgery, at least I'd know why.

Downstairs, Daisy got Ivan situated in his wooden bassinet and checked on the handful of other volunteers who were helping us with

Yellow Fever Day. It was, hands down, our most popular event, and every room was bustling with sickly-looking history buffs dressed to the nines. Or the mid- to late 1800s. As Daisy made her rounds, I headed down to the basement to grab some linen towels for feverish-forehead blotting from the laundry area. I closed the heavy door behind me and then flipped on the light switch that was hidden behind a squirrel-fur whisk broom. The bluish fluorescent light spilled up the staircase from the basement. The lights had been my idea. The basement was *really* spooky, and the lights helped a lot.

Feeling the heaviness in my heart and the tightness from my bad night's sleep in my shoulders, I headed down the stairs. There, sitting beside the washer and dryer, underneath a buzzing and flickering rod light, was one of the volunteers. She was an elegant older lady, with her white hair in a beautiful and complicated spray of curls on top of her head. I didn't know where Daisy found these people, but they were just fabulous. She sat on one of the spare chairs we stored down here, and I saw she was embroidering one of our linen kitchen towels. We had a few volunteers who liked to do that, and then we sold them to help support the museum.

"Hello, dear," she said with a very welcoming smile. The floral scent of her perfume filled the air. It was unlike anything I'd smelled before. Old-fashioned and delicate. Like roses, but not quite.

"Hello!" I said and grabbed the stack of towels. I saw one of her feet peeking out from underneath her dress. Her boot was like mine, but much, much more weathered and worn. Much more believable. "Gosh, your costume is incredible. Has Daisy seen it?"

She smiled at me again and passed the needle through the fabric. "Not yet." She'd stretched one of the dish towels in a small vintage embroidery hoop. In the center of the bottom panel, she was embroidering a single red heart. The work was fine and clean, and she was able to do it without even watching what she was doing. Amazing.

"Every time I embroider something, it ends up like I've got the wrong side out."

She chuckled a little and then paused with her needle halfway through the fabric. Even her needle was an antique—smaller than the needles I used and slightly rusted at the tip. "What a beautiful locket you have there."

Automatically, my hand went to it and clasped it tight. I had folded the paper with his name on it into a tiny square and placed it inside. As I touched it, a roiling sorrow made me feel sick to my stomach. "Thank you," I said, clearing my throat. "It means a lot to me. I'm Lily, by the way." I reached out my hand for hers.

"Lucinda Abrahams," she said and shook my hand. Her fingers were ice-cold and her touch so very delicate.

An unexpected chill made me shudder. Compared to the attic, it was downright glacial down here. I rubbed my arms with my hands and felt a shiver run up my back.

Lucinda continued to embroider the towel without looking. "Do you know, when I was a young woman like you, I had a locket very much like that one." She studied it, blinking slowly and pensively. "A man I loved very much gave it to me."

I swallowed hard and looked down at the gold oval with its enameled lily. Even though it made me ache to look at it, it hurt even more to think of not having it close to my heart. "Someone I love gave this to me as well."

She studied me, her eyes searching my face. It was as if she could read my anxiety—as if she knew exactly what I was feeling and why. I supposed it was written all over me, but as she studied me, I felt that she understood. That loss, that confusion, that wanting to do the right thing but not knowing how. Lovesickness like I had never known before. "If I had it all to do again, I never would have let him go." She passed the needle through the towel once again, tightening the embroidery floss with gentle tugs. "I regret that every day."

Her words had an almost physical effect on me, and I felt fountain of heartbreak come up through my stomach. I had been so, so happy with him. And now everything hurt so very much.

"You may feel a little better in time, dear girl." She tugged gently on the floss once more. "Though I never have. True love is the only thing that matters."

Feeling perilously close to the dam of tears breaking again, I managed to nod. I clutched the pile of towels to my chest as my chin began to tremble. I turned away and headed up the steps, pushing down a sob. At the top of the steps, in the shadowy darkness of the stairway, I collected myself. All I needed to do was get through a few hours here, and then I could go home and obsessively check my phone some more. The fluorescent lights flickered a few times, and I took a deep breath. I put my hand on the doorknob and then stepped back out into the museum, which was now slowly filling with visitors.

In the front room, I found Daisy pensively tending to Ivan in his nightshirt. Ivan, of course, was having a wonderful time, but Daisy was playing the concerned nursemaid to a T. And yet Ivan's cuteness outdid even the force that was living history, and my sister's "worry" cracked into a smile.

I leaned into the room, where she sat alone for the moment. I whispered, "That lady doing the embroidery downstairs? She's fantastic. So believable! And so . . ." I blinked a few times, still reeling from the intensity of what she'd made me feel. "So wise."

Daisy turned to face me. She wrinkled up her eyebrows and glanced down, as if she were looking into the basement. "Who?"

Glancing downward too, I said, "That lady. With the beautiful dress. Older, very pretty? Thin? She told me her name is Lucinda."

Daisy sat up taller in her chair. "There is nobody named Lucinda here today, Lily."

Ummm. What? "Oh, come on. Yes there is. I just saw her."

But my sister seemed *certain* that she was right. She glanced slowly side to side. "No, there is *not*."

A ripple of goose bumps prickled through me. My scalp tingled, and my fingertips went cold. "You're sure?"

My sister nodded slowly and deliberately. *"Positive."*

I tossed the basket of towels onto the fainting couch and ran down into the basement again, skidding down the last few steps, hooking my arm over the bare wood post at the bottom of the steps and twirling into the laundry room. She was gone. The chair where she'd been sitting was empty. There was no dish towel, there was no thread. There was no perfume in the air. And the basement felt about fifteen degrees warmer.

Oh. My. *God.*

She'd said her name was Lucinda. *Lucinda.* I'd heard that name before. Recently. *Very* recently. And then I remembered—it was when Gabe had given me my locket. Popping it open, I double-checked the engraving. *To L from G.* To Lucinda from George. This had been her locket. I knew it, as surely as if she'd told me herself. Even though she wasn't sitting there anymore, her presence lingered, and so did her words. *True love is the only thing that matters.*

Stunned and still covered in goose bumps, I sat down on the chair where Lucinda had sat and clutched my locket in my palm. From the inside, I took out the paper with Gabe's name on it. I hadn't dropped it in the trash, and I hadn't put it back in the jar either. Instead, I'd kept it as close to my heart as it could be.

I unfolded the page and stared at his name. That one simple word that meant so very much. The name of the man I loved. The name of the man I wanted to be with forever.

But I had been too scared to really open my heart to him at all.

And there was that word again. *Scared.* It was the bad penny that was always in my pocket. I'd done everything I could to stop myself from feeling scared—my career, my relationships, everything had been structured so that fear never got too close for comfort. But I was tired of my little golden cage. I didn't just want to stop playing it *scared*. I wanted to stop playing it *safe* too. I wanted to take the risks I'd never, ever been brave enough to take before. I didn't want to sit there, in my safe little world, wondering if he would text me or call me, scrambling for my phone and praying it might be him. I didn't want to lie awake wondering about pocket dials and calculating time differences. I wanted to be beside him—*with him*, in every way. I wanted to break free of what I knew and into the magic of what might be. I wanted to toss that bad penny into a fountain, make a wish, and never look back.

I saw now that my fear of flying had been the perfect metaphor for what was really happening. I had so been terrified of how or even if I could live in his great big world that I hadn't let myself believe it would ever work at all. Fear had stopped me from really opening my heart, which I had wanted so badly to do. But somewhere in the recesses of all my attempts at overcoming my fear of flying, I remembered that someone had said to me, *In order to turn fear into excitement, all you have to do is breathe.*

Clutching Gabe's name in my hands, I did. I took a breath so deep that it made my pleats and bodice darts groan.

And lo and behold, it began to happen. The fear started to fall away. And there in its place was excitement at the possibilities of what could be in store for me and for us together . . . if only I would give myself a fighting chance experience them.

If only I would let go of the fear.

By holding myself back, I had hurt the one person I had fallen harder for and loved more than I ever thought possible. But what if I stopped being scared of what might be? What if I reached out and burst my bubble, at last?

I imagined it around me, like a soapy snow globe. Gabe stood on the other side of it, smiling in the sunshine. He felt so close and yet still so very far away. And so I reached out toward him and all that he

Nicola Rendell

represented, and as my fingertip touched the surface of my bubble, it exploded with a champagne-cork *pop*.

Without the fear around me, the world began to open up and possibilities seemed to come at me from every direction, whizzing toward me like fireflies. All the no bloomed into yes. I saw *us* together, instead of him and me somehow kept apart. One way or another, we could make it work. I was sure of it. But I knew I had to take the first step.

Scratch that. The first *flight*.

Never in my life had I actually wanted to get on an airplane. Now I really, really, really did. With my whole heart. He was the love of my life, and there was no way I was going to play it safe anymore. Not literally or figuratively. I wouldn't sit and wait, hoping and praying and pining that he would come to me. Nope.

I would do just the opposite. Yes, I would get on an airplane for him. Yes, I would face down my fears. Yes, I would look him in the eye and ask him for another chance. In person. Half a world from where I stood. And if I did get another chance with him, I wouldn't push him away. Never again. This time, I would wrap him up in my arms and *never* let go.

I gave his name a big smooch and bounded up the steps with my petticoats rustling. It was time to say goodbye to no, hello to yes . . . and hello to Scotland too!

It cost a fortune, it would take forty-eight hours, and I looked like I was about to get booked into an 1870s women's penal colony in the photograph, but my new passport was officially in the works. The show was on the road! With my heart singing and Madonna blasting, I zoomed through town. I had lots to do and my mind was spinning like a disco ball, but I felt calm and steady—I was armed with a new shell of courage, and I didn't let my worry run away with me. Mr. Markowitz would be able to tell me where Gabe was staying. Google would help me get there. I needed to buy a plane ticket. I needed to buy as many external batteries as I could find so that I could play *Bejeweled* for the entire flight. I needed to see if it was still OK for me to bring my knitting needles on the plane. I needed to know if I could bring snacks. I needed to do *so* much, but it would all be so very, very worth it. Because I was going to be with back with him. With Gabe. My Gabe. My love. With my fingers crossed all the time in hopes that he'd give me another chance.

On the way to the museum, I had avoided going down Abercorn because I just couldn't stand the idea of passing the Willows with that pain in my heart. But now I barreled down the street with my engine roaring.

As I approached the house, though, I saw that in the front yard stood Robert E. Lee. No, wait. Wait. The pretend Lee. Jerry Whateverhisnamewas. The real estate agent. My heart sank, and I screeched to a halt. He was replacing the **FOR SALE** sign with one that said **BUYER INTERESTED** in big, bold, ominous red letters.

"No," I said. "Oh *no*." Even though I'd never really let myself believe it would belong to Gabe and me, the idea of someone else purchasing the Willows made my heart ache. In just a few days, we had experienced so much in that house. It had all started there for us, and it felt so awful to think of someone else living there so quickly after he'd left.

I rolled down my window, and General Lee leaned on the long plank in a way that was sort of weirdly reminiscent of a musket.

"Who is it?" I asked, stating the obvious and ducking down to admire the fish-scale scallop decorations and the stunning clematis in bright pink and white.

"The guy's around here somewhere. Waiting for the inspector." He looked slowly side to side as if he were considering something way more expansive than a suburban yard. Like, say, Shiloh or Manassas.

I gripped the steering wheel hard and took a deep breath. "Thanks," I said and began to take my foot off the brake.

And that was when I saw it. Sitting on the front porch, on the beautiful old porch swing, was a backpack. With a bright-orange patch sewn onto it.

Gabe. Gabe was *here*.

The goose bumps I'd gotten in the museum basement were nothing compared to these. I threw my van in park, flung open my door, and ran up the front walkway with my petticoats gathered in my hands like a cancan dancer. I thundered up the front steps and ran to the front door. But before I got there, it swung open. And there he was.

With his arms open wide.

Oh that hug, my God, that hug. His arms around me, his laughter, his warmth. I clung to him, and he staggered back, pulling me down on top of him on the shiny staircase. I showered him with kisses as a new wave of tears fell down my cheeks. Happiness tears now, though. Pure, unfiltered happiness. He took my cheeks in his hands and kissed me—a fairy-tale kiss from my very own prince that went on and on and on.

Finally, we both pulled away for a breath. Even though it was heaven to be in his arms, I had a lot I needed him to know, and I launched into a full-scale babble. "I was coming to see you. I got my passport renewed. It'll be ready the day after tomorrow. I was on my way to go home and buy a ticket. But now here you are." I gasped for a breath and pressed my finger into his chest. "*Here* you are. I can't believe it."

He drew his head back from mine, searching my face. "Really? You were going to come to me?"

I nodded, feeling my cheeks flush and still panting from the thrill of running up the steps and into his arms. "I don't want you tethered to me here. There is so much I want to see out there in the world, and I can't think of anybody I'd rather do it with than you."

He swept my hair aside and narrowed his eyes. "I don't know if I like the sound of that."

My heart sank, and I made a kind of strangled croak. I'd already preworried my way into the second in-flight movie and whether or not I'd do better in an aisle or a window seat. "Please just let me try."

Gabe answered first with that cocky, delicious smile of his. "Oh, I'll let you try all right," he said. "But I mean I don't like the sound of you buying your own ticket. *I* want to be the one to buy your tickets. And I want to buy you something else too."

And then, very slowly, he glanced around the foyer . . . and raised his eyebrow at me.

Finally, it registered what was happening. Robert E. Lee and the sign outside, and Gabe here too? He wasn't just back to visit. He was planning to stay. And he was planning to buy the Willows. For me. For *us*.

"But what about your job?" I asked, with the tears running down my cheeks now. "What about your life?"

He slid his hands down my body. He gripped my thighs, and I felt his strength through all my pleats and petticoats. "We will figure it out. You want to fly and you will. But I want to have my feet on the ground. I want a home, and I want it to be with you. In this house. Just like you said."

I let myself fall against him, holding him as tight as I possibly could. "Are we really going to live here?"

"Hell yes, we are." His deep voice made his chest rumble against my ear. "But I got you one more thing. I just need you to stand up for a second."

"Nope," I said, my voice a little muffled because my cheek was mashed against his rock-solid chest. "I'm staying here forever."

"You're going to want to stand up for this one," he said with a smile in his voice.

I squeezed him extra tight before I let him go and slid off him, straightening my dress as I stood.

He came up to sitting on the stairs, but he didn't stand. Instead, he reached into his pocket, got down on one knee, and looked up into my eyes. He didn't say anything at first. He just held my stare. Then he popped the ring box open. And I gasped. It was absolutely beautiful. But not nearly as beautiful as him.

"Will you?" he asked as he slid the ring on my finger.

My life had always had lots of love in it. But not until that moment did I have any idea at all what true love felt like. Because of him I did, and always would. I sank down onto my knees in front of him, wrapped my arms around him, and whispered, "I will, I will, I will," as we lay in the middle of that grand old foyer, in that grand old house, in our grand new life.

51

GABE

Eight months later

The opening sequence was now an ever-changing slide show of our life together—there were clips of us in Savannah, the Caribbean, Iceland, and even clips of her talking to the General, who now had his very own fan group. Lily had engaged her amygdala all the way to the top of the worldwide *Bejeweled* rankings, but we didn't travel as much as I had when I was on my own. I'd never been happier in my life. Every time I looked at her, I loved her even more. And no matter what shots made up the sequence, it always ended the same way.

THE POWERS OF SUGGESTION
WITH LILY AND GABE POWERS

Finally, we were back in Scotland. It was March, and the skies were deep gray and drizzling. The water was still and black. It was perfect. But then again, it always was with her by my side.

That morning, we'd done an interview with Mr. MacGregor. I filmed Lily as she interviewed him about what he'd seen and where.

We'd had lunch with him and his wife at the pub, as Mr. MacGregor and I sat across from our beloved terrible knitters, the happiest guys on earth.

Now Lily and I were out on the loch, in a kayak just like I'd imagined us that day that I'd been here without her. It was dusk, when almost all the Nessie sightings happened. Her cheeks were rosy, and her eyes were doubly beautiful against the bright yellow of her rain jacket. "We're out on Loch Ness," she said to the camera. "Obviously! So far, no Nessie." She leaned over the side of the kayak and peered down into the water. She tickled it with her fingertips, and small ripples shivered out from her hand. "Nessie? Are you down there?" she said to the water and then turned to the camera. She leaned even closer to the surface of the loch, cupping her ear to the water. She moved her lips off to one side. I figured everybody else would think it was cute. But to me, it was *so* damned sexy. Like every single thing she did.

She grabbed her oar with both hands and placed it in the water like I'd taught her. She pulled it toward her, making the kayak slip through the water. "Don't just sit there, Mr. Powers!" she teased. "Help me out."

I laughed, and it echoed out across the water and back at us again. Her big eyes followed the sound from one side of the valley to the other. "That's amazing," she whispered. "Hello!" she called out.

Hello-hello-hello echoed back, in that beautiful voice of hers.

"This is Lily Powers!" she called out. *Powers-Powers-Powers* said the echo.

Still, it was surreal to me. That she had taken my name. That any of this—my life with her—wasn't just a dream. I panned out to do a wide shot and then returned to her, finding her looking at me a little impatiently. "Seriously, now. Help me paddle."

"Right," I said and clipped the camera in place beside me. I reached down to get my oar from where it was fastened beneath my seat. But as I did, I saw something under me. It was a small box, navy blue with white ribbon. I heard Lily inhale, and I glanced up to see her watching with her fingers pressed to her lips. I picked up the box from the bottom of the kayak. It was featherlight and hardly more than four inches on each side.

"Open it," she whispered, now shifting her fingers into a steeple shape in front of her.

I pulled the ribbon off and slipped the lid from the top of the box. At first I couldn't even really process what I was seeing or what it meant. Because inside there were two little baby booties. Knitted out of yellow yarn.

Then it hit me, and I sank to my knees on the boat in front of her as her laughter echoed out and back again.

I took them from the box and placed them on my palm. They were so small, and yet the happiness they brought was so huge. Christ, happiness. More than I ever thought I'd feel. "Are you . . . ," I asked, on my knees in front of her.

She nodded. "I am," she whispered, and her hand moved down to her belly.

"Holy shit, Lily," I said as I put my head in her lap. I wrapped my arms around her, clutching the little booties in my hand. I pressed my ear against her stomach, as if maybe, somehow, I could hear a heartbeat. But instead of a baby's heartbeat, I felt her stomach contract as she laughed and sniffled. Turning my head, I looked up to see her wiping tears from her cheeks and smiling that beautiful smile.

I held her close and pressed my cheek against her leg. And there I stayed, on my knees in gratitude for her, for the home she'd given me, for the fireworks I saw around her every single day.

ACKNOWLEDGMENTS

Thank you to my husband for everything always; every night really is a sleepover when you marry your best friend. Thank you to Maria Gomez and the team at Montlake and Amazon Publishing for giving me a chance to spread my wings both creatively and professionally. Thank you to Charlotte Herscher; it's a dream to work with you, and I feel so honored to have your help. Thank you to Sybil and Sam for providing me with support, common sense, and laughter. Thank you especially to Sarah; I have no idea what I would do without you. And SL, through high and low. Thank you to Candi for helping me get this book off the ground and into the hands of bloggers and readers. Thank you to Melissa for your designer's eye and your Vitamix. Thank you to my agent, Emily Sylvan Kim, for your encouragement and steadiness. BR and CD, thank you for keeping my secrets and for cheering me on through all these many years. Thank you so much to the MBs, the Peaches, and the KOs for your support. An extra big thank-you to my family, my students, and my dogs for filling my life with joy. And thank you, finally, to my readers. It's all for you.

ABOUT THE AUTHOR

Photo © 2017 Emily Roembach-Clark/Emily RC Photography

Nicola Rendell, the bestselling author of *Shimmy Bang Sparkle*, loves writing naughty romantic comedies. After receiving a handful of degrees from a handful of places, she now works as a professor in New England. Nicola's work has been featured in the *Huffington Post* and the *USA Today* blog *Happy Ever After*. She loves to cook, sew, and play the piano. Her hobbies might make her sound like an old lady, but she's totally OK with that. For more information and updates, visit www.NicolaRendell.com.